NAKED PADDOCK

A Novel

NAKED
PADDOCK

A Novel

M.K. DUCOTE

TELEMACHUS PRESS

Cover Design by Asha Hossain Designs, Inc.

Cover photo of driver by Dan R. Boyd
Cover photo of crowd by Kyle Marcelli

Photo of M.K. Ducote by Studio Z

Second Edition

Published by Telemachus Press, LLC
http://www.telemachuspress.com

Visit the author website:
http://www.nakedpaddock.com
http://www.mkducote.com

ISBN: 978-1-939927-06-4 (eBook)
ISBN: 978-1-939927-07-1 (Paperback)

Version 2013.11.06

Printed in the United States of America

10 9 8 7 6 5 4 3 2 1

To:

Chloe & Cupcake
for their stubborn love
and for reloading my clips

pad•dock

\'pa-dək, -dik, -duk

noun

1. A fenced area used for pasturing or exercising animals; *especially* an enclosure where racehorses are saddled and paraded before a race.

2. An area of an automobile racetrack, near the pits, where cars are prepared before a race.

CHAPTER 1
PALM BEACH, FLORIDA

The Ferrari FXX lurched into sixth and for a split-second Palm Beach International Raceway was silent in the morning light.

Then the gears of the 6.3-liter V12 bit and the Italian engine roared with violence down the straightaway toward Turn 10. The sky was robin's egg blue and the only constant. Everything else blurred past the slim windows, stretched by speed.

"Ready for a real ride?" Coleton asked, checking on his passenger from the corner of his eye.

The man's lips were pulled back into a grimace, and a drop of sweat had splattered the inside of his visor, but his dark eyes glimmered. Coleton piloted through the double apex corner, then slapped the transmission paddle into fourth with more force than necessary.

"Let's give the nanny a break, shall we?"

Coleton leaned into the Momo five-point harness and switched the Manettino system to *Race*. To the untrained eye, nothing had changed, but Coleton felt the smallest shudder through the wheel. *Ahhhh … Pure Driving Experience.*

With a flick of the wrist he had disabled the ABS system, which prevents wheel lock under heavy braking, and various other safety measures and driver aids, relying on nothing but his own skill and confidence to keep the machine under control. Coleton coaxed the FXX even faster, opening her up and letting her run reckless like a thoroughbred on its first hot lap.

The rev limiter danced dangerously at 8000 rpms. His car was the only rig racing at PBIR that Thursday, but Coleton protected his line and pushed through the corners like he was fighting for the Championship at Atlanta with one lap left.

Like all racecar drivers, Coleton detested the "nanny" systems installed on today's supercars. These "electronic safety nets" are designed to safeguard normal drivers from the power of Formula 1 technology and protect against liability suits. Professional drivers, however, hate any dilution of complete control and are generally faster without them. Coleton was here to *drive* the FXX—not babysit the thing.

After one more hot lap around the 2.25-mile circuit, Coleton peeled off into pit lane and pressed his thumb on the Limiter button. The car instantly fell to 60 kph. The sound of the engine dropped to a low, chugging growl. The men could breathe more easily, and peripheral objects slid back into view, sharp and clear.

"See this button?" Coleton asked. The passenger nodded. "This button drops the gas to the engine and slows us down to the Pit Speed Limit. In a race, you get a penalty if you come into the pits too quickly."

The passenger nodded again, but Coleton doubted he was processing any information yet. His eyes were glazed, and his brain was still a swamp of adrenaline.

The instant the Ferrari FXX halted in the pits, people swarmed around it. Beyond the low pit wall, two models with identical blonde hair that fell to their waists jumped up and down in tiny leaps, clapping their hands with glee. One slid a diamond-studded iPhone from the back pocket of her cut-offs and took a picture of the car.

Coleton pulled his door handle, and the gull-wing door folded upward. He popped his five-point harness and ducked under the shoulder strap. At six feet, he was tall for a racing driver. His shoulders were strong and wide and tapered down to a narrow waist. Coleton was naturally athletic and built for speed like an Olympic sprinter, whereas most other endurance drivers looked like marathoners. When he worked out he had to be careful not to bulk up so he could fit in the cockpit. He swung his legs over the wide doorsill and hopped into the sunlight.

The passenger wasn't having such an easy time. He struggled to untangle the harness until Nicolas "Nico" Costa came over to help him. Once free of the belts, he stuck both legs out the door, but the doorsill was too wide for his feet to reach the ground. The fat man wiggled them up and down as he waited to be extricated. Nico motioned to one of his dealership employees, and it took both of them, working together, to hoist him out like a cadaver—feet first.

Nico owned Ferrari Fort Lauderdale, one of the largest Ferrari dealerships in the country. Sometimes he gained access to rare Ferrari supercars, but seldom could he convince even the richest buyer to cough up over a million dollars for candy they hadn't tasted. So, a few times a year he rented out PBIR for the day, and brought in a professional to give the buyer a bat-out-of-hell ride and a glimpse of what he could own. It was great PR, but he needed a good driver to prove the product.

Nico and Coleton had been friends for years, since before Nico ever dreamed of owning a dealership, when he was a senior studying business at the University of Miami during the week and playing on Miami Beach on the weekend. Nico's father, a Greek shipping magnate, agreed to bankroll the dealership, partly in hopes of making a businessman of his middle son, and partly as a way to guarantee himself access to the world's most exotic cars. For certain limited production supercars it doesn't matter how much money you put on the table; it's connections that secure the keys.

When the sparkle of this sale first surfaced, Nico knew Coleton was the driver for the job. Ferrari agreed to fly in one FXX from Italy for a single track day. Nico didn't have much time to close the deal.

Coleton unzipped the top of his racing suit to let in some air, and pushed his sweaty dark hair back off his brow. His face was classically handsome, and he knew it: high forehead, straight nose, full lips. His emerald eyes were startling at first glance, not hazel, but full-fledged green.

"Water?" Nico asked.

"Thanks."

In the distance, Coleton heard a low muted rumble. "Is that thunder?" he asked, turning. A few dark clouds had begun to gather in the east.

"Welcome to South Florida," Nico said. "Where storms roll in quick, and the money rolls in quicker."

"You're such a cheese ball," Coleton laughed.

Nico wiped sweat from his brow. His face was full and soft, with deep-set eyes. He wore his unruly hair thick and parted in the middle. The collars of his polo shirts were always popped upward, and he was rarely seen without a sweater draped around his shoulders—even on sweltering days like this one.

Coleton squinted at the bottle in his hand. "Do I look like a spring water kind of guy?" He tossed it back to Nico.

"What's wrong with spring water?"

"Nothing, if you don't mind drinking water animals have been pissing in for the past hundred years."

Coleton walked over to the bag that carried his racing gear and searched around in the bottom. He pulled out a bottle of Essentia.

"What's the difference?"

"That's like asking what's the difference between a taxi cab and my 1100 horsepower racing machine. Essentia water is purified by reverse osmosis, infused with electrolytes, alkalinized to 9.5pH and restructured using Ionic Separation Technology."

"Do you have any idea how anal retentive you are?"

"I'm a professional athlete." Coleton smiled his perfect print-ad smile, tilted back his head and took a long sip.

"I mean, the fact that you carry all that information around in your brain. It's disturbing."

"It's probably why my body looks like a temple, and yours, well, could use a little work." Coleton poked Nico in the stomach.

Panting, the buyer waddled up to them, still trying to connect the two sides of the built-in belt on his new Ferrari race suit, but they were too short to meet over his protruding belly. The models trailed behind him, their legs impossibly long, like stilted circus performers.

"That was amazing. Really amazing. We went fast!" he said, eyes gleaming. He had shaggy black hair, olive skin and the soft look of a man unaccustomed to manual labor.

"That wasn't fast," Coleton said distractedly, as he and Nico stared past him at the models. They were giggling and whispering in each other's ears.

"I think now *I* try," the buyer said, stroking his cropped black mustache.

"Oh, that wouldn't be possible," Coleton said. "There's no—" Nico grabbed Coleton by the shoulder before he could say another word.

"Come here," he hissed. He pulled Coleton into the catering tent. Behind them, one of the models tugged on the tab of the buyer's collar, while the other pinched his wide nose playfully.

"Look, Al-Aziz is Saudi money, okay? Stupid money. He's a *prince* for Chrissakes. If he likes this car he's going to order *two more* for his cousins. He owns—"

"Aren't there only 29 of these in the world?" Coleton interrupted. He tipped his head back for another sip of water.

"Thirty."

"How did you manage to get your hands on three?"

"I didn't. Not yet. But, I will. I had to put my ass on the line to get this one flown over. Tonight it gets sent back to Maranello. If we don't make this happen *now*, I'm jeopardizing my whole relationship with Ferrari."

"It's getting late in the day," Coleton said, lifting his eyes to the darkening cumulus clouds. "That storm's really moving in."

"Al-Aziz just bought an indoor racetrack in Dubai, modeled after the Monte Carlo Formula 1 track," Nico continued. "An indoor racetrack, man! The power of this car is intoxicating. Four laps behind the wheel and he'll be sold."

Coleton shook his head and moved to a folding table where he had left his helmet bag. "You're out of your mind if you think I'm getting in a car with that yokel at the wheel."

Unzipping a side compartment, Coleton pulled out his BlackBerry. He quickly checked his text messages. Nothing earthshattering. Then, opened his voicemails. One new message from a number he didn't recognize.

"Listen to me—" Nico began. Coleton raised his index finger, then held the phone to his ear and played the message.

"*Hi Coleton?*" a female voice asked. She sounded both perky and nervous, as if she had consumed a pot of coffee before breakfast. "*This is Candice. From last night. Your housekeeper let me out. I had a great time. We should do it again. I realized I never gave you my number. It's 305—*"

Coleton hit the delete button and dropped his phone back into his helmet bag. He turned to Nico and raised his dark eyebrows in a make-it-quick look.

"Al-Aziz will take it slow," Nico said. "I know that he—"

Coleton cut him off. "Forget it. I'm not risking a shunt in the off season for some rich asshole." Coleton's green eyes glimmered. "Not even for a '*prince*.'" Coleton made air quotes around the word. He picked up his helmet to pack it away. Nico glared at him.

"Listen—Al-Aziz used to drive Rally cars somewhere in the Middle East. He knows something about driving. It'll be fine." Nico grabbed the helmet from Coleton's hand and shook it at him for emphasis. "Just get in the car!"

"Just because he drove a Jeep in the desert doesn't mean he can drive one of the fastest cars on the planet. You want your sale?" Coleton asked. "Then *you* take him!"

"You know I can't take him. You can tell him what to do, how to take the corners, everything. He'll listen. Besides, he wants to drive with *you*. His son has a poster of you on his bedroom wall."

"Not going to happen," Coleton said. His voice was quiet, but he looked Nico right in the eye. "To that guy, this is all just a video game." Coleton motioned at the fire red Ferrari and the racetrack beyond. "Just a lap in Forza 4."

Then, Nico brightened with an idea. "I'll cut you in on the sale."

That was the magic incantation, and they both knew it.

"No," Coleton said, grabbing his helmet back. "You'll cut me in on all *three* sales."

A wide white smile lit up Coleton's face. The kind of smile that gets what it wants.

"Ten percent," Nico offered.

"Twenty," Coleton said.

"Fifteen and no more."

"Where do you own 'em?"

"One point seven each," Nico said through a smile, then bobbed his head. "And, he's paying two."

"Two million for a car that isn't even street legal?" Coleton whistled. He did some quick calculations in his head. He wasn't a math genius, but when it came to money Coleton could be quick on his feet.

"Four laps. That's it. For a hundred and thirty-five grand I'll eat a little shit," Coleton snickered as he pulled on his fireproof balaclava, then his helmet. Coleton loved when things fell in his lap.

"You must get some serious ass," said Al-Aziz, turning to Coleton. "Come on, you can tell me."

With three laps under their belt, Coleton began to relax. *One Hundred and Thirty-Five Grand.* For each corner, he had shown Al-Aziz brake markers long before the ones he used, and Al-Aziz had done well.

"Eyes on the road, Your Highness," Coleton instructed. "Into Turn 4, stay far to the right, then turn in for a late apex and clip the curb. See that red and while curbing?" Al-Aziz nodded.

Al-Aziz had really picked up his pace on the last lap, and Coleton was surprised by his creeping boldness. Maybe he was more experienced than Coleton gave him credit for and was finally settling in.

"Good," Coleton said, as they coasted through the corner. "Now make the right-hander through Turn 5. Go ahead and shift up to third."

"Too slow." Al-Aziz giggled. He paused at third before pushing the car into fourth, and the engine wailed an octave higher. Turn 5 came fast, but Al-Aziz managed the speed through as the RPMs dropped. He picked it back up, accelerating down the short straight. The speedometer waved to 80.

"Take third," Coleton instructed. He shifted his weight uneasily.

Al-Aziz pretended not to hear. Then mid-corner, he realized Coleton was right. He shifted down to third quickly, but the car still squirmed beneath them.

"Turn 7 is tricky," Coleton warned, his voice rising. Al-Aziz snuck back to fourth. "Slow down," Coleton ordered, as the car launched over an undulation in the pavement.

"I only go one way and that's up!" Al-Aziz shouted. The rear of the car skidded sideways, but Al-Aziz juggled the steering wheel and made it through the left right complex. His eyes were wide and bulging, as he pushed into the sweeping right-hander of Turn 8.

"Easy!" Coleton yelled. They narrowly missed fishtailing into the wall at the exit of Turn 8.

Coleton watched the tachometer wave into the red. Al-Aziz shifted to fifth, redlined, then sixth. They roared down the longest straight: 120, 130, 140, the fastest speed of his session.

"Okay, you got your speed. Shift back to fifth, fourth, slow down," Coleton demanded. A drop of rain splattered the windshield. 150, 160. "Slow down, *now!*" Al-Aziz would need to brake earlier and softer because of the changing weather conditions.

Suddenly it struck Coleton. *This asshole wanted to hit 180. Probably all day he'd held it in his mind, the roundness of it, like a hot babe. A mile every 20 seconds.* Now the pitch of the roaring engine swept higher. 160, 170. This was Al-Aziz's last chance to see the needle sweep across the dial to his target. He was going for it, and there was no way for Coleton to stop him. 175 …

"Brake, *now!*" Coleton screamed over the shrieking engine. On instinct his foot shot out and hit the foot well where the brake would have been, if he had been driving. They were coming in too hot. Way too hot for the wet conditions.

All professional racecar drivers have crashed, big. It's not a question of *if*, it's a question of *when*. Coleton's crashes fell under many categories: embarrassing, stupid, dangerous, asshole-puckering, and then there was that one crash two years ago—life threatening. Like his peers, Coleton could recall every intimate detail of each crash sequence. Even years later, he could describe a two-second crash with intense clarity: what he saw, heard, smelled. He was about to add another slow motion video to his mental library.

Al-Aziz nailed the brakes, and Coleton felt the wheels lock instantly. Recognition dawned. Without even a glance at the F1 style switches, Coleton knew what was happening, frame by frame. He had forgotten to switch the Manettino off its *Race* setting, and the anti-lock braking system was disengaged.

When the wheels of a car lock under heavy braking, professional drivers do the opposite of what human nature dictates: they release them gently, and can vaguely feel through the pedal the level of adhesion available to the tire. They keep just enough pressure on the pedal to extract every iota of tire adhesion before the tires lock and a slide begins. No more. No less.

An amateur, on the other hand, hits the brakes as hard as possible, aggressively trying to stop. Once the car starts to slide, an amateur never unlocks the wheels, which would allow the tire to rotate and use its adhesion capabilities to slow the car. The first mistake induces fear, which brings on panic and then the whole cataclysmic effect takes hold. Control is lost. Physics takes charge.

Al-Aziz's leg locked into place on the brake, as if trying to thrust the pedal through the floor. His brown knuckles went white, clenching the wheel. The huge Brembo brake calipers clamped like sharks teeth on the ceramic rotors, the wheels locked, the Ferrari slid.

Coleton knew they were going into the wall at the end of the straight. He also knew once they slid off the track the wet grass would accelerate their momentum. Physics. The 2,600 lb Ferrari flew off the asphalt and through the Michelin trackside banner like a bobsled on an Olympic run.

"Release the brakes and pitch the car!" Coleton yelled. "Turn the wheel!"

By throwing the car sideways at the last instant, a pro driver can enhance the deceleration and change the trajectory to a side impact. The broader surface area of a side impact dissipates more energy and reduces the severity of a crash.

Al-Aziz remained frozen, unable to process the order. His eyes stared straight ahead. Out the windshield, Coleton saw the Armco barrier approach, frame by frame.

"*Fuck me*," Coleton hissed.

Coleton spent most of his time in lightweight prototypes that slowed more quickly even when out of control and off of the racing surface. He had forgotten how much weight becomes the enemy in racing. The Ferrari was like a red missile careening into the wall.

The markings of prior visitors came into focus. Rubber marks, green paint, yellow paint, missing chunks of concrete the size of a fist. *Maybe the others walked away unscathed,* Coleton thought briefly. *Maybe.*

The wall grew larger. *Click. Click. Click.* His memory registered every frame.

"Hands off the wheel!" Coleton screamed the instant before impact, yet another counterintuitive step a pro driver takes a millisecond before going in hard to prevent a matched set of broken arms.

Al-Aziz released the wheel, as if electrified, all ten fingers extended in the air.

The initial crunch was surreal in its gentleness, as the bumper disintegrated. The front-mounted radiators exploded. The hood flew off as the Ferrari continued to compress into the Armco. Like taking a stack of crackers and bashing them with your fist on the counter, the bits and pieces disintegrated while debris shot outward: pieces of glass, shards of carbon fiber, bent aluminum from the chassis.

Coleton heard that familiar initial crunch, smelt the steam from the burst radiators. He could feel the mounting points rip out of the carbon fiber monocoque chassis. Then …

BANG.

Coleton felt the jolt and knew exactly what it meant. The expendable front of the car had been destroyed, its parts dissipating energy as the car slammed forward with huge kinetic force. Then came the last stand, Ferrari's Alamo, the safety tub: the thick carbon fiber structural element designed to stop the accordion effect of a frontal crash. The fist obliterating the crackers suddenly met the granite countertop. After thousands of engineering hours, the tub did what it was supposed to do.

The Ferrari stopped dead. The sudden stop with his right foot deep in the foot well shot fiery pain through Coleton's leg. There was a hiss of steam as hot fluids dripped into the wet grass. Then silence. Complete silence. Just the faint sound of a few raindrops splattering the wad of carbon fiber and steel that used to be a state-of-the-art Ferrari. Super toy for the super rich.

"You alright?" Coleton yelled, grimacing. The engine had cut out and his words came out louder than he expected.

Al-Aziz grunted and let out a string of words Coleton didn't understand.

"Yes or no?"

"Yeah … I think so," Al-Aziz said, his voice groggy.

"Your arms?"

"Good."

"You're lucky," Coleton said, as he pulled his harness release. "Somebody would've been wiping your ass for the next two months."

Coleton pulled the door handle but it stuck. He forced the wing-like door upward, and swung his legs over the doorsill. Electric pain shot up his right leg. Using his triceps he hoisted himself onto the doorsill. Then, he braced himself against the car and stood up on his left leg. He took a breath and tested the sole of his right foot on the ground like a lame horse. Pain exploded up his calf and the metallic taste he'd met more than a few times flooded his mouth. He lifted his foot off the ground, suddenly queasy, and knew. *It's broken.*

Coleton ducked his head to see Al-Aziz fiddling with his harness. He was in shock, but he appeared to be fine. *Let the paramedics pull the fat bastard out.*

Although carbon fiber shards littered the track, there was no fire risk. Coleton hopped away from the wreck, right leg cocked at a right angle, and sat on a stack of tires that made up part of the crash barrier. He felt his temperature rising with the pain, the first prickle of sweat, as a few drops of cold rain needled his scalp.

Nico tumbled out of the pit truck, his legs moving before they hit the ground. He looked at Al-Aziz still buckled in the driver's seat, but ran straight to Coleton. Coleton pointed to his right leg and shook his head.

"Is it broken?"

"Pretty much." Coleton shrugged.

"Maybe it's just a sprain. Let's get you to the hospital."

"It's not my first rodeo, Nico." Coleton looked him in the eye.

Coleton lay in the bed of the pit truck and they rumbled down the track toward the pits. He watched the paramedics struggle with

Al-Aziz, pulling him from the driver's seat headfirst. Coleton squeezed his eyes shut and cut the scene from view. *Fat Bastard.*

The truck shuddered to a stop on pit lane.

"Bring my car around," Coleton demanded, as Nico appeared at the tailgate.

"There's another ambulance on the way," Nico offered. "It should be here any minute. They'll check your leg out and take you to the hospital."

"It's broken. I told you. The paramedics aren't going to fix it. My keys are in my helmet bag. I'm not leaving my car here."

Nico recognized Coleton's tone of voice and knew there was no use digging his heels in. Nico pulled Coleton's silver Ferrari F12 streetcar next to the truck, hopped out and opened the passenger door for him.

"What are you doing?" Coleton asked, still sitting on the tailgate of the truck. Nico looked at him blankly. "You think I'm letting *you* drive? I'm driving."

"Your leg is broken," Nico scoffed.

"You think I don't know that?"

Using Nico's shoulder as a crutch, Coleton hopped to the car and lowered himself in. His leg was throbbing. He needed ice. But there, behind the wheel and in control, he immediately felt better. Nico got in the passenger seat and shrugged at his dealership employees as they stared open mouthed.

The F12 had a paddle shifter rather than a traditional gated Ferrari shifter with a separate clutch, so Coleton could drive it even with one leg. He had always complained that with paddles the F12 didn't stay true to the Ferrari tradition. Coleton was a purist in some respects and enjoyed heel-toe shifting. Then, why would he buy an F12, which only comes with paddles? Coleton's quick retort was always, "Because, it's the best."

They bumped along the road through the gates of PBIR. The rear tires of the F12 spun out, spitting gravel as they fishtailed onto Beeline Highway and sped past the Pratt and Whitney factory.

Coleton had always loved lines. Lines like that black delineation between playing it safe and turning your lights out. Riding those lines is always dangerous, and Coleton knew it. But, he also knew exactly where they lay and he loved playing with them. He loved taking a car just to the edge of out-of-control and keeping it there. So, driving at 98 mph on a public road with his left foot, while his right foot lay broken on the plush prancing horse floor mat wasn't even close to the edge. That was business as usual.

Twenty-two minutes later, they arrived at Good Samaritan hospital in West Palm Beach. Coleton pulled up to the Emergency Room entrance and revved the engine. It roared under the covered entranceway. The sliding glass doors opened and an attendant stuck his head out. He let out a long, low whistle at the car.

"We need a wheelchair, please," Nico called. The man nodded his head and disappeared. Returning with one, he wheeled it out the doors toward Nico in the passenger seat.

"Not for me, for him." Nico nodded at Coleton. The man looked confused, but wheeled the chair around to the driver's side. Coleton smiled at the man's disbelief, as Nico pulled him up out of the seat and into the wheelchair.

Nico wheeled Coleton through the sliding doors into the cold, sterile entrance. Everyone in the waiting room stared, not expecting to see a man in a full, Ferrari-red racing suit on a random Thursday afternoon.

"Name, please," said a woman behind the desk, looking over her glasses.

"This is Coleton Loren," Nico said.

"Oh, are you a race car driver?" She stood up to get a better look.

"What gave you that idea, sweetheart?" Coleton asked, giving her a good-natured wink.

The woman rolled her eyes, but a smile tugged at her lips. "Have a seat. And fill out these forms." She passed a clipboard through the slim opening in the glass to Nico.

Coleton's phone rang. He pulled his BlackBerry out of the jumpsuit hip pocket, and saw the name Ira Goldstein on the screen. Coleton stared in disbelief. *Already? Unbelievable!*

"What?" Coleton answered.

"Are you kidding me?" Ira asked. "You broke your *leg*?"

"How the hell do you know that already?"

"I've got ears," Ira said smugly. "You break your leg and your agent has to hear about it from someone else?"

"Calm down, asshole. It only happened half an hour ago. Hey, I gotta go. They're ready for me," Coleton lied.

"Where are you?"

"Good Sam."

"I'm coming over."

"Like hell you are. You have a plane to catch. And, Ira?"

"Yeah?"

"Try not to piss off Arthur Elrod. I want to race for Elrod Racing next year, and with the $10 million we have in sponsorship from Miller Sunglasses it should be a lay-up deal."

"Piece of cake. I'll be back Sunday and we can meet at the Breakers for brunch to celebrate."

"Why is everything with you about food?" Coleton asked with a smirk. "Fine. But, if you screw up the meeting tomorrow, Ira, so help me God, you may as well stay in New York." Coleton didn't wait for a response or a parting farewell before he hung up. He dropped his phone back to his lap. "Great. The word's out about my leg."

"Maybe Ira'll keep it quiet," Nico said.

"Are we talking about the same guy? The last time Ira stopped talking was in 1983 when he got his tonsils out," Coleton said, but Nico had already checked out of the conversation and was reading emails on his phone.

Coleton massaged his thigh muscle. The pain was creeping upward.

"Make yourself useful, will ya? Get me something to read."

Nico continued to stare at his phone. He finished his sentence, then looked up. "What's that?"

"Get me a magazine."

Nico strolled over to the wall, perused the clear plastic rack and returned with a tattered magazine.

"Really?" Coleton asked. "*Good Housekeeping*?"

"It's all they've got," Nico laughed.

"Sure," Coleton said, but flipped through it. He needed something to divert him from the pain.

"Coleton Loren?" called a nurse with curly, dirty-blonde hair and navy scrubs.

"It's pronounced LO-ren, not Lauren. It's French," Coleton said.

She looked down at her clipboard and adjusted her glasses. They were attached to a thin silver chain that looped her neck, and the movement sent the chains swinging.

"Whatever you say, Hero."

After Coleton convinced the nurse, whose name he'd learned was Margaret, that his leg was broken, she wheeled him straight to Radiology for X-rays. She then took him to an exam room and checked his temperature, pulse and blood pressure. When she began to pull up the leg of his racing suit, Coleton winced in pain.

"Okay, then. We'll do it the hard way."

Margaret unwrapped a pair of surgical scissors from a metal tray and set them to the edge of his pant leg.

"Are you crazy?" Coleton demanded, pulling his leg out of her hand and flinching again. "This is a five thousand dollar racing suit!"

"Fine," she said curtly. "Put this on however you want." She handed him a thin gown with small blue hearts scattered across the fabric. She picked up his chart and made a few notes.

Coleton unzipped the front of his suit and pulled it off his shoulders and down to his waist, exposing the fireproof Nomex long underwear underneath.

"Fair warning, Marge," he said, as he pulled the long-sleeved Nomex shirt over his head and exposed a muscled torso. "I'm not wearing underwear."

Coleton started to push the suit down past his waist. With a shake of her head, Margaret dropped his chart in a clear plastic box on the wall and left the room, but not without one last stolen glance.

Coleton managed to get the suit entirely off, except for the right pant leg. He was having a hard time pulling the suit over his toes without igniting fire in his ankle.

The door swung open, and Coleton froze. A beautiful woman in her mid-20s with long, straight blonde hair walked into the room, studying a clipboard. She didn't look up as she shut the door. She was wearing purple scrubs under a long white lab coat.

"Okay, Mr. Loren. How are we doing today?" she asked, looking up.

"I'm naked," said Coleton. "How are you?"

"Whoops," she said, laughing. She held up the clipboard to cover her eyes. "I'll give you some privacy while you work that out."

Coleton laughed.

"No, wait … help me."

She lowered the clipboard to her nose. Her eyes were large and bright blue.

"Can you just pull this pant leg off, please?" Coleton asked.

She grabbed the gown from the tray next to him, shook it open and handed it to him. Coleton leaned back on his elbows, extending his leg into the air. She gently pulled the suit over his foot, then turned her back while he finished putting on the gown.

"Okay, done," he said. She turned around.

"Right. I'm Dr. Harlow." She held out her hand.

"Sorry if I startled you," he said.

"It was nothing."

"*Nothing*?" he asked. He was still holding her hand. "I think I've just been insulted."

She pulled her hand away.

"Are you sure you're a doctor? You're too hot."

"I'm a Resident," she told him. "How about you? First time driving?"

"How tall are you?" he demanded.

"Why don't you let *me* do the physical?"

"It's just a question."

"I'm 5'11," she said. "Please lie back."

"That's a great height."

"Let's see, did the nurse check for HPI?" she asked, more to herself than to him, as she flipped through his chart.

"Oh God, I hope I don't have that."

"It means History of Present Illness," she said, trying to hide her smile. "Have you broken bones before?"

"I've broken everything except my femurs," Coleton said proudly. "Arms. Toes. Fingers. Ankles. Almost every rib, compressed some vertebrae, you name it. I even fractured my skull once."

"There's an achievement," Camilla said. She sat on a rolling stool, slid in front of a computer and entered some notes in the PATS software. Her fingers clicked on the keys. "Could explain a lot."

"Occupational hazard," he said.

"You're a racecar driver?" she asked, nodding at the suit that lay in a heap on the floor. "Were you in a race today?"

"No. I mean, yes, I'm a racecar driver, but the season doesn't start until March."

"So, you drive in circles really fast, risk your life and end up in the same place you started?" she asked, turning her head to blink at him.

"It looks more glamorous on TV."

"If you say so," Camilla said, standing. She bent over his leg. "Let's take a look."

"It's the other leg," said Coleton.

She startled, then glanced at his chart.

"Ha, made you look," he said, grinning.

She shook her head slightly and rolled her eyes. "I bet that works every night at the Holiday Inn bar."

"You wouldn't believe."

Coleton's leg was swollen and his ankle was turning purple, but no bones had broken the skin.

"Is the pain radiating?"

"Of course. It's broken," he said with authority. She raised an eyebrow and tilted her head.

"Let's see if your X-rays are in the system yet." Dr. Harlow went to the computer, clicked on a tab and an X-ray of Coleton's leg appeared on the screen. She leaned in to study it, then angled it toward Coleton.

"Your tibia is broken in two places. See here?" She pointed to two thin lines on the X-ray that Coleton could barely see. "But, they're only hairline fractures."

"*Motherf—*!" Coleton started, but reined himself in, his voice dropping off. "How long will they take to heal?"

"They aren't too messy. I'd say you'll be weight-bearing in two months. But, I'll have the orthopedist come downstairs and take a second look, since you're an athlete."

"I'll be walking in six weeks."

"Excuse me?" she said. "You'll walk when we say it's safe. Until then, I hope you have a comfy chair."

"Honey, testing starts the end of January. My comfy chair will be the driver's seat of an 1100 horsepower LMP1 Prototype." His voice softened. "This is my career. This is what I do."

She sighed, but humored him. "Testing?"

"Practice laps before the season starts. You ever been to a race? I could get you some passes. After all, you never know when I might need my doctor."

"First things first." She made some notes on his chart before placing it back in the plastic box on the wall. "What color do you want your cast?"

"Tell you what. I'll let *you* pick the color if you go to dinner with me."

"Okay, Hotshot. Get the pink," she said. She extended her hand to Coleton, and he held it a moment longer than necessary. "Someone will be in shortly." She smiled politely, then left the room.

CHAPTER 2

NEW YORK, NEW YORK

The Egyptian cotton sheet snapped tight across Ira Goldstein's naked body and the sudden movement woke him. He pried his eyes open, first the left, then painfully the right. Sunlight poured through the floor-to-ceiling windows of his suite. He had failed to pull the curtains. *What a night*, at least from what he could remember.

Rolling on his side, he peered over the edge of the bed. Sure enough, a bone-dry bottle of Patron lay on the plush cream carpet. Ira shook his head with a groan and ran his fingers through his hair, reflexively touching the first sign of a balding patch lightly with his fingertips.

Over a year earlier, a Mexican businessman who owned a share in the Waldorf Astoria had invited Ira to a free night at his hotel. Although they had met in the Salt Lake City racecar paddock and the introduction was made through Jose Gomez, Coleton's former and now hostile team owner, Ira decided to take a calculated risk that the businessman wouldn't remember how they had met. It paid off.

Apparently, the hotelier had been name-dropping invitations left and right for years, and his ego was too big to say no to an offer already made, whether he remembered the recipient or not. So, Ira had wrangled a free night at one of the best hotels in New York. The only unfortunate condition was that he had to leave his credit card on file for incidentals, which always made him a little nervous.

Someone groaned and the sheet snapped tighter across Ira's body. He was not alone. Ira tugged on the sheet, but it was yanked from his hand. He looked over his shoulder. The person had pulled the sheet overhead and a few chewed looking fingernails grasped it tightly: black polish with sparkles. She wasn't Miss USA, but at least she wasn't Mr. Universe.

Ira sighed and looked at his wrist. He bolted upright. His watch was gone. His solid gold Submariner Rolex with the sapphire bezel was gone. He looked at the digital clock on the nightstand: 10:00 a.m., exactly.

Unbelievable, Ira thought. *And, on top of it all, I'm going to be late!*

As Coleton's agent, Ira had scheduled a meeting with Arthur Elrod, the owner of the Le Mans racing team Coleton wanted to join the upcoming season. Ira hoped Elrod hadn't already heard about Coleton's broken leg. He wanted to get him under contract before the news broke. Either way, they were bringing $10 million of sponsorship to the team, so he wasn't that worried Elrod would turn down Coleton's offer. The meeting was a formality, but he couldn't be late.

He pinched the top sheet and peeled it slowly down. *Drum roll, please …*

The girl was no oil painting. Or if she was, she was more Picasso than Renoir. Black eye makeup raccooned her eyes and dark lipstick was smeared across her cheek. The harsh winter light did nothing to soften the ravages of the tequila.

Where did I find this whack job?

The girl flung her arm up to scratch her nose, then let it flop down, covering her eyes in the sunlight.

Ira was not picky. He had the best luck with perky college girls AWOL from school, who wanted a chance to visit Miami Beach and be seen in whatever sports car he happened to be leasing. Hooters girls were something of a self-proclaimed specialty.

Not bad bone-structure, really, Ira thought, looking beyond the ruined makeup. *She was probably a seven last night.*

Ira pinched the sheet again and pulled it slowly farther south. It slid down to reveal a pale clavicle and breastbone. He kept pulling. From the gentle slope of the sheet, he could tell he wasn't dealing with implants here, but he was willing to give them an honest look before he drew any conclusions. Just as the sheet rounded the top of her breasts, the girl slapped her arm across her chest, pinning the sheet to her body. She jolted upright, fully awake.

"Who the *hell* are you?" she demanded, clearly as unimpressed with his features as he had been with hers.

"Good morning, sweetheart."

"Where the hell am I?"

"Easy there," Ira said. "You're in a suite at the Waldorf. It could be worse."

"Where the hell are my clothes?"

She yanked the sheet off Ira and wrapped it around herself as she rose from the bed. She couldn't have been more than five-foot-two. She walked straight toward the bathroom with tiny measured steps under the sheet, and didn't look back at Ira sprawled naked across the bed.

As soon as he heard the bathroom door slam, Ira rolled out of bed. He opened the nightstand drawer. No watch. *Did she steal it?* He scurried to the kitchenette and found an empty bottle of 2005 Camus Cab in the sink, a cork screw with the red-stained cork still on it and a heap of crinkled Godiva wrappers, but no watch.

"I hope to God *that* didn't come out of the mini-bar," Ira said, picking up the bottle. He hurried to the armoire and pulled open the oak doors to inspect the mini-bar below the 52-inch LED. Everything looked intact, and he let out a long sigh. He must have bought the wine and tequila on the way back to the hotel. Then, he paused. There was a safe next to the armoire. He jiggled the latch, but it was locked.

"Shit! My watch!" Ira frantically tried code combinations, but realized in his drunken stupor he had been smart enough to lock his watch, and probably his wallet, in the safe, but not sober enough to remember the combination.

By the time Ira got off the phone with the front desk it was 10:20. He only had 40 minutes to get to his meeting, and the front desk couldn't send someone up for an hour. He would have to come back. Never mind the wallet, he needed the watch for one of his signature negotiation moves. He'd let it peek out from under his French cuffs. If they complimented the cufflinks, he knew they'd seen the watch. He didn't know why, but he never lost a deal if they complimented his gold checkered-flag cufflinks.

He hustled to her side of the bed and looked under the dust ruffle. A Jimmy Choo purse in black ostrich lay on the floor. Dior lipstick and unopened condoms, ribbed for her pleasure, were spilled across the carpet.

"A three thousand dollar handbag?" Ira mumbled. He yanked the purse from under the bed and pulled her wallet into the light. He couldn't believe it had come to this, but he was late, he didn't have his wallet, and he didn't have time to walk the 10 blocks to Fifth Avenue and Central Park South.

He took a $20 bill. Then, he studied her drivers license in the light. She was 19, and her name was Eileen Greenberg. Ira put her wallet back, then tossed the purse under the dust ruffle, leaving the lipstick and condoms on the floor. Was it wrong that he suddenly found her attractive because she was barely legal, Jewish and probably rich?

Either way, he had an appointment to make, and regardless of her financial stability, he was unwilling to leave the suite before her. It was very possible she would empty out the mini-bar and test all of the hair products and expensive face creams that hotels leave lying around for just this very reason: credit cards on file for incidentals.

Ira dressed quickly, zipped up his suitcase and tied his shoes, but the shower was still running. He looked at the nightstand: 10:40.

He tried the bathroom door. It wasn't locked, which surprised him.

"Sweetheart, think you can speed things up? I have a meeting to catch."

The steam was so thick Ira could barely see. She pulled back the curtain. Her eye make-up was now streaked down her face.

"Fuck. You."

She shot the shower curtain back across the rod. She paused, then grinned behind the curtain.

I'm not going to let some little slut ruin my best client's career, Ira thought. He lunged toward the shower curtain, threw it back and pulled her out by the forearm.

"Get your hands off me!" she screamed, but as she spoke, her center of gravity shifted and she slipped into Ira. They crashed to the floor.

"Oh shit, my back!" Ira groaned.

"Yeah, I bet it hurts, Grandpa."

They scowled at each other, their faces inches apart. The girl was naked and her arms and legs were splayed over him. His clothes were getting soaked. They struggled to get free from one another, but their limbs were entangled and she was slippery. She giggled. He chuckled. Soon they were laughing out loud.

"Hey, now that I see them, your boobs look a lot better than I thought."

"Yeah, well. You're still the fat Jew from last night."

Ira's jaw dropped. He glared at her, but her eyes sparkled with such mischief that despite himself, he broke into laughter again.

"Please, I'm not just blowing you off. I mean, I am, but I *totally* have a meeting to catch at 11, and if I'm late I'm, *like*, so screwed." It was his version of teenage girlspeak. He didn't know if it was accurate, but usually the girls lapped it up.

"Okay, okay. I get it," she said. She still had a smile on her face and those puppy-by-the-food-dish eyes that told him he would, *like*, totally have gotten some head. *This meeting better go well.*

"I'll be out of here in five," she said. "You should put on a dry shirt."

Arthur Elrod studied the bank of monitors arranged along the credenza behind his desk. He steepled his fingers and then pulled them to his lips. The landline on his desk rang, but he just narrowed his eyes and focused on the tiny blinking symbols. On the fourth ring, he swiveled around to sweep the phone from its cradle.

"Yes?"

"It's your pilot, *monsieur*. Returning your call."

"About time." Elrod gave a regent-like wave for his secretary, Marie-Claire, to proceed although she wasn't in the room. "Patch him through." He glanced at his impeccably manicured fingers, each cuticle pushed back into a perfect semi circle, while he waited for the click.

"When?" he demanded, unwilling to wade through pleasantries.

Elrod's pilot stood at a counter in the pilot's lounge at the Gulfstream factory in Savannah, Georgia, clutching the courtesy telephone. Elrod had stood there himself, more than once, but as a purchaser, not a pilot.

"Looks like Thursday, sir."

Elrod pulled the phone away from his ear to glare at it. He lifted it a few inches as if threatening to throw it, before slowly bringing it back into place.

With his thumb, Elrod slowly twirled the heavy gold ring on his ring finger: a sure sign he was about to lose his temper. The ring carried a five-carat, flawless ruby, and as Elrod believed the stone brought him luck in business, it never left his finger. Sometimes Elrod could just catch his reflection in the table of the blood red stone. He looked for it now, then frowned.

"Thursday will not work. You need to fix this."

A deep breath came over the line before the pilot spoke. "Well, sir—I *can't* fix the plane myself, and I'm not sure what else you'd like me to do?"

Elrod chewed the inside of his mouth for a moment, too enraged to speak.

"I'll tell you what you can do!" Elrod spat. "You can tell these assholes in Savannah, if I spend $52.5 million on a plane and it breaks, then they send me a new one until mine is perfect! What do they think I'm going to do? Charter some rat with wings for 20 G's an hour? I've bought four planes from these pricks over the years, which means I've spent more money with them than the GDP of some counties!"

The pilot said nothing, but Elrod could sense his discomfort. The man was round-shouldered and clam-like, with almost no muscle tone, which disgusted Elrod. If he hadn't been one of the best pilots in the world, Elrod would have happily canned him on looks alone.

"Now, you listen. Find something to fly back to New York tonight and pick me up tomorrow, and you can tell Mr. Howard that it's on his nickel! His boys screwed this up, so he can dip into his profit on the $52.5 mill I paid him and get me a plane that fucking flies."

"Yes, sir. I'll relay the message. I'm sure they will accommodate you. You're a great customer."

"Damn right, I am!"

Elrod dropped the receiver back to its cradle before his pilot could reply. The second it settled, the phone rang again. Elrod depressed the speakerphone button.

"*Monsieur*?" Marie-Claire's quiet voice resonated through the room again.

"Yes?"

"Blake Falcon from the pits in Chicago."

Blake Falcon was Elrod's lead trader on the Chicago Options Exchange. Elrod's business pursuits were eclectic: He dabbled in commercial real estate, fine art and the occasional undervalued common stock takeover or high yield bond. But his real moneymakers were commodities, specifically crude oil. He traded futures on the floor of the Chicago Mercantile Exchange and options through the Chicago Options Exchange. As he saw it, Blake placed the orders under his direction, but deep down, he knew Blake kept his account safe from his own bad habits.

"Put him through," Elrod directed, spinning to study the light, sweet crude futures chart.

A few seconds later, the roar of the floor came over the speaker. Elrod spoke first, his tone of voice rising again to almost the pitch he had used with his pilot.

"Blake, I'm looking at the one-minute chart. What the fuck is going on? I thought you said it was going to tank *today*? We are underwater and about two handles from getting stopped out!"

Blake always placed stop orders to limit losses should a trade go sour too quickly to get out manually. Pre-placed stops also took some of the emotion out of the exit decision. Like most smart day traders, Blake liked to get in and out quickly with a win some—lose some attitude.

Elrod, on the other hand, loathed stop orders, which set what he saw as an arbitrary level of loss and always seemed to stop him out seconds before the trade turned back his way. Elrod traded on gut, which was often the opposite of what everyone else was doing. Sometimes Elrod was wrong and took nasty losses, but when he was right he made fortunes.

"Yeah, it's not looking good, Boss. Do you want me to move the stop order up 50 cents?" Blake asked, still hoping to limit their losses. He knew Elrod would hold on, especially for a short sell. Even some veterans at the big banks and funds never shorted, because they just couldn't grasp the idea of selling first and buying back later. It was another thing that set Elrod apart from the sheep.

"No, I don't want you to move it, Blake," Elrod said slowly, as if speaking to a child. "I want you to *cancel* it! I don't want to watch it tick up just enough to blow our nuts off and then tank like we wanted in the first place. Cancel it."

"But, sir."

"I'll call you back. And Blake?"

"Yes, sir?"

"Stop with the fucking stop orders!"

Elrod pressed the button to end the call, his eyes returning to the screens behind his desk. After a few moments, Marie-Claire, buzzed him again.

"Yes?" Elrod asked, when the speaker crackled to life.

"Ira Goldstein is here to see you."

"Ira who?"

"Ira Gold-stein" said Marie-Claire.

"Who the hell is that?"

"Your 11 o'clock."

Elrod looked up at the carved, coffered ceiling of his office, but still couldn't remember.

"Coleton Loren's manager," she added.

It took him a second to shift focus. Elrod was in the market for new drivers for his Le Mans Series team. He had bought the team two years earlier for pennies on the dollar from a bankrupt team owner. He didn't know anything about racing *per se*, but had a penchant for fine cars and would buy anything at a big enough discount. Elrod knew how to wring the best from the people that worked for him. It had made him successful in just about every venture he had tackled. A race team would be no different.

"Right," said Elrod. "Send him in. Oh, and if Glen from the boat calls, put him through immediately."

"*Oui, monsieur.*"

Elrod scowled at the phone. She thought she was so smart. He knew she'd overheard him say, as she waited for her job interview, that he was looking for a French girl because he had new business in Le Mans, France. Apparently she'd looked up the Le Mans Wikipedia pages on her phone—both the race and the village—memorized their main points in five minutes, added "—Claire" after her name, Marie, and adopted the worst French accent this side of "Saturday Night Live." She was actually an Irish-Puerto Rican from Hoboken. But she was easy enough to look at, she did a decent job and it amused him to hire people who thought they were smarter than the boss. Someday, when she least expected it and it would hurt the most, he would lower the boom.

Ira Goldstein prided himself on having seen all manner of decadent wealth in his day, so that nothing really surprised or impressed him. But when he walked into Arthur Elrod's Fifth Avenue office, he couldn't help but take a step back. The room was cavernous with 20-foot ceilings and mahogany paneling. There were plush seating groups of Victorian furniture on either side of the towering double doors. Ira followed the secretary along the marbled mosaic that led from the entrance directly to Elrod's vast desk.

Elrod, himself, was equally impressive, with his fine Italian suit tailored to accentuate the broad shoulders of his once athletic frame, a crisp white shirt open at the throat, fat diamond cufflinks and a bright orange pocket scarf pointing at all the perfect angles from his breast pocket. Elrod had jet-black hair fingered through with gray and pushed straight back off his forehead.

"Anything to drink, Mr. Goldstein?" the secretary asked Ira, as she motioned for him to please-be-seated. He was still gawking at his surroundings.

"I'll have an ice water. Thanks," Ira said and watched the beautiful woman leave the room. Elrod seemed unfazed by her skintight pencil skirt, the delectable long legs underneath or her tantalizing French voice. Maybe it was because Elrod was busy, maybe he didn't want to mix business with pleasure or maybe he just didn't care, but Ira couldn't imagine any excuse worth not noticing a woman *that* beautiful. Ira shook his head and refocused on the task ahead.

"Good morning, Mr. Elrod," Ira said. His tone was cocky, as if to say, *I've just been under a soaking wet 19 year-old on the floor of a suite at the Waldorf. How's your morning going?*

"That will be all, Smith," Elrod said sternly. A large man in a black suit stepped from the shadows. Ira startled in his chair; he hadn't noticed him before. Smith's hair was shaved closely to the scalp, but his head was well shaped and the military cut suited him. His hands were clasped behind his back. "Report back at two p.m. I have a meeting downtown at the Bull Pen," Elrod said. Smith nodded, leveled a measuring look at Ira and then stalked from the room.

"Where were we?" Elrod asked, with his first, albeit forced, smile of the day. "Ira, is it?"

"Yes, Ira."

"So, how's Mr. Loren's leg?" Elrod asked with a raised eyebrow. He folded his hands and rested them on his desk.

Shit, he already knows. "He'll be fine. He breaks bones all the time and bounces right back."

"It's broken?" Elrod asked stiffly. "And, he'll still be ready for the test at Sebring?" They didn't sound like questions.

"Hairline fracture. He'll be a hundred percent by then," said Ira, brushing the matter away with his hand.

"And, how's the contract with Miller Sunglasses coming? Did you guys get that whole thing ironed out? What's the bottom line?" The intercom sounded, and Elrod pushed the button. "What?"

"*Excusez-moi—*" Marie-Claire said over the speakerphone. "You asked to be told when your boat captain called. Shall I put him through?" She sounded nervous to Ira, as if she was worried about interrupting the boss, whether he had instructed her to or not. Okay, so Elrod was a bully. Ira could handle him.

"Yes," replied Elrod. "Excuse me for a second, Ira. Weather problems this morning."

Ira shrugged and looked around the room, trying to indicate that he would not be listening in on the call.

"Glen, is it letting up yet? How far did you get?" Elrod picked up the receiver for privacy before he could respond over the speakerphone. Ira, who had every intention of eavesdropping, could only hear half the conversation. Elrod listened impatiently for a moment.

"If it's not too bad, let's push on to Barbados and drop the hook in the lee of that cove I like. You know the one I'm talking about? Where I taught Justine to water-ski."

Ira surveyed the objects on Elrod's desk. A model of a private aircraft that looked like a prototype, a model G-4, several models of exotic cars: Bugatti, Ferrari, McLaren, and an antique cigar box on the corner of a large leather writing pad. It was otherwise free of paper and clutter.

"Well if these assholes from Gulfstream get their shit together, I'd say about four-*ish*, but I'll have my assistant call you when we rotate."

That caught Ira's attention. Any mention of yachts or private planes got his blood flowing. He owned neither, but considered himself an expert on both. He savored the chance to display his knowledge and good taste.

Ira watched the monitors behind Elrod blink red and green, but the symbols and numbers meant little to him. Ira knew he was smart. He regularly impressed friends with the vast amount of information crammed in his brain and its search-engine-like ability to retrieve it in conversation, even after a tequila or three. But stocks, commodities, and investments in general, had him slightly foggy. Ira preferred words to numbers. He had great confidence in his patter— the ability to talk and charm and convince.

"Sorry about that," Elrod said, as he hung up the phone. Then he spent a good 30 seconds straightening everything on his desk before looking up.

"So … headed to the Caribbean?" Ira asked. "What kind of iron do you have down there? I'm pretty familiar with the yacht market."

"Feadship, 198 feet," said Elrod, as if he were talking about a Chevy Malibu.

"Oh really? Is that the one that launched this year? *Closing Bell* is her name, right?" Ira smiled. He would have Elrod's attention now.

"Yes, how do you know that?" Elrod asked, more suspicious than impressed.

"It was on the cover of *PMY* a few months back, right? The article mentioned a trader from New York owning the boat. I knew it had to be you." Ira beamed as if he'd just won Jeopardy. *I'll take smooth flattery for a thousand, Alex.*

"I did most of the design myself. It makes her harder to resell, but this one's a keeper," Elrod said proudly. Ira cleared his throat, but before he could show off any more of his knowledge of luxury goods, Elrod changed the subject back. "Coleton will be ready and Miller is on board, right?"

"Yes, Coleton will be ready. And Jack Miller has agreed to $10 million in sponsorship," Ira said. "The only thing is that he wants to break it up into four payments of 2.5 each. Which is pretty common, really."

"$2.5 million payments? What, like installments?"

"Yes. Sponsors do that for budgetary purposes. It's standard practice."

"Yeah, well what if they make the first 2.5 and then DK on us for the balance?" asked Elrod.

"DK?" Ira asked despite himself. Normally, he would have pretended he knew what it meant.

"Don't Know. It's an old trader standby—a trader makes a bad move and doesn't want to own up to it, so he pretends he doesn't know what you're talking about. DK. I may have invented it." Elrod smiled slyly.

"Well, I hate to say it, but I've been in motorsports long enough that I've seen that happen as well," Ira said, remembering a private aviation sponsor that had reneged on a substantial portion of promised sponsorship dollars the year before. "But I wouldn't worry in this case. We have a pretty tight contract. I think Jack Miller is an honorable guy, and as long as we are deploying for them in the paddock, I don't foresee any problems."

Elrod's face clouded over. "Yeah? Well, 2.5 is not enough of a down stroke," he said with a slight tinge of aggression in his voice. "I want five."

"Not gonna happen."

Elrod raised an eyebrow. "Those are my three least favorite words," he said in a conversational tone. "Most people who say them to me come to regret it. A great deal."

It suddenly seemed to Ira that he could smell tequila seeping out of his pores. He shrugged, his tongue thick and uncomfortable, aware this was an inadequate response to a not-so-veiled threat.

"How do you know it's not going to happen?" Elrod stared at Ira and narrowed his eyes. "Did you ask Jack Miller for a $5 million down stroke? Did you use those words? Or, did you offer him this chickenshit payment plan?" Elrod's eyes burned into Ira's.

A drop of tequila sweat dripped down Ira's temple. He wiped it away, but not before Elrod took full notice and steepled his fingers again.

"We always have installments in our contracts," Ira protested. "Like I said, it's pretty standard in the motorsports industry."

"Well it's not standard in *my* industry, son."

Ira was only 10 years younger than Elrod, but this comment didn't insult him. It alarmed him. For the first time during the meeting, Ira could feel the deal slipping from his grasp. Anytime Ira felt himself pushed in a corner, his strategy was to come out flailing. Coleton had chided Ira before about blowing easy layup deals because of his ability to generate personality conflicts.

His exact words had been, "You could make the Dalai Lama want to kick you in the nuts."

"Look, Arthur," Ira said, putting the fingertips of both hands on Elrod's desk, then withdrawing them a few millimeters. "I'll talk to Jack. But, I need to know that if I can't get it done for the five mill down stroke that we have a deal with the—"

"*Excusez-moi,*" the voice said over the speaker. Elrod held up his hand, stopping Ira mid-sentence, and smiled as if the interruption was right on cue.

"Yes?"

Ira looked around and realized the secretary had never brought his water. Apparently he wasn't expected to stay long. Or maybe he was just getting paranoid.

"Blake is on the phone again. He said it's urgent," Marie-Claire said.

Elrod spun his chair to look at something on the monitors. Ira had an uncanny ability to read body language, if not the stock tickers. As he watched Elrod, he had the sudden instinctual feeling in his bowels that never lied: Elrod was going to explode. *Of all the days I could have met this man, why does it have to be a day when he's pissed off about some stupid trade?*

"Fuck!" Elrod screamed, so loudly that Ira's chair rattled. "Fuck, fuck, fuck, FUCK!"

Elrod picked up the model Bugatti from his desk and shattered it against the wall behind the monitors.

He snatched the receiver off the hook.

"Blake, what the *fuck* is going on?"

There was a long silence, as Elrod listened.

Elrod rearranged the remaining model cars to fill the space left by the Bugatti, then cleared his throat to speak. "I'm staying put. You can put your asinine stops back in at a buck and a half. Fuck them, this thing is overbought. I'm not a sheep." His voice was resolute.

Ira wondered if Elrod had just DKed himself.

After a few more moments of silence, Elrod nodded and hung up. He looked at his monitors and then typed something on a thin wireless keyboard. A graph appeared on one of the screens. Ira squinted at it. Elrod, without looking behind him, angled the monitor away from Ira and studied the data.

For 10 minutes Ira sat bouncing his knee, occasionally hand-combing his hair back, and studying every detail of the office until he found himself actually staring at the ceiling.

Coffered ceiling, he thought. *Nice.* Then he remembered a call girl he'd paid for a month of Girlfriend Experience. A college graduate with an art history degree, she had been impressed by what she called the "lacunar" ceiling in their luxury hotel suite. He asked her to stop calling it that; he'd heard the word before. "Lacuna" means an empty space, specifically in the body, like, for example, in the mucous membranes lining the urethra, the ones that become not so empty and oh-so painful when you contract syphilis.

Ira gave a little cough. "Bad day with a trade?"

"You could say that," Elrod said.

"Well, I guess I'll get out of your hair then," Ira said.

"Good idea."

Ira stood up. But, before he walked to the door, he decided to make one final move.

"So, I'll try and get the larger down stroke from Miller, but if I can't, we still have a deal, right?" Ira regretted the question the second it left his mouth.

Elrod spun his chair around and leapt to his feet.

"Not with these insulting $2.5 million payments we don't!" Elrod screamed. "I just lost 2.5 million dicking around with you for 15 minutes!"

"Okay, well—" Ira began, backing up. His palms were low and outstretched as if to calm a spooked horse.

"Just get the hell out of my office before I lose another 2.5," Elrod said. He extended his right arm with his index finger pointing at the towering double doors and stood like that until Ira left the room.

CHAPTER 3
HOMESTEAD, FLORIDA

Sunlight beat down on the drum-tight blue tarp. Rather than providing shelter from the 10 o'clock heat, the makeshift tent barely dulled its edges. George Wachner could feel the sweat prickling his scalp, beading a slow course along his backbone.

"We should put entirely new rubber on the Burell before the race," he told Matteus, the Brazilian mechanic he had hired for the day. "And, let's widen the rear wheels a few millimeters. There was too much oversteer in the fast corners during qualifying."

George had been working shoulder-to-shoulder with Matteus for two hours on the racing go-karts—a Burell and two Tony karts—that sat elevated on their roll-bar trolleys like three split-open cadavers.

George was one of Matteus's favorite customers. Not only did his fame in the Le Mans series bring attention to Matteus's small but growing kart shop, but George always pitched in with the hard work on the day of the race. George was also able to communicate in detail how the kart handled around the track, which let Matteus showcase his skill. Most of his customers had more of a point-and-shoot philosophy.

"Dad?" a voice called out.

George looked up from the open chest of an engine overhaul in progress, and wiped his brow with a relatively clean forearm. George's son, Christopher, hopped out of the red trailer parked next to the improvised garage floor. He had a shock of dirty-blond hair that fell in his eyes.

"Dad. I'm not so sure I want to race today. It's too hot and I'm not really feeling that great."

"What do you mean … you don't want to race?" George said. "But you've already qualified!"

If George was honest with himself, he wasn't that surprised. He had managed to get Chris through the first and second practice sessions the evening before, and had talked him through the qualifying process earlier that morning, but barely.

"Qualified?" said Chris. "Dad, I came in last. It's embarrassing. I even have to start behind Megan—"

"It doesn't matter where you start, Chris," George said for the thousandth time. "Where you finish is what counts. As for Megan, she's smaller than you, so of course she's got a weight advantage." George found it hard to hide the disappointment in his voice. And he saw it in Chris's face.

On a karting race weekend, there are five race classes based on skill-level: Micro Max, Mini Max, Juniors, Seniors and then finally the Masters class. Chris was slated to run in the Juniors race. George had decided to bump him up from Mini Max, because he was just getting too old, but Chris clearly wasn't ready for the jump. He just didn't seem to have the racer gene, that raw aggression mixed with a certain patience of timing that it takes to win.

The boy kicked the toe of his shoe into the matted grass. "I'd rather just watch you, Dad. You're starting from pole! I knew you'd qualify first. You're totally going to dominate the Masters class!" Chris smiled up at his dad from behind his bangs.

"Well, your sister is going to race," said George. Chris just shrugged. George knew that Megan couldn't care less about racing. She only did it to prove she could beat her older brother with impunity.

"Yoo-hoo, hello there!" called a perky British voice. A short woman with sharply cropped red hair approached their tent. "Is that George Wachner, I see there? What a pleasure!"

"Hello, Sharon." George smiled his crooked smile despite himself. Before he could come off as cool and aloof, she had him in a lingering hug.

"I would love a quote for our website. You don't mind if I start this little tape recorder, do you?" Sharon pulled a chrome digital recorder the size of a lighter from the pocket of her khaki golf shorts. She wore squeaky white tennis shoes and a polo shirt decorated with the Homestead Raceway logo, a checkered flag rainbowing a curved stretch of asphalt.

"Sure," George agreed. He ran a hand through his thick hair. It was chestnut and only pinned through with gray despite his age. He had a handsome manly face, warm good-natured eyes and the skin around his eyes crinkled when he smiled. He was well past 40, which many considered beyond retirement age for a pro driver.

Sharon pressed a button, her eyes on him the whole time.

"*Le Mans Driver Embraces Off-Season Practice*, sounds like a nice title, don't you think, Georgey? I know a few teenage boys in this paddock, thrilled at the challenge of spanking one the fastest drivers in the Series."

"One of the fastest?"

"Second fastest, to be exact." Sharon smiled.

"And, that top spot is still debatable," George said, nodding.

"So, tell me. Are you excited?" she asked, holding the recorder to his mouth. The backs of her fingers brushed his chin.

"Sure I am. Although, to be honest, it's not so easy at *these* kind of tracks. It's definitely a disadvantage being a professional driver here. Every other guy is gunning for you, just so they can go home and tell the kids on their block or the friends in the break room that they beat a professional racecar driver. And, they'll run you off the road trying."

"Then, why do you do it?"

"You know why, Sharon," said George in his best interview voice. "Karting is the absolute best practice for a racecar driver, other than getting in your team's million-dollar racecar and taking it for a spin around a full-sized track. But, budgets only allow *that* a couple times a year."

Sharon's phone rang and she pulled it from her pocket.

"He's here?" she exclaimed. "No!" She stared at George in disbelief. "You've got to be kidding! Klaus Ulrick? To *race*? He hasn't had a single practice session. He hasn't even qualified. He's going to just jump into a kart and start from the back of the pack?" She shook her head, impressed. Drivers who fail to show up for the qualifying session are still allowed to race but are penalized by starting from last position.

At the name Klaus Ulrick, George's mood soured. Klaus Ulrick was the star driver for the Porscheworks LMP1 team in the Le Mans series. George may have been the second fastest LMP1 driver the previous Le Mans season, but Ulrick was the one ahead of him.

Ulrick drove for a "works" team, which meant it had the full factory support of Porsche for engine and chassis parts, and an exorbitant budget that could be written off as a business expense. Porsche, Corvette, BMW, Audi, all sponsored factory Le Mans teams to vie for the Constructor Championship title, awarded to the team whose car wins the most races in the season.

The counterpart to the Constructor Championship title is the Driver Championship, which goes to the driver with the most points garnered over the course of the season. The previous year, George had raced for a privateer team called Ignite Racing, owned by a midwestern entrepreneur and car enthusiast, not an automobile empire. This meant that although they had similar-looking LMP1 machines and attended the same races, George's racing budget was a fraction of Ulrick's. George was convinced that on an equal playing field and with the same resources, he would surely dominate.

"What a rock star!" Sharon gushed. "Ulrick just rocks up and knows he'll win even if he starts from the back! Did you see Heidi? Is she here too?" Sharon squealed. "How does she look? Oh, how exciting! Right now, I'm coming over right now!"

George rolled his eyes in disgust. If Ulrick was there, the stakes had surged. There is a natural aversion between true competitors; however, George's distaste for Klaus Ulrick veined deeper than any dislike. George specifically and whole-heartedly loathed Klaus Ulrick, what he stood for, his co-drivers, his team, his team owner, even his perfect supermodel wife with whom the whole world appeared to be in love.

Now was his chance to show his skill, and George could feel the pressure, that quickening of the blood that all real racers live for, tighten the veins in his neck.

"The Seniors race is almost over," Matteus told George, pulling him from his thoughts. "Then there will be a 15-minute break before the Masters is called to the starting grid. And that bolt is already tight, man." Matteus took the wretch from George's hand. "Why don't you cool off in the trailer for a few minutes?"

George nodded. His face was flushed. "Drink some water, relax," he heard Matteus say.

The loudspeaker crackled to life. "The track is now ready for today's final race. Will the Masters class please make its way to the starting grid?"

Mechanics and drivers emerged from rows of tents and trailers, and pushed their go-karts atop their trolleys toward the gap in the chain link fence and onto the track.

It takes at least two people to lift a go-kart from its trolley. All along the miniature replica of a real starting grid, karts were lifted by their crash bars and set carefully down on the pavement, lined up in rows of two in the order in which their drivers had qualified. George looped the nylon strap of his helmet through the double ring and pulled it tight under his chin. It was the same helmet he had worn in his Le Mans races the past season. It had large chrome stars spilling across a red and blue streaked background.

Like all drivers, George was obsessed with his helmet. A driver's helmet is his only real avenue of self-expression in the whole racing get-up, and drivers regularly shell out three to five thousand dollars for custom paint jobs. And, like the backpacks of spoiled school children, helmets must be new each year. This red-white-and-blue number had served George well. He already had three Driver Championships under his belt over the course of his long career, but still second place was nothing to scoff at. He decided to work some of the same elements into his helmet for the next season, just for good luck.

George allowed himself one long survey of the back of the grid, but Klaus hadn't arrived. If he didn't show up in the next few minutes he wouldn't be allowed to start. George turned back and focused his eyes at the start/finish line. Maybe it had just been a nasty rumor to rile him up. He placed his hands on the seatback of his go-kart. He hopped both feet into the bottom of the seat before jumping them forward onto the pedals and dropping into the seat. This was the proper way to get into a racing go-kart, and as if following his lead, the drivers behind him began leap-frogging into their karts as well.

Leading the pack from the grid onto the track for the warm-up lap, George set the pace. With a few corners to go, he slowed down to a crawl to bunch up all the karts. Like most experienced drivers, George used his pole position to his advantage by manipulating the pace, clustering everyone up and then slingshotting ahead at the last moment.

George got away clean and fast from the starting line. His right foot pinned the accelerator flat to the floor. He managed to edge in front of the kart next to him, the one that qualified second, just far enough to gain the advantage into the first corner, a sharp left-hander. As in real racing, there is no coasting in go-karting. You are either flat or braking for your life.

At the last second, George pumped the brake hard with his left foot and turned into the corner. Professional drivers develop enough sensitivity in their left feet to brake hard, but in a smooth, squeezing motion that keeps the rear wheels from locking up. George felt his left wheel hit the red and white raised curbing on the apex of the corner, then he tracked out by letting the momentum push the kart out to the far right side of the lane and onto the outside curbing.

The second corner of Homestead is what professional drivers call a throwaway corner, since Turn 3 is more important. Corners leading onto a long straight are key, because the more speed you carry through the corner the more speed you will carry down the *entire* straight. Rather than cutting in sharply for Turn 2, George waited an extra second for a late apex, setting up for a perfect Turn 3. This would give him a quarter to a half second on the kart behind him.

All of a sudden, George's head snapped backwards. He felt the rear end of his kart skid to the right. His adrenaline surged and he looked down at his hands on the wheel. They were straight; it wasn't him. He hadn't done anything wrong. In confusion, he turned to look over his shoulder, but his back wheels locked, jerking him into a spin. The second blurred, then he saw the bottom of another kart launch over his left shoulder, barely missing his helmet. A third kart t-boned him pushing him off the track.

Cutting in for an early apex, some amateur had hit him, and his kart had done a complete 360 in less than two seconds. George watched the other karts skate through Turn 3 and head down the straight toward the first hairpin. In a flash he recognized Ulrick's neon green and black helmet. In only three corners Ulrick had sprinted to second place. It would be a clear win for the German.

"Hey, kid. Did you race today?" Ulrick called. He tossed two duffel bags into the trunk in the hood of his Porsche GT3RS and walked toward Chris.

Chris held a helmet bag in each hand and was heading to their car to load up. He squinted into the sun as he looked up at Ulrick and shook his head no. Ulrick had sandy blond hair and gray eyes. He wasn't tall, but his shoulders were wide and square, matching the shape of his jaw.

"Can't say I blame you," Ulrick said. "Why battle your genetics?"

Chris looked up at the famous driver, and used his shoulder to push his bangs out of his eyes. It made him feel special that Klaus Ulrick was talking to him.

"Don't you know, boy? Real champions inherit their talent. Seems you're out of luck." Ulrick winked. Chris suddenly realized the conversation wasn't meant to be friendly. He was shocked, and didn't know what to say. He had never experienced open hostility from a grownup.

"Hey, Ulrick. You got something to say? Say it to me." George shuffled up quickly behind Chris. "What did he say to you?" George asked Chris through clenched teeth.

Ulrick smiled and held out his hand to George. "Just wanted to shake your hand, friend. As I was telling your son, I hear you did a great job qualifying on pole today." George looked down at his outstretched hand and refused to take it. Ulrick continued, "*Almost* as good as winning a race. At your age, it must feel like a Championship." George glared at him. "Exactly how long did it take you to auger in today? Fifteen seconds?"

George wanted to drop kick Ulrick. But, just as he was about to unleash his worst, George's wife, Grace, walked up behind him and put her hand on his shoulder.

Grace wore a lime green and pink Lily Pulitzer dress and had a slim silk scarf tied around her light brown ponytail.

"Hello," she said to Ulrick, shading her eyes with her right hand. "I didn't see Heidi here, but you will give her my best?" She had never met Heidi Ulrick, but she always tried to be pleasant.

The men glared at each other.

"Don't *ever* talk to my son again. Or you will regret it," George spat. Then, with his arm around Chris's shoulder he pushed past Ulrick. Grace sucked in her breath and hurried after her husband.

"In a fair race, I would have killed that pompous prick!" George hit his fist into the steering wheel and depressed the accelerator another inch. The Tahoe's rev limiter jerked in a quick wave. Outside the window, orange groves and tall stands of cord grass blurred past.

"George, language ..." In the back seat, Christopher held the latest *AutoWeek* a few inches from his nose, while Megan looked out the window. Grace turned up the radio. "I don't like it in front of the children."

"Nothing they haven't heard at school," he said.

George's phone rang in the cup holder. *"Bam, bam, bammm."* Grace turned her head and shoulders to look at George. *"Oh baby, baby ... I'm so into you,"* the phone sang.

"Nice ring," Grace said.

George ignored the call. But the caller wasn't going away. Britney Spears continued to sing, *"You drive me crazy. I just can't sleep."* He snapped up the phone and turned off the ringer. When the screen cleared, he dropped it back into the cup holder.

"The kids must have been playing with my phone again."

Grace leveled her gaze out the window and watched the fruit trees whiz past. After a minute, she cleared her throat. George turned at the sound. She seemed far away.

"Who was that?" she said, the way she might ask if it was supposed to rain that day.

"It was noth—"

"I asked *who?*" Grace said, her voice sharpening. She leaned forward and flipped up all the air-conditioning vents so they stopped blowing at her. "It said Cheryl Grayson."

"Cheryl?" George shifted in his seat and looked back at the straight road in front of him. "She must be … she's the girl in Mitchell's shop. My new helmet is probably ready."

George hadn't meant to broach the subject of the next Le Mans season with Grace, not yet. He needed a few months, at least through the holidays. That was the plan, but now it hung in the air between them, covering an even larger betrayal.

"George?"

The wheels were in motion and George knew they couldn't be stopped. He didn't even try.

"I … I thought it was decided," she said. George kept his eyes on the road, his face impassive. "I thought last season was your *last.*" Her voice quavered with emotion; he couldn't tell if it was grief or fury.

"This isn't really the time to get into this," George said.

"But, George," she said, pleading. "We don't need the money."

"It's never been about the money." They both knew that thanks to her family trust fund this was true.

"But you're at the top!" Now the emotion rang clear: she was angry. "You've already made it. Second Place in the Driver Championship—at your age, George, that was incredible."

George just drove, letting her spend her anger in words.

"You know I stay out of it, George. I always have. Even though I hate what it does to you, that it keeps you away from us. I'm beginning to think you love the danger more than you love your family—" It took all George had not to react to that. "I've stayed quiet. But not now—I'm stepping in. Someone has to."

George drove on, silent. There was no way to win this argument. Grace thought he didn't miss her and the kids when he was out on the circuit, but she was wrong. He could not explain to her the passion he felt for the track, the joy he got from being mentor to a talent like Coleton Loren.

He broke and glanced in her direction, checking her polarity. Her usually warm brown eyes were dark and hard. His look only provoked her.

"You think the guys in this business care about you?" she demanded. "You think you're in this band of brothers and you're willing to put your lives on the line for each other. It's all such a farce." She laughed without humor, pulling the silk scarf off the root of her ponytail and balling it up in her fist.

"You've been in it too long, George. I'm the only one who sees how long it takes for you to recover from a race weekend. You've had a great run, but you've got to let it go."

George made no reply. They rode in silence for a while, the fields of southern Miami-Dade sliding past the windows. George ground his teeth and twisted the steering wheel in his hand, angry at this sweet woman he loved and her inability to understand how much the track meant to him.

"Are you ready to hear me out?" George finally asked. He did not raise his voice, but there was steel behind his words.

Her eyes were blazing, but she didn't respond. He waited a moment, then continued.

"Coleton is making a move. The word hasn't hit the street yet, but I know he is. And, he's like a son to me—"

"Like a son? You have a son! And he needs you to be home for *him*." George didn't flinch.

"Coleton is going to a new team. Arthur Elrod knows Coleton has vision and real talent and he'll back him with whatever hardware it takes to win." Grace shook her head, but let him continue. "If Coleton starts a new team—" He looked at her steadily. "Then, I'm there with him."

He snuck a glance at Grace, and he hated himself for what he saw on her face. It was that look of sadness and resignation she got when she knew he would do what he wanted, no matter how she felt about it. He wished she would cry. Even tears would be better than that mournful look, but she had been through this wringer too many times for that. George shook his head briefly. It didn't matter. He knew his course, and he would not veer from it.

"Coleton just needs some experience. I've always been there to direct him when he needed help. I've watched his career from the very beginning, and it's just about to skyrocket. His potential is unlimited, Grace, and I've never said that about another driver—ever."

George couldn't keep the rising excitement out of his voice, even though he knew what it cost Grace to hear it. By God, they were going to win this year. This year.

"You'd be doing Coleton a disservice, and you know it. You've been in this too long and it's wearing you down. Your reflexes are not what they used to be ..." Her voice dropped off at the end of the sentence.

"You should see him in the rain. Coleton has this uncanny sixth sense in the rain. I've never seen anything like it. There'll be other cars sliding all over the track, crashing into each other, and he'll drop a second off his lap time. It's not even possible, but he does it. No one taught him that."

Grace said nothing, and he could feel her pulling into herself. She might not speak to him again for days; he'd seen it before. She would sink back into her daily routine—move through the rooms of their house, do homework with the children, bake a lasagna, fix the shower curtain in the guest room, all the while pretending he wasn't there. As if the more carefully she ignored his presence, the less shocking the dichotomy between a whole and happy house, and the hollow place that echoed with the final click of the door every time he left.

"This is his year, Grace. I still have a few things left to teach him. Give me one year with Coleton. Then, I'm out. I promise. I'll be happy with my career and I'll settle into a quiet retirement just like you want."

Grace accepted what she had to, like swallowing a pill, but the color drained from her cheeks. Outside her window, the blur of passing orange and grapefruit trees turned to a Monet of tropical colors: mangoes and lychees, passion fruit, star fruit.

CHAPTER 4
PALM BEACH, FLORIDA

Frank took Camilla's hand without looking at it and parted his way through the crowd of people waiting for a table at Cucina.

They walked past the maitre d' with hardly a nod, straight toward the small lounge area.

Camilla unbuttoned her coat and let Frank slide it from her shoulders. He pulled out a chair for her at one of the tables, and they sat with their backs to the wall, looking out over the lounge. They could see the throng of people through the open French doors, and beyond the milling bodies Camilla could make out puzzle pieces of night sky. Industrial heaters hung from the ceiling, pushing the chill back onto Royal Poinciana Way. The music was loud, and she nodded her head in time to the beat.

"Shall I order us some oysters?" Frank asked.

"Not too hungry, but I'll take a glass of red."

Frank looked across the restaurant. He squinted his eyes and then laughed. "The party just got more interesting!" Two wind-blown men wound their way through the crowd. "That's my friend Enzo Ferrini. There, in the black leather jacket."

Camilla's eyes fell on Ferrini without effort. With thick dark hair that brushed the top of his collar, olive skin and that jaunty swagger that for Italian men is predisposition, he would stand out in any crowd. The other man was taller, also with dark hair, and he certainly didn't pale in comparison to his dashing companion. Although Camilla couldn't make out his face well, she recognized his wide, white smile, and the crutches and cast were a confirmation.

"And his friend? What do you know about him?"

"Cheers," said Frank, as soon as the waiter set down their glasses. He waited for her to turn back toward him.

"Cheers," Camilla returned. Then she looked across the room again, pretending to survey the crowd.

"I'm not sure, a friend of Enzo's," he finally answered. "Think I met him once. Enzo comes from big money."

"Oh?" she asked.

"No, I mean *big* money, like owns his own airline kind of big, or at least his family does. He's also one of the best drivers in the Le Mans series. He drives for BMW."

"So, are you going to leave me for him now or later?" Camilla smirked. Frank was watching his friend intently and didn't hear her.

Frank stood up and waved to Enzo at the bar. It took a few tries before Frank attracted his attention. Enzo held out his hand, index finger extended at Frank like the barrel of a gun and winked. His companion leaned towards him and whispered something. Camilla lost sight of them in the crowd.

A few minutes later, Enzo appeared, leading a tall blonde waitress with a tray of sparkling drinks. "Mojitos for everyone." Without taking her eyes off Enzo, the waitress set each Collins glass slowly onto the table.

"Thanks, *bella*." Enzo dropped two hundred-dollar notes onto her tray. "Keep 'em coming, eh?" He slapped her behind, palm open. She jumped, then forced a smile.

Out of curiosity, Camilla followed the waitress with her eyes. The waitress looked back, eyebrow arched. But by then, Enzo was looking at his reflection in the mirrored wall behind her.

"Yeah," Enzo announced, shrugging out of his leather jacket to reveal a tight V neck t-shirt that hugged his muscled torso. "Tapped that once," he said, nodding toward the waitress. "Maybe twice, but who can remember?" He passed his jacket to Frank, who added it to Camilla's, then sat across from him. Enzo's friend pulled out the chair opposite Camilla.

Frank did not introduce her to either of the men. As soon as Enzo sat, Frank leaned forward to tell him something over the loud music.

"Hello, Doc," Coleton said with a smile and held out his hand to Camilla. His hand was not calloused, but strong. "Remember me?"

"Of course. How's your leg, Carlton?"

"Coleton. Coleton Loren," he said with a wink, like he was saying something clever. He didn't let go of her hand. Camilla could smell his cologne, warm and dry like vanilla and … bergamot? Involuntarily, she took a deeper breath.

Enzo banged the table with his fist. They both jumped.

"Yes, on the way *here*!" Enzo's eyes glimmered. "The bitch just rear-ended me on Okeechobee Boulevard. You'd think she would notice a $300,000 McLaren sitting at a red light in front of her. She better have insurance." Enzo grabbed Frank by the lapels with a sudden look of supplication. "Who's your attorney? Is he any good?"

Coleton was still holding her hand, as he watched Enzo, smiling. She pulled her hand loose and sat back.

"Poor Enzo." Coleton leaned toward her. "This housewife in a minivan just wrote off his car on our way here."

The tea candle lit Coleton's face, and Camilla realized with a little catch of breath just how good looking he was. Hair she'd taken for black in the emergency room was actually a dark, dark bronze. Not only did he have handsome features—broad brow, strong jaw, the works—but there was something more: an energy. He had a youthfulness that seemed brash and boyish, though he must be close to 30, a personal charisma driven by confidence. And the softest looking lips. When he made a particularly crude joke, he always seemed to bite his bottom lip, just a little, if only for an instant. *I bet not many resist him*, she thought. But she planned to do just that.

"You should have seen it," Coleton said. He sat back. "Enzo couldn't look at the lady, just called his PA to come handle the mess and call us a cab. And here we are."

"Isn't that like a hit and run?" Camilla asked, and then took a slow sip from her red wine.

"More like a *get* hit and run," he said confidently. Then, after a pause, "At least, I don't think so."

"Well, you've got some luck."

"You mean the accident or finding you here?" he asked, taking a sip of his drink.

"Two accidents in one weekend? I think you're in the wrong profession."

"Didn't take you long to figure that out."

"Don't these things come in threes?" she asked. "Remind me not to get in a car with you."

Coleton laughed. He swirled the ice in his glass and took a sip of the mojito.

"That's not a good idea," Camilla said. "You shouldn't be drinking on that pain prescription I wrote you."

"Relax, Tiger. I threw it away."

"You what?"

"I never take that stuff. As often as I get injured, I'd be drugged up half the time."

"So instead you drink Captain Morgan."

At this Enzo turned, surprising them both that he was listening, and said, "Please! This is Havana Club Selección. The finest Cuban rum."

"Hear that?" said Coleton. "The finest. So, Enzo?"

"Yes?"

"What do the *men* in Cuba drink?" He winked at Camilla and drained the glass.

As she tried to suppress a smile, Coleton changed the subject. "So," he said, and nodded toward Frank. "Is that your boyfriend?" She glanced at Frank, but he was still engrossed in conversation with Enzo. Probably not, though she had no intention of admitting it to this man. Frank was handsome, and rich, kind and thoughtful, but for some reason they had no real chemistry. He was pleasant to be around, fun even, but he seldom came to mind when they weren't together. In some ways, he was *too* nice. She suspected she would soon have to sleep with Frank, if she wanted to keep him. The prospect filled her with no great feeling one way or the other. Camilla shrugged.

Coleton pulled his straw out and jabbed at the remaining shards of crushed ice.

"That bitch!" Enzo yelled and smashed his fist into his palm. Frank placed a hand on his shoulder.

"Hey—" Coleton leaned toward Camilla. His eyes danced with mischief, bright green in the candlelight.

"What?" she asked, but knew what was coming.

"I'd like your phone number."

"What's that?" she asked, cupping her hand to her ear.

"I want to call you."

She leaned her ear towards him and frowned as though she couldn't hear, daring him to speak louder. But he was the wrong man to dare.

"Give me your number!"

Camilla startled, then looked cautiously at Frank. His eyes were bright, his face flushed with excitement as he listened intently to Enzo.

"You don't even know my first name," she whispered harshly.

"Just say your number. I'll remember it."

"I think you've had too many mojitos, Mr. Loren." She picked up her red wine by the stem of the glass.

"Do you like my cast?" he asked, pointing under the table. "Go ahead, look."

She gave in and holding the strap of her dress with one hand, leaned down. Below a fine linen pants leg roughly cut off at the knee, he wore a bright pink cast, covered in autographs and, she noted, more than a couple phone numbers. Hidden under the table, she finally let herself smile.

She sat up to see him grinning. "A deal is a deal."

"This is not the time or place," she said.

Coleton pulled a stark white card from his wallet and placed it on the table. He glanced over at Frank. Frank was laughing, almost giggling, and Enzo was gesturing wildly. He placed his fingertips on the card, looked her in the eye and slid it toward her. It sat white and floating on the dark tabletop. "When the time *is* right."

She sat for a moment and nodded her head in time to the music, thinking.

"You know, I *am* on a date!"

"We all make mistakes."

Her mouth dropped open.

"Just put it in that little Prada bag of yours."

"It's Chanel and you're out of your mind if you think—"

"Put it in your purse!" Coleton raised his voice again to a level that threatened to spark Frank's attention. The couple at the next table turned for a second before they went back to flirting.

She snatched the card off the table and slipped it under the flap of her purse. She hooked it back over the arm of her chair.

"Happy?" she snapped. Out of the corner of her eye, she looked at Frank, but he hadn't noticed a thing.

"Ecstatic," Coleton replied. Did he have to have such goddamn green eyes? Medically speaking, they were no big deal. Just a result of low melanin concentrations in the iris epithelium combined with Rayleigh scattering of blue frequency light … sparkling above perfect white teeth in the candlelight on a cool starry evening.

"Well, boys—" Coleton clapped his hands, and Frank and Enzo turned toward him. "Early morning tomorrow. Enzo, we sharing a cab?"

"Can't believe its come to this. A fucking cab." Enzo shook his lowered head, but stood up. He looked across the restaurant and saw a beautiful woman with lush red hair take a seat at the bar. She was petite and almost too thin, not Enzo's normal type—he favored tall, busty blondes—but she was striking, with angular cheekbones. There was an empty barstool next to her. "I think I'll stay for one more drink. I'm sure she can drive me home."

"Don't you ever get full?" Coleton asked with a good-natured laugh. He stood, then turned to Camilla and extended his hand.

"Early morning on a Sunday?" Camilla hated herself for asking, but she wasn't quite done with him yet. "You don't look like a church-goer to me."

"First, you should know that I'm *very* pious. And, second, I've got to meet my agent for an early brunch at the Breakers. Care to join us?"

Camilla took Frank's hand and pressed close to him. "We'll be sleeping in," she said. Frank bounced his eyebrows and smiled.

Thirty minutes later, she walked out of Cucina with Frank into the brisk air. It was an unusually cool winter in Palm Beach, and she pushed her hands deep into the pockets of her coat.

"Be careful, Camilla," Frank said.

"What do you mean *be careful*?" she asked with a pinprick of attitude, but felt her stomach go cold and hard. *Had he seen through the whole thing?*

"The men in Palm Beach aren't all like me." She stared straight ahead as they walked to Frank's car. "Be careful, that's all I'm saying."

"Right," she said and pulled the car door shut.

Frank put the top down and they raced through the black night down South Ocean Boulevard. The car hugged the curves and they flew through the dark, with the beach stretching out on their right, wide and white, as they made for the north end of the island.

The cold air numbed their faces, but Frank turned the heater to the max. Camilla smiled up at the starry sky, confident he couldn't see her in the dark. She clutched her purse to her chest, as if she could feel the indentation of the white card within. She was not going to call Coleton Loren.

By instinct, she knew he was a womanizer. He was brazen and obvious. She despised men like that. The fraternities in college had been full of them, and the doctors she had studied under, some of them handsome, had been little different. Cocky and privileged and expecting to get whatever they wanted, whenever they wanted it. That's why she gravitated toward the moody complicated type, like the creative writing major who had broken her heart as an undergrad. Or the actor-slash-waiter she had dated in Paris during her semester abroad. Or poor Frank here, owner of a tony art gallery on Worth Avenue.

Of course, she was flattered by the attention of a powerful and attractive man like Coleton Loren, regardless of his moral standards, a man who could have any woman he wanted. But, that's all it was. Flattery. So, she smiled into the night, content with the wind whipping through her hair. Above her, the stars glimmered, thousands of loose diamonds in a black velvet box.

"Where am I taking you?" Frank turned down the music.

"Home, please," Camilla stated, as if that was the only possible response. "My sister's house on Everglade."

Camilla had graduated from Columbia medical school and agreed to her first residency at Good Samaritan Hospital. Her sister had convinced her to give Palm Beach a try and offered up her pool house for incentive.

"You sure? We could stop by my place on North Lake Way. Sit outside with a great view of the Intercoastal, have a bottle of Taurasi. Have you heard of it? Great Italian red." It was a solid attempt. She gave him that. But, it would take more than booze and a view.

"I'm really very tired. I have a 12-hour shift starting at five a.m. Thank you, though."

He dropped her off at 925 Everglade, and as she walked up the large stone steps toward the side door that led to the pool house, she heard him roar off into the night. He didn't wait to make sure she got in okay. Camilla shook her head, peeled off her black heels and hugged them to her chest while she dug through her purse looking for her key. She wondered if it was the last time she would see Frank Gilleno, but shrugged off the thought.

As Camilla turned the key and felt the door give way to her shoulder, she remembered with a start: the waitress never returned with Enzo's change, nor did she return with even a single refill for his $200. Camilla smiled into the dark at the thought. *Good for her.*

CHAPTER 5

PALM BEACH, FLORIDA

On Sunday, Coleton woke with the sun. He could never sleep in on Sundays, even if he tried. At six o'clock like clockwork, he would sit up in bed, heart racing and ready to ride his road bike. Outside the weather was perfect. The sky was bright and clear, and the morning air still held last night's chill.

Coleton rolled down the windows of the Ferrari as he pulled through the black iron gates of his family estate, and made a sharp left onto South Ocean Boulevard. The cold morning air poured in through the windows, as he accelerated south toward the Breakers. He pulled the knot of his cashmere scarf tighter, but refused to turn on the heat. There's nothing like icy air to clear your head. He just wished he was on his Pinarello, hurtling break-neck at 35 mph.

As he rounded the bend in front of the Palm Beach Country Club, Coleton down-shifted to second just in time to avoid wiping out an entire pack of professional racing bikes, domino-style. The V12 purred in the morning air, warmed up and ready to run. In an instant Coleton recognized his boys in their bright racing colors and carbon fiber bikes. Coleton looked down at his Panerai: 8:30. The peloton of bikes had already reached the cut at the north end of the island and were re-tracing their track down South Ocean Boulevard. Now they were on race-pace towards Manalapan.

Coleton laughed and revved the engine, raw and loud and rude against the quiet waves crashing on the beach to their left. A few of the bikers turned their heads to see who had the nerve. Immediately, the pack recognized the silver Ferrari and knew the driver. Coleton pulled up alongside the pack, tracking their speed.

"Hey there, cowboys!" Coleton yelled through the open passenger window. "How's the ride?"

"Well, look who it is," the closest rider called. His name was Charles Foist, the senior manager of a billion-dollar hedge fund who at 40 had retired and turned to professional biking. "That doesn't look like a racing bike," he added, nodding to the Ferrari. "I guess it's the only way you can keep up with us!" The other riders hooted and laughed into their handlebars.

"Look, assholes." Coleton lifted his leg up as far as he could without bumping it into the dash, and pointed to his cast. "I'm out of the saddle for six weeks at least."

"Yeah? How'd you do that," Charles asked. "In the sack with your girlfriend?"

"No, your wife!" rejoined Coleton. "Hey, be thankful. I'm giving you a few weeks of head-start training, boys! I suggest you exploit it!"

Every Sunday that Coleton was in Palm Beach, he rode with this pack of professional cyclists. Coleton was the only amateur. As professional athletes themselves, they respected his career path, but more importantly, he could keep up. Coleton spent only about one long weekend a month at his family's place. But, when he was there, the cyclists welcomed him.

Cycling is the best cardiovascular training for a racecar driver. It is the only sport that can elevate a heart rate into the 190's, a remotely similar pace to what a driver experiences in the racecar, and keep it there. Not to mention, learning to ride in the pack, maximizing the slipstream of other riders and negotiating riding positions mid-flight, is a direct correlation to the skills needed to pilot a racecar.

Coleton inched the Ferrari to the front of the pack, nodded in respect to Don Peters, the lead bike, and then floored it. A few miles later, Coleton pulled left into the long drive of the Breakers hotel from South County Road. Its two flag-tipped spires seemed to motion him in like an air traffic controller.

Originally called the Palm Beach Inn, the Breakers acquired its new name from the lips of its elite guests, when the stars of early twentieth-century high society such as the Vanderbilts, Astors,

Rockefellers and Carnegies requested rooms in that hotel "over by the breakers." Living up to its name, and growing only grander with time, the Breakers still sits in its splendor like a Medici villa just above the sand dunes.

"Good morning, Mr. Loren," said an older valet with graying hair. Mickey was such an icon at the Breakers that many joked he had been there since Flagler built the place in 1896. He certainly acted as if it were true, with his stately grace and perfected manners. He was the only valet that Coleton let handle his F12, and he paid for the privilege accordingly.

A maroon Aston Martin DB9 already sat to the side of the red brick drive, just past the entrance. It looked like Ira's, but Coleton knew it wasn't. Ira refused to valet at the Breakers. He claimed they had scratched his door once, but Coleton knew Ira just couldn't stomach the $25 ticket.

Coleton crutched his way into the lobby, turned left past the plush couches arranged into small sitting areas under the 30-foot, frescoed ceilings and headed toward the Circle restaurant, where "Sunday Brunch is a Palm Beach Tradition."

At the reception desk, Coleton halted mid-stride and let his legs swing forward on his crutches and then back to a standing position. William Crowne, his iconic white hair brushed back into a pompadour, was leaning against the counter. Coleton smiled with genuine delight and made straight toward him.

"William, long time."

William Crowne pivoted toward the sound, maintaining with ease his perfect posture. His crisp, light blue shirt brought out his impeccably tan skin. He didn't look a day over 50. In reality, he must have been nearing 70. When it came to racing, there was almost no name on the planet to rival the legend of William Crowne. In 2007, he purchased BMW Racing division for $70 million, considered an absolute bargain by many aficionados, and turned it into one of the most competitive packages around. Currently, Crowne put his name to teams in the Le Mans, Indy and NASCAR racing series.

"Coleton Loren." Crowne smiled, then glanced down at Coleton's cast. "Look at you. You know, I heard you'd broken it, and I have to admit—I believed it without question."

"Yeah, it's broken in two places." Coleton pointed at his cast. "But, I'll only be out for a minute."

"When will you be back in the car?" Crowne asked.

"I drove here!"

"Of course you did." Crowne shook his head and smiled. "And, Victoria? How is your mother?"

"Oh, she's well, thank you," Coleton answered, but Crowne stared, waiting for more. "Oh, you know, still the Queen Bee of Palm Beach. I've heard it's harder to wrangle an invitation into her book club than to get a t-head slip at the Sailfish club." Crowne smiled broadly, the tan skin around his eyes crinkling.

Coleton continued, "And, you? How is your family?"

"Oh, Hilton's still the quintessential journeyman driver. You know, roving from team to team with his helmet in his hand, hoping for a ride. If he would just settle down and focus for once, he could really make something of his career. He certainly has talent. But, you know, he always waits for me to pull something together for him."

"Hilton's still young. He has time to mature yet," Coleton said, thinking that if he had William Crowne to fall back on, it would have taken him a few more years to collect himself as well.

"He's not *that* young anymore! Drivers are getting younger and younger these days."

"True." Coleton nodded in agreement. "And, Juliette? She's well?"

"Juliette—" Crowne sighed, thinking about his daughter for the first time that day. "—is, well, still Juliette, I'm afraid."

Coleton nodded. That was all the explanation he needed. Although he hadn't seen her for a long time, he knew the beautiful Juliette Crowne well. Coleton had grown up just down the road from Hilton and Juliette in Palm Beach, and although he was a bit older than the twin siblings, he had spent many a weekend racing go-karts with Hilton, with Juliette tagging along to watch. Later in life, Coleton had partied with Juliette in Miami Beach a few times, and would never forget the night at Set nightclub when she bought 40 sparkler-topped bottles of Dom Perignon for her newest boyfriend's birthday. While her acting career hadn't exactly taken off yet, she never failed to make the tabloids with her extravagant lifestyle.

"And, tell me—" Crowne changed the subject. "How is your Italian friend doing? You know I'm fronting Enzo a new works BMW team next season."

"Really?" Coleton replied. "No, I didn't know."

"I hope he grows to deserve it. His immaturity worries me, but that boy has real, raw talent. I want you to do me a favor, Coleton." Crowne motioned Coleton closer. "I want you to keep an eye on him, keep him focused."

"I'll do what I can. He's like a brother. He really does mean well, but he just attracts trouble like a magnet." Coleton smiled, then continued. "But, I'll do what I can."

"And, what about you? Have you finalized your plans for next year?"

"I've got a great new sponsor, Miller Sunglasses, which is bringing a lot of money to the table." Coleton looked into Crowne's eyes and paused to consider his next words. He decided to be honest. "But even so, I'm a bit worried about trying to talk my way into a ride while still on crutches. I hope to finalize a deal with Elrod Racing, but it's still up in the air."

Crowne nodded. "Just remember—" he said, leaning forward to place a fatherly hand on Coleton's shoulder. "Sponsor dollars are not your only bargaining chip. Connections and the right introductions can also be of great value to a man like Arthur Elrod." Coleton nodded slowly, processing the advice but unsure how to apply it.

"And you know—" Crowne leaned even closer. "The Porscheworks team is going to be stiff competition for you again this year, but there is a chink." Coleton's ears perked up even more. "Did you know Porsche is pulling their factory support?" Coleton shook his head no.

"In today's economy, Porsche can't spend the kind of money on R&D to perfect their chassis that they need to, so instead they're pulling it. You know the Germans: if it's not perfect, it's nothing." Coleton nodded. "Porscheworks is scrambling. They were counting on their winning works car again this year: Porsche chassis, Porsche engine, full factory support, but that deal is long gone." Coleton held his breath, not daring to interrupt Crowne with even the hint of a head nod; this information could be crucial.

Crowne thought for a second, as if weighing the motivation to go on, then he continued. "So, the Porscheworks team has picked up the new Stewart chassis, and are powering it with the same Porsche engine as last year. Everyone knows that overall the new Stewart chassis is a big question mark, but I'll tell you something you don't know—"

All of a sudden, to Coleton, the hotel lobby went silent. "And this is not public knowledge, but the Stewart chassis has serious down-force issues. Unless Porscheworks spends a fortune in the wind tunnel before Sebring, that chassis will carry a real weakness on any fast track, and they can throw in the towel if it rains." Crowne sighed and leaned back to a more comfortable speaking distance. "Just a word to the wise." He smiled, then clapped Coleton on the shoulder.

"Noted," Coleton said, still absorbing the information. "And appreciated."

"Anything for Victoria's boy."

"What is this? Kiton?" Coleton asked, reaching out and taking an inch of Crowne's khaki blazer between his thumb and index finger.

"Run only the best; wear only the best. Isn't that how it goes?" Crowne winked.

"It does when you're William Crowne," Coleton joked, but with an undertone of true reverence.

Crowne chuckled. "Give Victoria my best."

"Of course, I will," Coleton agreed.

Crowne reached out, shook Coleton's hand and turned back to the front desk, where the GM still stood, waiting to complete his paperwork.

Coleton passed through an oak doorway into the grandly appointed dining room of the Circle. Ira was the only one seated there. Brunch did not begin in earnest until 11 a.m. Ira had chosen a small round table at the far right side, by the picture windows that overlook the ocean. As Coleton crutched to the table, Ira took a long sip from one of the signature Seafood Bloody Marys and looked up at him.

"So, what? You think nine o'clock means nine-fifteen these days?"

"Who the hell eats breakfast at the Breakers at nine, when they could wait for brunch at 11?"

"We need some peace and quiet. We have a lot to talk about."

"Meaning you can't stomach the hundred dollar price tag."

"Yeah, yeah, screw you." Ira giggled. "But, seriously, who can eat 30 desserts and make a real dent in a raw seafood bar. I can't eat a hundo worth of food before lunch."

"Brunch is lunch." Coleton glanced at Ira's sizeable paunch and raised an eyebrow. "Never mind."

"Well, for a racecar driver, you're not very prompt. Guess that ten-thousand dollar watch doesn't keep time so good."

"Twenty, and chill out," Coleton replied. "I just ran into William Crowne in the lobby." Ira froze, his eyes wide.

"Really? What is *he* doing here?"

"I don't know. Checking out."

"Did he recognize you?"

"Of course he recognized me. He's been a friend of the family for years."

"The family?" Ira said. "Or your mother?" Coleton lowered his chin and gave Ira a look. They both knew what it meant. It meant: don't cross the line.

"He dated Victoria years before she met my father," Coleton said. They sat back in their chairs, allowing that to be the final word on the subject.

"Well," Ira said, lifting his empty glass into the air and clinking the dry cubes at the waitress. "You missed a crazy party last night."

"I'm sure it was elegant," Coleton scoffed.

"You've got to see Landon's new boat. It's immaculate."

"The Lürssen 170? I've been on that boat a hundred times."

"No, the 200. The new custom one. It's sick. There were so many beautiful girls, the average ones were walking the plank of their own free will. You should have seen this one girl I scooped up."

"Only one?" Coleton joked. "What did you do? Give the poor girl intravenous Patron?"

"Nah, man this girl was all over me. We were drinking, but she couldn't get over the stories from when I represented Schwarzenegger."

"Crutches and boats don't mix. Besides, if I showed up it'd wreak havoc on your bell curve."

"Yeah, whatever. It wouldn't have mattered. This girl was a huge Schwarzenegger fan. I'm telling you, she was so into me. Especially when I imitated him. I do a great Arnold. I'll be—"

"Great. Can we talk about your juvenile conquests later? Ten to one she's got major buyer's remorse this morning, not to mention anything else you gave her."

"My dick's so safe, it's insured," Ira said.

"Really? What'd you do with the money?"

"Hysterical."

"Let's talk sponsorship."

Ira shrugged, then dove in. The only thing he enjoyed talking about more than his conquests was money.

"You want the good news first or the bad?" Ira began.

"The bad, of course. Let's get to the point, instead of you jerking me off for half an hour."

"Okay but first some quick good news," Ira said. "The Java Juice deal is done. The contract is signed; the ink is dry."

"Did you read the whole thing this time, or was it TLRD again?"

"I read it, I read it." Ira grimaced. "You should probably split the five hundred grand 60/40 with your new team."

"Yes, my *new* team. And what team is that going to be? Did you finalize everything with Elrod in New York?"

"So, that's not a bad start to the season—a good little kicker," Ira said, ignoring the questions.

"Yeah, good thing I pulled the deal together," Coleton said.

"Now that's seriously fucking debatable, Colt. And, you know it."

"Really? Do you know Geoffrey Bennison? Hmm?" Coleton asked, then continued without waiting for an answer. "Did you talk to their CEO *one* time about this deal? Did you negotiate even *one* contract point with even *one* single Java Juice employee?" Ira just stared into his drink.

"Look," Ira said. "Let's just stick to the facts here. We're never going to agree on your sweeping conclusions."

Coleton shrugged. "Fine, you know what I want to hear. Tell me the meeting with Elrod went well, and we have a deal."

Ira moved to the edge of his seat. "Well, the meeting went—let's just say it went okay."

"Okay? What do you mean *okay*? You tell this guy we're bringing him $10 million from Miller Sunglasses over one year, and he's not ready for me to father his next child? How the hell did you screw that up?"

"Now, hold on a second," Ira said.

"I thought the deal with Elrod was done. I've already been spreading the word that it's me and George for Elrod Racing next year. You're telling me we don't even have a deal yet?"

The waitress arrived to take their order.

"Just the normal stuff, sweetheart." Ira waved her away. The waitress had her pad and pencil ready and stood looking down at him, confused. "Scrambled eggs, bacon, hash browns, toast, food, okay?" She looked to Coleton, and when he nodded, she shrugged and spun toward the kitchen.

"Elrod wasn't satisfied with Miller's payment plan," Ira said. He shook out his yellow napkin and dropped it in his lap before putting his elbows on the table.

"Okay, so why didn't you negotiate the payment schedule? Who the hell cares? We're talking about big money here. I could waltz onto any team in the series with this sponsor."

"Yeah, so maybe we're aiming too low with Elrod. Maybe we should set up a meeting with Phillip Floyd? Maybe we can get you into a works car with full factory support."

"No, Elrod Racing is the way to go. I had them in mind when I kissed Gomez and his motley crew goodbye last year. You know that asshole served me at Jack Miller's birthday party on Star Island?"

Ira's mouth dropped open. "Seriously?"

"Seriously. The process server was waiting next to that huge Moroccan door, loitering around in a Brioni jacket. What process server wears Brioni? He waited until I gave my name and then handed me the envelope. Classic. I thought it was a party favor!"

Ira threw his head back at this and laughed.

"It's not funny, but the best part—" Coleton leaned forward. "—is that no one saw it! I was so late getting there that no one was outside. How dare he serve me on Star Island. It's all such a joke."

Ira sobered at this.

"No, Colt. It's not all a joke. You've got to take this lawsuit seriously."

"Like hell I do!" Coleton said. "Thanks for the advice, but opinions are like assholes. Everybody's got one."

"Gomez was a name in this business for a long time, and he's not playing around." Ira took a sip from a fresh Bloody Mary and shook his head slowly. "We don't want him as an enemy."

"Who cares? He's finished in racing. Our racing budget fell to basically zero last year. He just stopped writing checks with two races to go. When you own a team you have a responsibility."

"Well, I still don't get it. How do you *not* make money in the titty bar business? I mean, come on. Strip clubs, adult bookstores, the sleazy bastard has got to be printing money," Ira said. "Why's he crying poor?"

"He either spends more than he makes, which can happen to anyone, or he's saving his money for a different series next year. Either way, it's not my fault his team fell apart."

"Of course not."

"And, now he's trying to claim money from my sponsor? *I* found Phantom Jets, *I* grew the relationship and *I* introduced them to the paddock. Screw him! Phantom is mine." Coleton drank his water in two gulps and tapped the table with his knife.

"All right, easy," Ira said. "It's brunch for Chrissake. We'll deal with this."

As if on cue, the waitress arrived with steaming plates of food.

"So how bad did you fuck up the deal with Elrod?" Coleton asked, forking a piece of scrambled egg into his mouth. "Did you piss him off in that patented Ira Goldstein way, or is he still willing to negotiate? We've got to make this happen."

"Well, I wouldn't say he's pissed off, but it might smooth things over if you meet with him."

"Smooth things over? Christ! In one meeting? You screwed things up so badly in *one* meeting that I've got to fly to New York to salvage my ride?"

Ira cleared his throat. "Actually, I think he's in Chicago now."

"Great. Thanks for that. And, while we're on the fucking subject—" Coleton was warmed up now and on a roll. "I'm not going to compete with every swinging dick for Organic Valley Market. I hear they're talking to Jerry Falco now? Screw it. If they want the best they know where to find me."

"Now Colt, listen," Ira said. Ira was heating up now too, ready and willing to match Coleton's tone. "Organic Valley wants you. But you've got to put in a little effort. All their marketing director wants is a little face time. I'm not asking you to pull down your shorts. Just go see the guy."

"Do I have to close every fucking deal?" Coleton snapped. "Seriously, what do I pay you for?" They glared across the table at each other for a few seconds in silence. "Am I going to have to sign autographs and walk South Miami grannies to their cars carrying their bags of gluten-free cupcakes? If so, tell me now."

Ira broke into a laugh. Coleton watched, then shook his head and smiled. Ira had a genuine belly laugh, and Coleton enjoyed hearing it, even when he was pissed off.

The waitress reappeared. "Whenever you're ready," she said, as she set the check down in the middle of the table between them. Ira reached out, overshot the check and grabbed Coleton's last piece of bacon. He popped it in his mouth and pushed his chair back from the table.

"I got the last one. I'm hitting the head."

Coleton just shook his head, unsurprised. The last time Ira paid had been eight-dollar Cuban sandwiches on Calle Ocho. But Coleton knew when it came down to it, Ira would lie down in the street and die for him, and that kind of loyalty can't be bought. Coleton paid the bill without animosity, over-tipped the waitress to compensate for Ira's abuse, and left the light-filled restaurant without looking back.

CHAPTER 6
PALM BEACH, FLORIDA

With both hands firmly on the desk, Camilla twisted the office chair left and right to stretch her back, and then refocused on the computer screen. She needed to check the lab work on a few of her patients and had planted herself at a desk in the nurses' station. After a long slow night in the ER, the hospital corridors began to pick up with the morning buzz as the nine-to-fivers came in.

She copied a few notes from the screen into a paper chart. She closed the file, stood it upright, tapped it on the desk and added it to a pile on her right. Above, she heard the industrial air conditioner click to life with a shudder, revving up to a hum. Camilla pulled the lapels of her white lab coat together, before she even felt the re-circulated breeze on her face.

The cursor on her screen blinked in the patient search field. She watched it wink and rested her right hand on the keyboard. L-O, she typed with her ring finger, then R with her index finger. Enter with her pinky.

"Hello, handsome," she said.

She felt giddy, but maybe it was just sleep deprivation. "Hospital Hot" is a common syndrome in the realm of 12-hour shifts, where suddenly a co-worker or patient can seem devastatingly attractive, when in the outside world they'd barely invite a second glance.

She skimmed his vital statistics: *Sex: male, Age: 29, Hair: brown, Eyes: green, Weight: 180 lbs.*

A nurse walked behind the counter and grabbed a stapler from Camilla's desk. Camilla sat up straight, following the nurse out of the corner of her eye as she moved back down the corridor. She rolled her chair closer and kept reading. *Non-smoker. Patient uses no recreational drugs. No STDs. That's a plus*, Camilla smirked. Besides the fractures in his leg, he appeared to be in perfect health.

She clicked on the Contacts page and stared at his cell phone number. It had been almost two weeks since she'd bumped into him, but surely he'd remember her. Before she could change her mind, she snatched the phone from its cradle and dialed the number.

"Hel-lo?" Coleton answered on the third ring. He sounded annoyed, or busy.

"Hi, Coleton. I just wanted to follow up on a couple things–"

"Who's this?" he asked, interrupting.

An impulse to play with him swayed her. "Guess."

The line went silent for a moment. "Susan?"

"No," she said. "Try again." Another pause.

"Oh, it's you, Ashley. So you got early parole after all?"

"No ..." Camilla laughed. "Come on, Coleton. This is serious."

"I don't know any serious girls."

"Why doesn't that surprise me?"

"I give up—before I get into too much trouble."

"It's Camilla," she said. Silence. "Dr. Harlow ..."

"Ohh," Coleton said. "Hi, Doc! I thought you were never going to call."

"I'm sure you were holding your breath."

"I was, and now I feel special."

"Coleton," she said as dryly as she could. "I call to check up on all my patients."

"Right ... tell you what, let me take you out, and you can observe my leg in person—all night."

"A superficial chat will suffice."

"But *Dr. Harlow*," he said. "The pain really is terrible."

"Is it? Around the fractures?"

"No, higher."

"The pain's radiating?"

"It's my heart," he said. "It's aching, Camilla. Because you won't let me take you someplace fun tonight."

Camilla groaned. "Has that line ever worked?"

"That depends on whether you text me your address."

She smiled, but didn't make a sound. "Doctors aren't allowed to date their patients."

"You're fired."

Her smile broadened. She pulled the phone cord toward her, then let it snap back. She watched it bounce up and down until it slowed to a stop.

"Okay, eight o'clock sharp. Though I'm a little apprehensive about what you consider fun."

"I know a great place. We can do some bowling, eat some ice cream—"

"How wholesome."

"—naked."

"Enough!"

Camilla hung up the phone and laughed out loud. She looked briefly over her shoulder, but no one had heard her conversation. Maybe a fun evening with a pretty racecar driver was just the prescription she needed.

At 7:55 there was a knock. Camilla turned on the patio lights and pulled back the curtain. Her sister, Katherine, stood outside the sliding glass door, holding a bouquet of flowers.

"Why is there a strange but attractive man in my living room?" she asked. "Not complaining. Just curious."

"Forgot to tell him I live in the pool house! He's here already?" Camilla leaned against the table to strap on a pair of lanky black heels. "Go ahead. I'm sure you already have an opinion."

"Charles certainly does," said Katherine. "I think he's still in the driveway, licking that fancy Ferrari."

"And you?"

Katherine shrugged. "Well, he's not hard to look at. And you've got to give him points for the flowers."

"Hmm? Oh yeah, pretty." Camilla stood, and wiggled her toes.

"Look again."

"What?"

"They're *camellias*, Camilla."

"Okay, points for originality."

"Double points!" said Katherine. "You know how expensive these Japanese ones are?"

"Fess up, Kat. You're more charmed by it than I am."

"Of course, I am. That's the luxury of being married. I can flirt all I want, as long as I go home with Charles and keep from screaming another man's name."

"That's totally not a disturbing thought."

"But seriously, Milla. Just be careful. Pretty and charming is great, but you don't know this guy."

"That's why it's called a date. No courthouse, no shotgun, and, though it's none of your business, no sex."

"Just don't get swept off your feet. I know you're a smart girl, but the guys in Palm Beach can be ... predatory."

"Your Palm Beach predator swept you off your feet and into five bedrooms, three cars and a statistically perfect 2.5 children. All wrapped in an actual white picket fence."

Katherine began to speak, but Camilla cut her off. "I've put myself through med school and lived on my own for eight years. Don't worry, Mom. I'll be home by curfew."

"Okay, fine." Katherine rolled her eyes. "All I'm saying is—just be careful."

"Sure." Camilla grabbed her Pashmina from the table and the purse that lay underneath it.

"Is that my Chanel purse again?" Katherine asked. Camilla smiled mischievously. "You better take good care of it, and it better be back in my closet tomorrow."

"I better get in there." Camilla lifted the hem of her dress with her fingertips, then let it drop. "I hope this works. I have no idea where we're going."

"That's a good sign," said Katherine, then frowned. "Or a bad one."

"There's some useful advice."

"You look beautiful, Milla. Really." Camilla wore a fitted black dress. It fell off one shoulder and displayed her porcelain collarbone. She had just finished drying her hair and it fell well past her shoulders.

"Thank you. How will these heels look?"

"They look great!"

"I mean when they're up around my ears."

"You're horrible!" Katherine gave her a mock serious look. "Use a condom."

Camilla gave her sister a hug. "You're worse than I am," she said, and hurried toward the main house.

"By the way, what's with his pink cast?" her sister called after her.

"Long story," Camilla said without turning, but she smiled to herself.

"I s this an automatic transmission?" Camilla asked, as Coleton pressed the button between them marked "R" and backed out of the driveway.

Coleton's mouth dropped open with indignation. "Automatic? No … it has a built-in dual clutch."

"And you're sure you can drive this thing with a broken leg?"

"This *thing* is a Ferrari F12, and I could drive it in my sleep."

"Please don't."

Coleton straightened the wheel and revved the engine. They pointed west on Everglade, the wrong way down the one way. She thought about mentioning it, but he hit the gas and pushed the car from first straight into third. The force threw her back in her seat, and she gripped her purse to keep from grabbing the door.

Coleton skidded left onto Bradley Place. Camilla tried to fasten her seatbelt, but the car kept jerking back and forth. She squinted out the windshield. Coleton was swerving quickly and efficiently, but almost violently, around indentations in the pavement, to protect the lowered chassis of his car. Camilla tried again, her hand extended in the air like a painter, but she couldn't get her seatbelt buckled.

"Are we late or something?" she finally asked. Coleton looked at her. She had her feet planted on the floor mat, bracing her back against the seat and her seatbelt buckle was still extended in her right hand. "Or, do you always drive this fast?" she asked exasperated.

"Baby," Coleton laughed. "This isn't fast!" He floored the engine.

Camilla let her seat belt fly backward. She closed her eyes and reviewed the facts. She could die in a crash, but he was a professional. She consciously chose to accept the danger, chose to enjoy it, like a roller coaster. The tightness in her throat, the racing in her chest, the fear—became fun. The car slowed and she opened her eyes.

A line of cars stood at the entrance to the Palm Beach Grill waiting for valets. Coleton accelerated toward the stopped cars, and at the last instant, he pulled into the oncoming lane and continued down the line. They passed a Maserati Spyder, an Aston DBS, a Bentley GTC. Camilla shook her head. For the friends she grew up with, this would be a scene from a movie, but in Palm Beach, it was just an average Tuesday night. Coleton swerved in front of the first car and pulled the e-brake. The valet hustled to open Camilla's door.

"Welcome to Palm Beach Grill."

Coleton's crutches were wedged in next to her doorframe. She angled them out and passed them to the valet. He jumped to attention as she began to get out.

"Wait, let me help you!"

Camilla smiled. "They're his." She nodded at Coleton. The valet hurried to Coleton's side. Camilla expected a cacophony of car horns and irate outbursts from lowered, limo-tinted windows at Coleton's blatant line-cutting.

She hurried around the front of the car. Coleton was waiting, resting on his crutches. He leaned forward and moved her closer with a palm on her back. "Did I tell you? You look great tonight."

Camilla shook her head. He was in no rush to get inside. He tossed the keys to the valet. Camilla heard the window of the Bentley behind them lowering. *Here it comes*, she thought, expecting expletives.

"Heya Colt! You gonna be back in the car by Daytona?"

Coleton turned and gave a thumbs-up.

"Who was that?" Camilla asked, as they passed the line of people waiting to slip the maître d' folded up $20s.

"How the hell should I know?" Coleton laughed.

A tall woman in a short black dress met them where the maître d' table dead-ended the entranceway: left to the bar, right to the restaurant. She had straight blonde hair slicked back into a chic ponytail that accentuated her long graceful neck and a gap between her front teeth. Past the towering vase of exotic flowers, Camilla could see the room was packed with full tables. The Palm Beach crowd was out *en masse*, decidedly aged, decidedly billionesque.

When the hostess saw Coleton, her lips curled back in a knowing, hungry smile. Camilla glanced at Coleton, but his face betrayed no secrets. The woman slowly peeled her eyes from his face and forced a smile at Camilla before gathering two leather bound menus and motioning for them to follow her into the dark restaurant. She hadn't asked for a name or reservation.

The woman led them toward a table for two in the back corner, separated from the rest.

Coleton moved slowly on his crutches through the crowded tables. Women sat up in their chairs, eyes widened; wealthy gentlemen inclined their heads and smiled. Camilla saw him through their eyes. *Maybe he's more famous than I thought.*

Beautiful in her black dress, she felt the approval of lingering gazes. She rolled her shoulders back and allowed herself to bask in the feeling of being in a fashionable place with a powerful man at her elbow. It was a world away from Good Sam.

They sat and shook out their napkins. Now, it was only them, and Camilla was suddenly nervous.

"So, tell me about racing. What kind of car do you race again?"

Before Coleton could answer, the waitress arrived and handed him the wine menu. He accepted it without looking up.

"Would you like red or white?" he asked, his eyes not leaving Camilla's.

"Red," she said confidently. "A Pinot would be nice."

Coleton raised his eyebrows in approval.

"The lady will have a glass of Cakebread Pinot Noir." The waitress nodded. "A 2005 if you have it."

"I'll check, sir," the waitress said.

"And, I'll have a double Johnnie Blue. Neat." Coleton handed back the unopened menu.

"You know ... I never drink," Coleton said.

"How's that working out for you?" Camilla joked, eyeing the waitress as she jotted down his order.

"No, really." He smiled. "During the season I rarely drink. But, I figure a little scotch is better than those horse tranquilizers you prescribed me."

"You really haven't taken one?" she asked. "Your leg is broken in two places!"

"I didn't even fill the prescription. I told you, I get hurt too often to start the pain pill cycle. I'd be an addict."

Camilla had the sudden urge to reach across the table and rub her thumb over the stubble on his cheek. He hadn't shaved in a day or two, and she thought it only improved his looks, tiling the scale from pretty toward rugged.

The double doors of the restaurant opened wide and a raucous group entered. Everyone turned to watch the colorful flock of socialites, younger than the other diners, and too beautiful to really fit in. The girls wore short jewel-toned dresses. Their tan necks and wrists sparkled with precious stones; their faces shone with flawless white smiles. Before they were even escorted to their table on the bar side, champagne bottles began to pop: one, two, three, heralding their arrival.

"Do you know them?" Camilla asked, nodding toward the newly arrived.

Coleton narrowed his eyes for a second, then smiled. "That's Juliette Crowne, and her entourage."

"Juliette Crowne," Camilla said, frowning and sitting up.

"She's an old friend," Coleton said. "Will you excuse me for a second?"

Without waiting for a response, Coleton lifted his crutches from the floor and made his way to the bar area. Camilla looked at her hands folded in her lap; her knuckles were white.

Camilla heard a shriek and looked up. The girl in red at the head of the table leapt up to give Coleton a bear hug and almost knocked him over. She was in her early 20s and had long softly curled hair that reached her waist. *Clearly hair extensions*, Camilla thought and rolled her eyes.

Juliette Crowne's red Alaïa dress fit like a corset and flared out around her hips, the hem resting mid-thigh. It was a gorgeous dress, but paled in comparison to her rope-like diamond necklace. From where she sat, Camilla could see the size of the diamonds, not just their sparkle, but the actual size of each glittering stone.

They talked animatedly, as each girl kissed Coleton hello. Camilla sipped her water and straightened her napkin. When what seemed like 10 minutes had passed she asked herself, *should she: (a) Walk confidently over and claim him? Lead him back to the table and finish their first and possibly last date, or (b) walk out of the restaurant dramatically and hail a cab. Who was he to make her wait around? Or (c) Sit patiently at the table, because maybe she was getting ahead of herself.*

As if reading her thoughts, Coleton motioned for Camilla to join him. Juliette pointed at a waiter and told him something. He turned and scurried to look for more chairs.

"I'm fine here," Camilla mouthed to Coleton and pointed at their table. Coleton shrugged, gave Juliette a hug and began to make his way back.

"Sorry about that." Coleton sighed, as he settled back down. "I haven't seen Juliette for a year at least."

"Oh?" Camilla asked. "Did you want to join her?"

"No," Coleton said. Then, he added, "I told her we'd maybe catch up with them later for drinks."

"Oh." Camilla nodded. "Okay."

The waitress placed Camilla's glass carefully on a cocktail napkin in the center of her plate, and then set down Coleton's double shot of Johnnie Walker Blue in the same manner. Arranging a napkin over her forearm, the waitress poured a small sample of the dark liquid into Camilla's glass, but before she could sample it, Coleton reached across the table and wrapped his fingers over hers. He took her glass by the stem. He swirled the wine, brought it to his nose and inhaled a long, slow breath.

"It's good." He winked at her and nodded to the waitress.

He set her glass lightly back on her side of the table for the waitress to fill it.

"I'm quite capable of tasting my own wine," Camilla said. "You didn't even sample it."

"My olfactory senses are sharper than the palates of most wine experts." He winked. "But I don't care for the taste of wine. Too vinegary."

"*Vinegary?* That just shows you have no idea what you're talking about," Camilla said, then stopped when she saw his big grin. "You're teasing me."

"It's my charm," he said.

"So, how do you know Juliette?"

"Juliette? Sweet girl. She's the daughter of William Crowne—the biggest legend in racing. I mean, he's the Godfather of the motorsports industry. They lived down the street from where I grew up, here in Palm Beach, so I've known her and her twin brother, Hilton, for most of my life, and all of theirs."

Sweet girl? Camilla thought, remembering the tabloid photos of Juliette, clearly drunk, flashing an unobstructed crotch shot as she exited a limousine. "She's very beautiful," Camilla said lightly. Coleton eyed her, as though reading her mind.

"Oh, I guess so. She's had a crush on me her whole life, but she's like a little sister. Between her absolutely psychotic brother, who I was friends with growing up, and my respect for her father, I'd never go there. Don't worry ..." He laughed and put his hand over hers.

"Worry about what?" Camilla said sweetly. She took a slow sip of the wine. He was right; it was good. *Rose petals, sandalwood and brown spice.*

"Back to your question."

"Which was?" she asked.

"I race in the Le Mans series."

"Oh, yes." Camilla loved when someone could circle a conversation. Come back to a question, rather than wandering along.

"In an LMP1 prototype car," Coleton continued. "Last year I was with Gomez Racing, but this year I'm racing an ORECA chassis powered by a Ferrari engine, with Elrod Racing—or at least I hope so. We're still in negotiations."

"Le Mans?" she asked. "That sounds French."

"It is."

"Is it like NASCAR?"

"Are you kidding?" Coleton scoffed. "We have more technology in our braking system than NASCAR has in their entire car!"

"Really?" Camilla asked. "So, it's a higher level of racing than NASCAR?" Coleton nodded. "Then Le Mans drivers must really rake it in? My sister's friend's husband drove NASCAR and he made millions."

"The economics of racing is complicated. NASCAR is much more popular in the US, so the drivers make a much bigger salary in that series, not to mention the purses are out of control." Camilla picked up her glass and took another long sip of wine. "Le Mans, on the other hand, is more popular globally," Coleton continued. "It's actually televised to over 60 million people in 107 countries. I mean, we are televised in the US, but we don't have near the viewership here that NASCAR does."

Coleton swirled the amber liquid in the bottom of his glass. "But, the real money in racing comes from sponsorship. The more ambitious and business-savvy a racecar driver is, the more sponsors he will attract, and the more money he will make, no matter what series he drives in."

The waitress came to take their order.

"Can I order for you?" Coleton asked, sitting forward with a grin. Normally, she would have found it antiquated and presumptuous for a man to order for his date, but for some reason, at this moment, she wasn't insulted. Did she already trust his taste, or maybe she was surprised by his bravado or was she just curious to hear what he would choose?

"Go ahead," Camilla said. "Let it be a test. We'll see if the wine selection was just a lucky guess."

Coleton grinned. For starters he ordered a dozen Blue Point oysters to share. Next, he ordered the Chilean Sea Bass for himself and the eight oz. filet, medium-plus and with truffle mash, for her, adding a side of almandine green beans for the table.

As the waitress left, they both resettled themselves, sipping their drinks, refreshing their postures. Camilla had never heard someone order a steak medium-plus before. She liked it: the precision.

"So," Camilla said. "You take me for a carnivore?"

He laughed. "Am I wrong?"

"You'll have to wait and find out."

"Fair enough." Coleton took a sip from his water glass. When he spoke again, he returned to the subject of racing.

"The more sponsor dollars a driver can wrangle, the more attractive he is to all the teams in the paddock. In fact, even if a driver isn't that skillful, he can muscle himself onto a great team if he brings a lot of cash to the table."

"The paddock?" Camilla asked. "Isn't that a term for horses and cattle?"

"It's the behind-the-scenes area of a racetrack where all the teams set up their tents and trailers, where the drivers hang out when they aren't in the car, where the deals are cut, where all the drama and gossip goes on."

"Oh," Camilla said. "And, wait … the team gets the money a driver solicits from sponsors? But, I thought you just said that sponsorship was how drivers make real money?" Camilla leaned forward over the table, where she knew her eyes would catch the glimmer of light from the tea candle. Just because she didn't go out with fast men *usually*, did not mean she didn't know how to play the game. "How does that work?"

Coleton noticed for the first time how beautiful her eyes were: large and blue and curious. He smiled and leaned closer.

"Do you know how blue your eyes look right now?"

"What?" she asked, sitting back with a coy smile.

"Oh, nothing." Coleton drained the last sip in his glass with a full smile on his lips, then dropped it back to the table. "A driver can decide how much of the sponsorship money to give the team and how much to keep for himself."

"Really?" Camilla asked. She pushed her long bangs back off her cheekbone. Her cheeks looked flushed, and Coleton knew she had heard his compliment and had processed it. "I wouldn't imagine racecar drivers to be of the altruistic persuasion."

"It's a balance. You give what you have to in order to get on the team you want. If you're a talented driver, you might keep a larger percentage and still score the team of your choice. Other drivers don't have that luxury and buy their way in, either bringing their own cars onto the team with them, or by filling the team coffers with fresh sponsorship money."

The waitress arranged a large silver platter between them with 12 Blue Points perched on a mountain of ice, and set down a fresh drink in front of Coleton.

"Would you like a glass of Sauvignon Blanc to go with your oysters?" Coleton asked Camilla. "It will bring out the metallic taste of the ocean in them." He nodded at the rock-like shells.

"How very Hemingway of you." Coleton gave her a quizzical look. "I'm fine," Camilla added with a smile. "But thank you."

"Sure?" he asked again. She nodded, so he continued. "Have you ever seen a Formula 1 race?" he asked. He removed an oyster shell from the ice and seasoned the meat with lemon juice and Tabasco before passing it to her on a white bread plate.

"A few. I watched Schumacher win a race, once, with an ex-boyfriend," Camilla said, proud that she could drop at least one pertinent name. Coleton chuckled.

"Schumacher's retired now, for the second time. But, at least you're not completely new to the sport."

"Really I am. We didn't date long."

"Well, Le Mans is very similar to F1. The main difference is that our cars are slightly slower and we have longer races so there are at least two drivers per car."

Camilla nodded and pulled an oyster from its shell with her cocktail fork.

"Oh, and there are different types of cars in Le Mans, all running at the same time, whereas in F1 they all look the same." Coleton looked at Camilla to gauge her interest. She nodded politely. "First, there are prototype cars. They're the big boys. That's what I drive, the fastest ones."

"Why does that not surprise me?"

"There are also GT cars, which look like different streetcars: Ferrari, Porsche, BMW, Jaguar, Ford GT40, Corvette, but only in silhouette. Everything under their skin is dramatically different from their streetcar counterparts. I'm boring you?" Coleton asked abruptly.

"Oh, no …" Camilla said, but really, all that kept her engaged in this discussion was the man across the table. Instinctively she knew it was better to feign interest. "How do different types of cars all race at the same time, aren't the GT cars holding you up all the time?"

"Exactly!" Coleton seemed delighted she was paying attention. "It can be frustrating to get stuck behind lap traffic, but that's why you've got to be a great driver in Le Mans. There are a lot of moving parts."

He paused to sip his drink, then looked up at her intently. "Enough about Le Mans. Tell me about you."

The sudden change in trajectory took Camilla by surprise. She looked up at him, an oyster poised mid-air on her fork.

"What do you want to know?" she asked, and slipped the oyster between her lips.

"The good stuff. Where'd you grow up?"

"Just outside of Miami. We moved to New York when I was 14."

"Good thing you got out of Miami."

"What's wrong with Miami?" Camilla asked, taking a sip of Cakebread.

"It's not that. I live in Miami Beach, actually—"

"You don't live in Palm Beach?" Camilla interjected, confused.

"No. My parents live on South Ocean Road, where I grew up, and I spend a weekend or two here a month to relax. I love Palm Beach, but it's a little too quiet for permanent life."

"So, why is it *good* I got out of Miami?"

"Miami doesn't produce real people."

"Excuse me?" Camilla asked, ready to take offense.

"I mean Miami is not the most family centered environment. People who grow up in Miami are a little messed up in the head."

"That's a sweeping generalization. You know three quarters of the people in Dade County are Latin American, right? There are no more family centered people in the world."

"Maybe I'm just jaded by the dating pool. But, stereotypes—well, they save time. Take this for example—are you parents still together? That's why you moved to New York, right?"

"You have no idea what you are talking about," she said, bristling.

"Hmm … well are they?" he said smugly.

"My mom died when I was 14. We moved to New York because my dad couldn't handle it and quit his practice for a teaching position at Columbia medical school." She twisted her glass to let the light roll through the garnet liquid.

"Shit, I'm sorry." Coleton pulled back his bottom lip, then put his hand over hers. She pulled it back.

Her eyes burned. She sat in silence while her emotions sorted themselves out. "Let's talk about something else."

"Do you have brothers and sisters?"

"That's not something else," she said, an edge in her voice. But maybe she was being too hard on him. "Just the sister you met. Katherine's four years older."

"She's a doctor too?"

"No, she started at NYU Business School when we moved. Then got a job on Wall Street with Goldman Sachs, working 70 hours a week. She met her husband Charles at a pool party in South Hampton. And, that was it for her: love at first sight. She gave it all up and moved here, so he could start an investment firm in West Palm Beach. It's so funny to see her as this docile housewife after she's painted the streets of New York with investment banker blood for years."

"So, you're the youngest then?"

"I'm the baby."

"That could be a problem." Coleton leaned forward. "Because, I'm the baby too."

"Big surprise."

"What?" Coleton laughed, feigning offense.

"You reek of spoiled brat syndrome."

"Is that a technical medical term?"

"Very technical, and *very* serious I might add." She worked hard not to return his smile. "We've been trying to find a cure for years."

Two waiters arrived out of the dark restaurant and set down their entrees. Coleton looked over at her steak. "That looks great. I may be interested in a trade."

Camilla looked down at her perfectly cooked steak, tender and juicy. "Keep your eyes on your own plate." She turned her plate half an inch, then picked up her fork and steak knife. "So, how much younger are you?"

"Than my brother? Seven years."

"No!" Camilla exclaimed. "What have I got myself into?"

Coleton looked at her and cocked his head with curiosity.

"Look—" she said, setting down her fork. "The dinner's been great, but I might have to abort now." She pretended to throw in her napkin. "You're telling me—" She sighed. "Not *only* are you the baby, but you're the functional equivalent of an only child?" Coleton laughed, she continued. "I mean, *really*?

This information was *not* fully disclosed before I accepted your dinner invitation."

"And to compound matters … you should know, I was a complete mistake."

"No."

"Complete! My parents are very vocal about that fact."

"They've admitted it?" she asked in mock horror.

"I've known since I was 10," he said. "My parents were completely done after my brother. He and my dad are inseparable: look alike, dress alike, act alike. They were completely happy, and then, surprise—Coleton Loren!" He pointed to himself with an evil grin. "I'm the original party crasher."

"How horrible for your psyche," Camilla smirked. "I can see your self-esteem has really suffered. In fact, you should probably be submitted for testing. I'm sure there's a study you can join about spoiled little rich mistakes who are angry at the world and take it out on the Miami Beach party scene."

Coleton erupted in laughter. "Now, what makes you think I'm rich?"

"Ok, Mr. Ferrari! Clearly, you grew up on the wrong side of the tracks. No? On the gray, plaid polyester couch of a double-wide?"

Coleton looked at her, his eyes gleaming. "You are too funny," he said, then sobered. His eyes never left hers, as he took another sip of scotch, testing his motivation to continue.

"I've never gotten along with my dad. We're so different it's crazy. He hates that I race cars for a living. He took my choice as a personal affront."

"What does *he* do?"

"He and my brother run an oil company together, based in Texas. He thinks that's the only real occupation for a man. I've been cut off from him financially since high school, and emotionally, well, for as long as I can remember."

"Really?" Camilla asked. "But you seem so privileged."

"What I have, I've earned behind the wheel."

"But, isn't he proud of your success?"

"Dad? He thinks it's a joke. He keeps waiting for me to fail, hoping I'll come crawling back one day." A cloudy expression passed over Coleton's face, and Camilla wondered what wounds it hid. "He doesn't have the balls to do what I do for a single afternoon."

"The prodigal son?" Camilla asked.

Coleton smiled. "I make prodigal *look good*."

The waitress arrived and set down a three-tiered serving tray of mini desserts.

"We didn't order this," Coleton said.

"It's from your friend over there. The blonde one." She nodded at Juliette's table.

"That was nice," Camilla said.

Another waitress set down two dessert wine glasses with a tasting of wine in each.

"And what's this?" Coleton asked.

"A 1819 Madeira from Portugal."

"*A what?*" Coleton asked, leaning forward as if he'd misheard.

"This wine was made when Napoleon was alive?" Camilla asked.

"You sell this here?" Coleton asked. "The wine list must be better than I thought. I should have looked at it!"

"No, Miss Crowne brought it from her personal cellar."

"You mean—her dad's cellar. Poor William."

"Who is she again?" Camilla asked.

"Someone not cut off from her dad."

Coleton held up his petite glass, and she lifted hers in turn. "Cheers," he said, looking directly into her eyes and took a slow sip of the sweet wine. She tasted hers, and the thought of putting something with so much history in her mouth, something that was on the earth almost 200 years ago, gave her a giddy chill. She liked it, the sweet, syrupy taste, and the sensation.

"I thought you didn't drink wine?"

"I was just pulling your leg." He grinned.

"That's not nice," she said, gracing him with the first unrestrained smile of the night. "Especially on a first date."

"Oh," he said. "Is that what this is?"

Coleton took a heart-shaped cookie from the top tier and bit it in half. Crumbs dusted his lips, as he stared at her and chewed. She held his gaze unabashed. He broke into a lopsided, little-boy smile.

He popped the rest of the cookie into his mouth and raised his hand to call the waitress for the check.

Somehow the restaurant had gotten even fuller over the course of their meal. It was difficult and slow-moving work for them to make their exit. Camilla inched toward the door in front of Coleton, making way for him and his unwieldy crutches.

"I need to make a quick stop at the maître d's," Coleton said.

"Oh?"

"You always take care of the guy on the way out, never on the way in," Coleton explained with a wink.

As they passed the desk, Coleton stopped to clap him on the shoulder. There was a crowd of people waiting to get in, pressing slowly forward, passively fighting to get close to the maître d' to attempt a stealthy slight of wrist, a quick divestiture.

"Mr. Loren," the maître d' said with a broad smile. "As always, it's a pleasure to have you at our humble establishment." Camilla could just discern the corner of a bill slip into the maître d's hand as Coleton shook it.

At the curb sat a black Rolls Royce Phantom with closed curtains in its backseat windows. As Camilla stepped into the cool night air, the driver opened the back door for her.

"That's not us," she said with a polite smile. "We drove here."

Coleton placed his hand on the small of her back. "Yes, it's us. Get in, doll."

She looked over her shoulder at him, confused. "But, where's your—"

"They picked it up. This is Victoria's. I wouldn't presume to drive you anywhere after a few drinks. I respect you, as well as the art of driving, too much."

Camilla raised an eyebrow.

"Not to mention, they could take my racing license over a DUI."

"So *that's* the reason," Camilla laughed. "Who's Victoria?"

"My mom."

"You call your mom Victoria?"

"Is that weird?"

"Suddenly, I don't feel so bad for you. *Boo hoo*," she said, pretending to wipe her eyes. "My family doesn't support me."

"They don't put food in my mouth, but I guess being a Loren does come with a *few* perks."

A few minutes later the boat-like car wallowed up in front of her sister's house on Everglade. Camilla glanced into the front seat. The driver was staring fixedly out the front window. Somehow he knew not to open her door, but to give them a few minutes. She felt that awkward anticipation at the end of a good date. Should she invite him in? All her instincts said no.

"Do you want to—" Camilla waved her hand toward the house. "My sister always has good coffee."

Coleton's smile beamed in the dark. "Thank you, but I should be getting home."

"Well, as your physician, I agree that rest is the best policy."

Coleton pushed her long bangs back off her cheekbone. "It looks like I'll be heading to Chicago on business." She was suddenly very aware of her own shallow breathing. "So, you may not hear from me for a while."

A while? Camilla realized she had no say over this sudden feeling of disappointment. She sucked in her breath, waiting.

Coleton leaned toward her until his face was inches away. She continued to hold her breath and forced her gaze down from the front headrest to look at him. The second their eyes met, he moved even closer. He kissed her lightly on the cheek and let his lips linger on her skin for a moment. Then, he leaned across her, and with a yank, pulled the handle and pushed the door open for her.

Camilla sat up, breathless and dismayed. *Didn't he know she wanted him to kiss her—properly?*

"Goodnight, Camilla," he said, his devilish smile illuminated by the soft light of the streetlamp.

"Goodnight, Coleton," she said, composing herself.

Camilla stepped into the silent street. She was confused, but didn't look back. She walked confidently up the driveway. It wasn't until she let the wooden gate that led to the pool house close behind her that she heard the Rolls Royce motor away into the night.

CHAPTER 7
MIAMI BEACH, FLORIDA

"Heya, Johnny!" Coleton called into his BlackBerry with more volume than necessary; the call was an important one. "It's Colt."

"What's happening?" Johnny asked. "How's my favorite JW?"

"Oh, I'm doing alright," Coleton replied, quieter now.

"Hey, I read in *AutoWeek* that you broke your leg racing?"

"Not racing. Some asshole testing an FXX ran me into a wall while I was trying to teach him a thing or two."

"No way!" Johnny laughed. "So your leg is really broken?"

"Yep, and I need to get to Chicago … yesterday," Coleton said. "You got any deadheads or one-ways?"

"Mmmm, let me check." Coleton could hear the quick tapping of a keyboard in the background. He held his breath. "Actually—"

"Yes?"

"Ah, nope."

"Come on, Johnny!"

"There really isn't much out there, Bud."

"Gimping through a commercial airport with the GFP is not an option."

"GFP?"

"General Fucking—"

"Public. Got it," Johnny laughed. "Well, I may have a Lear 25 deadhead from Detroit tomorrow."

"That's a start," Coleton said, but his hopes dropped. A re-direct from Detroit would be almost as expensive as a charter from scratch. "Got anything that isn't older than I am?"

"Let me call around. Give me an hour."

"Thanks man. I really appreciate it," Coleton said.

"I'll do my best."

At his Breakers breakfast, Coleton realized that a face-to-face with Arthur Elrod was his only hope of saving his season. So, he hit the phones calling all of his friends who owned jets to see where they might be going. Even under normal circumstances, Coleton shuddered at the thought of flying commercial. However, as he didn't own a plane this conviction required the not infrequent phone call to bum a ride from a friend or acquaintance. This made him what his circle of friends affectionately coined a "JW" or Jet Whore. Coleton was willing to embrace this moniker if it meant he could avoid security lines, re-circulated air, possible exposure to an Ebola outbreak, screaming babies and seatmates so large they had to raise the arm rest.

Coleton had invented, and mastered, the four rules of jet whoring: never be late, never sit in the boss's seat, pack light, and never crap on the plane. Sticking to these tenets had made Coleton one of the most successful JWs in Miami. However even for the best, a JW's seat is never guaranteed, especially if his route is out of the "golden triangle" of Miami, New York and Los Angeles. On any given day, dozens of private jets travel these routes, and a savvy JW has a decent chance of bumming a ride *gratis*.

Growing up on the tarmac of private FBOs, Coleton traveled with his family on his father's various planes. An interest in private aircraft was pretty much the only thing Coleton and his father had in common. On their travels, Coleton would rattle off which planes were the fastest, which were safest and most efficient, which would hold their value, all the while looking for a reaction in his father's face. At 12, Coleton could tell from a glance the difference between a Gulfstream 4 and a Bombardier Challenger.

More than a decade later, Coleton used the same knowledge to impress a private jet broker called Phantom Jets and convinced them to sponsor him at his former team, Gomez Racing. To monetize the sponsorship Coleton agreed to sell time-shares, called jet time or jet cards, on behalf of Phantom Jets to wealthy individuals who weren't quite wealthy enough to buy their own planes. It was a win-win: Coleton made commissions and Phantom got new customers.

New to this symbiotic breed of sponsorship, however, Phantom Jets cut a deal with Coleton that was too rich in his favor if he delivered as many sales as he predicted. The CEO, Howard Starkly, saw the deal as a lucrative entrance pass to the paddock and its legendary business network, which he hoped to pillage, and expected Coleton to fail as a jet time salesman.

Coleton jumped on the deal and quickly brought in a host of new customers. He developed a new strategy, negotiating sales of jet time to other aviation operators and brokers, who in turn re-packaged and sold them to their own networks of clients, which resulted in millions of dollars of commissions, rather than the thousands Starkly expected.

Coleton collected some of his earned kickbacks, but by the end of the year Phantom Jets had declared bankruptcy. Coleton was unsure whether this move was thanks to his over-achievement and their outstanding debts to him, or whether perhaps the rumors of embezzlement by its corporate officers were true. Either way, Phantom stopped paying him. Coleton was forced to comfort himself with the only lasting benefit of the Phantom deal—the friendships he made in private aviation by spreading around his juicy deal and cutting in other brokers.

As soon as he hung up with Johnny, Coleton began flipping his mental Rolodex, trying to come up with a friend, business associate, acquaintance, or anyone else he could think of with a private jet that he hadn't already tried. After an hour, he had still come up short. His friends were staggered around the country but no one was flying Miami to Chicago: two were in Aspen, one in Las Vegas, one in Miami but not going anywhere, and one in Los Angeles for maintenance.

Coleton looked out his broad kitchen windows across Biscayne Bay, then down at his watch. Johnny had taken his hour and had turned up nothing. Coleton picked his phone up and stared at it, dreading the call he knew he needed to make. He held down the number six and the phone dialed a number.

"If you're going to borrow our things, then you better learn to respect them."

"Hi, Dad. I respect them."

"Good, then I'll send you a bill for the chauffeur's overtime for the Rolls Royce and a tank of gas."

"Okay," Coleton said simply.

"So what do you want?"

"I have to have a reason to call my old man?" Coleton asked, but the joke fell flat.

"What is it?"

"I need a favor."

Coleton heard his father scoff and then the shake of ice cubes in the bottom of a glass. On the other end of the line, a polite voice asked if he'd like another.

"I need to borrow the G-4 to Chicago. I know it's just collecting dust at Galaxy Aviation."

"For what?"

"A business meeting."

"What do you know about business?"

"I made north of seven figures last year, so I must be doing something right."

"You're like a model with a very definite expiration date. You better save every penny you make."

Coleton pulled the phone away from his ear and bit back his anger. He inhaled a long breath through his nose.

"As you know, I have a broken leg, Dad. It would be very difficult for me to fly commercial across the country. I'm asking you very politely, if I may borrow your plane. I will of course pay for fuel."

"I thought you were a fancy professional athlete, too good for the oil business. Buy your own plane."

"Fine." Coleton ground his teeth, wishing he'd never hit the call button. "Listen closely. I will never ask you for another thing. You hear me?"

"What's that? A threat? More like a relief."

Coleton hung up and shook his head. His chest ached as if someone hit him in the solar plexus. Not that he didn't expect it. His dad had never supported his racing career, but it still stung.

Coleton heard a scuffle and a soft bump in the hallway, the sound of a body part against dry wall, the back of a heel or an elbow.

"I can hear you," he said. Silence. "If you want to listen in on my conversation so bad, then come right on in."

Part of a head peaked around the corner, half a forehead and one hazel eye, then Gigi strolled into the kitchen with a laundry basket on her hip, as if she'd been headed his way the whole time.

Gigi had shoulder length brown hair that gained a reddish hue in the sun, and she wore rectangular purple glasses. In the proud set of her eyes, her high cheekbones and trim figure, it was easy to see that she had once been a beauty.

"What wrong, Cole-ton?" she asked. She dropped the basket to the marble topped island, as a frown wrinkled her forehead. She had a hard time pronouncing Coleton, a trait he secretly found endearing.

Coleton never got the full story about her former life, but he knew she'd been through hard times. Back in Brazil, she'd had two sons of her own, a little older than Coleton, but only one was still living. To her, Coleton was her third son. She carried a picture of him in her wallet and took pride in his every accomplishment.

"Nothing's wrong."

Gigi frowned again and put her hand on her hip. She wasn't going anywhere. "I no like your father talk to you like that." She made a tsking sound in her throat.

Coleton looked down at the tiled floor and nodded in agreement. He picked an ice cube out of his glass of iced tea, shook it off and placed it on top of the soil of a potted orchid growing in the kitchen window.

"You need me help to go somewhere?" she asked, then brightened with the solution. "I drive you!"

Coleton chuckled softly. "You can't drive me to Chicago, you crazy old bird."

"No?" she asked, looking downtrodden that her idea wouldn't pan out. "Maybe I make you something special for lunch?"

"I'm not suicidal," Coleton laughed, and she narrowed her eyes.

Gigi was a great housekeeper, but they both knew she couldn't cook to save her life. Once when Coleton had the flu, he thought scrambled eggs would be a safe and easy request, until he saw the plate of yellow Play-Doh she brought him. To avoid hurting her feelings, he had to force down half the plate before he could feign fullness. After that, the only meals he allowed her to prepare were from plastic containers bought at the hot bar at Whole Foods.

A flash of orange in the laundry basket flagged Coleton's attention. He stepped forward and peered over the edge.

"Noooooo," he said. He looked at Gigi with wide eyes, then back into the basket. "No. No. No." He snatched a tiny orange sweater from the basket and held it up with both hands, yanking it to its maximum dimensions. "You washed my new cashmere sweater?"

Gigi frowned. "No, that not yours. It too small."

"Gigi, you washed it and it *shrank*. You can't wash cashmere!"

"Ohhhh," she said, and clucked her tongue, realizing her mistake. "I forgot, but it okay."

"Explain me," Coleton said, using one of her stilted phrases and trying to look stern. "Why it okay?"

"I find it good home for someone little," Gigi said, hiding a giggle. She patted him on the back and yanked it out of his hand.

Coleton shook his head. But, what could he do? Who else would put up with his completely neurotic OCD behavior? Who else would iron every article of clothing, including underwear and pocket scarves, and fold his T-shirts to squares of precisely the same size and arrange them in color-coded stacks? When Coleton would request some strange task like cleaning under the refrigerator, or going over every indentation in the egg and dart molding with a damp washcloth, she'd just roll her eyes and oblige.

His BlackBerry vibrated on the white marble. With the reflexes of a cat, he snatched it up.

"Johnny, tell me something good," Coleton blurted out. "Please."

"You are a lucky fucker, you know that?"

"Whatcha got?" Coleton asked with a wide smile.

"It ain't perfect, but it's free. You've got to drive to Naples, and I mean now. I found a flight to Chicago, wheels-up in an hour. And tomorrow I diverted our Lear 25 from Detroit to pick you up."

"You're the man!" Coleton roared. "But, I don't know if I can make it to Naples in an hour—"

"—said the champion racecar driver."

"I'm leaving now."

"Get there quick. The owner will be on-board, and you know those guys don't wait for anyone. But, he happens to be a huge Le Mans fan and he's psyched to meet you. Take an autographed Hero card."

"Hero card? I'll give him a goddamn kiss on the lips," Coleton laughed. "And, how the hell did you get the Detroit re-direct for free?"

"Well, considering how much you helped us with numb nuts before he went under, I figured I'd eat the fuel on a quick cycle for ya."

Coleton muffled the phone against his chest and yelled as loud as he could, "Gigi!"

"Thanks, Buddy," Coleton said back into the phone. "I won't forget this."

Gigi scurried back into the kitchen as Coleton hung up. "We're going on a field trip, you hot old broad."

Her eyes widened, but working for Coleton, she'd come to expect the unexpected. "*Norte?*"

"No, Naples. Then, me *norte.*"

"Okay, I pack you sweater," Gigi said, then she grinned. "But … not orange one."

"No, not orange one." Coleton smiled despite himself and grabbed an apple from a crystal bowl. He tossed it up, snatched it from mid-air with one hand and took a huge crunching bite. "*Muito rapidamente,*" he said through a mouthful of apple. Then, as an afterthought, he added, "*Obrigado!*"

Gigi quickly packed an overnight bag, and fresh fruit, nuts and three bottles of water into a brown paper bag, then loaded up her 172,000 mile Honda Civic. Coleton took the wheel and drove at the very limit, tearing across Alligator Alley. Gigi sat stiffly in the passenger seat. She covered her eyes and gripped the rosary around her neck with both hands when Coleton careened onto the shoulder to pass a slower car. Coleton laughed at her horror when he slipped between two semi trucks with the accelerator pegged to the floor. He wiggled the tips of his toes that poked out of his pink cast in her lap and gave her a winning smile.

Coleton navigated under the green scalloped awning of Gibson's Bar and Steakhouse on his crutches. He picked his way through a fleet of tables topped with green and white plaid tablecloths, along a row of rust red leather booths and past the bar lit by smoked-glass Art Deco drop lights to a private dining room in the back.

A burly man in a dark suit, with a closely shaven head stood outside the door to the private room with his hands clasped behind his back. Coleton didn't recognize him, but knew he must be part of Elrod's security detail. He inclined his head when he saw Coleton and motioned him inside.

"Would you look at this guy!" said Elrod. He stood up from the head of a 10-person table set for two and extended his hand. Coleton had to balance on one crutch before he could accept the gesture. "You feeling alright?"

"Never better. I'm used to this shit." Coleton gestured to the few inches of pink showing at the hem of his dark, boot-cut jeans.

The men sat down and without further ado, ordered like kings: Alaskan king crab cocktail with Bombay cocktail sauce, two bone-in filet mignons, a giant buttery Lobster tail, double baked potatoes and loaded wedge salads. The food arrived quickly and disappeared just as the small talk grew to be an effort. Coleton decided it was time to get down to business.

"Look, Arthur," Coleton said. "I know Ira may have pissed you off, or maybe you were just having a bad day—it doesn't matter." Coleton spoke slowly, trying to make eye contact. Elrod didn't look up from the final crab claw that he was taking his time to crack. "We need to make a deal. I have a ready, willing and able sponsor that has a good track record of paying his bills, so what's the problem with the payment schedule? It's pretty normal."

Coleton knew that not many people dared to speak to Arthur Elrod so frankly, but he could read people, and he knew Elrod would respect him for it. Besides, Coleton Loren did not kiss ass. Ever.

"I understand it's a decent deal and all. I just need more upfront. What if this guy DK's on me halfway through the season and we're way ahead of him? What then?" Elrod shook his head slowly, took a sip of wine and shrugged. "I just can't do it."

"Arthur, it's $10 million! That's got to be the absolute biggest single sponsor in the paddock. Why aren't you jumping up and down? Just because it's spread out over the season?"

"First off all, I never jump up and down," Elrod began. There was a sly look on his face that Coleton recognized, but didn't like. "And I've got Roberto Gonzalez waiting in the wings for an LMP1 ride, and he's committed to seven mill from Citgo. All upfront."

"Roberto Gonzalez?" Coleton said in shock. Ira hadn't mentioned a word of this to him. Usually his dog on the street could sniff out all the gossip and potential deals that were brewing. "Gonzalez is a mediocre driver. And, you know that seven million is a sweetheart deal from Venezuela. His family is friends with the president, who's dodged three assassination attempts, by the way. What if the politics change? Talk about DK. They'll DK you out of existence and take their money back."

"Now, let's be fair. Gonzalez is relatively quick, when he can keep it out of the wall."

"Seriously, Arthur?" Coleton poured the rest of the bottle into Elrod's glass. "You would rather have seven million up front than ten over time? Even on a present value basis, you'd still be way ahead with Miller."

"Well," Elrod said, ignoring the wine, then he cleared his throat. "I mean let's be frank—Gonzalez doesn't have a broken leg. At least it's a sure thing he'll be ready by Sebring."

The waiter arrived, set down their desserts along with two glasses of Château d'Yquem and left without a word.

Coleton looked down at the perfect pistachio crème brulée in front of him, but didn't even see it. Elrod had brought up the leg, and there wasn't much wiggle room around that topic. He picked up his glass by the stem and took a slow sip of the golden dessert wine, buying himself a second to think. He needed to come up with something big, and quick. *Sponsorship dollars are not your only bargaining chip,* he remembered William Crowne saying at the Breakers. Coleton smiled and leaned back in his chair, wiggling his toes. *Introductions are also valuable.*

"What are you doing here?" Coleton asked.

"I beg your pardon?" Elrod leaned forward and the tea candle in the middle of the table lit up his face.

"Chicago, why are you here?"

"I'm meeting with the traders at my office here. I have a seat at the CBOT. Top step," Elrod said. Only the best traders had a berth on the top step overlooking the pit.

"Right," Coleton said. "You trade crude oil?"

"Bonds, index, grains, meats, anything with a trend. And yes, I take positions in crude if the opportunity presents itself. But it's an insider's market."

"Meaning?"

"Meaning it's manipulated and as far from a free market as it gets. And I'm not a Saudi sheikh. But if you're good, you can profit without inside info."

"What if I could deliver one of those opportunities?" Coleton asked with a wry smile.

"What do you know about futures?"

"More than most," Coleton said. "My dad owns a few wells, but that's besides the point." Coleton took a sip of wine, letting Elrod wait. "Let's assume I know a very wealthy Arab with a massive stock of crude in his refinery. And, let's next assume this Arab may be looking to take a huge short position to hedge against a drop in price? Would that sort of introduction interest you?"

Elrod froze, then set down his dessert fork and made the first real eye contact of the entire evening. "Continue."

"What if I could arrange a meeting?" Coleton stared deep into Elrod's eyes.

"You have my attention," Elrod said, absent-mindedly noting Coleton's piercing green eyes. "Who is this mystery man?"

"All in good time." Coleton relaxed against the back of his chair as Elrod leaned toward him. "For now, I can tell you he's Saudi royalty and we're talking about a $100 million trade."

"Okay, Mark Rich. Put it together!"

"Arthur, now listen." Coleton leaned in and rested his elbows on the table. "These people are serious and if I put this meeting together you have to perform."

"So do it already."

"Consider it done," said Coleton. He picked up his spoon and gently cracked the center of his crème brulée, scooping up half of it in one go. Now he could enjoy the French delicacy. "But," he continued. "I have two conditions."

"Tell me," said Elrod, finishing his Macadamia Turtle Pie and wiping the tar-like chocolate residue from his lips with his napkin.

"First, I want a 10% commission as soon as the trade is placed, in cash, hard currency. And second, I want your word here and now that we have a deal with Miller at the installments he agreed to and we can start racing together." Coleton ate the other half.

"Done," Elrod said. He extended his hand.

"Done," Coleton said and shook it. He wiped his hands with his napkin and dropped it to the table.

Elrod stood up and started toward the men's room. He paused mid-step, and turned back.

"Let me ask you a question," he said. He put a hand on the back of his chair and leaned over the table toward Coleton. "You're a smart businessman, Coleton. Why do you have that obnoxious douche bag for an agent when you negotiate the deals?" Coleton laughed and tipped back his head, careful to drain the last precious drop of Château d'Yquem into his mouth.

"Because," Coleton responded without even thinking, "everyone needs a fat, pushy friend to cover their ass."

CHAPTER 8

SEBRING, FLORIDA

"1:44.623," said Nelson Webb over the radio. "Solid lap, Colt! One more hot lap, then pit."

"Roger that," Coleton replied as the LMP1 ripped past the pit wall at 190 mph.

The morning of Saturday, February 5th dawned bright and clear, and despite Florida's hot and humid reputation, there was a chill that the whole Elrod Racing crew appreciated. It was the first official winter testing session at Sebring International Raceway. Twelve Hours of Sebring was to be the first Le Mans race of the season, so a few teams had made the trip to the small Florida town to get in a couple of practice laps before the real thing. In a few weeks, the 10,000 residents of Sebring would welcome over 100,000 diehard fans camped out around the track for the practice sessions, qualifying session and finally, the long-awaited race on Saturday. Today the infield was quiet and swaths of scrawny grass stretched in all directions.

The Elrod crew had arrived the day before, and Arthur Elrod's bleacher-like pit cart, larger and more luxurious than any other, had already been carefully erected next to the track on the rumor that Elrod himself might attend.

Elrod's favorite business tactic was to overwhelm initial expectations, at all costs, and he carried this stratagem into racing as well. When the crowd already expects you to win, triumph becomes a foregone conclusion. Elrod was not exactly a hands-on owner. He was busy with other ventures and knew little about the mechanics of racing or operating a team. But he had invested enough money to want a voice in major decisions and he tolerated no imperfections. Elrod's temper was infamous. He staunchly believed enough money thrown at any problem could buy success, and demanded nothing less than podium finishes.

At the last minute, the crew got word that Elrod had canceled his Sebring trip for a meeting with an investor. The glossy pit cart with its plush leather seats and bank of television monitors remained empty, with only Nelson Webb, the team's lead engineer, and Coleton's teammate, George Wachner, perched at the center of the bench.

George hovered under the monitors that displayed Coleton's lap times, fidgeting like a worried parent. Coleton had convinced Camilla to remove his cast early—late enough not to be malpractice, but too early for her better judgment. He had promised her that he would begin careful "rehabilitation," but this turned out to mean jumping back in his car for the first test of the season. He still couldn't put weight on his leg and had to crutch his way to the cockpit.

"Don't let him push himself too hard," George warned Nelson. "Sometimes Coleton's pain tolerance is higher than his IQ."

Coleton flashed by on the front straight and his new lap time appeared on the screen. Nelson nodded approvingly. Then, he flicked the switch on his headset.

"1:44.423. Nice lap, Colt," Nelson said. "Keep up the temps and pit now."

Nelson was a lanky, serious man with silver hair and a high widow's peak. He had a hawk-like nose, and sharp, keen eyes that he kept behind wire-rimmed glasses. In high school he had worked as a mechanic at a race shop a few miles from the Silverstone track outside London. He wasn't a great mechanic, and his clumsy fingers were perpetually battered and oil stained, but by the time he graduated he was hooked on racing. The pure physics of the sport was his first and only true love: the predictability of forces, the play of gravity and inertia, and the mathematics of tire wear and fuel strategies.

While other engineers shied from bad news or murky results and receded into the data, Nelson's fast, clear response to upsets made him an incredible engineer. His career had peaked as a second engineer at Audi for two years, but he soon found the stress distasteful. Elrod had been lucky to find such talent for his start-up team, and had only dared to negotiate Nelson's salary down 10% for fear of losing him.

The Elrod Racing machine roared into pit lane. Coleton depressed the limiter button the exact moment he crossed from track to pit entrance, and the car lurched down to 60 kph.

"On pit lane. On pit lane," Coleton warned the crew. His voice sounded calm over the radio, but faraway like an astronaut.

Coleton swerved in to a perfect halt on his marks in front of the Elrod pit box. A Michelin engineer ran around to check the tire temperatures and make sure they matched the temps on his screen. Another engineer jumped over the pit wall and plugged a laptop into the dashboard to transfer telemetry data. A jack man stuck an air hose in the back of the car, lifting it several inches above the ground. Two other crewmembers ran around the back to remove a side panel and peer into its dark interior.

"How's the car?" yelled Max Cross, the Crew Chief, so Coleton could hear him even through his helmet.

Coleton flipped up his tinted visor. "A bit of mid-corner understeer in Turn 1 and a bit of snap oversteer at the exit of the Carousel."

Drivers encounter understeer when the front tires lose their grip, and they turn the steering wheel, but the car keeps going straight. Oversteer, or fishtailing, is the opposite: the rear tires lose their grip. Some drivers prefer understeer and will manhandle a headstrong car through a turn, while others prefer to rein in the after-effects of oversteer.

When the crew sets up a car, based on the ratio of corners to straightaways, they also factor in a driver's preferences. Coleton's team knew what he liked, often better than he did.

"Wanna make a change?" Max asked.

"Why don't we soften the front bar a little *and* add a bit of rear wing for down force," Coleton said in the same radio voice.

Coleton hated making two changes at the same time. It made it harder to tell if either change did the trick. But, he knew a softer bar would put more front tire rubber on the ground and give the car better grip into a corner.

The rear wing instruction, however, was one of those the crew followed without asking why. The more wing angle, the more down force a racecar has in the corners, which mitigates oversteer, but adds more aerodynamic drag on the straight-a-way. Drivers look for the perfect balance of straight-line speed and cornering down force, and in the end it was Coleton's call. He needed to test the new angle now, before the practice session ended.

"No problem," said Max. He radioed the mechanics on another frequency, ordered the changes and hurried off to supervise.

Nelson hopped down from the pit cart with his laptop under his arm, and made his way over the pit wall. "Your laps are looking good, Colt. I'm going to let you settle in before we get too technical about your brake and throttle applications." Nelson watched the mechanics buzzing around the car. "And, for the big question—how's the leg?"

"It's not going to last the rest of the session," Coleton replied darkly. "Not without a fitment change." Nelson rested an elbow on the tub of the car to peer into Coleton's visor. He nodded, then stood up and motioned for Max.

Max hurried over and leaned close.

"Tell Junior to grab some foam and black tape," said Coleton. "And fix a pad next to my knee." Coleton pointed to his right leg. "It's banging like hell against the tub."

Max nodded grimly. He switched radio frequencies and quickly described Coleton's request. Another mechanic scrambled over the wall. Ninety seconds later, the pad was in place.

"Are you sure you want to finish the session? We can throw George in if you want to take a rest," Nelson said.

George was peering over the pit wall, trying not to get in the way of the crew. Although he usually saved it for race weekends, George had grown his lucky mustache for the practice, and even though he was slated to run the second practice session, he was already suited, helmet under his arm, and ready to take over.

"No, the pad is fine."

"Okay, then. We're going to stay on this rubber for the rest of the session," Nelson told Coleton. "The temps were great, so give me two more hot laps and then a cool down. There are six minutes left in the session."

"Six is plenty." Coleton grinned and slapped his visor down into place.

A mechanic unhooked the hydraulic jack and the car slammed to the ground. The second the tires hit the pavement, Coleton lit them up in a plume of smoke. Coleton quickly depressed the limiter button and rode toward the exit of the pit lane.

Ira pushed his sunglasses up the bridge of his nose, and smeared the beads of sweat on his brow into a solid sheen across his forehead. He gazed up at the white peak of the Gomez Racing tent and felt the sun beating down through the industrial plastic. It wasn't the heat that got his blood pumping; he was in the enemy's camp and ready for war.

I wonder what this tent will go for at auction, Ira wondered. Then, he re-focused, elbows on the table. He lowered his eyes and glared into the bulging round eyes of Jose Gomez, Coleton's former team owner. Gomez sat smugly thrown back in his chair and at the sudden re-direction of attention he folded his arms across his protruding belly. His body language left nothing about his mood to the imagination.

Gomez Racing had won respect on the Le Mans circuit for eight years running and had proven to be a competitive package. But, at the end of the previous season, the well had seemed to run dry. Gomez had cut the budget so drastically that the team barely made it to the last race.

It was one of the year's biggest sources of paddock gossip. Was Gomez broke? His appearance at this winter test had come as a shock to everyone, and by-mid morning the rumor mill was already in high gear. Maybe the black clouds of bankruptcy weren't gathering on the horizon.

Gomez had served Coleton with a lawsuit several weeks earlier. Ira had to negotiate a settlement, which meant he first had to strut and swagger, embellish, and without question, bluff. Although his poker face wasn't exactly going to snag him the Penthouse at the Wynn, Ira made up for this weakness with sheer aggression.

"Come on Jose, you know Coleton brought Phantom Jets to the team on a silver platter. This lawsuit is a joke. They were never a team sponsor, they were *his* sponsor. You guys didn't do shit."

"We didn't do shit?" Gomez slammed his fleshy fist on the table, upsetting their *cafecitos*. Ira caught his without taking his eyes off Gomez. This thimble-sized injection of sugar and caffeine reflected the mood: all business. "We convinced Phantom Jets to write the check in the first place, and you guys stole them *from us*!"

"Stole them? Look, Phantom was *my* deal, if you want to get technical. I gave it to Coleton and he could have taken it to any team in the paddock. But, Coleton was with you, and so we brought it to your shop." Gomez stared at Ira darkly, but let him continue. "Now, since your program can no longer offer Coleton the resources he needs to win a Championship, it's time for him to move on. And win one with somebody else."

Ira searched Gomez's sweating face. "How's the titty bar business these days? Sorry, do you prefer 'gentlemen's clubs'?" Ira asked with air quotes. "Are you in the Series this year, or are you out of it?"

Gomez looked down at his hands, too small for his chunky frame, and folded them on the table. That, Ira knew, was his tell. Gomez muttered something to himself, but refused to answer.

"The whole point is moot, anyway," Ira continued. "You really want to continue this sandbox fight? We both know Phantom is bankrupt. We still have a contract, technically, but we haven't seen a dime in months. Even if you sue us and win, you won't get a drop of blood."

"If Phantom is bankrupt, then I'll get what I'm owed from Coleton's pocket. I know they paid him two mill last year."

"Yes, they did. And Coleton already paid you 50% of what he got, you greedy asshole. One million isn't enough, now you're going after Coleton's half?"

"It was a two year deal," Gomez growled. "I'm still owed another million for this year."

"But, Phantom isn't even paying *him* this year. They took a dive into Chapter 11. Not to mention, Coleton isn't driving for you anymore! Can't you get that through your fat head? Why should he pay you anything if he's not under your tent? Coleton's not under contract to drive for you, and he can go any—"

"What makes you think we even want him?" Gomez cut him off harshly. "I saw Coleton this morning. He can't even walk! His leg will never be ready by Sebring. We're glad he's—"

"What makes me think you want him?" Ira said. "He's the hottest driver in the Series! If you don't know that you're stupid as well as bankrupt." Ira smiled to himself. "Coleton is going straight to the top this year. You saw his lap times in the November test. No one can touch him."

"That was before he broke his leg—what is it? In three places?"

Ira looked across the tent at a monitor set up on a folding table. It listed the lap times of each car on the track and updated every few minutes.

"Heya kid," Ira yelled at a boy who was filling a white cooler with bottles of water. "What's the last lap time for #37?" The boy took a minute to run his finger down the list of cars.

"A 1:44.322."

Ira looked smug. "Best lap of the session, I'd wager. If you even make it to the 12 Hours of Sebring, just so you know, you'll have your ass handed to you publicly."

Gomez's cheeks were red, and his eyes bulged farther from their sockets.

"Let's not blame this on a sponsor. You couldn't keep Coleton. You're pissed. It's okay. Just admit it," Ira said with a shrug. "He has every right to leave. Trying to punish him with a frivolous lawsuit just because you're pissed—is ridiculous."

"My lawyer doesn't think it's ridiculous."

"It's *so* frivolous," Ira scoffed. "That any lawyer who takes it up is risking Rule 11 sanctions."

Gomez raised an eyebrow. "You may have brought Phantom Jets to the paddock, but we harvested them for you, and we are entitled to some consideration." Gomez banged his fist against the table a second time.

"Harvest my left *nut!*"

"Gentlemen, let's be reasonable," interjected Gomez's new business manager, Jim McKenzie, in a British accent that Ira was sure was fake. Ira and Gomez jumped. They had both forgotten he was at the table with them.

"A settlement is in everyone's interest," Mr. McKenzie continued. "Coleton doesn't want a lawsuit following him to his new team, and Jose, you know the legal fees involved."

Ira and Gomez turned to glare at the manager. Neither of the men, their bodies pumping with testosterone and guided by billboard egos, were in a mood to be reasonable.

"One hundred grand," Ira spat. "That's what we'll pay you to leave us alone, and not a penny more. And, that's a *gift*. If you want to take this to the mat, you are going to lose." Ira peered through his sunglasses at Gomez waiting for a response.

"Why should I settle? I will sue for my 50% percent of the Phantom Jets contract. If you're too incompetent to enforce your contract and get the rest of the Phantom money, then I guess my share will have to come out of Coleton's pocket."

Mr. McKenzie cleared his throat. "Jose. Though the law is on our side, the expense of litigating this may be higher than your final award, especially considering the financial circumstances of Phantom Jets."

"What do *you* know?" Gomez grumbled, glaring at his business manager with what Ira could only describe as hatred.

"Don't you pay this guy for his advice?" Ira asked. "Get some value for your money. Listen to him!"

"Fine. You want a settlement offer?" Gomez glared at Ira. "The total contract was for four million. You paid us one, and you owe us one more—" He lit a fresh Cuban cigar, puffed it to life, and blew a leisurely cloud. "But, I'll take two hundred and fifty grand to walk away and keep your boy out of the headlines."

"No fucking way," Ira spat without even pausing to consider the offer. "Even if Coleton *wanted* to pay you, I'd cut his fingers off before I'd let him sign that check. A hundred grand, or we'll take you to the mat." Ira pushed back his chair and rose, thumbs in his waistband. "You have my number."

Ira paused to stare at the monitor as he left the tent. God, he was proud of his boy. He had a full smile on his face as he stepped out of the tent into the sunshine and turned toward the pits. Battle suited Ira Goldstein. Going toe-to-toe with an unreasonable asshole before lunch meant business was booming, and to Ira nothing could be better.

"1:43.901—that's the quickest of the session! I knew you had it in you. Pit next lap, and cool down," Nelson encouraged Coleton.

"Where did Gomez's jockey finish the session?" Coleton asked.

"P4, but more than a second off your time. They got a ways to go."

"I'm sure Jose is happy about that."

"Great pass in Turn 17," Nelson said. "Ulrick didn't even see you until he was kissing your tailpipe. The Germans are pissed!" Nelson looked to his left. The Porscheworks pit box was next to the Elrod box, and their lead engineer, Andreas, was screaming into his headset.

"Yeah, they're not so tough now that they've lost the full support of Porsche! The Stewart chassis they're stuck with may be the best thing that could happen to us!"

"They've got some bugs to work out, at the very least."

Coleton swerved into pit lane and depressed the limiter. He had a huge smile on his face. It felt great to have a solid lap time under his belt. The car sputtered down the lane. The crew had set out the #37 pit board at the far end of his marks, and Coleton knew where to turn in. But, as the car approached its pit box, Coleton slowed to a crawl. Klaus Ulrick in the #99 Porscheworks LMP1 was right on his bumper. In the narrow lane, Ulrick had to brake to match Coleton's crawl. Ulrick was already furious about Coleton's final pass and this just tilted the scale. He threw his right hand up to flick Coleton off, then swerved back and forth, but couldn't get around him.

Coleton moved to the right, inches from the Porscheworks pit board, and slowed even more. He flipped up his visor and winked at Andreas, who had one foot perched on the wall. Andreas's face was blotched red with fury, not only at the insolent American, but also at the incompetent maneuver of his own driver. Coleton gave a thumbs-up before he sprinted forward and swerved into his own pit box.

Of all the drivers in the series, Coleton disliked the Porscheworks drivers the most, specifically the #99 LMP1 drivers Klaus Ulrick and his teammate Hans Vanderscot. Both drivers were familiar with success and had Formula 1 careers under their belts. Klaus had stepped down at the peak of his, because he "didn't like the politics of the sanctioning body." And, although he claimed the Le Mans series was more relaxed and fun, he certainly didn't appear to be having fun today.

"Is the session closed?" Coleton asked Nelson, as a mechanic leapt over the wall with Coleton's crutches.

"There's 2:26 left," Nelson said, as he squinted at a monitor. Coleton waved away the crutches.

"The car feels good. I think I can shave some time off the entry to the Carousel. I can go deeper; I just need to trust the brakes. They are much better than the ones I had last year. The changes we made are perfect."

"You can snag another lap if you hurry."

The crew jumped back over the wall. Coleton lit up the rear tires and headed toward the pit exit.

"Go for it, then head in," Nelson instructed, now over the radio.

"Roger that," Coleton said with a smile.

Ira watched Heidi Ulrick's signature runway strut down the path behind the pit boxes. She carried her head high, her shoulders thrown back, and she stared straight ahead, ignoring the catcalled whispers of the mechanics. Heidi had warm blonde hair that spilled past her shoulders in soft waves. Her large blue eyes were wide-set, her nose perfectly straight and her pink lips were pouty-full even when she smiled. She had a deep tan, but her skin was smooth and flawless, as if she'd been born that golden color.

Heidi made a beeline for the Porscheworks pit. She was wearing four-inch, peep-toe sandals that gave her extra height she certainly didn't need. She was six feet tall barefoot. Although only closed-toed shoes were permitted in the pits, Ira was not surprised to see her perfectly manicured, Chanel-red toes. Security was so star-struck they hadn't noticed her footwear.

"Wow," Ira said, as he pulled a headphone off Max's ear. "She is beyond hot."

"Yeah, mate. Too bad she married a bloody idiot."

Ira watched Klaus in the pit box next to them. He seemed to be the only man oblivious to Heidi's arrival. Klaus was staring at a computer screen and waving his hands angrily at a mousy engineer.

"How can such an asshole attract such a fine piece of ass?" Ira implored a nearby mechanic.

"A piece of ass with plenty of her own money," Max chimed in.

"Formula 1 guys always get the babes," said George, as he walked over from the pit cart.

Heidi Ulrick was more than a model; she was an icon, a brand name. She had moved to the States from Sweden as a high school exchange student and landed campaigns for Victoria's Secret. She quickly migrated to more high fashion work for Gucci and Chanel. By 25, Heidi was the face of L'Oreal Paris, and *Forbes* ranked her as the world's highest paid model. Then, two years ago she married one of the greatest drivers in Formula 1, and the merger-marriage catapulted the pair to the echelon of "power-couple." While her bikini-clad *Sports Illustrated* swimsuit cover still graced a large percentage of high school boys' bedroom walls, Hollywood gossip began to obsess over when she and Klaus would start popping out devastatingly beautiful blond babies.

"My God, she's so beautiful it's painful," Enzo said, as he walked up unnoticed to stand next to Ira and George in the Elrod pit. "If she was mine, I'd put a padlock on it and give her the key."

Enzo had just finished the practice session for BMW Crowne with respectable lap times and had stopped to visit Coleton before heading to his driver debrief. His helmet balanced on his right hip, he pushed his sweaty jet-black hair off his brow. His tan skin glistened.

"Monogamy wouldn't suit you, believe me," Ira said, without detaching his eyes from Heidi's skimpy pink tank top. One of the spaghetti straps had slipped down over a tan shoulder. She leaned against one of a long line of concrete pillars that held up the grandstand above the pits, bleachers that would be packed with spectators on race day but were quiet this February afternoon. She swung her boxy Louis Vuitton purse in front of her, then lowered it to the ground at her feet. A little palomino colored head poked out, and looked around, blinking its large black eyes in the light.

"What is *that*?" Enzo asked.

"One of those rat dogs," said Ira. "Looks like a Chihuahua."

Klaus was still engrossed in the data, and in reaming out the sweaty little mechanic who quietly accepted the abuse, but looked as though he was about to throw up.

"Watch and learn," Enzo said, as he pushed past Ira.

"Oh, dream on!" Ira said, as Enzo turned and walked directly toward Heidi. As he crossed the yellow painted line of the Elrod pit box, Enzo stooped and with one hand he flipped open the team cooler and grabbed a bottle of Essentia before the lid could bang to a close. He sauntered up to Heidi, who straightened and stared in disbelief.

"Could you hold this?" Enzo asked. He held out his helmet and looked at her, his black eyes dancing. With her high-heels on, she was an inch or two taller than him, but then again, she towered over everyone. Enzo's helmet was off white and shimmered in the sunlight with an Italian flag outlined in gold. Enzo shook the helmet at her, and she accepted it abruptly with both hands.

"Thanks, *Amore*," Enzo cooed with nonchalance, as if talking to his little sister. He took a knee, wiped a few drops of condensation off the bottle and let the dog's tiny pink tongue flicker over his fingers. Enzo noticed a worn book in the purse, standing upright. He wiggled his fingers to attract the dog and moved him to the side so he could see: it was an old, worn-out copy of *Romeo and Juliet*.

"Napoleon likes you," she murmured with a small, tight smile, as if making an effort to ration its radiance.

Enzo straightened and twisted the cap off the water bottle. Then, he tossed the cap in a nearby trashcan, took his helmet back and held the bottle of water out to her. "Want a sip?"

She shook her head no, then collected her hair and pulled it over one shoulder. She adjusted the position of her purse with the toe of her shoe.

"Holy shit!" George whispered to a nearby mechanic. "Enzo's making Heidi Ulrick nervous!" The whole team stared. "What a legend!"

"Oh, come on." Enzo smiled at Heidi, unleashing a row of perfect white teeth. "I brought it all the way over here just for you and it's super hydrating water." He pushed the bottle closer. "Hydration is very important."

She smiled shyly, then abruptly grabbed the bottle. She looked over her shoulder before taking a long, slow sip. She watched Enzo watching her fine throat and smiled while the bottle was still at her lips. When she lowered it, a few drops of water remained on her upper lip. Enzo stepped forward to wipe them off, but she stepped back quickly, just out of his reach.

At that moment, a hand grabbed Enzo's shoulder pulling him backward.

"Hello, *Mauselein*," Klaus's deep voice greeted his wife. He grabbed the bottle of water from her and in one long gulp drained the rest of it. He tossed the bottle into the garbage can and took her hand, brushing Enzo aside as if he didn't exist. When she picked up her purse, the little head growled softly in Ulrick's direction, then disappeared inside. Klaus led her to the walkway and toward the pit exit. Neither of them looked back. Her gallery of admirers watched the slow swing of her hips, and it took a few minutes before the teams were able to resume their work.

On his final and quickest lap of the session, Coleton's foot decided to stop working. His brain told it to move, but it numbly refused. The fracture coupled with the stress of racing had pushed his not yet healed bones and the muscle and cartilage that surrounded them to the limit. At the exit of Turn 15, Coleton's foot was too fatigued to modulate the throttle properly, and he had too much speed to save the car from crashing into the Armco barrier.

"Confirm that you are okay," Nelson said over the radio.

There was a moment of silence.

"Confirm that you are okay!" Nelson repeated, his voice now worried.

"Confirmed. I may have fucked up my leg, but I'll make it."

"Good. The hook truck should already be on its way to get you."

"No, the engine is still running. I think I can get her back to the pits on her own power. Just make sure there is a bag of ice waiting for me, will ya?"

Coleton limped the car back and pitted on his marks, but by the time the engine shuddered to a stop, the pain was throbbing well past his knee. His ankle had swollen to the limits of his racing shoe and he could feel it pressing against his laces.

"Junior, bring my crutches please," Coleton said over the radio.

Coleton grimaced in pain and had no idea what the extent of the damage would be. Even before the shunt, Coleton couldn't apply full weight. It hadn't been a major crash, but the jolt could easily have re-broken the leg. Camilla was going to kill him. Or she might just end it before they knew what they had. That instant, Coleton realized, he *wanted* Camilla to be furious with him, to care that much.

Coleton hoisted himself out of the cockpit. George leapt over the pit wall and steadied him so he could swing his legs over the carbon fiber side skirt.

"Can you put any weight on it? I think you should go to the hospital," George said. Coleton sat on the side of the car, his leg suspended in the air.

"No, I need to debrief first." Coleton looked up into George's strong, square face.

The team gathered around the car, which still creaked with heat and smelled of hot brakes.

"It could be re-broken, Colt," George said, voicing the truth that everyone was thinking.

"It sure as hell could be," Coleton said. His eyes were luminous with pain. "But, we need to debrief now before any details are lost. Get the boys together. The car has issues we need to address."

"Get me that missing chart *now*," Camilla demanded. She had already asked nicely, twice. She was on hour nine of her shift at Good Samaritan hospital. She was tired, over caffeinated and her patience had evaporated like a pool of rubbing alcohol, with only a hint left hanging in the air. "Room eight has been waiting for over 30 minutes, and I can't do anything until I get the full story."

"I've got to get these samples to the lab," her nurse replied. She paused and leisurely raised a bag full of plastic cups. "Then, I'll get right on it."

Camilla rolled her eyes. Her regular nurse was on vacation, and the temp she was stuck with was making her job infinitely more painful. Even her speech was slow.

"Is it going to be a full moon tonight, or what?" Camilla asked no one in particular, as she walked down the hall and pulled a chart from a plastic box on the wall. She flipped it open to peruse its contents and pushed open the door to see her next patient.

"Dr. Harlow. Please report to the emergency room, Dr. Harlow," a steady voice said over the PA system.

Camilla stepped back out into the hallway before she even greeted the patient. "What now?"

She started down the hallway, her stride quickening. Her cell phone vibrated in the pocket of her scrubs.

"Yes?" she asked, slowing her pace.

"It's Ira. Coleton's agent."

"Oh," Camilla replied. She had met Ira before. Once, briefly. Coleton had shown up at the hospital unannounced a week earlier with Ira in tow, and then sat quiet and shameless while Ira begged her to remove his cast early. She couldn't imagine why Ira would be calling her now. "Yes, Ira? How can I help you?"

"It's Coleton. We have a little problem."

"What *little problem*?" She didn't have time for this, but even so, she felt a jolt at the sound of Coleton's name.

Camilla hadn't heard from Coleton since she removed his cast, and before that, she hadn't heard a word since he gave her a kiss on the cheek and practically pushed her out of the car. She had decided she was better off without him, and besides she needed to focus on her career. She didn't have time in her life for a man, let alone a Palm Beach playboy.

"Coleton got in a little accident at the track, and I think—"

"What the *hell* was he doing in a racecar?" Camilla said.

"Well, see, we were at this winter test at Sebring—"

"Ira," Camilla said, shaking her head. "I know the world revolves around Coleton Loren, but I don't have time for this. Tell your *friend* I wish him luck, but honestly I'm done. I'm not treating him if he ignores my medical advice."

"Camilla," Ira said, his voice soft as though they'd entered a place of worship. "No one wants an injured driver. Coleton's had to fight harder this season, than ever in his life. But it's more than that. He has this energy that wells up inside, and he has no way to express it."

"I understand why you're protective of him, Ira. I do. And I want him safe, too. But—"

"That's all I'm asking."

"You *both* promised he would stay out of the racecar if I took his cast off. I'm not in business to hurt my patients. There's a little thing called the Hippocratic Oath. Look it up. He lied to me, and used me, and honestly, I don't have time to discuss it. Take him to the Heartland ER."

"Camilla, he's *hurt*," Ira said, squeezing as much pathos into the word as he could.

Camilla froze. The thought of Coleton hurt, the idea of his beautiful face in pain, shifted something inside her. Maybe she did care.

"For crying out loud, Ira," she said, annoyance snapping in her words. "Where are you? When can he be here?"

Camilla saw Ira buzzing around the nurse station and barking into his cellphone. She watched him for a second, his face red, his free hand gesturing wildly. She tucked Coleton's chart under her arm and pushed open the door to Exam Room #3.

"Hello, Coleton," she said.

"Camilla!" Coleton's face broke into a smile. "See how far I'll go to spend time with you?"

"Sit back, please."

"I even got dressed up this time."

"Excuse me?"

"I meant at least I'm—" His voice trailed off. "—wearing underwear."

"Please don't try to be charming."

"Hey, I *am* injured here."

"Yes, I saw that on your chart. But it doesn't list the cause. What might that be, Coleton?"

"I did have the fastest lap time," he said, hoping boyish might work. It didn't.

"Ah, so you spent thousands of dollars and gallons of fuel to take half a second less to arrive at the same place you started?"

"More like a hundredth, but who's counting."

"Clearly a job that needed to be done, even if it meant injuring yourself. And here I spent the day delivering a baby whose mother has no insurance, reviving a heart attack victim and stitching up a sorority girl whose boyfriend likes to use her as a punching bag."

She moved to the computer and brought his new X-ray to the screen. She stared at it for a long moment in silence.

"So?" he asked.

"It's *not* re-broken, you lucky bastard." Coleton broke into a loud laugh, as his nerves released. Camilla turned to him and narrowed her eyes. "But, it could have been!"

"Okay, I'm sorry. I didn't—" Here Coleton paused, as if considering various phrases to be sorry for. Then he picked just about the worst choice. "—didn't take better care of myself."

"Didn't *what*?" Camilla groaned, then took a step toward him. "That's not what this is about."

"Well, no. When we spoke, I may have slightly understated my future physical commitments."

"Coleton, your job may be going around in circles, but I don't have the luxury. If you understand, say it. If you don't, don't."

He looked down abashed, like a scolded boy, concealing those green eyes with thick black lashes, and a warmth broke inside her—but she pushed it down. This was too important. It was important to her as Coleton's physician. It was important to Coleton's career, whether he understood it or not, and how long he would be physically able to drive at the top of his profession. But mostly it was important to her dignity. His response, right here, right now, would determine whether she ever saw him again, in any capacity.

"I lied to you," he said in a small voice. "I'm a liar."

"No, Coleton," she said, her voice softening. "You're not a liar. But you did lie to me."

"Will you forgive me if I take you to brunch next Sunday?"

"I've already forgiven you. And no, I'm busy."

"How can you forgive me if I haven't apologized yet?"

"Forgiveness is something you do for yourself."

"What?"

"Think about it."

Camilla turned to the counter, assembled a row of bottled vitamins and minerals, and laid out a needle tip and an eight-inch syringe.

"You want me to fix you?" she asked. "Then you better start listening." She pushed up the sleeve on his right arm. He flexed his bicep and winked. "Stop it," she said sternly, but she smiled, eyes on the rubber tourniquet she wrapped above his elbow.

"Then tell me," he said, rising slowly and carefully. Balanced on one leg, he pulled her toward him and held her two hands in his. "What do I have to be to get you to go out with me again?"

"In one piece, for a start. Coleton, don't." He leaned toward her, but stopped when the door opened. A nurse ducked in. "They need you in the E.R. Car accident. Hit by a no-helmet drunk on a donorcycle."

"Darn it!" said Camilla.

"Darn it? How about 'Motherfucker!'?"

The nurse laughed. "Good luck, Buddy. She never swears."

"Can you do his IV? Just give us a minute."

"Come on, just once. Motherfucker! It's very liberating. Musical, almost."

"I'll tell you what you can be," she said as she wrote out his prescription and handed it to him. "You be the one to go handle that mess. I'll drive around in circles."

"Ouch."

"Look, I'm busy. I'm exhausted. And I'm about to be very sad and angry at what's out there. I don't have time for your games."

"Camilla, you're not a game." He put his arms out and offered a hug. She took it before she knew what she was doing, and there was that damn cologne again. *Warm vanilla and bergamot.* She wanted to curl up in it.

He lifted her chin with his finger, fixed her with green eyes, and said, "I will never lie to you again."

"Good."

The nurse came back and Camilla broke contact. She passed the syringe of amber liquid to the nurse and looked over her shoulder on her way out.

"Goodbye, Coleton."

Hours later, exhausted, she slipped back into the exam room to be alone with her thoughts, if only for a minute. The motorcyclist had died of head injuries no doctor could have repaired. She saw one of her prescription pads with her gold pen next to it. Coleton had scribbled a note on the blue paper.

Lovely Camilla,

Let me make it up to you. Brunch next Sunday? My place: 14 San Marco Island, Miami Beach. Boat embarks at 1pm.

Truthfully,
CL

CHAPTER 9

MIAMI BEACH, FLORIDA

Coleton's BlackBerry vibrated on the white marble countertop. He hobbled across the kitchen on a leg throbbing with pain. His leg still couldn't bear his full weight, which Coleton was finding increasingly more difficult to accept. He didn't have much time left to rehab his atrophied calf muscle before the 12 Hours of Sebring. Coleton's self-inflicted physical therapy regime was simple: put as much weight on it as possible without passing out.

"Ira, that better not be you," Coleton said. "My blood pressure's still high from our last conversation." Ira always called, and it was always urgent. Coleton glanced down at the screen.

It wasn't Ira.

"Mr. Elrod, Good Afternoon."

"How's the leg?"

"It's great. Doing just fine," Coleton said, as an electric stab of pain shot up his shinbone. "The cast has been off for almost two weeks now. Rehab is going really well."

"That's not what I heard," Elrod said. "I heard you lost control and crashed my car at the Sebring test. Is this true?" They both knew it was. Coleton couldn't believe he was making him say it out loud.

"I had a small shunt, but the cast had only just come off. Now that I've had a few days to walk around on it, I can't believe my improvement! I've started weekly IV therapy—Meyer's cocktail, they call it—B6, B12, Vitamin C, Selenium, Magnesium, all right into the blood stream. It has been a quick recovery."

"Well," Elrod said, clearing his throat. "My yacht is headed up from the Caribbean toward the northeast. My wife wants to spend the fourth of July in the Hamptons, and I want to stop in Miami along the way. Let's meet up for lunch."

"It's great here this time of year," Coleton said. "Where are you going to dock?"

"Miami Beach Marina," Elrod said. "Justine wants to do some shopping at Bal Harbour, and if I can still afford to keep my boat after that excursion, we'll spend next Sunday in Miami."

Coleton's eyes lit up. He had already planned a boat trip for Camilla on Sunday. He could easily switch the location of their brunch plans and kill two birds with one stone. He loved when things fell in his lap.

"Have you ever been to Fisher Island?" Coleton asked.

"I hear it's impossible to get in."

"It comes down to size and politics. What are you? About 200 feet?"

"198," Elrod replied.

"And what do you draw?"

"About seven feet."

"That'll fit. And, as for politics, you're covered."

"You know someone?" Elrod asked. "I hear there's a two year waiting list for new members."

"Sounds about right." Coleton smiled and let the silence drag.

"Well," Elrod said. "Can you get us in?"

"Sure."

"Don't you want to check?"

"Yeah, sure. Hold on." Coleton paused for emphasis, then exhaled as he said, "I checked. It's fine."

The line went silent. Elrod furrowed his brow. He wasn't going to show up at Fisher Island Yacht Club just to get turned away. Maybe Coleton was confused and talking about another place.

"I'm sure there aren't many 200 foot slips. Maybe you should call."

Coleton smiled. Clearly Elrod was not used to being toyed with.

"Arthur, relax. My great grandfather was one of the founders. If they have to kick a Trump out of your slip, they'll do it for me."

Coleton arrived early and picked a four-top in the sand. Saturdays at La Piaggia Beach Club are always busy, and the tables were filling quickly. The waitress gave him a lunch menu and a smile, before she turned to open a magnum bottle of rosé at the next table.

"I'll have the same, but not a magnum," Coleton said, squinting at the label. It was a decent table wine.

Through the patchwork of tables, Coleton could see a few topless cougars lounging in the orange and white striped recliners near the pool. Each bare breastbone offered up a pair of implants round and hard as citrus fruit, their sunbaked skin like handbag leather. Coleton refocused on his tall menu—nothing he hadn't seen a hundred times before.

Coleton toed off his loafers and dug his feet into the white sand. Someone reached over his shoulder and smacked a magazine onto the table. Coleton jumped, then looked up into Ira's shining face.

Ira smirked, happy with Coleton's reaction.

"Take a look at that." He pointed to the cover of *Maxim*, as he pulled out a chair. A gorgeous blonde in a revealing purple halter-top graced a 1959 Mercedes SL convertible somewhere in rural Europe, or maybe southern California. Coleton recognized her at a glance: it was Heidi Ulrick, and beside her, in the driver's seat was Klaus.

"Way to ruin my lunch." Coleton skimmed through, looking for the article.

"It's not worth reading," Ira said and pulled the magazine out of Coleton's hands. "Heidi is a perfect Barbie, blah blah blah. Highest paid model in the world, blah blah blah. And, Klaus is a BSD and the Le Mans Champion. Who cares? It's a joke."

"No. It's good PR," Coleton said, feeling sick to his stomach.

"What's a BSD?" a smoky voice asked. They both looked up. A woman in her late-30s in a neon pink bikini and a white crocheted sarong stood behind an empty chair. A lit cigarette dangled from her fingers.

"Big Swinging Dick," Ira said. The woman's eyes widened and the tan skin around her eyes wrinkled.

"I'll have to use that one. Mind if I sit?" she said. "I'm Rhonda."

Coleton glared at Ira, who was sizing her up.

"Why don't you circle back in half an hour, sweetheart? We're in the middle of something."

"Okay," she said with a smile. Above each of her capped teeth was a slim black crescent at her gum line.

"Really?" Coleton asked, turning toward Ira with a mocking look.

"Where's our waitress?" Ira asked, looking past Coleton to the U-shaped wooden bar. Hundreds of philodendrons were strung from the white-tented ceiling, their tendrils swaying in the sea breeze over the tabletops. The sunlight through their leaves made them glow like strands of emeralds.

The waitress arrived clutching a bottle of Cote de Provence rosé by the neck, and a busboy set up a bucket of ice. "You already ordered the wine?" Ira asked. Coleton nodded, and Ira shrugged.

"Here you are," she purred, pouring them each a glass with a flourish.

They ordered a plate of truffled carpaccio and an arugula salad, two entrees of mussels, and Ira added a side of French fries for himself. Ira took a long sip of rosé, then smacked his lips.

"Landon's hosting a blow-out on his yacht tomorrow. Leaves from the Mondrian at two."

"Not my scene," Coleton replied.

"Since when? You missed the last one. It's worth it just to see the boat, never mind the 50 plus smoking asses."

"I know the boat. It's nice, but not worth getting stuck on, listening to trance music for 10 hours in Hurricane Hole, when all you want is a good night's sleep."

"Colt," Ira said, tilting his head. "I already told Landon you'd come."

"Well that was stupid. I can't even if I wanted to. I've got brunch at Fisher tomorrow."

"With who?" Ira asked. Fisher Island can only be reached by private boat or the member-supported ferry. This wasn't a casual

Sunday brunch and Coleton was probably meeting someone important.

"Hey, there's Richard Foxley," Coleton said and pointed at someone over Ira's shoulder who arrived with two skyscraper blondes.

"With who, Colt?"

"I don't know them. They look foreign."

"No," Ira snapped. "Who are you going to Fisher with?"

"Elrod."

"What?" Ira said, raising his voice. "Why didn't you tell me? I need to be there."

Two waiters arrived with their food.

"Take it easy," Coleton said. The waiters set down two plates, two cast iron pots and a cone of French fries. "The salad and carpaccio were supposed to come out first," Coleton told the waiters.

"Oh, you want us to take them back?" one of the waiters asked, reaching for a bowl of mussels.

"No. Forget it."

Coleton motioned for them to carry on. Ira had already dug into the fries, stuffing a handful into his mouth all at once. Coleton seized the rare moment of silence.

"First, we only planned the brunch a few days ago, and second—no, you don't need to be there, and *that's* why I didn't tell you."

Ira crossed his arms, slumped back in his chair and tucked in his chin as he chewed.

"I need to salvage this deal," Coleton continued. "Not jeopardize it. You can be a real liability."

"Oh, yeah?" Ira said after swallowing. Coleton knew Ira's arms wouldn't stay crossed for long. He was right. Ira reached for another handful. "Well, what are you going to do when Elrod tries to back out?"

"I have a plan. You're going to have to trust me."

"Coleton, you're the talent. I'm the agent. I'm going to the meeting."

"Like hell you are. This isn't just business, it's social. I'm taking Camilla; he's bringing his wife. It's better to keep things light."

They dug into their pots of mussels, scooping the shells from the broth, then snapping them apart to get at the slug of meat.

"That's fine. I'll bring someone too."

"Who?" Coleton asked, then continued before Ira could answer. "Is she a straight-up hooker—like ding, dong?" Coleton made the motion of pushing a doorbell. "Or is she a Hooters girl?"

"Fuck you. I'm seeing a really nice one at the moment." Ira glared at Coleton before scooping up another mussel.

"Where'd you meet her?"

"Believe me, you'll like this one."

"*Where?*"

"Vegas," Ira said, then looked into the bottom of his empty wine glass. He swiped the bottle from the silver bucket and filled his glass.

"Which strip club?"

"Judge not lest ye … I forget the rest."

"She's not coming," Coleton said. "And neither are you."

Ira wiped the last drops of salty broth from his chin and crossed his arms over his belly again. "Speaking of women, I don't know about this Camilla chick."

"What do you mean?"

"She's nice and all, but she's a little *much*."

"A little much?" Coleton said. "Are you jealous that she's going and you're not?"

"She's the kinda girl, you wake up one morning and she's taken over all your drawer space, and picked out names for all your future children."

"That sounds like the wack jobs *you* date. Camilla's career-oriented and fucking smart. You'd like her if you gave her a shot."

"I don't care how smart she is. You've got to focus on your career. She's different. You might be the one to get hurt this time."

"That's why I like her."

"So she's not just a fling?" Ira asked, more worried than ever.

"I've got the situation under control."

The waitress skated past, saw the empty dishes and dropped a leather folder with the check onto their table.

"Oh, sorry, sugar," Ira said. "Separate checks."

"What?" Coleton asked. "Don't be ridiculous." Then to the waitress, he said, "This is fine, just split it." Coleton picked up the folder, placed his card on top, then held it out to Ira.

"But you ordered the bottle of rosé," Ira said, jutting out his chin.

"And you drank it you fat bastard." They both looked at the empty bottle.

With a sigh, Ira laid his card on top of Coleton's. "I would've preferred a bottle of Fat Bastard."

Past the sand dotted with pots of lipstick-red hibiscus, past the pool and the sunbathers and the bright orange cabanas, lay Government Cut. A cruise ship was migrating out of the Port of Miami and into the Atlantic. It was so large Coleton's eyes couldn't take in the whole ship, only a section, as though one of Miami Beach's high-rises had been tipped into the water and made to float. Tourists lined the balconies, row upon row of them, waving goodbye to the city.

By the time the waitress returned with the check, they were both antsy, ready to go. The cruisey French music had steadily increased in volume and was now thumping in their chests. A girl near the bar was standing on a table, spinning and dropping in time to the music with one hand in the air.

"One hundred and twelve dollars!" Ira gasped, as he opened his leather folder.

"Welcome to St. Tropez." Coleton chuckled.

Ira muttered to himself, "St. Tropez my ass. I remember when Miami Beach was nothing but *alter kockers* waiting to die." But he picked up the pen and scribbled his name.

Ira stood. "I'm going to see if Francesca is working."

"Who?"

"You know, the girl who works in the beach shop. She's been around forever."

"No, I don't know the girl who works in the beach shop."

Like the great beach clubs in the south of France, La Piaggia has a shop that sells bejeweled sandals, sheer cover-ups, straw sunhats and hundreds of colorful string bikinis that are priced per ounce more than platinum. These pop-up shops capitalize on the inevitability of gold-digging escorts and their aging dates buying them a few overpriced items on the way to the bathroom.

"Francesca's pretty good looking. Spent too much time in the sun as a child, so her skin is shot, but she's got some great bags on her."

"Lovely," Coleton said. "You're not waiting around for Rhonda?"

"Life's too short to wait."

As Coleton limped toward the barn-sized blue door, he saw several familiar faces. But, familiar is not always the same as pleasant, so he ducked his head and made straight for the circular valet ramp.

Coleton looked at his watch again, shading its face. The thought had never occurred to him that she might not show.

"Want me to untie the lines, sir?" the Rent-a-captain asked.

Since its christening, *La Vie Vite*, Coleton's 78 foot Magnum had never had another person at its helm. But, with his leg still weak, Coleton wasn't sure he could move quick enough to tie and untie the lines by himself.

"Let's give her five more minutes."

Coleton leaned back against the padded bench in the helm station and looked out across the sparkling water. He had already confirmed with Elrod, and he was bringing his wife. He should have called Camilla, but he knew she'd find his note tucked carefully under her gold pen, and he knew she'd come. He felt an unfamiliar weight in the pit of his stomach.

"Sir?" Rent-a-captain asked, after exactly five minutes. The sun beat down on the backs of their necks and the tops of their shoulders.

"Unbelievable," Coleton said, looking down at his watch again. "Let's get the fuck out of here."

Rent-a-captain leapt to the port side to untie the lines. Coleton, propped against the driver's bench with his right leg poised a few inches above the deck, busied himself with gauges and switches.

Coleton edged away from the dock, then pushed the throttles forward. A massive rooster tail rose from the Magnum as it cut east, then circled around Monument Island and moved south through Biscayne Bay toward Government Cut. Coleton remained behind the wheel.

Maybe she didn't get the note? Of course she did. Maybe she was angrier than I thought about the lie? Coleton felt sick to his stomach, but pushed the feeling down. Anger bubbled up in its place. He turned left in Government Cut toward the ocean.

Rent-a-captain yelled above the roar, "Are you really going in the front side? It's almost low tide."

"I am," Coleton said. "And, yes, I know."

As soon as Coleton rounded the rock jetty at the furthest end of Government Cut, he spun the speedboat and made for the long white beach that stretched the length of the eastern edge of Fisher Island.

"What are you doing?" Rent-a-captain yelled above the wind. Coleton had his hand pressed to the dash, holding the throttles flat, and his eyes were wild with speed. "We're going to run aground!" Rent-a-captain covered his eyes with both hands, but peeked through his fingers.

Just before the boat ran into the sand, Coleton sprang left at full speed, sending a spray of water onto the shore only feet from a row of aging sunbathers on the most expensive real estate in the county. He pumped the wheel back and forth as the boat ran just off the beach. He glued his eyes to the ocean in front of them, narrowly escaping the coral reef heads that broke the surface of the water. The prop blades skimmed inches above the ancient rocks buried in the sand. Coleton knew that if he reduced his speed even a little and came off plane the boat would hit bottom.

Coleton loved to flirt with disaster, and he knew these waters well. He drove his boat right on the edge, as he did his racecar. The difference was if he went over the limit his team wouldn't shoulder this repair. Even though it didn't seem like it to Rent-a-captain, who looked like he was tempted to jump overboard, Coleton knew what he was doing. Being stood up had just made him a little less risk averse.

The sleek vessel made the final sharp right turn around a concrete jetty that was meant to keep boats in deeper water. Coleton kept the throttle pegged for a few extra seconds to compensate for the falling tide. Finally, he throttled back and idled towards the marina entrance. Rent-a-captain let out his breath in a long slow whoosh.

"Was that supposed to impress me?" Rent-a-captain asked.

Because La Vie Vite had Arneson drives that hung off its back, rather than drive shafts mounted beneath, it was difficult to dock. In fact, most captains with Arneson-powered boats depend heavily on their bow thrusters to maneuver into a slip. Coleton considered this cheating.

"No, but this should," Coleton said.

He cut off the 4000 horses and let the boat coast into the slip, timing its momentum. It slowed into perfect position. The dockhands scrambled to tie the lines, taken off guard at the sudden arrival. They had never seen a vessel of its size put in position so quickly.

Once the lines were tied, Coleton said, "Whew, I've never done *that* before!"

Rent-a-captain looked at him with astonishment, then scowled. "That might seem cute, son, but that stunt back there is called reckless showboating," he said. "Next time you need a captain, call someone else."

He leapt onto the dock with an agility surprising for a stocky middle-aged man and stalked away. Coleton paused to watch him go, making a note to remember his name so he could recommend him to his friends. *Good man.* He hated an ass-kisser.

To the west, far across Biscayne Bay, rows of towering Brickell skyscrapers rose from the wave tips. Coleton wished Camilla was there, and not just because he had planned on her help. He would have liked to see the city dancing in her eyes. His disappointment extended past the personal, however. Coleton knew Elrod meant to use this meeting to check on the rehab of his leg. Having Camilla there as his doctor as well as his date would have been a great witness to his recovery.

The Fisher Island Beach Club sits right above the beach on the southeastern tip of the island. White pavilions stand along the glittering beach looking out to the Atlantic, with long white curtains that flutter in the wind. In his mind's eye, Camilla wore a white dress and smiled at the scene he'd visited so many times he'd stopped noticing its beauty.

Elrod sat at a six-top on the edge of the sand. He and his wife stood to greet him. Coleton walked slowly, purposefully forward, making sure to hide any sign of a limp. The pain from walking flat-footed was excruciating, but Coleton's smile was broad and fixed.

"Coleton! What a place!" Elrod beamed and clapped Coleton on the back.

Coleton was surprised by the warm gesture; it certainly wasn't the business-like manner they'd left things in Chicago. Then, Coleton remembered the extra C notes his assistant had spread around to the dockhands who would be taking care of them during their stay. Bribery works wonders.

"This is my wife," Elrod said.

"Thank you for your hospitality!" An attractive, petite woman with glossy dark hair stepped around Arthur to embrace Coleton. She clung to him, brushing against him a second too long. Coleton pulled back a step.

"My pleasure, Mrs. Elrod."

"Please call me Justine," she said with a subtle wink. She wore a tightly fitted Pucci dress printed to look like a shattered mirror of blues: indigo, turquoise, sky. On her ring finger rested a diamond the size and shape of a quail egg, at least 20 carats.

Elrod motioned for Coleton to have a seat, and he sank into a plush white couch facing them.

"Where's your girlfriend?"

"She had an emergency. She'll take the ferry over if she gets out of the O.R. in time."

"Well, everything has been just wonderful," Elrod said, without waiting for him to ask.

A waiter arrived and handed out white book-like menus, casting an appreciative glace at Justine, who seemed to expect it. Coleton took a second, longer look at her. Her skin was creamy and flawless, despite her age. She had a soft and pampered, expensively-maintained look, but something in the proud set of her flashing eyes told Coleton she was not someone to mess with.

"Well, hey! Seems like you're walking okay," Elrod said. "I forgot to look for a limp!"

Coleton tightened his lips into a smile, but knew that was exactly what Elrod had been looking for.

"None to look for. I've had the cast off for more than two weeks now. Rehab is going great. Couldn't wish for anything better."

"Surely you'd wish you hadn't put my car in the wall?"

Elrod had jumped to the point quickly. Coleton sat up in his chair and took a deep breath. *Now or never.*

"Oh, come now, boys," Justine said. "Enough talk of business!"

She lifted her glass of rosé into the air and rocked to the side and back, as if she was still aboard her yacht. "Waiter, one more glass, and another bottle of this beautiful wine."

Elrod gazed out over the sparkling water. "Did you see that yacht? What is it, a 260 Lürssen?" Elrod motioned toward a massive ship loitering in the clear blue water just off shore.

"310 Heesen," Coleton corrected. "Crazy boat."

"You know what they say, if it's not Dutch, it's not much." Elrod grinned.

"I'm not Dutch, darling," Justine said, leaning over the table. A drop of wine spilled from her full glass.

A low-flying Sikorsky S-76 buzzed the Beach Club, fluttering fringed umbrellas along the waters edge, and continued out to the yacht.

"It's going to land on the yacht," Elrod said, pointing.

"Probably," Coleton agreed, as if he'd seen a helicopter land on a 310 foot yacht every day of his life.

Elrod refilled his own glass of rosé, then cleared his throat. "So, you think your leg will be up to par by Sebring?"

"I know it will," Coleton said, as the waiter appeared to take their order.

"I will start," Justine announced over the lip of her wine glass. "I will have the California Cobb with no dressing, no croutons, no bacon, no cheese, and boiled chicken, not fried. Nothing fried. And make sure they don't put salt in the water when they boil the chicken."

The men stared at her.

"What?" she asked. "Nothing tastes as good as skinny feels."

"Do you have that embroidered on a pillow?" Coleton asked, but not loud enough for her to hear.

"What now?" Elrod asked, his attention settled on the mega yacht. A crane on the top deck had kicked to life, and they watched a jet black Wally speedboat lift from the deck, pivot and descend to the surface.

Elrod shook his head to refocus and placed his elbows on the tabletop. "You know, I'm still not convinced. I've got Gonzalez perfectly fit and itching to get in the car. Maybe we should slot you in for the second half of the season."

Coleton froze, his glass of rosé halfway to his lips. He felt a rush of blood around his temples.

"Arthur, we had a deal."

"We had a nice dinner in Chicago, but that's the extent of it. We're both businessmen, and nothing's in writing."

"We shook on it."

"Well, I'm having doubts. Serious doubts, and after Sebring, can you blame me? That was a $40,000 shunt and the season hasn't even started. I want a Championship this year, and ..." Elrod's voice trailed off.

The waiter passed their table carrying a magnum bottle of Cristal champagne with both hands. He plopped it in an oversized silver bucket at the pavilion next to theirs.

When they arrived there had been only two people sitting in the neighboring pavilion, but now there was a small party. Several corks had already been popped, and a man who seemed to be organizing the festivities kept asking the waiter to turn up the Café del Mar music.

"This is ridiculous. My leg is fine. Do you really want to throw away the oil opportunity I offered you in Chicago?"

"That introduction never materialized and I'm still not happy with the Miller deal."

"The Miller deal?" Coleton asked. "That's what this is about? We've been over this." Coleton was heating up, but he saw Elrod had checked out again.

"I think they're coming *here!*" Elrod said, pointing out to sea. They watched the Wally skim the water and curve around to dock in the marina. "Who do you think it is?" Elrod asked. "That's well over a million dollar tender."

Coleton sat back. The conversation was officially on hold, possibly over. He shrugged, disgusted at the realization that all of this—the race team, the drivers—was just a hobby for Elrod, an ego-stroking amusement. He shook his head slightly, but he could play the game.

"There are lots of celebrities who live on Fisher," Coleton said, leaning back. "We've lost a few the last three or four years, but some pretty big names still winter here."

Elrod's body was tense like a hunting dog at the sound of a bird falling through the air, as he watched the Wally dock.

Fisher Island yachties converged on the speedboat to help extricate its passengers. A long bronze leg extended, then the other, as they pulled a beautiful South American model onto the dock turned fashion runway. Next, they dredged up two stick-thin girls with matching white-blonde hair that fell to their hips.

"It's the Neilson sisters!" Elrod panted excitedly. "I'm sure of it."

A single Neilson would have stormed the international modeling scene, but these were not only sisters, but twins, by God, and it was as if the world's male population was entirely incapable of controlling its delight. The sisters had amassed a cult following and graced the cover of almost every magazine in their signature metallic string bikinis. To enhance their mystique, they refused to give interviews.

"Coleton, do you know them?" Elrod asked. "I've got to meet them."

"Why, are they Dutch?" Justine giggled, then drained her glass of wine.

"Yes, I know them," Coleton said.

The three girls huddled on the edge of the dock, skittish like gazelles on the open Serengeti, while the staff joined in to hoist the final passenger from the boat: an overweight Middle-Eastern man with jet-black hair and beard. He was wearing a white V-neck shirt, neon yellow Vilebrequins and brightly mirrored '80s sunglasses.

The conversation at Elrod's table did not resume until the four new guests had taken their seats at the neighboring pavilion. As if on cue, the bartender increased the volume of the music, and waiters paraded by with silver trays of steaming seafood.

"They already monopolize our oil. Do they have to monopolize the best women as well?" Elrod shook his head. Coleton looked at Justine, who stabbed at her salad.

Coleton cleared his throat, but Elrod jumped in. "So, all I'm saying, and I don't want you to take this the wrong way, but the point of today's meeting is to make clear that nothing is settled and I haven't made any final decisions."

"You want to play?" Coleton asked, and his eyes grew icy. Elrod's lips parted in surprise. Coleton stood and threw his napkin on the table.

"It's a shame you don't want me, because there is someone I wanted you to meet—an old friend." Coleton turned and walked straight to the neighboring table.

"What's he doing?" Justine asked, craning her neck. "Does he really know them?"

Seconds later, Coleton returned with the Middle Eastern man.

"Elrod, I'd like you to meet my friend, Fahid Abd Abdullah Abd Al-Aziz."

"Call me Al-Aziz. Everyone in this country does. At least, to my face," the heavyset man chortled. "May I sit?" Without waiting for an answer, he passed the couch facing Elrod and pulled up a chair next to Justine.

"Tell me, Coleton. Is this beautiful woman yours? You racecar drivers and your women!" He picked Justine's hand off the table and kissed the massive rock.

"She's my wife," Elrod said.

"The affection of a beautiful woman is Allah's greatest blessing," Al-Aziz said, pointing upward.

"Just one?" Coleton joked, looking back to Al-Aziz's table full of models.

"Well, Allah blesses some more than others." Al-Aziz turned to look Elrod in the eye. "In my country, Coleton Loren is the most famous driver. I tell my sons, the fuel in his tank comes only from Saudi oil."

"Surely not *the* most famous." Coleton smiled.

Al-Aziz continued to address Elrod. "My favorite son, my oldest, has a poster on his bedroom wall—a poster, in the *palace*—"Al-Aziz paused for emphasis. "—of Coleton taking the checker at Sebring last year." Al-Aziz smiled, then continued. "Imagine pure gold-leaf walls, priceless crystal chandeliers and a ten-dollar poster of this guy's smiling mug!" He grabbed Coleton's shoulder and shook it. "It's preposterous!"

Al-Aziz gave himself a moment to savor his laughter, then motioned for the waiter. The waiter heeled like a well-trained spaniel.

"A magnum of DP for my friends here."

The waiter bowed and disappeared. Al-Aziz settled himself, crossed his legs and turned serious. "Mr. Elrod, our mutual friend here has told me many good things about you. And, when a close friend tells me there's a business opportunity I cannot miss, well then, I seize it. That's how we succeed, don't you agree?" He banged the table with his open palm.

Elrod nodded, his face tight and pale with greed.

"Now, it's a lovely day, and I would hate to bore this beautiful woman," he said, nodding at Justine. "But, I have 150 million barrels of oil that I would like you to hedge. I assume you can buy put options for me? Can you find market-makers?"

Elrod nodded. "Yes. I can."

"It's a little brazen for me to buy put options openly." Al-Aziz leaned toward Elrod. "Because I know the price of crude will begin falling a week from Monday. It will begin Sunday night in Tokyo and Australia—I'm going to make a few bucks on the Yen-Aussie carry trade once the volatility kicks in. Then Chicago and New York will speed things along with the electronic trade, all those little people with their big dreams, trading in their cubicles when the boss isn't watching. It will continue south for the next five weeks."

"And all those little traders will lose their kids' college funds," said Elrod. "Some people shouldn't be allowed to trade."

"Free country, free market! They have a right. As my friend Warren Buffett says, 'Be—'"

"Be fearful when others are greedy. Be greedy when others are fearful?" Elrod asked, and leaned back into the couch with a smile.

"Ah, you know Warren?"

"Well, not personally—"

"Nice guy. I'll introduce you. Anyway, a wise trader once told me something I will never forget." Al-Aziz spread his fingers out on the table and paused. "Everyone gets what they want from the markets. Everyone. Some want drama, some secretly want to be punished, some want something to brag about to their mistress. Everyone gets what they want from the market."

"How profound!" said Justine. "Isn't that profound, dear?" None of the men acknowledged her words; they were suddenly engrossed in business.

"Five weeks of hedging," Al-Aziz said. "And if we time it right, we'll make a small fortune on the puts before crude rallies again."

"Five weeks? How can you be so sure?"

"The faucet turns both ways, Mr. Elrod. Surely a man of your sophistication knows this." Al-Aziz bucked his eyebrows twice.

"Of course, but—"

"My cousin Hassim is cutting the ribbon on three new fields, each one bigger than any in existence. The press conference is on Friday, but of course no one else knows that. His first TV interview will be Friday evening."

"You're going to bury the story at the end of the news cycle."

"Those who find crude oil more interesting than suntan oil will know. I like to help my friends, Mr. Elrod."

Elrod's eyes widened greedily, as he swept his phone off the table, and quickly typed a reminder into his phone. Al-Aziz wiggled his eyebrows again, happy little caterpillars.

"Well, it appears that my party is warming up, and I hate to leave my guests unattended," Al-Aziz said. "Naturally, we have much to discuss. Will you be staying overnight?" Elrod nodded.

"Good," Al-Aziz said. "I will send someone to bring you to my yacht at three p.m. tomorrow."

"I look forward to it."

Al-Aziz pushed his chair back from the table, and gave a slight nod of his head to Elrod, half bow, half dismissal. Coleton stood with Al-Aziz and accompanied him back to his table.

"So, we're friends again?" Al-Aziz asked, once they were out of earshot. "Your leg seems much better."

"Yes, we're friends," Coleton said, then he added, "But so help me God, next time—I'm driving!"

"Fair enough. Fair enough, my friend," Al-Aziz chortled.

Coleton sat on the dock and let his legs dangle toward the water. The rough wood bit into the back of his knees, but he let them swing idly back and forth. The sky was streaked with red as the sun sank below the Brickell skyscrapers across the bay, and the warm glow lit his face. Dark plumes of towering cumulus clouds billowed high into the troposphere, as if the Miami skyline was ablaze.

He looked over his shoulder at his house. Gigi was gone for the night, and it was completely dark. Hopefully, she'd left something for him in the fridge. Hopefully, something she'd bought pre-made.

With his thumb and index finger, he pulled on his bottom lip and stared at the cell phone on the dock next to him. He sighed and ran his hand through his hair. Sure he was a little rough around the edges, and maybe he hadn't put in the effort she deserved, but had she really given up on him? He'd never made a grand gesture in his life, but for the first time he was interested. He snatched up the phone and hit Call.

"Hello?" Camilla answered after a few rings. Her voice sounded strange, close. The phone was touching her lips.

"I've never been stood up before."

"Oh, Coleton ..."

"You missed out on a lovely afternoon at Fisher Island. I had everything arranged—boat ride, elegant brunch, I can't take credit for the beautiful sunset, but I reserved a front row seat."

"I can't talk right now. I'm sorry." Camilla bit her lip. "Goodbye."

"Wait, wait," he demanded. The blood drained from his face. "Are you brushing me off? Is it because of the accident? I told you I'm sorry. I promise I'll make it up to you." Coleton paused, but the line was silent. *Shit, she hung up?*

"This isn't about you," she said finally. Her words came out quick and clipped. "I'm at the airport."

"Why? Where are you going?" Coleton asked. His adrenaline kicked in, and his finely tuned arteries began to pulse under the skin.

"Nowhere. That's the problem." Her voice shook. "I have to go now."

"Wait! Camilla, *please.* What's wrong? Are you okay?" Coleton used a dock piling to pull himself up on his good leg. He stared into the water just off the dock, his brow wrinkled. "Did someone hurt you?"

He heard her cover the phone, then sniffle.

"Why are you at the airport? Where are you going?"

"I'm at the airport with Katherine. We're trying to get to New York, but all the flights *are booked*," she said, her voice rising in panic. "Every single *one*."

"It's going to be okay," Coleton said. The taste in his mouth went metallic, and he felt his heart beat against his ribs like a kick drum. At least she was talking. "What happened?"

"It's my ... dad." Camilla sobbed. "Something happened, he's in the hospital." Her breath came in ragged bursts, as she gulped back each breath. "They, they think ... he had a ... heart attack." Her voice crumpled inward.

"Oh, Camilla. I'm so sorry." He didn't know what to say.

Coleton felt like a block of houses blacking out one by one. Then, a hand shoved up the emergency generator switch. His head filled with blinding white light. He squinted into the brightness of the idea.

"Listen to me. Go to Galaxy Aviation in West Palm Beach right now," he said, but he only heard Camilla crying softly. "Put Katherine on the phone." He heard the phone handed over.

"Hi, Coleton, is it?" Katherine asked. "This isn't a good time. Camilla will have to call you later."

"Katherine, listen to me," Coleton said with authority. "Do you have a car at the airport?" Coleton could hear Camilla in the background. Each sob felt like a knife between his ribs.

"Yes," she said.

"Go to Galaxy Aviation. Put it in the GPS: Galaxy Aviation. By the time you get there, I'll have a plane on the tarmac to take you to LaGuardia."

"You can do that?"

"Go," he said softly.

"Thank you, Coleton."

Coleton hung up, scrolled through his phonebook and called Johnny's personal cell phone. No answer. He tried it again. No answer. *Fuck.* He tried his business line, but knew on a Sunday it was unlikely. Answering machine. *Fuck!* Coleton left a message: "Johnny, I need a plane from Galaxy to LaGuardia in 15 minutes. I don't care if it's a BBJ, I'll charter anything you find. It's an emergency." Coleton knew the impossibility of his request, but he was going to make this happen.

He stared at the phone in his hand, bit his lip and without another thought held down the number six.

"Didn't take long for you to come crawling back. *Oh, I'll never ask you for another thing*," his dad said, mimicking Coleton's words. "What do you want now?"

"It's not for me. I need to borrow the G-4, and I'll pay the full charter rate. It's an emergency."

"Who's it for?"

"A friend."

"Which friend?"

"You don't know her."

"*Her?* You think I'll let one of your South Beach rats on my plane?"

"She's not a rat. You think I'd pay thirty grand for a rat? It's an emergency. Her dad had a heart attack and she's got to get to New York."

"Ooooh, so Coleton has a *girlfriend*?"

"Dad, don't start with me. This wasn't an easy call to make."

Coleton heard another voice in the background. "What? He has *what*? Is that Coleton? He has a *girlfriend*?"

"Your mother says hi."

"Is something wrong with Coleton?" He heard his mother's voice, closer to the phone now.

"His *girlfriend's* in the hospital."

"No, it's her—" Coleton started.

"Help him, Lawrence." Victoria's voice sounded slightly slurred. Coleton heard a struggle as she tried to grab the phone, then she leaned her head close to the receiver. "Hi, Coleton, dear. How wonderful, of course you can borrow the plane—for your girlfriend."

"Thanks, Mom," Coleton said, but his expression didn't waver as he waited for the final word from his father.

"Don't you have *any* pride? Didn't at least that *one* trait rub off on you?"

Coleton remained silent. He knew this was as important to his father as making Coleton send a wire for the plane. He let the snide comments pummel him. He didn't even hold up his hands to protect his temples. They were worth it—for her.

"Your brother never had to come begging on his knees to borrow my plane. Because *he* has one, because he has a real profession."

Coleton held his breath, which made it easier to hold back the retorts that were building up in his throat.

"Fine," his father finally said. "But, this is a one-time thing." Coleton let out his breath in a rush. "And don't think you're not going to pay for fuel, overnight pilot rates, reserves, wear and tear, the works."

"That's fine," Coleton said. "I'll pay whatever you want as long as she can use it." Relief washed over him, and although his pride was tender, his face felt warm again. As if he'd been able to reclaim those last dying rays from the red sky at dusk.

CHAPTER 10
SEBRING, FLORIDA

Camilla's Pandora app kicked out a new song. *Journey!* In one long twist of the wrist, she ratcheted up the volume until the speakers vibrated in the doors of the car. She pressed down the accelerator another half inch, and a smile broke over her face.

"Anyway you want it, *ba-bam*, that's the way you need it, *bam*, any way you want it." She sang at the top of her lungs, and airbanged her head in time to the blaring music.

She rolled down the windows and stuck her hand out the window, riding the currents up and down. On impulse she pulled off the road and held down a button. The roof of her black BMW 135i peeled backwards, and hot sunshine poured into the convertible. She drummed her fingers on the steering wheel and seat-danced as she waited.

"I was alone. I never kneeeew," she yelled, as the roof locked in place. "What good love could do!" She threw the car into drive and floored it back onto the open road of Highway 98.

"Oooh, then we touched, then we sang." Camilla gripped the steering wheel with one hand and stretched the other past the top of the windshield into the roaring wind. "About the lovin' things!"

She bobbed her shoulders and sang into the wind, "Oooh, all night, alllll night. Ohhhhh, every night."

She had been at the wheel for almost two hours and could feel she was getting close. With every mile she raced closer to Sebring International Raceway, the anticipation grew.

Her phone rang, and the music cut out. She pressed the Bluetooth button and the line crackled to life.

"Is this Camilla?"

"Yes—" she said calmly, as if she hadn't just been screaming into the wind like an '80s rock star.

"This is Barney. Coleton asked me to call you. You're driving in?"

"I'm just turning onto Airport Road," she said, as she swung the wheel to the right and accelerated through the intersection.

"Then you're here! Park in the first lot you see on your right. I'll meet you there in five minutes."

Camilla pulled into the grassy lot and parked in line with the rest of the cars. She closed the roof, got out and stretched her arms into the air. She popped the trunk and began to lug out a large red suitcase.

A golf cart spun to a stop behind her car. "You Camilla?" A man with graying hair and a thick salt and pepper beard asked.

She nodded.

"Well, come on, girl!" He smiled. "I'm Barney."

Barney jumped out and secured her suitcase on the backbench.

"Where's Coleton?" she asked, holding her purse to her chest.

"Oh, he's in the paddock. He sent me to pick you up. I've worked for the Loren family for years."

"Okay," Camilla said tentatively.

It only took a minute for the golf cart to reach the gates of Sebring International Raceway.

"I can't believe the traffic," Camilla said. "And it's only Friday! It's going to take forever to get in." Even though the 12 Hours of Sebring wouldn't begin until Saturday morning at 10:45, a line of cars, trucks, motor homes, trailers and golf carts waited to check through the gates and parade down the flag-lined entrance toward the packed infield.

"Not really." Barney pulled the cart onto the shoulder, dangled a red pass from his outstretched hand and floored it. "The funny thing about working for Coleton Loren, it changes your whole attitude toward driving." He smiled at Camilla. "I used to drive like a granny, but after a few months with him suddenly I'm Mario Andretti."

Camilla watched the cars blur past, locked into a grid, waiting for their chance to make for the infield and stake a claim for the coveted spots along the inside edge of the racetrack: Turn 7, Turn 17 and most notably "the Carousel" at Turn 5. Like the settlers in the great Oklahoma land races in the late 1800s, the spectators at Sebring waged their own pedestrian race of sorts, camping out for days in advance to ensure a choice square of earth, the perfect vantage.

Once inside, spectators would have little chance of getting back out through the crowd with their vehicles until Sunday, so some of the less committed opted to park in one of the surrounding lots and walk in. As the golf cart turned south and headed toward the paddock, Camilla saw through the chain link fence, thousands of spots were already claimed along the edge of the racetrack.

The golf cart bumped down the main road that ran between the pits, where teams set up their tactical race-day headquarters along the track, and the paddock, where they set up base camp.

They came to an intersection and saw a large black man directing traffic from the middle of the road. He was tall and stocky, and his biceps bulged under his 12 Hours of Sebring t-shirt. He had a baseball cap pulled down over his eyes, a mesh neon vest and fresh white gloves on his hands. He bent forward at a 45-degree angle and his arms, perfectly flat all the way through the fingertips, jerked up and down energetically. Each motion started in his hips, then torqued through his body. His arms: a full extension, snap, quick flection. Camilla was amazed. His motions were so precise, but full of happy energy, as if he was dancing.

"Yep," Barney said. "That guy's here every year. He's a legend. Tomorrow, he'll be here for the entire race. I've never seen him take a break during a race."

"But, the race is 12 hours!"

"You'll see. It's incredible."

They got the cue to proceed, and Barney made a right, then a left onto Paddock Road. Each team is allotted a space along the Paddock Road to arrange their team transporters, tractor-trailers full of equipment, and motor coaches into a team commune centered around their main tent turned garage floor where the cars live while not on track. The paddock immediately reminded Camilla of a zoo. As the golf cart careened down Paddock Road, she caught quick, short glimpses into the different team tents and saw the bright, pampered cars crouched like animals in their cages.

"Here we are." Barney looked kindly at Camilla. "The epicenter of the chaos we motorheads call Sebring."

Barney pulled up to a large, white tent and jammed the brake down until it stuck. Like the others, this tent opened onto Paddock Road and was attached on the north and south to large semi-truck transporters that had flung-open doors in their sides.

Camilla picked Coleton from the ranks of men working under the white canopy, even with his back turned. Red racing suit pulled down off his broad shoulders and tied at the waist, he talked animatedly to an older man in a black mechanic's jumpsuit. There was a black, red and white LMP1 car in the middle of the tent, perched proudly on jacks a few feet off the ground. Coleton let out a loud, easy laugh and clapped the man on the back. He radiated such excited energy, a drastic change from his often bored, smug demeanor. She watched him move, quick and easy, free of pretension. This was Coleton happy, and she liked it.

"I'll just put your suitcase in the coach, then?" Barney said from behind her. He had been watching her watch Coleton. Barney smiled. "You two can move your things over to Château Élan later on."

"Château Élan?"

"You didn't think Colt would make you sleep in one of these roach coaches did you?" Barney laughed. "No, no. There is a really nice hotel here called Château Élan. Resort and spa, really. We passed it on the way in."

"Thank you, Barney."

"Camilla!"

Camilla turned just in time. Coleton snatched her up in a full bear hug, arms too.

"You made it!" Coleton breathed into her ear.

Coleton grabbed her face in his hands. He kissed her slowly, full and square on the lips. His eyes flickered open, and he let them linger on her lips. Her purse slipped out of her hands.

Camilla couldn't help the smile that spread across her face.

"Barney gave me a mini tour of the infield," she said, slightly breathless as she picked up her purse. "Wow, you've really got a dedicated fan base. But, I thought you said this was *classier* than NASCAR? On the way in, I saw a deer head mounted on the front of a pick-up with Mardi Gras beads strung through its antlers!"

"Yeah, Sebring is a different crowd," he said. "Wait 'til you see Long Beach!" Then, he grew serious. "But, more importantly, how's your father?"

"Oh, Coleton. Thank you again for everything," she said. As she looked into his emerald eyes, hers misted over. "Thank God it wasn't serious. He had a bad one last year, so when Katherine and I got the news, we panicked. We've always been so protective of him, after everything that happened with my mom. But, he's going to be fine."

"Good," Coleton said. He pulled her back into his arms and kissed her lightly on the temple. "Did you eat breakfast yet?" She shook her head no. "Great! I'm starving."

He grabbed her hand and led her out of the tent and picked the black team golf cart. It lurched forward as Coleton jammed down the accelerator. He spun in a donut and Camilla clung to the metal handle against the centrifugal force.

"Hold on," Coleton laughed. "This isn't a normal golf cart."

"Clearly!"

"The boys were waiting for a few parts to arrive for the LMP1 car on Monday and got a little bored, so they jacked this thing up!" Coleton grinned from ear to ear, as proud of the machine as if it had been constructed from his own rib bone.

It only took a few minutes to traverse the length of the paddock. Coleton weaved between slower carts and pedestrians and pulled up to a large, white, closed-in tent. Coleton bailed out of the cart before it came to a complete stop. Camilla let it roll its final few feet, then thankfully swung her legs onto solid ground.

"Welcome to Pamela's," Coleton said.

Inside, a large dining hall was cut in two by a long buffet table with a row of steaming silver trays. Twenty folding tables were neatly arranged and covered with checkered tablecloths.

Coleton nodded to a man in a blue and orange racing suit at a table near the entrance. His face lit up and he gave Coleton a little salute, exposing a row of crooked yellow teeth. He had a ruddy complexion and warm sparkling eyes.

"That's Anderson Green, factory Aston Martin driver. Great guy. He's got a Cockney accent you'll love."

At a table in the corner, Camilla immediately recognized Enzo from Cucina in Palm Beach; his bravado was unmistakable. He whispered in the ear of a girl next to him. She had bleached blonde hair and wore a skin-tight red jumpsuit with a checkered stripe running up both sides. Her folding chair was so close to Enzo's that the skinny legs were tangled together.

"Enchanting," Camilla mumbled.

"Fine specimen, huh?" Coleton chuckled. "Hey, Asshole!" he yelled toward the couple.

Enzo looked up, his black eyes flashing. Then, a boyish smile lit up his handsome face. "What can I do?" He shrugged. The girl swooped in to kiss his neck, ignoring the new arrivals. Enzo drained his glass of orange juice, as if undistracted by her determined advances, and winked at them. His other hand remained unaccounted for under the table.

"That's a Flag Girl."

"A what?" Camilla asked.

"You know, a podium girl. They hold team flags on the grid before the race, hand out the trophies after races and get soaked with champagne."

"Really?" Camilla asked sarcastically. "What else do they do for you?"

Coleton laughed. "It's what we do for them. They'll do anything for a little limelight with an up-and-coming driver."

"Riiiight," Camilla said, stifling an eye roll.

"I guess Enzo doesn't follow the Rule. Or maybe that's all for show."

"What Rule?"

"The No-Sex-Before-a-Race Rule."

"*What?*"

"Drivers are very superstitious. For example, a lot of us think it's bad luck to shave the morning of a race, and we all have a special routine for putting on our gear. If one step's out of place, watch out! Above all, almost every driver believes it's bad luck to have sex the night before a race. I guess the theory is that sexual energy makes you faster and more aggressive on the track."

"No. Way. With all these Flag Girls flouncing around, you mean to tell me there's no action going on?"

"Little to none," he said. Camilla's mouth dropped open. "Now after the race, that's a different story."

"And you follow this rule?" Camilla asked shyly. Coleton's cheek dimpled with a held-back smile, and he nodded solemnly.

"Come on." He took her hand. "Come meet the Queen."

He led Camilla to a table at the back of the tent. A woman with thick glasses sat bent over a clipboard, making notes. She had silver hair pulled loosely back into a French braid that fell past her shoulders. As they approached, she looked up at them through large watery blue eyes. "Coleton!"

"Kill the calf," Coleton laughed. He gave her a warm hug. Then, with an arm still around her shoulders, he turned. "Pamela, I want you to meet Camilla."

"So you're the Camilla we've been hearing about," Pamela said. "It's about time someone domesticated this animal." Pamela poked an index finger into his side. "I'll be the first to say this boy's always had potential, but I've never known anyone like him for not using it."

"Great to meet you," Camilla said.

"You are a lucky lady," Pamela told her. "Coleton really does deep-down—" Here she looked at him. "—very deep down, know how to treat a woman. He is always helping me around here."

"He's definitely full of surprises."

"Well, you guys didn't come in here to visit an old lady," Pamela continued. "Go get some food while the gettin's good."

Coleton gave her shoulder a squeeze. Pamela nodded and winked at Camilla.

Coleton led Camilla toward the row of steaming silver trays.

"You told me you were a street devil and a house angel," Camilla said. "So, I guess Pamela's hospitality tent counts as domestic territory?"

"You remember me telling you that? You remember everything! I have to be more careful what I say."

"It comes from memorizing all that anatomy."

Coleton opened his mouth.

"Don't! say it," she said. "I know what your dirty mind just thought of."

"Takes one to know one."

Camilla opened her mouth, then snapped it shut and giggled.

Under the silver lids were scrambled eggs, plain and with cheese, eggs Benedict, pancakes, waffles, bacon, sausage, home fries, plain and with onions, hash browns, grits, croissants and a variety of fresh fruit.

"This is a feast!"

"It's like this for every meal," Coleton said, pointing at her plate already piled high. They were only halfway down the row. "I promise this won't be the last time I feed you."

"How does this work?" Camilla asked, as she looked for cash registers. "Do you have an account?"

"Each team signs up at the beginning of the season. It's all you can eat, every meal, and the team pays for it."

"It's just for the drivers, then?" Camilla asked.

"It's for the whole team. Plus special guests and sponsors."

Camilla followed Coleton to a table on the other side of the tent from Enzo and the Flag Girl, who were now lip-locked. It didn't look like Enzo was in control of the situation anymore, at all.

A purple, potted orchid adorned each table. Camilla liked Pamela's attention to detail. It would take a lot of effort for orchids to survive the race circuit with its constant traveling. Camilla pictured their proud purple heads packed into crates, shaking in their pots as Pamela careened down the highway.

"Pamela's is Switzerland," Coleton said through a mouthful of scrambled eggs. "God, I'm starving," he added, shoveling in another mouthful.

"Switzerland?"

"Neutral territory. Most of the teams eat here. A few have their own tents and a few eat at Myrtle's, which is a competing hospitality tent, but most eat here. Imagine this place filled with a lot of hungry, competitive lions."

Camilla nodded.

"A lot of egos and testosterone manage to fit under this tent," Coleton said. "Because of our respect for Pamela. She's like the godmother of the circuit; she keeps everyone in line. Well, for mealtimes, at least."

"The power of the apron strings?"

"Definitely," Coleton agreed.

"I'm sure it's worth it," Camilla said. "This food is amazing!"

"Speaking of egos—" Coleton nodded over Camilla's shoulder as an attractive man entered the tent followed by two tall blondes. His racing suit looked tailored, his gently waved dark hair fell down to brush his collar. His swagger suggested a man who'd been told his whole life that he's the star.

"Who is that?" Camilla asked.

"Who is *that*?" Coleton rolled his eyes. "Ony Fernando Garza, one of the best drivers in the world. He's racing for Peugeot tomorrow, along with Nicolas Sagat."

"I didn't know that Peugeot was one of your competitors."

"They aren't, really. They only come over from Europe for the endurance races, not all the races. So, they aren't really competition for us. I mean, of course we want to crush them, but they aren't in contention for our Championship."

Although Fernando Garza was not tall, he filled out the shoulders of his suit. He ran his fingers through his wet hair, slicking it off his high forehead. Clearly he had just finished up a practice session, but he looked and acted as if he had recently surfaced from a dive off his mega-yacht in St. Tropez. He spotted Coleton.

"Oh, no—" Coleton laughed, sitting up straight. "Brace yourself."

"Well, if it isn't Coleton Loren! Is this seat taken, my friend?" the man asked Coleton directly, apparently making a point not to look at Camilla.

"Of course not." Coleton rose and shook his hand. "Have a seat."

Camilla was aware that she was a beautiful girl. Not perfect lipstick and matching fresh manicure, but naturally beautiful, so strangers, especially men, gave her a second glance she had come to expect. An admirer once quoted her something Clark Gable had told Carole Lombard: "You may not be the one I'd look at first, but you are the one I'd look at the longest."

When someone failed to look, it was usually on purpose. Camilla did not resent Fernando for it, rather she saw it as a misguided sign of respect for Coleton.

Fernando sat on the corner of the seat, turned slightly away from her, his back straight and one angled arm resting on the top of the folding chair. The two models pulled out chairs and sat on either side of him. Coleton cleared his throat.

"Fernando, this is Camilla." He motioned toward Camilla. "Camilla, this is Fernando Garza." Fernando raised his eyebrows. When he turned slowly toward Camilla, his dark eyes sparkled.

"Oh, I see," he said. *"Ciao, Bella."* Fernando unleashed a row of gleaming white teeth, bowed his head and kissed her hand.

Fernando did not introduce the models. "Yes. Just stopped in for a quick, short black," Fernando said, holding up a tiny paper cup of espresso and then making a circular motion with it in front of his chest. "My trainer, he says, it is not good for the cardiovascular." His words were thick and heavy with accent, but Camilla couldn't tell if it was European or South American, Italian or Spanish. "But, I say—it is the *aqua vita.*" He raised his tiny paper cup a few inches higher in a "Cheers" to Coleton. Then, he threw back his head and took a miniscule sip. Coleton nodded and drained his glass of orange juice.

"Well, it should be good weather for our little race tomorrow, no?" Fernando said, crossing his legs.

"Yeah, it should be good, but too hot for my taste," Coleton replied. "This Florida heat really separates the men from the boys."

"Indeed." Fernando leaned forward. "You know, I would rather drive two 24 Heures du Mans in France than 12 hours of Sebring. Between the heat and this bumpy American track. I will tell you, I do not look forward to this race."

"Well, there she is!" a man boomed from the doorway.

"There's George," Coleton told Camilla.

George strode toward them and clapped Coleton on the shoulder. Coleton began to rise, but George leaned into his shoulder, keeping him seated. Camilla was beginning to notice that the best racers hovered around five-foot-ten. George was no exception. He had chestnut hair fingered through with gray and warm, playful eyes.

George nodded tersely at Fernando.

"You must be Camilla," George said, turning with a smile. "I've never heard Coleton gush about anything but a car before. Or maybe himself." He smacked Coleton roughly on the back, then, shook Camilla's extended hand heartily.

"I've heard a lot about you, too," Camilla said.

"Oh, Garza," George said, turning. "I just came from the pits. They're starting the 11 o'clock practice session and Nikki Street from SPEED TV was asking around for you—something about an exclusive for Telemundo?"

"Interesting," Fernando murmured, sitting up, clearly more than just interested. "Interesting. Yes. Well, in that case I shouldn't wish to keep her waiting." Garza tilted his head back to finish the last drop in his tiny cup, one pinky extended in the air, and pushed his chair back from the table.

"*Senorita*." He nodded at Camilla, displaying again his million-dollar smile, but his eyes were already vacant. He was gone before he made his exit, the two models following silently.

"What ya got, Georgey?" Coleton asked with a smile. "Now, tell the truth. Nikki Street won't grace us with her presence until tomorrow morning. You just wanted to get rid of him?"

George shrugged, but a mischievous smile played on his lips. "I just came from the pits. Put Trotter in the car for the practice session. He looked so nervous! He's a decent Indy driver, but that just doesn't translate."

"That kid is lucky as hell. If he weren't Elrod's nephew, he would never be our third shoe. I don't care if he's a goddamn Indy *legend*, he should prove himself in Le Mans before he waltzes onto a serious team."

"Third shoe?" Camilla asked.

"Yeah, for most races in our series there are only two drivers, but for the few endurance—" Coleton stopped and turned.

"What?" George asked, looking across the tent where Coleton had fixed his gaze. But Coleton wasn't looking. He was listening.

Camilla realized the sound of the cars was missing—that low, ragged monotonous growl that she had already grown used to. Coleton looked at his watch.

"It's only 11:15," Coleton said. George looked at his own watch and nodded. Then, George added the two words they were both thinking, "Red flag."

"Pamela! The TV!" Coleton yelled. Across the room Pamela was on her feet. From the tiptoes of her white Keds she could just reach the TV, which broadcast the Sebring track cameras live from various strategic locations, perched on a broad industrial refrigerator. Around the track grounds, TVs broadcast these channels to help the engineers, mechanics, drivers and crew chiefs keep abreast of on-track events.

The pixels crackled to life as Pamela switched on the screen. George, Coleton and Camilla went to Pamela's side, inching close to the screen. Channel 6 showed the Carousel, the tricky Turn 5, clear in the morning sun. The road was deserted. Pamela clicked to Channel 7, Turn 17. Still no cars, but a red flag rippled in silence.

Pamela clicked again. Channel 1 was hazy. Camilla caught her breath: smoke filled the screen like a war zone and crumpled carbon fiber shards littered the track.

"Someone augured in at Turn 1," George stated the obvious.

"Who is it? What car is it?" Coleton asked, but no one could make out the car through the smoke.

"Shit, it's us!" George exploded.

"No!"

George spun toward the door. Camilla could not peel her eyes from the screen, unable to believe it was real and happening only a few hundred yards away.

Coleton grabbed her wrist. "Camilla, come on!"

They raced after George, catching glimpses of his broad shoulders as he pushed through the crowd. When they reached Pit Row, their car had already been pulled back the wrong way down the front straight from Turn 1. The crew was slowly pushing the wreck out of the pits onto the narrow road that led to the paddock, but pieces of carbon fiber dragged along the ground, making it slow going. Nelson gave Coleton a meaningful, wide-eyed look.

Coleton checked his watch. "We're on the clock now, boys!" The men put their shoulders into the mass of wrecked metal. "Twenty-two hours and counting."

Coleton turned to Camilla at his side and explained, "They have 22 hours to put that animal back together. Perfectly back together before the race begins."

Camilla just nodded. *Twenty-two hours.*

Then they saw the third shoe. Camilla knew it was him immediately, and not just from his suit that was streaked black with dirt. His shoulders slumped forward, his dirty blond bangs fell into his eyes and he held his helmet laxly at his side.

George followed him, yelling. As they got closer, Camilla could hear the barrage: "You idiot! You really shit the bed this time! Why would you try to not lift through Turn 1? Because Coleton does it?"

Coleton shook his head. Camilla saw the tension in his jaw and knew he was biting back his own barbs because she was there.

Spectators packed the road to the paddock. They followed the car as it ground forward along the asphalt, like a funeral cortège.

At the intersection of the main road and the narrow thoroughfare that connected Pit Row and the paddock, Camilla noticed the black man she'd seen that morning in the very same spot. His movements betrayed no hint of fatigue. He continued to swing his hips energetically back and forth, pumping his arms, his muscles pulsing under a solid sheen of sweat.

At sight of the wreckage, he stopped all traffic with a quick spin, then motioned them confidently forward, his white perma-smile replaced by a grim mask of concentration as he got them safely to the paddock. A tangled, jostling mass of people had already collected in front of their tent, cameras ready, hoping for a glimpse of carnage.

"Get back!" Nelson yelled. The crew joined in, waving their arms and yelling at the crowd, driving them back from their front row view of the spectacle, the chaotic surgery of a mangled million-dollar racecar.

"Shit, it's Paddock Pass time," Coleton muttered as they reached the tent.

The day and morning before a race, officials open the paddock to lucky fans who have bought or bribed Paddock Passes. Each team ropes off the front of its tent to keep the spectators back a pace, and fans can walk down Paddock Road, peer into the workshops, take pictures of the shiny, bright cars, try to glimpse a driver or team owner, and maybe even finagle a quick autograph.

Coleton wrapped an arm around Camilla, guiding her through the crowd and safely into their roped-off garage.

"Do you think Trotter should go to the medical tent?" Camilla called after him, but Coleton's attention was focused on the car, as he walked around the battered vehicle with an assessing eye. For Trotter's driver debrief, Coleton needed to channel his anger into a few perfectly sharp, to-the-point comments.

The crew grabbed tools and crawled over the car like ants on a carcass. They peeled fiber from its frame and cast it roughly to the side. Coleton and George exchanged a few quick words near the back, then turned solemnly into the southern transporter, to the room in the back of the semi used for debriefs.

The room was just big enough to hold five or six men. On three sides, it was lined with narrow benches attached to the walls, and it had a flat screen TV on the fourth wall. Trotter trudged up the three iron steps, holding an unopened bottle of water, looking pale and stunned.

When a crewmember brushed roughly past Camilla, she realized she was in the way. She didn't know where to go or what to do. She had nothing to offer. She belonged outside the ropes with those faces thirsty for each drop of panic.

She walked to the transporter. With a sigh, she sat on the top step, pulled her knees to her chest and made herself as small as possible. Every once in a while she heard an angry outburst from George through the closed door of the debrief room.

As the minutes passed, Camilla settled in, watching the team move in orchestrated mayhem. In time, a discernable change occurred. Each crew member, as if flipping a switch, went from a panicked rush into his own rhythm of quick and efficient movements.

No one spoke. No one bumped into another. They functioned like a single sentient being. Camilla watched silently from her perch as they swarmed over the car, paring it down to its boney carcass.

Camilla sat up in bed, for a second forgetting where she was or why. She rubbed her eyes trying to see the face of her watch.

Moonlight seeped through the thin polyester drapes, and she could just make out the right angle of the hands: 3:15. She felt the sheets next to her with a blind hand: empty, and still smooth. Coleton had not been to bed yet.

Château Élan had not been in the cards for them after all. Coleton decided to stay near the wreck and Camilla refused to isolate herself in the luxury of a hotel while the team sacrificed a night of sleep to make the starting grid.

She swung her legs out of the bed and felt the floor for Coleton's team jacket. It lay where she'd dropped it. She slipped it on, pulled back her hair in an elastic band and felt her way down the length of the coach. She had to throw her weight into the heavy door to swing it open into the night.

Outside, it was quiet and pitch black. Camilla pulled her jacket closer although she wasn't cold and made her way around the end of the transporter into the blinding light of the tent. The crew buzzed away like moths under the fluorescent bulbs, working as hard as when she had first retired to the coach. Their movements were just as quick, but now they seemed less hurried, more determined. None of them had rested since word of the crash had descended like an unexpected verdict the day before.

Coleton sat alone on the transporter steps, his head bowed over his bent knees. A thick silence now muffled the gentle clanking of metal against metal, tools against carbon fiber.

Camilla watched Coleton for a second, then made her way toward him. The mechanics and crew didn't notice her. She sat next to him, put her arm around his shoulders and leaned close to his ear. His breathing stirred. "Coleton, come to bed."

He nodded, without lifting his head from his arms.

"Don't forget, you still have to drive tomorrow." Camilla ran her fingers through his hair, combing it back from his forehead. "You need some real rest." He nodded again.

All of a sudden, a shout shattered the heavy quiet.

"Who's hungry?"

Heads lifted, backs straightened, the crew blinked tired eyes and peered into the dark. A golf cart shot through a gap in the ropes and skidded to a stop on the rubber garage mats. A whoop of joy went up, as they recognized Pamela's shining, smiling face. The air crackled with excitement, high-fives were exchanged and smiles broke through masks of concentration. Pamela began unstrapping plastic bins of food, metal canisters of coffee and baskets of fruit and cookies from the back seat.

"I said," she yelled. "Who's hungry, boys?" With another gigantic whoop, tools were dropped to the ground and everyone pitched in, clearing the tops of tall tool boxes to make buffet tables, prying open containers with excited, curious faces, their movements just as precise as when they worked on the car.

"Pamela!" yelled a young mechanic, who couldn't have been more than 20. "These aren't your world famous truffle grilled cheese sandwiches, are they?"

"You think I could hold back from my favorite team?" Pamela's impartiality was a well-known and obligatory fact, but she made each one feel like the first-born favorite.

Pamela grabbed a wide plate, brought it to Coleton and Camilla where they still sat, happily watching the men dig into their feast, and pulled off the cellophane.

"I knew you'd still be up," she told Coleton. "Although, if you were smart, you'd be sleeping like a baby." Coleton took the plate.

"A tuna steak!" Coleton said. "My favorite."

Pamela ruffled his hair and winked at Camilla. "On one condition."

"He has to share it with me?" Camilla joked.

"Sweetie, don't even try—"

Coleton fed Camilla a bite with his fork.

"Well, that's a first," Pamela said. "Must be love."

"Oh, it is," Coleton mumbled, his mouth full. "She loves tuna."

"Brat." Camilla laughed.

Pamela rolled her eyes. "Get your ass to bed when you finish."

CHAPTER 11
12 HOURS OF SEBRING

Camilla woke with a start. Morning light flooded the egg-colored "master suite" of the coach. She hadn't heard Coleton leave.

Although they slept in the same bed, the sleeping arrangement had been a product of necessity rather than romance. A racecar roared past and rattled the window. She sucked in her breath and pulled back the thin drapes.

The coach was parked against the chain-link fence that fronted the Ullman straight. From the window above the bed, she could see a 50 yard stretch of the track and the entrance to Turn 17. A red Ferrari GT roared past, then a Porsche GT. The morning warm-up session had begun. If she focused her eyes, she could just make out the type of each car before it shot into the turn.

Camilla held her breath until her lungs burned and watched, hoping for a white, black and red LMP1 to shoot past with a huge Miller logo across the side. Then she saw the red Ferrari again. Coleton's car had not made the warm-up.

Bolting out of bed, Camilla splashed water on her face, dressed, and hurried toward the tent. As she rounded the corner, she saw the crew carefully lowering the hood of the car, buckling it into place. Exhaustion etched their pale faces, but the crew still moved quickly. Someone dropped the air jack, and the car settled onto its tires. She couldn't believe it was the same car, now perfect and shining in the morning light.

She scanned the tent for Coleton, then bounded into the Transporter and looked in the window at the debrief room. All the Chiefs were gathered: the Chief Engineer, Crew Chief, Chief Mechanic, instructing the drivers, rallying their warriors suited in bright red. Their faces were serious and confident: war ready. Coleton motioned for her to come in. She shook her head no; she didn't want to interrupt. He motioned again. She backed up. Coleton jumped up and swung open the door.

"Camilla, come in!" Coleton whispered. "I want you to hear what a driver debrief sounds like." The men slid down the bench to make a space for her. Their eyes remained glued to a map of the track on the flat screen.

"George, you've got to brake release quicker into Turn 1," Nelson said, his nose a few inches from the spreadsheet on his laptop. "Then gas earlier. But, don't just lift, really brake, unless you're pressed to make a move on someone, and you better be really pressed."

George made a note on the paper diagram of the track in front of him. The chief engineer glanced meaningfully at Trotter, who did *not* have the option not to lift into Turn 1 under any condition.

"Between Turn 3 and 5, into the Carousel," Nelson said. "I want to see you at full throttle—I'm talking to the floor. As for Turn 5, brush brake earlier." George nodded and underlined something on his paper. "And, make sure you hit the apex at Turn 5 for a better exit. Then, get quicker to full throttle after Turn 7." Camilla could see George write "More speed!" next to the exit of Turn 7 on his diagram.

Although not yet fluent in "Enginese," Camilla was grateful to be there. It made her feel like part of the team. Coleton took Camilla's hand under the table and placed it on his knee. Then he picked his pencil back up and continued to make small notes in the margins of his diagram.

As they filed out of the transporter, Camilla smiled to herself. The three men in their red racing suits swaggered down the stairs in slow mo, ready for their comeback moment.

The car sat proud and perfect, aloof in the middle of the tent, which had in seconds transformed from O.R. to showroom. A crowd pressed in on the ropes, and flashbulbs burst off its lacquered paint like fireworks. The floor had been swept clean, tools put away, and not even a screw remained behind. Most of the crew had disappeared, probably to Pamela's for breakfast, but a few mechanics lingered around the garage. One young mechanic lay on his back in the corner with his knees in the air, eyes closed.

"Ira!" Coleton called and waved. Ira's head appeared shoulder-high in the crowd, his cheeks pink in the cool morning air. Coleton waved him through the ropes.

He clapped Ira on the back. "You've missed all the action!"

"Action?" Ira demanded.

"Action, romance, tasteful nudity—Camilla can fill you in. Hey, listen," Coleton said, making eye contact. "Watch out for Camilla today. Get her suited up, take her to breakfast and meet me on the grid in 30."

"Sure, Colt," Ira said. Then he added with a grin, "Did the fat fuck show up?"

"Yeah, you're here."

"Funny. I mean, Gomez."

"No, he's off licking his wounds."

"I knew it." Ira turned to Camilla. "Let's get you suited up, honey."

Ira led her to the other transporter that was packed with gear, car parts and crates of bottled water. He burrowed into the truck, only his large backside visible. He unwedged a trashcan and said, "Pick one." Camilla wiggled her nose at the mass of tangled clothing. "You've got to wear a racing suit."

"Are they clean?" she asked.

"Yeah, sure." Ira looked away.

"Hmmm."

Camilla pulled out a few suits before finding one that looked relatively clean and relatively her size.

"You know," he said off-handedly. "I could get the equipment manager to order one in your size."

"That would be great."

Ira loved doing favors for people, especially for people that could be of use to him in the future. Sometimes this trait was misinterpreted as magnanimity. But, Ira had a great memory for certain things, namely the full shape and flavor of indebtedness. His world ran on quid pro quo.

By the time Camilla had slipped into the borrowed fireproof suit, Ira was already at the team golf cart waiting for her.

"Come on. Keep it moving, kid!" Ira called. She jumped into the golf cart. "The race is starting in 20 minutes."

As they sped past Pamela's and she got a passing whiff of warm pancakes and syrup, Camilla suddenly realized with a sinking feeling that breakfast was no longer in the cards.

By the time Ira and Camilla reached the front straight, it had already been converted into the pre-game grid. All of the bright racecars were lined up like pageant contestants on the track, parallel to pit lane. Milling around them were spectators, photographers, race officials and team sponsors. Flag girls stood near the hood of each car, team colors fluttering, skin-tight jumpsuits unzipped just north of indecent exposure.

Since Trotter had crashed, Elrod Racing hadn't made the qualifying session and was relegated to the back of the grid. Past the other cars, Ira and Camilla finally found their white, black and red beauty. Camilla felt a surge of pride. She felt singularly familiar with it, special in the crowd because she knew what lay underneath its shiny shell. She had seen its parts flung in every direction, a mayhem of metal across the rubber garage floor mats. Now it was a work of art again.

"Ohhhh, yeah," Ira said, winking at the Elrod flag girls who stood by the hood of their car. Instead of red jumpsuits with checkered sides, they wore matching wife-beaters, with the necklines and armholes cut wider to make them even more revealing, and black spandex mini-shorts.

"Nothing says class like side-boob," Camilla muttered. Ira laughed out loud.

Camilla brushed past the flag girls. Coleton was mid-interview, one eyebrow arched, hand on his hip, while Nikki Street from SPEED TV held a microphone to his mouth.

"It's been a wild ride, and the race hasn't even begun! The fact that we're even here on the grid is testament to the quality of our crew. We have some of the best guys in the business."

"Talk in the paddock is that *you're* one of the best guys in the business."

Coleton smiled at her, not entirely sure how to respond. She tilted her head and unleashed a well-insured smile that dimpled her cheeks. She pushed the microphone closer to his mouth, staring at him with restrained hunger.

"And your leg? How is your injury coming?" She turned to the camera and looked deeply into its lens. "Only two and a half months ago Coleton Loren broke his leg in two places." She held up two fingers.

"I'm good as new!" Coleton smiled and did a little dance, as the camera zoomed in on his shinbone.

"Well, we certainly wish you luck. The race is only minutes away! I'm Nikki Street, and we're here *live* at Sebring International Raceway."

The cameraman lowered the heavy camera from his shoulder, and the producer cut to Nikki's counterpart Brian Horn farther down the grid. Now that the camera was off, Nikki inched closer to Coleton. She put a hand on his shoulder and leaned in to whisper in his ear. Coleton began to laugh and pulled away to look her in the eye, as though shocked by what she'd said.

Just then, Coleton saw Camilla watching them. He broke into a wide, easy smile. Coleton set his helmet on the hood of the car, and not even saying goodbye to Nikki, walked straight to Camilla, grabbed her face in both hands and gave her a loud, smacking kiss.

"Heya, Stranger," she laughed. "Who was that?"

"Oh, that's Nikki Street. She's a SPEED reporter."

"I see," Camilla said. His response did nothing to calm her imagination. She had a sinking feeling that something more than a simple interview had been brewing. Her gaze followed Nikki Street as she walked away, head high and looking for the next attractive driver to interview. Camilla shook off the feeling.

"Aren't you worried about all these people so close to the car?" Camilla asked, gesturing to the teeming mass of fans and pressing her hip into his. Occasionally a spectator would fall against the car, pushed by the crowd. "You're not worried they're going to damage a splitter or something?" she added, testing out a word she'd heard in the driver debrief.

"This car is gonna have the hell beat out of it for 12 hours straight. A few sunburned fans leaving fingerprints on its hood isn't going to hurt anything."

Three steel gray F-16s roared over the track, leaving silvery smoke trails in their wake. Camilla shaded her eyes, trying to pick them out, but they were too fast and the sun was too bright.

"Clear the grid," a voice boomed over the track PA. "It's now time to clear the grid." Track officials in blue vests began to shoo people off the grid, growing more insistent as the clock ticked.

Camilla looked into Coleton's eyes, framing his face in her hands. "Time for you to go," she said. "Please be careful." He kissed the top of her head. "I mean it, Coleton. Please, be careful."

"I will," he promised, but his emerald eyes were lit with mischief. Camilla shook her head and ran her fingers lightly across the stubble on his cheek.

"No time to shave?" she asked.

He pulled on his balaclava, ducked under the HANS device and fastened his helmet before slipping on his red racing gloves. As he stepped into the cockpit, he looked back at her. "It's good luck," he said, then flipped his visor closed. Camilla saw the skin around his eyes crinkle and knew he was smiling. He lowered himself carefully into the tub, then wiggled his legs forward, as the driver assistant belted him in place.

Camilla caught sight of Ira through the thinning crowd, speaking animatedly to a flag girl. She had a grin frozen on her face, looking into the distance, her flag at a perfect 90-degree angle. Ira cracked a joke and laid his hand on the girl's shoulder. Her eyes flicked down to glare at it icily.

"Ira, let's head to the pits!" Camilla called.

She threw her arm protectively around Ira's neck and glared at the flag girl. Ira gave the girl a missed-your-chance-Cookie glance, then wrapped his arm around Camilla's waist. She was a good three inches taller than he was. Camilla tossed her hair, and the flag girl blanched. Her eyes didn't leave them as they walked away. Out of eyeshot, Ira dropped his arm from Camilla's waist and gave her a wink. Camilla smiled back, glad that he recognized the gesture of goodwill for what it was.

Camilla and Ira walked down pit lane until they found the Elrod Racing pit box, and then stepped over the pit wall. Elrod Racing had lucked out and gotten the last space on pit lane. This gave their car an easy entry and exit to their pit box.

The Elrod team of engineers and mechanics amassed in their pit box, milling around, but careful not to leave the vicinity of their appointed positions. Ira led Camilla to the pit cart, and they climbed up into a row of bleacher-like seats. A bank of live feed screens hung along the top of the cart.

"Gentlemen, start your engines," the loudspeaker boomed. The immediate roar of the engines startled Camilla. The sound was abrasive. Fifty-six cars was a new entry list record at the 12 Hours of Sebring.

"Here. Listen to this." Ira put a set of team headphones over Camilla's ears, deadening the sound of the engines. She could just make out a calm voice in the headset saying, "Take it easy. I know you hate starting in the back, but remember, it's a long race."

"They're talking to Coleton," Ira told her.

"He can hear them in the car?" Camilla asked. Ira nodded. "Can he hear me?"

"Hell, no! Only the lead engineer."

"Get some heat in those tires Coleton, first thing," Camilla heard through the headphones. The engines revved loudly and plumes of smoke rose as the cars peeled out in their qualifying order for the parade lap.

"Was that the start?" Camilla asked confused by the cars streaming down the front straight.

Ira chuckled. "No. Le Mans has rolling starts. The cars make one lap in their qualifying order to warm up, and when they come down the front straight again, an official will wave a green flag, which means game on. You'll hear the difference."

Quiet settled over the track, as all 56 cars bunched up on the far side of the track, skating through the turns. Any moment, the pack would descend down the front straight and the green flag would fly. Camilla's stomach was tight and nervous with excitement.

"Here they come!" Ira yelled. They both jumped to their feet and craned their necks to see the cars round the corner. "Down the front straight!"

"Hold steady, hold steady," Nelson instructed Coleton over the radio. "Almost there ... GREEN! GREEN! GREEN!" The cars exploded past the Elrod pit. The sound of 50,000 horsepower was deafening. Camilla pushed her headphones tighter to her head to lessen the roar that shook her body.

Ira laughed at Camilla's flushed cheeks and bright eyes, then pointed to the top left television screen: Turn 1. The cars were already there. They sat down on the bench, eyes glued to the screens.

Her headphones clicked to life again.

"Okay, Colt. Good out of the gate," Nelson cooed. Coleton had skated past two cars before Turn 1. Nelson was great at calling a start. The key was staying in constant radio contact with the driver and calling the green the microsecond the race official *began* to lift his arm with the green flag. Nelson could spot this first muscle twitch and tell Coleton long before he could see the green flag for himself.

"The GT cars are crazy. Stay patient," Nelson instructed. Coleton was going to have to fight through all the slower GT cars. "Get cleanly through lap traffic when you can. It's a long race."

"Roger that."

Constant activity buzzed in the Elrod pit. Crew members rolled fresh tires to the front of the pit box, straightened fuel hoses, and prepared for the LMP1's next pit, whether planned or not. The engineers sat on barstools, mining telemetry data from a bank of shiny black laptops.

The engineers were so focused on their computers that they could have been in a concrete, windowless room in Wichita. They didn't look up, didn't even flinch, when the cars roared past and sent their keyboards rattling. When Coleton came in to take fuel and tires after the first hour, and the choreographed panic of mechanics set in, they just hunched their shoulders and moved their noses closer to their screens while directing calm instructions into their headsets.

Camilla was thankful for her small perch in the pit cart, out of the way, but still in the middle of the action. When the cars roared past on the far side of the wall that divided the track from pit lane, Camilla could just make out the roofs of the passing GT cars, but not Coleton's prototype, which had an open cockpit.

Ira had disappeared right after the start, so Camilla stayed glued to the SPEED channel monitor for information and glimpses of their car. Here she was, with the most restricted and coveted access to the 12 Hours of Sebring, but in reality, she had the same view of the race as the millions of viewers at home, sitting on their couches in their underwear.

"Nelson," Coleton's voice crackled over the radio, calm and cool. "We've got good mid-corner speed, but I'm getting a wicked push at corner exit."

The live SPEED broadcast had picked up Coleton's in-car camera, and now millions worldwide watched Coleton dodge and dive through slower lap traffic, methodically picking his way to the front of the pack. Camilla wondered how his voice could be so relaxed despite the violence she saw on the monitor.

The G forces slammed him left and right as he swooped through the corners. It looked like an invisible hand was shoving his helmet, first toward one shoulder, then the other. The in-car camera shook as the car rocked around the bumpy track.

"There's not much we can do about the push. Keep it up, Colt. You'll be in contention in five laps if you keep this pace," Nelson said.

Seeing the track from Coleton's point of view gave her a sudden jolt of anxiety. What exactly was a *wicked push*?

"Heya, Shorty!" Ira called. Camilla turned. Ira gave her a thumbs-up, but it was a question with raised eyebrows. She smiled and returned the signal with a nod. He waved her toward him, peeled one of her headphones off and yelled, "Want to check out the infield?"

Maybe she would have a better view of Coleton from the infield. She followed Ira to one of the team golf carts, and as they sped away from the pits, the noise subsided so that they could speak.

"Where you been?" Camilla asked.

"Around. You know, doing what I do. Cutting deals and making money."

They went northwest, then over a bridge that spanned the live track. Camilla looked over the railing and saw the cars zoom below them.

"You been to the infield yet?" Ira asked.

"No, not yet."

"Get ready for a real shit show."

Camilla watched the steady stream of spectators inch toward the infield. Seconds before they would have crashed into the mass of cars, Ira spun the golf cart onto the shoulder of the road.

When she had righted herself, Camilla glared at Ira. "Even the drivers' agents ignore traffic rules?"

"See this?" Ira tapped the corner of the windshield glass with his knuckle. "That pass means this is a Team Elrod cart." Camilla nodded. "It means … there are no rules."

Once in the infield, Ira zigzagged through the cars, golf carts, motorcycles and motor homes. Beer-can garlands clattered in the dust behind open jeep Wranglers jacked up on three foot wheels and parading doughy, sun-burned Peroxide blondes on their roll bars like backwoods beauty queens, their worth measured by the number and size of faded tattoos and their prowess at draining and crushing beer cans. Golf carts were decorated with Christmas lights and wired with speakers to blare *Sweet Home Alabama* on repeat. Concession Row attracted lines of people with funnel cakes, root beer, corn dogs, and an assortment of deep-fried foods that could be meat or pickles or something a vendor found in the field while setting up.

"Glamorous, isn't it?" Ira laughed and pushed the accelerator flat.

"Two more. Then pit for fuel, tires and driver change," Nelson told Coleton over the radio.

"I can triple, no problem," replied Coleton. He had taken fuel and tires at the end of his first stint, and was now nearing the end of his second. The tires still felt good, and his adrenaline was pumping.

"We know you can, Marathon Man, but let's get George in and put on some fresh rubber."

A racecar needs to be refueled every 50 to 60 minutes, one stint, and the quickest pit stops are when only fuel is taken. Tires are changed after one or two stints depending on a variety of factors, such as time of day, track temperature and the wear and tear a driver's style puts on them. Driver changes take the most time, so teams try to change drivers and tires in the same pit stop.

"We can double these tires if you guys want to do a splash and go," said Coleton, suggesting an audible. He didn't want to relinquish his seat.

In the cool of night a team can double stint tires, as cooler temperatures mean less heat in the tires and less wear. But on a hot Florida day, double-stinted tires erode fast and lose their grip, and if they get too hot they can blow out and end a team's day at the races.

"I don't want to risk the tires going away," Nelson said. Double stinted tires and a triple stinted driver wasn't a great combination and the race was still young. Nelson didn't want any mistakes. "Bring her in, next lap."

Coleton grimaced in his helmet. They would lose a few seconds, but he couldn't challenge the call, at least not with 10 hours left in the race.

"Roger that," said Coleton. "I'll pit next lap."

The golf cart tossed a wave of dirt in the air as it spun to a stop. Ira bailed out and walked off. He yelled over his shoulder, "This is Turn 5, the Carousel. Let's watch from here. Lots of action."

They started up a slope that overlooked the turn. Loose rows of beach chairs were scattered down the hillside with Coleman cooler footrests filled with icy American beer. As they neared the top, heads began to turn. Just one or two at first, then as those glances fixed with interest, more heads joined in. Soon a good portion of the hill had turned to stare at Ira and Camilla.

"What are they looking at?" Camilla asked.

"First, you're a hot piece." Ira smiled. "Second—" He reached over and pinched an inch of her red racing suit. "The suit. You're the closest they'll get to the pits, Shorty."

"Oh." Camilla smiled, looked down and brushed her hair behind her shoulder.

At the peak of the hill, a plywood platform had been erected and topped with two beach chairs. Two men with gray hair, big bellies and t-shirts with the arms cut off sat like kings on thrones with a perfect view of the track. Lit cigars dangled from their mouths and their beers were tucked into bright foam cozies.

"Hi there," Ira called to the men. "Mind if we borrow your seats a minute. I need to show her something."

The men looked Ira slowly up and down, from his dirty white Nikes to his double chin and thinning hair, and lingered on the team credentials around his neck.

"Okay," one of the men grunted. "What team are you with?"

"Elrod Racing," Camilla said shyly. She was not comfortable with Ira's pushy request, and she didn't want to put the men out of their seats. "Want to listen to my headset?" Camilla pulled the team headset from her neck. "You can hear our driver talk to the pits."

The man's eyes widened. He snatched the headset and jammed it onto his head.

Camilla followed Ira onto the platform and it swayed under their weight.

"You want a beer?" the man called to Camilla, ignoring Ira.

"Oh, no. Thank you."

"Look here." Ira pointed out a car roaring through the Carousel. "That's Stu French's Jaguar. I give it another 20 laps before it DNFs. Maybe 10. And that's Fernando Garza in the Peugeot."

"I had breakfast with him!" she exclaimed. A few neighboring heads turned to look at her, as the Peugeot hummed past. "It doesn't make much noise, does it?"

"It's a diesel. They're quiet, but fucking fast."

"Now that's what a racecar is supposed to sound like!" Camilla exclaimed, pointing at a yellow Corvette GT that rumbled though the sharp turn, shaking their platform.

"Look, there's Coleton!" Ira pointed out the white, red and black LMP1. "He should be getting out soon, unless he's going to triple stint."

"On pit lane, on pit lane," Coleton radioed his crew to prepare for his arrival.

"Colt, I've had a chat with Max. If you feel the tires will hold, stay in the car and triple," responded Nelson.

"Not a problem, I'll stay in," Coleton replied with a smile, happy to contribute to the strategy.

Nelson switched radio frequencies to talk to the crew. "Okay boys, were going to do a splash and go: NO tires, NO driver change."

The strategy worked. They had a blistering pit stop and Coleton was back on the track in fourth place with only a three second margin separating him from third. Coleton ripped through the Carousel, maneuvering the tight hairpin with skill, and passed a Ferrari GT.

Camilla leapt to her feet. "Look! Coleton smoked him!" She shook both fists in the air, filled with pride at the pass. The spectators surrounding the platform joined in, jumping from their chairs and cheering, they gave wild thumbs-up to the two Elrod emissaries perched on their borrowed beer throne.

In a split second, euphoria turned to devastation. A black and green GT spiraled through the air and crashed on its roof a few feet from Coleton, who accelerated safely out of the turn. Carbon fiber rained down on the track and smoke erupted, obstructing the accident from view. The car rolled onto its side and skidded down the track before it rocked to a stop.

Already on her tiptoes, Camilla shaded her eyes with her hand, trying to get a better view. "How did—what just happened?"

The driver-side window was smashed, and its sparkling pieces glinted in the sunlight. She could just make out movement beyond it. The driver was moving, trying to pull himself out of the window.

Camilla didn't think; she just reacted to her training. She jumped from the platform, sprinted down the hill, pushing people out of the way and hurdled over the guardrail. She reached the car in seconds and covered her mouth and nose with the sleeve of her racing suit to keep from choking on the smoke.

The driver managed to pull himself out of the window. Blood seeped through the fabric of his racing suit. *His left arm is cut. Assume it is broken.*

Camilla threw her shoulder under his right arm and walked him away from the car. With each step, more of his weight slumped against her. By the time they stopped he was almost unconscious. She lowered him onto the ground, flat on his back, and started triage. She straightened his neck, carefully laid his arms out at his sides and put pressure on his arm to stop the bleeding, using the thick fabric to her advantage, knowing better than to try to remove it or examine the wound.

"Stay with me," she said, tapping his face. His cheek was rough with stubble. He hadn't shaved that morning, either.

His eyes fluttered open. They were hazel and she leaned over his chest to look into them. "You're going to be fine. Hold on. They're coming for you." He was young and tan and had a thin Mediterranean look. For a second, the world was quiet, and they were the only ones in it.

Camilla looked up and realized there were still racecars roaring past her. She looked for the medical truck.

On the other side of the track, a corner worker leaned through a hole in the chain link fence and jerked two yellow flags back and forth, which meant: full course caution. The pace car would come out and the cars would line up behind it with no passing allowed. She looked back toward the hill of spectators. Ira was there, his belly pressed against the guardrail, arm flailing. His face was bright red and he was screaming at her, but she couldn't make out his words.

She looked down again at the boy. His eyes fluttered and he tried to say something, but he couldn't form the words.

"Shhh," she said. "I know. You don't have to say anything."

The track grew still. The remaining 55 cars threaded past, trying to avoid the debris. Her adrenaline began to slow, and she could feel a heavy thumping in her chest.

She looked over her shoulder and down the track—still nothing. The driver was losing a lot of blood.

"Where is the medical truck?" she yelled.

She saw the flashing lights seconds before the truck appeared, hurtling toward the wreckage of man and machine.

"**W**ow! Phillipe augured the fuck out of his car. It's all over the track!" Coleton announced over the radio. Coleton accelerated a bit once he passed the accident. The pace car was only a few cars in front of him.

"Yeah, it looks messy," replied Nelson. "Be careful with those bits everywhere and watch your language over the radio." Coleton rolled his eyes.

If a driver curses over the radio and race control happens to be monitoring the channel, they will fine the team for a vulgarity infraction. Nelson had highlighted this rule in several driver meetings, but habits are hard to break.

"Add it to my tab," Coleton said smugly. "I've got more important things to worry about."

"If you say so."

"Is Phillipe out of the car yet?" Coleton asked.

"Yes, and it appears your doctor girlfriend is helping him."

"Very funny," replied Coleton. Nelson blanched.

Under a double yellow flag, it's customary for team members to joke with their drivers over the radio while the cars trail the pace car to help them steal the moment to relax, to release their tense shoulders, if only for a few minutes.

In a flash, Nelson realized that even though a yellow flag was out, he should never have told him. This kind of emotional distraction could be dangerous. Regardless, three minutes later on his next lap, Coleton saw for himself, and nothing could shelter him from the news.

"That *is* Camilla!" Coleton yelled. "What the hell is she doing? Is she out of her goddamn mind? Where is Ira?"

"Ira's with her, Colt," Nelson said. "She's climbing back over the wall now. We're watching the live feed. She's fine, just focus on the car."

Coleton suppressed a few pages of curses, knowing they'd do nothing but earn them fines if race control was scanning his frequency. "That's great," he said. "I've been in for a triple stint, cool as a cucumber, and now I'm hot—over this!" *Motherfucker!*

Coleton hit the steering wheel with his hand.

I ra pulled the golf cart into the Elrod pit and jumped out. Camilla remained behind and looked down at her left sleeve. The blood on it was already turning black. Camilla's eyes welled with tears.

She was shocked by her own reaction. She was an emergency room doctor, but still she couldn't control the shaking in her hands. It was as if her nervous system, a new tyrant, decided to block out her brain and all of its reasoned, logical orders to the rest of the parts of her body. In the emergency room it was different. In those bright, sterile rooms she was ready for whatever flew through the double doors, but here, new emotions overwhelmed her.

She saw Coleton, helmet in hand, striding toward her. The first hot tear slipped down her cheek. Relief rose from the heat of the track, filling her legs, stomach, lungs, choked hot in her throat. She was so glad to see Coleton, safe and done with his stint that she could barely breathe.

She leapt out of the cart. Coleton held out his free arm to her and she ducked under, letting him embrace her.

"Oh, Coleton," she murmured. He let her rest there for a second. Then, he couldn't stand it and he pushed her an arm's length away.

"What the *fuck* were you thinking?"

His words hit her like a slap in the face. They were not what she expected. His face was contorted with rage.

"You could have been *killed*!" he yelled. "Don't *ever* do that again!" She stared at him, studying his eyes and face. Her tears were gone, just hot streaks remained on her cheeks. "Do you hear me? How the *hell* am I supposed to drive a racecar if I have to worry about you killing yourself on the sidelines?"

She felt her own anger tingle her fingertips.

"I have to focus," he continued. "What the *hell* were you thinking jumping over that wall?"

Her eyes clicked back to life. She took a step toward him.

"If that happens again," she said, her voice unsteady, but loud. "I will do the *exact* same thing."

Now it was Coleton's turn to look shocked.

"That's fucking stupid! You jumped over the wall for some dumb asshole? You could have been killed!"

"That asshole could have been *you*, Coleton!" Didn't he understand that? "That boy bleeding on the asphalt—could have been you! And for what? For some dumb sport? For money? For your precious ego?" Coleton tried to interrupt her, but she ignored him and raised her voice even louder. "You're going to write yourself off, Coleton Loren! And you don't even care."

She tried to push past him, her eyes welling again, this time with furious tears. Coleton dropped his helmet and grabbed her shoulders with both hands, stopping her abruptly.

"Camilla, when I saw you by the side of the road I would have given up the whole race to make sure you were okay. I can't have that kind of distraction when I'm driving. Don't you understand?"

Camilla refused to meet his eyes. He gave her a little shake by the shoulders, but she just stared at the ground, seething.

"I think you should go."

"Go?" Camilla asked, looking up. "What do you mean?"

"You should leave. This is *exactly* why I never bring girls to the track." His eyes were hooded.

"Girls?" Camilla lowered her chin and her eyes darkened. "I'm just *some* girl that shouldn't be here?" Camilla let her breath out in a whoosh. "Well that explains a lot, Coleton. That's why you've barely touched me. That's why you flirt with other girls right in front of me." She pushed herself away from him. "It makes perfect sense."

She spun and stalked down Pit Row, tears on her cheeks. She pulled her sunglasses out of her hair and covered her eyes.

She was almost to the exit from the pits to the paddock, planning her departure. She would gather her things from the coach, pack them in her car and drive south.

"Camilla … wait."

She heard the words, but didn't slow her pace.

Coleton jogged up and grabbed her shoulder. He pulled her around. "Don't be such a drama queen."

"Bad choice of words."

"Come back to the pits."

"Coleton, this isn't going to work. It was silly of me to think it would. It's over. You're right, I should go." She tried to turn back, but he held her shoulder.

"Camilla, wait. You can't break up with me. You can't—it's not possible."

Camilla raised an eyebrow.

"You can't break up with me, because, well—because we aren't technically dating."

"You did not just ... You're such an—" she sputtered, but he put a finger to her lips. She pulled back, unwilling to let him touch her.

"Hear me out," Coleton demanded. "If you leave now, I'll crash. I can't focus knowing you're walking out of my life."

"That's not fair."

Coleton wiped the palms of his hands on his racing suit. "Will you go out with me?"

Camilla put her hands on her hips and glared at him.

"Look, I know I'm bossy and a hopeless flirt. I'm OCD and overbearing. I'm fully aware of that and more, but if you will be my girlfriend, if it's official, then I promise—you'll see a change."

Camilla was too angry and offended to yield—even though a part of her thrilled at his words. Would an update to her relationship status on social media really change anything? "In a relationship" instead of "Single."

"Camilla, please?" Coleton asked.

Camilla saw something new in his eyes, a glimmer of something hidden—maybe true, maybe good. She recognized sincerity in his words, the effort he was making, and she started to give in. She wanted to believe in this man, so different from her, so different from anything she had ever thought she wanted.

Camilla let out a long sigh. "All right, Loren."

"So, it's official?"

Camilla nodded gravely. "The probationary period starts."

"Fuck! I have a girlfriend!" Coleton beamed and danced a quick happy circle.

"You have a real way with words. You know that?" she said, smiling at last.

He pulled her into a bear hug, squeezing all the air out of her lungs. Camera bulbs began to flash, as fans recognized him. He pulled back, his face still flushed, his eyes shining.

"And, Camilla, just so we're clear—it's been about impossible to stay away from you. I want nothing more than to ravage you on the hood of that car—right now!" He pointed to a car stopped in pit lane.

"Coleton!" Camilla blushed.

"Wait. No, not the Jaguar. The green one." He pointed at a different one. "That's better." He gave her a mischievous, crooked smile.

"Seriously baby, I knew from the start you're different and that's how I want to treat you. For the first time in my life I've tried to take things slow."

Camilla nodded, although to her the conversation had suddenly turned uncomfortable.

"Can we go back to the pits now?" Coleton asked. "I kind of have a race to win."

Camilla sniffled theatrically, then wiped her nose slowly with the sleeve of her race suit and smiled up at Coleton, knowing full well this gesture would normally invoke indignant reproof from Coleton's OCD. He shook his head, trying not to smile.

"Come here, you little animal." He grabbed Camilla into his arms, and she buried her face into his shoulder.

"I'm just glad you're okay," Camilla said.

"Me? You're the one who could have been killed!"

Softly into his shoulder, she said, "I would do it again."

"I know," he said and sighed. "I know."

Suddenly, they were both aware that a crowd circled them, gawking: mechanics, photographers, and behind the chain link fence, a bevy of spectators. Camilla lifted her head from his shoulder. A nearby pit crew ignored their ongoing responsibilities to watch. Someone started clapping, someone else started snickering, then laughing.

"Okay, okay," Coleton said. "Show's over. Everybody back to work! Nothing to see here, you assholes."

Back in the Elrod pit cart, Camilla scanned the monitors for Coleton's car before it shuttled out of the frame. Ira climbed next to her and held out a sweating electric blue Gatorade.

"No, thanks," Camilla said. "I've actually got to find a bathroom."

"Use the coach. By this time of the day, the Port-o-lets might asphyxiate you." He pronounced it, "ass-fixate." She couldn't tell if he meant it as a joke.

Camilla squeezed past him and dropped to the ground. She stretched out her arms and legs, and stifled a yawn. The constant commotion and energy of the pits, hour after hour, had grown monotonous, and Camilla found herself dazed. Even the rhythmic roar of the cars seemed to dim in volume, as she grew used to the sound.

The gray clouds and white sky looked like a swirling, milky marble, darkening as the sun began to set. Camilla picked her way out of the pits. At the main intersection, she saw the traffic director again, as energetic as ever in the falling light. The black man stopped all traffic and motioned her through the intersection on foot. As she walked past, he dipped the brim of his baseball cap, gave her a wide, white smile, then snapped back to work.

Inside the coach, on the beige couch, Camilla saw a bright green Hermès Kelly bag.

That wasn't here before, Camilla thought. *Who brings a $15,000 handbag to a racetrack?*

She walked toward the bathroom, but stopped short. She heard a loud moan from the bedroom. Her adrenaline raced. Should she leave? Who was in there? Was her overnight bag still safe in the closet?

She inched forward and peered through the cracked door.

She gasped. She saw the naked back of a woman, rising and falling. Long auburn hair tossed over a bare shoulder. Then she heard George moan, "Oh, baby."

Camilla stifled a gasp. Either he was breaking the "Rule" or he wasn't planning to get back in the car. Either way, from what she'd heard about George's wife, this was not Grace.

The sun had set an hour before, unnoticed by the focused teams, and the temperature was dropping. Coleton shoved his hands into the pockets of his racing suit, thankful for the first time that day for his two heavy layers.

Nelson sat on a barstool in front of a bank of monitors analyzing data. George and Coleton hovered over his shoulder, shifting from one leg to the other, watching and waiting. Cars roared down the front straight, intermittent, but unceasing.

"Where's Elrod?" Coleton asked. "I haven't seen him all day."

"In a VIP suite sucking up to Miller and his wife," Nelson said without looking up.

Coleton dropped his head back to see the grandstand that rose above the pit boxes. Each glassed-in VIP suite was lit with bright, golden light, and painted below the boxes were the names of every team that had won the 12 Hours of Sebring since it started in 1952.

Coleton wondered briefly if they were watching—Elrod, the sponsors, his whole cheering section, were they plugged in? Did they know the entire race hung in the balance, or were they distracted by that last awkward shrimp, bowing into a martini glass of crushed ice, and who was going to claim it? Coleton shook his head and turned back to the track.

"If this kid augers in, I'm going to kill him," George growled.

"Trotter's doing well," Nelson said over his shoulder. "We have to keep him in for his minimum drive time or he won't get any Driver Championship points."

"Who cares if that little prick gets points?"

"Elrod," Nelson stated simply. "This kid's his nephew."

"But, he's a third shoe," Coleton said after waiting for a lull on the front straight. "He's not driving all the races, so he's not in contention for the Driver Championship. George is right. Who cares?"

"I guess he's still trying to get a full season ride with another team," Nelson said.

"The shitty little traitor," George mumbled.

"How much time's left in the race?" Coleton asked.

Nelson pointed to a countdown clock in the corner of one screen: 1:03.05.

"Damn it," George snapped. "We need a strong driver this close to the end."

"Agreed," Nelson said, shaking his head. "But Trotter's time is almost up."

Their original strategy had folded like a deck of cards, and they had resorted to playing by the yellows and reacting to the obstacles the race threw their way. Luckily, it had played into their hands so far, except that Trotter was behind the wheel for the next-to-last stint—that fighting time when most teams throw in their powerhouse drivers to grapple for the checker.

"Trotter, pit in five laps," Nelson said over the radio. "Repeat: pit in five laps for fuel and driver change."

"No tires?" Coleton asked when Nelson finished.

"We don't have time," Nelson said. "We'll lose a position. We've got to make this a quick one."

George and Coleton looked at each other. This was going to be a hell of a final stint, double stinted tires and a battle just to keep the bottom step of the podium.

Nelson swiveled and faced his drivers. He was exhausted and annoyed, and asked the question that should have been decided, planned on and stuck to from the start. "Who's gonna bring it home?"

"I'll drive," Coleton said. He noticed one of his shoelaces was loose and bent to re-tie it. As he took a knee, he felt a dull ache begin in his bad leg. He knew George was watching him.

"And your leg?" George asked. "How's it holding up? This is not the time for bravery."

Coleton paused mid-bow and smiled to himself. He knew what was coming. He finished the knot and straightened, eye-to-eye with George.

"So," George paused. "You go!"

"Thanks, Cassidy." Coleton grinned at George's quote from his favorite movie. Nelson did not smile. This was game-time and he did not, could not, appreciate the jest. Also, he hated movies with sad endings.

"Right-o." George clapped Coleton on the shoulder. "I knew you'd take it home for us." His smile still wrinkled the corners of his eyes, but it was gone from his lips.

"Coleton, suit up," Nelson instructed.

Coleton grabbed a bottle of Essentia and drained it. He carefully twisted an ear bud into each ear: red for the right, blue for the left. He pulled on his Nomex balaclava, still damp from his earlier stints. He ducked under his HANS device and pulled on his helmet, carefully looping the nylon cord and pulling it tight under his chin. He double-checked that the radio cord wasn't tangled or zipped into his suit, then stuck it to the Velcro on top of his helmet, so he could find it when he was getting belted in. Finally he pulled on his lucky red racing gloves and stepped onto the pit wall, waiting.

Trotter zoomed into their pit area, but overshot his marks.

"Fuck me!" Coleton yelled. He jumped down onto pit lane, as the panicked pit crew rushed forward and pushed the stalled car back within reach of the fuel probe. The fuel man jammed it in and Coleton heard the rhythmic chug of fuel.

Trotter hadn't loosened his belts properly as he drove down pit lane, so it was hard for him to wiggle out. Coleton grabbed the steering wheel, pulled it off its column and laid it on the dash, which Trotter should have done. Trotter finally stood up in the cockpit.

Coleton grabbed him by the shoulder and yanked him out of the way. He pulled out Trotter's foam seat insert that held the skinnier driver in place and threw it over his shoulder into the pit box without looking. He leapt into the seat, and the driver assistant belted him in. In a flash, Coleton got the go-ahead signal from Max, a quick succession of circles drawn in the air with his finger. Coleton started the engine, dropped the clutch and burned out his tires, fishtailing into pit lane. Before he was even past the pit exit, he was on the radio. "How much did that son of a bitch cost us?"

"Relax," Nelson said. "About 10 seconds, but you're still in third."

"*Motherf—*"

"Watch it, Coleton," Nelson warned, before he could get another fine.

"May I please win this race?" Coleton said, and went after Ulrick.

He soon had Ulrick in his sights and gained on him each lap, a tenth in Tower corner, a half-second into Bishop because he refused to lift and muscled the speed through. With five laps to go, he was on Ulrick's bumper, but an Aston LMP1 rode Coleton's own bumper. He could afford no mistakes.

Coming out of Turn 11, Coleton felt something go, a sudden jolt. Coleton pegged the accelerator through the left-right sweeper of Corner 11 into 12, but then had to slow as the car began to shake and shudder.

"Houston, we have a problem," he said over the radio, gritting his teeth as he manned it through Turn 13. "I've got a nasty vibration!"

Nelson peeked between two monitors at Max on the other side. Max shrugged.

"Must be a flat spot on a tire," Nelson said. "Drive through it."

"*Not* a flat spot," Coleton responded. "I haven't locked up the wheels once!"

Nelson began checking levels and gauges, flicking from window to window on his screen.

"Anything?" he called to Max. Max looked just as puzzled as he was.

"Nothing, Mate."

"Nothing's showing on our end, Colt," Nelson said. "Can you drive it to the end?" Coleton felt like his teeth were going to rattle out of his head.

"If-f-f you promise to pay for my dentissisist!" He bit down against the vibration.

The faster Coleton accelerated the worse the vibration got. As he shot down the straightaway at maximum speed, his thoughts drifted to the cause: most likely the failure of a wheel bearing. Coleton knew if this part let go into Turn 1, it would turn his lights out for good.

He shook his head to clear his thoughts. He didn't have enough bandwidth to process the implications. His job was to drive the hell out of the car and keep Aston behind him. Coleton pressed down the accelerator. His vision blurred, but he held it down, unwilling to give up third place.

"Shit!" Coleton yelled. "I can't see my reference markers!" That was the last thing the crew heard before Coleton hurtled at 160 mph into Turn 1, the most dangerous corner of the track.

Coleton threw open the French doors to the night air, before dropping spread-eagle onto the king-sized bed. Across the room, the TV blinked into the darkened room, as SPEED's live coverage began to wrap up. Coleton looked with pride at the trophy on the desk, but couldn't help wondering how much bigger the first place one would have looked. Peugeot on the top step was to be expected, and third was a great result, but it was still difficult to watch Ulrick claim second.

Coleton gingerly placed a gallon-sized Ziploc of ice onto his shinbone, the cubes clinking and clattering as they settled into place. His leg throbbed, but it had held out through the rattling, which was more than he could have hoped. Coleton picked up the remote and turned up the volume. Nikki Street had finally cornered Nicolas Sagat, the Peugeot driver who had taken the checker, and was extracting an interview from the excited Frenchman, his face flushed red from champagne.

"How does it feel to win at Sebring?" Nikki beamed, holding the microphone close to his thin lips.

"It's *fantastique* … fuck!" the Frenchman blurted, raising his fist. He froze, realizing his mistake. "I mean, oops … beeeep," he said, slapping a hand over his mouth, as if this could edit out the expletive that was already streaming live across the nation.

Coleton laughed out loud, a tired husky laugh. That little slip of the tongue could cost Sagat his job at *perfectionniste* Peugeot. Coleton adjusted the ice bag and felt that familiar cold ache creep up on the pain, silencing it, covering its head with a black cloth bag.

"Well, there you have it!" Nikki pulled the microphone back and raised her chin to signal the cameraman to zoom in on her face. "The excitement here at Sebring is—nothing short of overwhelming!"

Coleton saw Ulrick lurking in the frame behind the pair, clearly hoping for the next interview. As soon as they presented his trophy, Coleton had made a run for it, under the theory: *Don't bask in the glory of third, save that for the win.* Coleton leered at Ulrick; he looked like a puppy hoping for some tossed scrap of praise. Coleton turned off the TV, then let the clicker drop to the bed, and his arm with it.

If it hadn't been for the mechanical, Coleton would have taken Ulrick. This smarted more than his leg—the sudden, but obligatory acceptance of bad luck.

But in a way, this Sebring was a victory beyond all measure, marking a new stage in his driving skill. He flashed back to his last stint, savoring the memory. Not only is the apex of Turn 1 a concrete wall, but the exit of the corner has no run off, no margin for error. Though Coleton's eyes had been open as he approached, the vibration was violent and the night was dark. He had to negotiate the corner by feel, something he had never done, relying on his talent and the thousands of laps he had set down on this track to guide him through.

In the end, he hadn't needed his reference markers, as he swept cleanly through the exit of Turn 1. As Coleton sprinted toward the Carousel, he had clenched his teeth against the vibration, but to him it was a smile. And now he smiled at the memory.

Camilla emerged from the bathroom and looked past the checkered curtains, which fluttered into the wind and revealed a sliver of the track. The hairpin of Turn 7 was now quiet. The fireworks display, which had danced for 15 minutes following the podium ceremony, had ended. Eyes shut, Coleton heard her move toward the bed and lifted his arm to form a right angle. Camilla snuggled into his shoulder, her head resting just below his collarbone.

Outside, tens of thousands of spectators partied like it was New Years Eve. In the small town of Sebring, Florida, the 12 Hours of Sebring was *the* event of the year regardless of who won and who lost. The first trailers wouldn't begin to pull out from the tangled mess of muddy infield until mid-afternoon, once the hangovers had been slept off or at least mitigated by hair of the dog.

For now, the party continued in full swing, but Coleton and Camilla barely noticed the noise: blaring country music, car horns, jubilant drunk voices, firecrackers. Neither bothered to peel down the comforter. They were tired and the night breeze was a cool, delicious counterpoint to the warmth of their bodies. Camilla nuzzled up to Coleton, kissing him lightly on the lips. They fell asleep in each other's arms, fully clothed.

CHAPTER 12
CAT CAY, BAHAMAS

"What's that?" Camilla yelled through the wind. She lifted her arm to point at a line in the open water. The color of the sea beyond the line changed to a different shade of blue, not darker, but visibly different.

"The start of the Gulf Stream," Coleton said. They were standing at the helm, shoulder-to-shoulder, as *La Vie Vite* sprinted at 40 knots through the rolling waves toward the Bahamian island of Cat Cay.

"It will get a little rougher as the Gulf Stream pushes on our port side. We're in international waters for the next 30 minutes, then things will calm down," There was something about the words "international waters" that excited Camilla; a certain promise of adventure.

"You doing okay, girlfriend?" Coleton asked with an anxious smile. He repositioned his hand from the throttles that were flat to the dash to Camilla's shoulder. The maritime forecast had called for two to three foot seas, but until you were actually in the Gulfstream all bets were off. Today was quickly turning from a pleasant two to three foot sea to a character-building six to eight. "Sure you're not feeling seasick?"

"No, I'm great!" A wild smile broke through her excitement. Officially a couple, they had scheduled their first get-a-way together on her "golden weekend," the only full weekend she would have away from the E.R. for the rest of the month. Nothing could dim her mood, not even a faint queasiness. She held it at bay, determined not to be seasick.

"That's my girl!"

The wind beat against their chests and faces, and Coleton kept the bow into the wind to reduce the roll of the hull against the waves. Camilla secured a baseball cap to the top of her head with her hand. Her arm grew tired and she gave up, peeled it off and shook her hair out into the wind. For her, this simple gesture marked the start of the weekend. A letting go, a quick release and a forgetting. As the Florida peninsula disappeared from sight, she let all her other thoughts and cares remain there.

It took 58 minutes from door to door, from Miami Beach Marina, where they stopped for fuel, to the small marina of Cat Cay, a tiny private island positioned at the start of the Bahama Banks. For a brief moment, as the Magnum rounded the palm covered northern end of the island and turned south toward the Cat Cay Yacht Club, Camilla felt transported in time, like an explorer arriving on the far side of an ocean. An antique cannon, green with salt and corrosion, pointed at the harbor entrance to their right as they idled into the marina. On the left stood a whitewashed lighthouse with a painting of a black cat balanced on the edge of a key.

"Look, it's *Hidden Order*." Coleton pointed. "That's Peter Smith's yacht."

"Peter, that's the guy we're staying with?"

"Yes, he's been a friend for years. He's a very successful hedge fund manager. And by successful I mean he spends a million a year just on landscaping!"

A dozen crew members in white polo shirts scurried around the 198 foot Trinity yacht, securing it to the long, protected dock that ran along the eastern side of the marina, between the airplane landing strip and Cat Cay harbor.

"I can't believe they're just docking now," Coleton said. "They left Peter's house in Bal Harbour six hours ago!"

"Six hours? It only took us one!"

"Less than one," Coleton corrected, as he patted the helm station.

"Yeah, those big boys don't have the speed of a Magnum, especially through big waves. But, they do have longer legs."

Camilla wrinkled her brow. "Longer legs?"

"They can travel a lot farther on a full fuel load."

Camilla nodded, and Coleton looked back the way they came through the ocean. "You thought our crossing was bad? Anybody onboard *Hidden Order* must be beat to shit."

As Coleton spoke, they heard a low buzzing sound and over their left shoulders a white Caravan with a blue pinstripe dropped onto the Cat Cay runway, ran its full length and sputtered to a stop a few feet from jagged rocks and sparking blue water.

"This place is booming!" Camilla said.

"Not exactly a sleepy Bahamian town, is it? Easter weekend is one of the biggest weekends of the year on Cat Cay."

As Coleton idled *La Vie Vite* alongside *Hidden Order*, they saw a long line of people waiting to disembark. A tall young man leaned over the rail and projectile vomited. Down the row, a blonde girl followed suit, losing what was left of her own lunch over the side of the yacht.

"That must be the orchestra," Coleton said. The passengers waiting to disembark were all dressed alike in crumpled white shirts and black trousers, and they carried black cases of varying sizes.

"Orchestra?"

"Symphony orchestra. Peter is hosting a cocktail party and a concert on the 18th green tonight."

"An orchestra concert on the 18th green of a golf course … in the Bahamas?" Camilla asked incredulously.

"They're supposed to be on-stage in a little over an hour. Should be an interesting concert." Coleton chuckled. As if punctuating Coleton's observation, a young Asian violinist appeared and instantly threw up, but she didn't quite make it over the railing.

As *La Vie Vite* coasted toward its boat slip, Coleton brushed Camilla's salt-flecked shoulder with a quick kiss and said, "God, I'm glad you've got sea legs!"

The chauffeur opened the back door to the limousine. Streetlight angled into its darkened interior and lit up a pair of toned legs, crossed at the ankles. There was already a crowd gathering on the cobbled street, jockeying to get into the newest and by definition hottest restaurant in the Meat Packing district. A cell phone began to ring from within the depths of the long car.

"Darling, you won't answer that. I'm sure," Justine said with a calm smile. Elrod knew better than to trust her polite words or the façade of her face. Justine Elrod was a smiling assassin.

Elrod nodded and silenced the phone before the next ring. Together, they emerged into the flood of streetlights and sauntered into the restaurant, guided by a set of red velvet ropes like a cattle shoot, neither of them noticing the waiting crowd on either side. The darkened interior of the restaurant looked more like a nightclub than a fine culinary establishment.

"Why do you insist on dragging me to these kid places?" Elrod demanded. Justine pretended not to hear him and stalked to the hostess station. Although Elrod gave her a hard time, he was pleased that his wife kept them in the society pages.

"Do you have a reservation?" the hostess asked getting right to business. In New York, hostesses are generally nasty and pretentious, and it seems the ruder they are the better, because the worst ones run the best restaurants.

An Italian man in a tailored suit scurried over just in time, seconds before Justine could answer the hostess with a face-blistering lecture on how reservations were for little people, flavored with aspersions on the hostess's patrimony.

"These are my friends," the man said. "My very personal friends. Please show them to table 11." He inclined his head to Elrod. "It's the best in the house."

A smug, satisfied look settled like a mask over Justine's face. She turned abruptly toward Elrod, "See, dear? A little more gratitude for my efforts would be appreciated." She smacked Elrod's chest with her sparkling clutch for emphasis.

"*Your* efforts?"

Justine spun to follow the long-limbed waitress, lankiness being another mark of a good hostess in New York City.

"Your efforts?" Elrod repeated with a gruff sigh, as he followed them. "I loaned that asshole half a mill to open this place, and she gets the credit for our table?"

Just as they arranged themselves at table number 11, Elrod's phone began to ring again.

"I told you to turn that thing off!" Justine barked.

"You asked me not to answer it, not to turn it off. I never turn it *off*."

The waiter cleared his throat, and they both glared at him with such burning aggression, that he took a step backward. Elrod silenced his phone again, waved the waiter forward and snatched a menu. The waiter disappeared, and Elrod's phone began to ring yet again. The tone of the ring was the same, but to them both it sounded increasingly more urgent on repetition.

"It's Blake. For the third time. I have to take this." Elrod said, looking down at the Caller ID.

"Blake?" she asked.

"Blake Falcon. My lead trader."

"Blake?" Justine narrowed her eyes, trying to place the name, "Oh, yes. Blake. Hot piece of ass." Elrod ignored her comment. He stood and dropped his napkin to his chair.

"Oh, it's always life or death. Isn't it, dear?" Justine stood, swaying slightly, atop her spike heels. The bottle of Château Margaux she had finished in the limo was beginning to warm her up. She put a hand on her narrow made-by-Pilates waist. "Don't put yourself out. Stay. I'll be at the bar."

"This better be fucking important," Elrod said, answering his phone. He sat back down at the table.

"Would I call you on a Friday night if it wasn't?" Blake asked. "Your wife scares the shit out of me!"

"Speak."

"We've got problems. Big problems." At these words, alarm shot through Elrod. He didn't like anyone telling him he had problems.

"I bet you five bucks the first violinist doesn't make it to the second movement," Coleton whispered to Camilla.

The concert had just begun, and the orchestra was sawing away bravely at their instruments. Five conspicuously empty chairs sat on stage, like unturned cards in a game of Memory.

"You're on!" Camilla giggled, but she had to admit the odds weren't in her favor. The poor girl's face was completely green.

All of Cat Cay had shown up in their finest attire for the annual Easter Weekend orchestra concert. And everyone was checking out each other more than the musicians: who was there, who had gone broke and wasn't; who looked fabulous, and who looked like another trip to rehab was in order.

Coleton took Camilla's hand in his and placed it on his knee. The fleet of white folding chairs had been set up on the 18th green as promised, and the sun had just set, but the light was tenacious, taking its sweet time to filter slowly into darkness through the heavy clouds.

There was a sudden crack of thunder. The audience jumped and gasped, and a few musicians lifted their horsehair bows from the strings. The music continued, but its tempo had shifted from *allegro* to *presto*.

A fat droplet of rain splattered Camilla's shoulder. Her head snapped toward Coleton's.

"I just felt a—"

"Me too," he whispered. His eyes widened, and an oh-shit smile broke over his face.

Coleton leaned over Camilla's lap and motioned George closer. Grace inclined too to see past both George and Camilla to where Coleton sat.

"This is going to be a cluster," Coleton said.

George smiled and nodded. His eyes twinkled.

They looked around at the crowd and watched as other people came to the same realization. A murmur rippled through the crowd, registering the news like a flock of roosted birds ruffling their feathers.

For an instant, no one knew what to do, but at the sudden crashing downpour the crowd leapt up in frenzy and ran in different directions, as if someone had thrown a flashbang grenade down the center aisle.

"I have a golf cart. Follow me!" George called. Camilla pulled Grace close to her and tried to cover them both with the wide brim of her sunhat she held overhead. They had only just met, but Camilla already like her.

They chased after George through the short slippery golf grass, as the rain poured down, and piled into the cart. Coleton favored his leg as he ran. The cart was already rolling by the time he reached it. Coleton leapt forward and pulled himself onto the backbench with Camilla, as the cart picked up speed.

George raced down the dark bumpy road toward Peter's property on the south end of the island, and skidded to a stop in front of Coleton's guesthouse.

"Goodnight, Brother," George said, reaching a strong hand back to shake Coleton's shoulder.

"So nice to meet you," Grace said with warmth.

"Same. See you tomorrow!" Camilla said, as Coleton grabbed her hand and pulled her into the rain.

Tall saw palmettos bordered the path and sheltered them from the worst of the rain, as they ran up to the doorstep and pushed open the door, which hadn't been locked since it was set on its hinges.

Coleton moved through the British Colonial guesthouse, clicking on the soft glow of a lamp here and there. The décor was a mix of rustic island chic and true luxury. Old, weather-beaten objects decorated the walls, but Baccarat stemware and Havilland china filled the kitchen cabinets. The walls were rough-hewn and whitewashed, but the bathrooms were set with intricate glass mosaics and Waterworks fixtures. Beat-up antique furniture was upholstered with Robert Kime fabrics imported from London. Coleton walked into the master bedroom at the back of the house, past the canopied, black walnut bed made up with the finest Leontine linens. He threw open the glass double doors and stood on the doorsill, watching the rain fall in rolling sheets into the choppy ocean.

Camilla came up behind and wrapped her arms around him. She put her chin on his shoulder and watched the waves crash against the high seawall behind the house. The moon was just beginning to rise over the wave tips. She shivered.

Coleton turned. "You're cold." He ran his hands from her elbows to her shoulders and back. She nodded.

"Let's get you out of these wet clothes," he said, leaning in to kiss her.

Their lips were slick with rainwater. He pushed her sopping hair past her shoulders. Her silk blouse sucked tight to her skin, transparent. He ran his hands down either side of her chest to its hem, then pulled it slowly up and over her head. He watched her chest rise and fall. He moved in and kissed her neck, right above the collarbone, and felt her pulse quicken under his lips. Her heart was at a full gallop.

As they kissed, he guided her backwards and pushed her against a dresser. He picked her up by the waist and set her on top of it. He moved forward parting her legs, until the dresser stopped his movement. She wrapped her legs around his waist and tangled her fingers in his hair. She pulled his head back, then kissed him hard on the mouth. He ran his hand down from her throat, cupped her cleavage through her lacy bra, then traced his hand down past her flat stomach. He slid both hands under her full short skirt, drew them lightly up over her thighs, and gripped her hipbones.

With a growl, he picked her up from the dresser and turned toward the bed. He tottered for a second, and she clung to him.

"*Ohhhh, shi—*" His bad leg gave way, and they toppled to the floor.

Camilla burst out laughing.

Coleton held his right leg with both hands and rocked back and forth on the floor, a smile fighting through the grimace.

"Are you okay?" Camilla asked, through peels of laughter. She held her right elbow, then tested it, hinging and unhinging. She wiped away a tear of laughter.

Coleton flopped back on the hardwood floor, spread eagle. "Owwwww," he said. Camilla rolled on her stomach and propped herself up on both elbows, looking into his face.

"Are you okay?" she asked, suddenly serious. For a moment he was her patient, not her boyfriend.

"Owwwww," he said. "My egoooo." They both laughed.

"Come here," he instructed. He put his palm behind her head and brought her lips to his. They were both smiling as they kissed, then the kiss began to deepen and grow as before. He reached out the other hand to pull her closer. His tongue slid past her teeth.

She pulled back. She placed her palms on either side of him and rested on her extended arms, pulling her shoulder blades close.

"I'm sorry, but we can't do this." Camilla shook her head as if to clear it.

"What are you talking about?"

"We can't. Not tonight."

"Why not?"

"Because. It's not a good time."

"It couldn't be more romantic, and you know I care about you."

"It is romantic, but we still can't."

"Why not?"

"Just drop it—" Coleton sucked in his breath to speak, but Camilla cut him short. "I have my period, *okay*? I should have told you before, but I really wanted tonight to be special."

"No way. That's the oldest trick in the book."

"What?" Camilla said, shocked. She screwed up her face. "'Let's get you out of these wet clothes.' Now *that's* the oldest trick in the book."

"If you don't want to have sex, just say so."

"You think I'm lying?" Her face flushed with sudden anger. Coleton pulled his shoulders away from the floor, shrugging as though dismissing the conversation—and her. "Then I'll prove it, you bastard!" She grabbed his hand and yanked it toward the hem of her skirt.

With lightening reflexes, Coleton pulled his hand back. "Okay, I believe you!" He broke into laughter again. "I believe you!"

Camilla toppled back onto the floor, with her knees still in the air, and flopped an arm over her eyes.

"Come here," he said softly. He reached out and spun her toward him like a beetle on its back. He lifted his right arm, so she could tuck under it and rest her head on his chest. He kissed the top of her head. She sniffled, then smiled shyly into the dark.

"Ohh, Camilla. We're a pretty pair."

The pages of *The New York Times*, Sunday Edition, were crunchy from the salt air. Camilla shook them out and began the largest and most important looking article about a series of terrorist attacks in the Middle East. A staff member had arranged two sun chairs on the beach a few feet from the lapping water, and she had settled into one of them after a quick breakfast of scrambled eggs and turkey bacon.

Camilla tried unsuccessfully to stifle a large feline yawn. She waved down the beach at George and Grace. Coming back from a walk, they picked two chairs in the shade of a small grove of palm trees. Grace shielded her eyes from the sun, recognized Camilla and gave a wide wave overhead. She dropped her Longchamp bag to one of the chairs and picked her way through the hot sand toward Camilla.

"Good morning," Grace said.

"Hello." Camilla reached out and patted the chair next to her.

"What a catastrophe last night."

You have no idea, Camilla thought with a hidden grin.

Grace untied her sarong, sat on the beach chair and extended her shapely legs in the sun. She was not striking, but she had sturdy, ordinary good looks, like an aging prom queen from a small-town high school. Despite childbearing, she had maintained a good figure, giving in to only a little maternal plumpness.

"With the rain, you mean?" Camilla asked. "Yes, what a shame. It really was a beautiful concert."

"I keep thinking about all those poor ruined instruments."

"Do you really think they were ruined?" Camilla asked, frowning.

Grace shrugged. "Couldn't have been good for them."

"No," Camilla agreed. "It couldn't."

"Have you and Coleton been dating long?" Grace asked, getting right to the point. But Camilla didn't mind.

"No, not long at all."

"But, you really like him." Grace smiled sheepishly. "I can tell."

Camilla dropped her paper to the sand. "You mean I'm not keeping it to myself?"

"We've known Coleton track-side since he was in middle school. He's always been the sweetest boy."

"I've heard him called many things, but never sweet." *And never boy*, she thought.

"Oh, he is," Grace said with a smile. She leaned toward Camilla and nodded her head. "You'll see. His upbringing wasn't very— loving, what with Lawrence Loren in the house, but he really does have a big heart. I think he's just learning how to use it."

"Hmm." Camilla frowned. "Do you know Mr. Loren?" She'd heard bits and pieces about this Lawrence Loren, but she wanted the full story.

"Not well. You *do* have sunscreen on, don't you, dear?"

"Oh, yes," Camilla said. She let her head fall back, closing her eyes, letting the sun warm her face. She imagined she could feel her skin soaking in the Vitamin D. "And, you and George? How long have you been married?"

"Ages. We have two children in middle school now."

Something had been nagging at the back of Camilla's mind, ever since the orchestra concert when she'd met Grace, and now it suddenly hit her. She sucked in her breath.

"What is it?" Grace asked.

"Oh, nothing," Camilla said. She pushed her dark sunglasses tighter to eyes. She remembered walking into the coach in Sebring, the sexy pale back, arching above the sheets, and the thick auburn hair. *George is a cheater.*

"Do you come to many of George's races?" Camilla asked. She couldn't come right out with it. Not to a woman she barely knew, but she couldn't leave it untouched either.

"Not many, no."

"Don't you miss him?"

"After all these years?" She smiled and tucked in a shoulder to scratch her elbow. "I guess so, but during the season, we kind of live our own lives. Me and the kids at home, and poor George always on the move."

"Maybe you should start coming to more races?" Camilla said, nodding her head encouragingly. "I'm sure George would love it, and I'll be coming to as many as my schedule permits."

"Gracie!" someone down the beach called. They followed the sand with their eyes to George. A female staff member sat next to him with a silver tray and a few umbrella-topped drinks.

"Wanna drink?" he called.

Grace didn't respond. She looked out to the ocean. "I can't believe he's starting again. He had people over at our cabana playing poker until three a.m." She sighed, then stood and tied her sarong back around her still narrow waist. "You're right. Maybe I'll come to the Toronto race." She smiled down at Camilla, then walked back up the beach.

Camilla picked her paper up from the sand and re-focused on her article. *More terrorism. What's this world coming to?* A movement in the water distracted her eyes from the page.

She canopied her hand over the top of her sunglass and peered into the harsh sunlight glinting off the water. It was a paddle boarder, and as the board drew nearer to the shore she recognized Coleton.

"Hello, sleeping beauty!" Coleton called from a distance.

"Hello, stranger."

With a final deep stroke, Coleton pushed the board the final few feet and leapt onto the sand as it came to an abrupt halt.

"I had to make sure you were still breathing when I left this morning." Coleton laughed. "God, you can sleep!"

Camilla smiled back shyly. "Must have been the sound of the waves."

"Maybe you just need more sleep for that abnormally large brain of yours."

With a dog-like shake, Coleton shook the water droplets from his bangs and smoothed them back from his forehead. He turned back to the board. Only then did Camilla notice the long spear shining in the sun and the fish held with a bungee cord to the top of the board.

"Wow!"

"Yeah, he's a big boy. It's a Hog Snapper. They're really hard to spear, real skittish. But, I sat on the ocean floor about 40 feet under and threw pinches of sand above me." Coleton pointed his left arm straight and pulled back his right arm like an archer. "And, when he came over to see what was going on … *wham!*"

"I didn't realize you were such a hunter."

"Yeah, baby!"

Coleton smiled with pride, and as he untied the slippery fish, a staff member jogged down from the main house.

"Think the chef can cook him up with some lemon and butter for lunch?" Coleton asked as he brandished the fish. The young woman pinched its rubbery bottom lip and held it up appraisingly. Its burnt orange cheeks had already begun to fade in the sunlight.

"Sure thing, Mr. Loren." Her smile lingered in Coleton's direction.

Coleton stooped and washed his hands in a swell of salt water, then padded to the sun chair next to Camilla. He moved her magazine off the chair.

"*The Economist?*" he asked, holding up the magazine. His voice sounded both impressed and mocking. "Just a little light reading while on vacation?"

"Look at this article." Camilla shook the page of her newspaper and pointed to the headline. "There was a terrorist attack in the Middle East."

"There's always a terrorist attack in the Middle East," Coleton said as he dropped into the lounge chair. He folded his arms behind his head and crossed his ankles, basking in the sun.

"Not one that destroys 30% of the oil supply in Saudi Arabia," Camilla said.

"What?" Coleton asked, sitting up. "That could affect OPEC supply."

"Sure could. Looks like there were five simultaneous explosions. Is this going to hurt your friend, Al-Aziz?" Camilla asked. "The Saudi you told me about?"

Coleton took the paper from her and perused the article.

"No, Al-Aziz is golden. Supply and demand, baby. This will only make the value of his supply skyrocket as demand increases." Coleton folded the paper in two and dropped it onto the sand. "Guess he didn't need the hedge he placed with Elrod." Coleton shook his head. "Still, it was a pretty cheap insurance policy."

Coleton sat upright. "Okay, next activity."

"How can you possibly have any more energy?" Camilla groaned.

"Ready for a romantic Jet-Ski ride?"

"Don't you ever chill out? Take a nap? You're like a hamster on crack."

Coleton laughed and shook his head no, trying to fling a final few drops of water from his hair at her. He stood and padded toward the water.

Wading into the swells, salt water crashing around his thighs, Coleton threw a leg over a large Jet-Ski tied to a mooring ball about

10 feet off shore. There were two other bright Jet-Skis tied to other mooring balls, but the one he sat on looked slightly newer, slightly bigger.

Camilla heaved a sigh and waded out after him into the clear blue Bahamian water. He tossed her a life-vest. She slipped it on, buckled the three plastic buckles and pulled her hair free from the back of the vest. Water sparkled around her knees.

"Romantic Jet-Ski ride?" Camilla scoffed. "Sounds like an oxymoron. I know you well enough to know this little ride will be high speed, terrifying and possibly death-defying. But not romantic."

Coleton shrugged. "Try me." His green eyes sparkled.

Elrod's phone buzzed on the antique mirror-topped nightstand. In the silence of the bedroom, it sounded like a percussion grenade. Elrod rolled out of bed and snatched it up in one fluid motion. He tucked it under his armpit and ran forward, legs spinning and his right arm extended, through the dark bedroom, dodging plush armchairs and the corner of the coffee table like a running back.

At the double doors, he skidded to a stop, his nose only inches from the fine French paneling. He looked down sideways and hit Answer, before the caller could hang up. He gently turned the oval glass nob, and the door unlatched with a loud click. He looked over his shoulder at the lump in the bed. Justine was still asleep, her black silk eyeshade secured over her dreaming lids. He heard the air-conditioner whoosh to life and breathed a sigh of relief. He slipped out the door and closed it behind him, careful to keep the egg-like nob turned to 90-degrees until the door was flush.

"Talk to me, Blake," he whispered harshly.

"The Japanese markets are closed, sir."

Elrod pulled the phone away from his ear to look at its clock in the dim hallway light.

"Yes. And? How did oil close?" Elrod pushed the phone tight to his ear.

"One hundred and twelve dollars a barrel."

"*Shit!*" Elrod whispered, pushing the word out with a rush of air.

"The price of oil has skyrocketed since the terrorist attacks, and the Japanese markets are a good indication of how New York and Chicago will open."

Elrod picked his way sideways down the grand staircase, taking one step at a time. The pant legs of his striped pajamas were two inches too long, and he was afraid he might slip banana-peel style.

"That's ridiculous. It's all theatrics. I have it on good authority that market forces will push oil prices *down* in the very near future."

"The reports about the explosions are saying they effected OPEC supply, sir. I don't think the price is just reflecting media hype."

"I'm not a sheep!"

Blake sighed. "Yes, sir. What should we do? We have an insane amount of our portfolio tied up in this. I think we need to pull back."

"Fuck that!" Elrod said loudly, his voice rising as he reached the bottom step. "I want to sell *more* calls. The price of oil couldn't possibly go over 117 a barrel. Sell *more* calls at 118. It will pull us out of this hole."

Elrod walked into his expansive professional-grade kitchen and flipped on the lights. Shielding his eyes, he lumbered to the industrial refrigerator and lugged open the heavy door.

"Or blow a hole in our ship, sir."

"Only if we pull out too early. We'll ride through this media hype, and be there when the price plummets to rake in the gains."

Elrod stared blankly into the refrigerator at row upon row of glossy packages, then shivered. There was an entire shelf of the bottled water arranged in neat lines. Elrod grabbed one, cradled the phone against his cheek with his shoulder, twisted off the cap and tossed it onto the marble countertop.

"If the price continues up," Blake continued. "We won't have enough money in our margin account to cover the loss."

"Then, we'll have to add some, won't we?"

"From where, sir? No offense, but I've been studying our numbers, and—"

"Let me worry about that, Blake. *No offense*," Elrod said, twisting up his face and mimicking Blake's voice. "But I was trading the floor when you were in diapers."

A sigh came over the line. "Whatever you say, sir."

Elrod hung up and chucked the bottle of water onto the counter without taking a sip. The drink skidded sideways a few inches, then tipped over. For a moment, Elrod watched the cold clear liquid puddle on the glossy marble, then he strode across the kitchen and switched off the lights.

CHAPTER 13

LONG BEACH, CALIFORNIA

The limousine door opened, and Camilla extended one long leg, then the other, onto the asphalt. She dropped her head back to look at the highway of sky left between the tops of the skyscrapers, and was surprised to see a tangle of stars, bullying their way through the electric buzz of city lights.

The driver set her weekend bag down on the pavement. Camilla hunted in her large purse for her wallet.

"Everything has been taken care of, Miss."

Camilla raised an eyebrow. "Even the tip?" He nodded solemnly. "Who doesn't shoot for the double tip?"

"I was very generously compensated," he said. "Good luck." A large, beefy older man, he gave her an awkward pat on the shoulder and returned to the driver seat.

Camilla picked up her bag and looked around. She was standing in the middle of a street dead-ended by a 10-foot chain link fence, reinforced at the base with concrete guardrails. She looked back up the street. The wide city streets were empty in every direction. Camilla shivered. It was only nine p.m.

She wasn't really sure where to go. Coleton's instructions did not extend farther than, "You're flying Delta, first class. I'll have a car waiting for you at LAX to bring you to Long Beach."

Camilla had learned over the past few months that Coleton hated unnecessary questions. And to him, an "unnecessary question" was any interrogative, provided you were clever and had access to Google. She was saving her allotment of questions for more than: Wait, how am I supposed to find you?

Surely, she could locate a famous racecar driver in Long Beach, California, on the weekend of the Long Beach Grand Prix. She was a doctor, for crying out loud. A doctor standing in the middle of a dead-end street. At night. By herself.

Camilla could just make out the serpentine racetrack beyond the fence, winding through the city streets in the darkness. She walked along the guardrail, and after a block, she saw a square of yellow light, a plywood guardhouse with a single window.

Camilla knocked on the door. A burly guard packed into a black polyester uniform opened it.

"Well, hello there," Camilla said with a warm smile. His expression did not waiver. He stared down in stony silence.

"Um, well, I'm looking for Coleton Loren." Camilla paused, but the guard made no sign of recognition. "I'm supposed to meet him here, tonight. He's a driver in the Le Mans series." She realized how she sounded, like a groupie desperate to get in. Her cheeks reddened. He wasn't giving her anything.

Then, she remembered. "Wait!" She dug through her purse, holding it open to the gentle light from the guardhouse doorway, and pulled out her annual credential on its fire red lanyard. "Here. Look!" she exclaimed, brandishing the pass and pointing to her smiling picture on it.

It was the open sesame. The guard's eyes widened slightly and he nodded. He shut and locked the door to the guardhouse and led Camilla to an adjoining gate. The imposing walls and all-business guards gave her the distinct feeling of being escorted into a prison.

"What team are you with?" the security guard demanded. They were the first words he had said to her.

"Elrod."

The guard pointed at a golf cart. "I'll take you. You'll never find them." Camilla had had about enough of him at this point and just nodded.

The golf cart hurried through the semi trailers and tents of the paddock, zigzagging left and right, then swinging into a long right hand curve. Unlike Sebring, the makeshift Long Beach track did not have a single, straight Paddock Road. Rather, the teams were arranged into a haphazard grid. The soft glow of the tents pooled around the shining, lacquered bodies of the racecars. The light reached Camilla's eyes in flashes like Morse code, as the cart hurtled down the dark, narrow paths. The scene reminded her of the Matthew Brady photos of the Civil War encampments the night before battle.

The golf cart skidded to a stop under the bright fluorescence of a broad white tent. The guard tossed his head at Camilla in a clear signal: Get off. She jumped down, grabbed her duffle bag and looked around. A circle of people sat in folding chairs at the far end of the tent, but she didn't recognize any faces. She started toward them.

"Camilla!" someone called.

The circle turned. It was Nelson, the chief engineer. Then, someone else stood, smiled and walked toward her, hand on his hip.

"You made it, bella!" Coleton smiled. He wrapped her in a quick, tight hug. "I'm so glad you made it," he whispered into her ear. "Wait until you see our coach! Ira somehow negotiated a new sponsor. All on his own, can you believe it? I can't," Coleton continued, without pause. "And he got us two brand new coaches for the rest of the season."

"Really? Wow."

"It's so much better to stay on site than at a hotel. Especially when it's nicer than that roach coach at Sebring." He dropped her bag by the steps to the semi with the debrief room. "Come on, I'll show you the track."

Coleton took her hand, and they walked onto the dark lane.

"This place is so much bigger than Sebring!"

"Much," Coleton agreed. "It's not just Le Mans that races here." He motioned toward another area of the paddock, all the tents facing inward. "That's the Indy paddock. They race tomorrow as well."

"What's Indy car like?" Camilla asked.

"About the same speed, but open wheel cars, and only one driver."

The lane dead-ended into a wider, north-south road. "This is one of the main roads. See that big building?" Coleton pointed to a large dome shaped building to their right. "That's the convention center. Tomorrow that place will be packed with people and filled with vendors selling God knows what … souvenirs, t-shirts, Silhouette sunglasses made for driving, you name it."

"Anything with your picture?"

Coleton looked at Camilla and could just make out the contours of her soft pale skin in the moonlight. "No."

"They should. It's American consumerism at its best. They're selling an idea more than any product."

"What do you mean?" Coleton asked. "I'm an idea?"

"If you buy something at a sporting event, it makes you feel like a part of the action. Those people won't get close to you or your car this weekend, but if they buy a t-shirt with your smiling face on it, then they feel like part of the team. It's a form of transference."

"Are you trying to say you want a t-shirt with my face on it? I can get you one." Coleton laughed. "What sort of idea am I to you, by the way? I'll bet it's X-rated." Camilla punched him in the shoulder, glad he couldn't see her smile in the dark.

"Easy," Coleton retorted, rubbing his arm. "I'm going to need that tomorrow."

Hand in hand, they turned left onto the main road and walked toward the track. The clouds shifted and moonlight silvered the path in front of them. Camilla looked up.

"Full moon?" she asked.

"We still have a few days, I think. The moon is never as full as it looks."

"So, how's the car?" Camilla asked. She was learning. This was the appropriate question or rather the obligatory one.

"I don't even want to talk about it," Coleton mumbled, which meant it was exactly what he wanted to talk about.

"What? Why?" Camilla asked. Coleton sighed, as if pausing on the edge of a pool, then dove in.

"Well, Elrod bought a new LMP1 car from a bankrupt team. It should run marginally faster than the one we fielded in the last race, but more importantly it's two years newer. So, it should be more dependable."

"And, it's not turning out to be more dependable?"

"No, it's not that," said Coleton. "Elrod bought the car from Jose Gomez. He doesn't know anything about the politics of this sport or its players, and he didn't bother to research Gomez. I raced for Gomez last year." Coleton paused to let this information sink in.

"I left because his bankruptcy was written on the wall and I had to move to a competitive team, but the greedy asshole hates me, if hate is a strong enough word. We're actually in the midst of a lawsuit, but that's not the point. I couldn't care less about the lawsuit." Camilla nodded. "The bottom line is, Gomez delivered the car, but he won't give us the engine codes."

"Engine codes?"

"Yeah, these engines are so sophisticated they're more like computers. While the car is on track, our engineers are able to pull data—engine temps, fuel levels, tire and brake pressures, more information than you can imagine—which they translate to us so we can improve lap times. After every running, our engineers download hundreds of pages of telemetry data and study it for the next one. They help the mechanics make adjustments and the drivers learn how to 'sweet talk' the car. Racing has become like a NASA mission."

"And, you can't get any of this information now?" Camilla asked, grasping the enormity of the problem.

"Nothing. Without the engine codes, we're driving blind."

"Can't you get the codes somewhere else? Like the factory?" Camilla said. "Just call them and explain what happened."

"Of course. We called the manufacturer in Europe, but they want a fortune. The code only comes for free when the car is bought from the factory. If a new buyer needs it and the seller won't share it, the factory makes a killing."

"That's not fair!"

"No kidding."

"Well, Elrod is loaded, isn't he? Why doesn't he just buy the codes again?"

"Exactly! I can't understand it. Legally, Gomez *has* to give us the codes, so I guess Elrod's idea is to hang back and sue it out of him. But, that takes time and the race is tomorrow! We've already lost valuable practice time, and the data we mine after a major race in particular is priceless."

"This Gomez character sounds like a real jerk."

"Well, it's not a total loss. Luckily, George is pretty old school, and we've just been doing everything manually. We've had extended driver debriefs after every session, which is a lot more work. We tell the lead engineer and car chief about every errant tic in the engine, every minor problem, and we've all put our heads together and tried to pull together the best machine we can."

"Well, that's got to be great for camaraderie, at least," Camilla said, looking for the silver lining. Coleton chuckled to himself.

"Want to know a secret?" Coleton put his arm around Camilla's shoulders and pulled her closer. "No one knows about the problem. And, I don't just mean the press. No one on the *team* even knows, no one except me, George, Nelson, Max—a few key people. If the rest of the team found out, they might stop working so hard because our chances of success are so diminished."

"What about your other car? Can't you just drive your old one?"

"Nelson sent it to France to get refitted when we bought the new one. We could never get it back in time. No one thought Gomez would stoop to this." Coleton sighed. "It's more work for us, but we still qualified third. We're still in it. It's just that I really wanted to school Ulrick here. I know I could have crushed him on a street circuit."

"You're fast on street circuits?"

"You could say that," Coleton said, his eyes sparkling. "On a street circuit, there's no run off. If you screw up, you put it in the wall. Hard. This makes some guys pull back a notch."

"And you don't?" Camilla asked, aghast.

"Nah, I think I actually ratchet it up a notch. I just go for it. The closer the wall, the more I push. If you're going to write yourself off, you may as well go all the way. It's not like I want to end up in diapers."

Camilla's mouth dropped open. She didn't know how to respond.

Coleton chuckled softly. "What? That's just how it is. You've got to be on a first name basis with death if you're going to get in one of these machines. Otherwise, you may as well take the bus."

"Coleton, I like all your parts. Your arms—" She poked his bicep. "Your legs, try to keep them all attached, will you? I mean, it *is* just a sport."

"It's not a sport, baby." Coleton pulled her close and kissed her on the forehead. "It's my life."

There wasn't much she could say to that. She inhaled deeply.

"But for you, I'll try to keep it out of the wall." Coleton ruffled her hair. When she looked up, he had a big nerdy grin on his face. It made her smile, too.

A metal barrier cut across the road, and alongside it a guard leaned in the shadows of a tree, almost hidden. He straightened, and began to inch out into the moonlight, but Coleton flashed his driver credential. With a curt nod, the man receded to his post.

"The night before a race, I have a tradition. I like to walk the length of the track," Coleton told her. His arm was warm and heavy over her shoulders. "It's even more important tonight, without the data. I try to walk the exact line I will drive, hit each apex perfect, then track out, just like tomorrow. Walking a track really helps you to feel your line, something that is invaluable when you're lapping it at 180 with your hair on fire."

They turned right again, and made their way in the dark down Pit Row. The moonlight painted the ground with just enough light for them to see team boxes outlined in white.

"These are the pit boxes?" Camilla exclaimed. "They're so narrow! How do the teams fit here?"

"It's tight," Coleton agreed, wincing. "Very tight. It's a bad race for sponsors and team guests. There just isn't room."

"I remember we filled in every free space in Sebring and those pit boxes were three times as big."

"Yeah, you don't have that luxury on a street track. You've got to make do."

Finally, they reached the end of the pits and walked out onto the track. Camilla followed Coleton closely as he walked the exact line he would track the next day down the front straightway.

"To be really good at racing, you have to segment the race in your mind and you've got to systematize your actions, or rather your reactions, to certain reference markers."

"Reference markers?"

"Sometimes a reference marker is an official brake board with the exact measurement of the distance until the corner, but usually they are just random visuals, like a tree or a specific window in a building alongside the road, or a man-hole cover, or even a black mark on a guardrail."

Camilla nodded, starting to understand.

"Markers are really just mental notes that guide a driver through the track, since the visibility from our cars is so horrible. After a driver's got his markers set, he will trust them so implicitly that he merely starts reacting to them, rather than watching the contours of the actual track."

"What do you use here?" Camilla asked as they neared Turn 1 at the end of the long front straight.

"Here? Well, I turn in at that Sargento advertising banner. It's my super late braking marker." Coleton pointed to the sign that had been plastered to the guardrail. "I brake later into this corner than pretty much anyone else on the track. I turn in at the S in Sargento. You've got to be careful with banners though because they often repeat, so you want to make sure you are depending on the right one."

Together Coleton and Camilla walked the remaining length of the 2.6-mile track. Coleton pointed out what parts of the track required special attention, what parts he loved to take flat, pedal to the floor, and where the best places to press for a pass were.

They exited the track through a gap in the chain link fence behind the pit boxes and followed a serpentine city sidewalk to a park below the convention center, comprised of a large flat lake with a few bridges arching over it.

"This way." Coleton guided Camilla toward the main bridge over the water. Coleton's strides were longer and more relaxed. He was ready for tomorrow.

"Where is Ira?" Camilla asked, as they ascended the gentle slope of the bridge over the dark water. "I would have thought he would be loitering around the new coaches, trying to soak up every bit of credit he could."

Coleton laughed out loud. "You've got him pegged. It's actually a little scary. But, he's out with his GFE."

"Is that a car?" she asked. They rested their elbows on the railing, peering at their silhouettes in the dark water below.

"You don't know what a GFE is?"

Camilla shook her head no.

"It's short for Girlfriend Experience." Camilla still looked confused, and Coleton sighed. "It's a rook who specializes in giving the Girlfriend Experience."

"A rook?"

"Prostitute."

"*What*?"

"Except a GFE doesn't necessarily look like a prostitute, not the streetwalker, stripper kind," he added. "She goes out to dinner with him, holds his hand, and lets him make believe that she's his girlfriend and that she really likes him and that he won't have to pay up in the morning. But, she doesn't and he will."

"That's horrible! I've never even heard—"

"Sure you have," Coleton said, cutting her off. "Don't be naïve. Julia Roberts was a GFE in *Pretty Woman*. She gave Richard Gere the experience for a week, but he paid up too."

"That's horrible!" Camilla exclaimed again, the shock still plain on her face. "Ira actually pays a hooker for sex?"

"Yeah," Coleton said. "He's got this one GFE in Long Beach. He's 'met up' with her—" Coleton made air quotes. "—for the past three years on Grand Prix weekend. And, I've got to hear about his escapades for the rest of the year."

"I can't even express how gross that is." Camilla shook her head. "Every weekend it's a different girl with him. Doesn't he ever get depressed about how meaningless it is?"

"Not depressed, so much as exhausted. You just get tired of it. The really scary part about it is that you lose track—of time, and people. It just gets exhausting chasing it all the time, always thinking about the next conquest."

"Exhausted?" Camilla bristled. "It's not like it's a job. And, why do you sound so familiar with the feeling?" Camilla was heating up. "Have *you* ever had a GFE?"

Usually, Camilla was careful to sidestep questions about Coleton's past. The facts spoke for themselves. He was an attractive, young, wealthy racecar driver, and women had been throwing themselves at him for years. But, when she looked at Coleton, she didn't see a womanizer. And anytime she heard something to the contrary, her reaction was anger. Deep down, she felt like it somehow debased not only her boyfriend, but her as well.

"Camilla, please," Coleton scoffed. "No, I've never paid to have sex with a girl." They both realized the conversation was beginning to spiral.

"But you've had enough meaningless sex to know it gets exhausting? Not depressing, just exhausting!" She had pushed it too far, and knew it, but it was too late to pull the words back into her mouth, to salvage the night and the beautiful almost-full moon floating on the lake beneath them.

"I've never hidden my past from you," Coleton stated darkly. "And, I haven't slept with as many women as you probably think. I'm really quite picky. I mean, you wouldn't believe how many girls I've given the Heisman at the last minute."

"You're picky? I should draw comfort from that? At least, you're superficial and judgmental, as well as promiscuous."

"You know what?" Coleton raised his voice, deciding to change the trajectory.

"What?"

"You should be glad! You should be happy that I've had those experiences."

Camilla stared at him in shock, waiting for him to continue, but he remained smug and silent. "I should be glad that you took down everything that could walk for the past 10 years?"

"*Fifteen* if you want to get technical," Coleton spat back, but he immediately throttled down. "I have things in my past I'm not proud of, but I've gotten them out of my system. I've slept with all the women I need to."

"I'm so happy for you. And, might I add—how thoughtful to get that out of the way."

"Camilla!" Coleton grabbed her by the shoulders. "Camilla, you should be glad that's out of my system. Because, I can honestly say that I just want one woman in my life: a good, smart, quality woman—like you. I'm over that stage. For good."

"Like me?" Camilla looked away from his eyes.

"No, not 'like you.' You."

She looked up at him from beneath lowered lashes.

He sighed, deeply. "I'm not going to have a mid-life crisis like those other guys and run out and cheat on you all over town. And *that's* why you should be glad I've had those experiences."

Camilla remained silent. Maybe what he said did have some truth to it. Granted, she would rather have a man with ironclad integrity who could come to that conclusion without a parade of sluts, but at least she knew now that he appreciated the goodness she had worked so hard to protect.

Coleton glanced at his watch. "It's getting late." Camilla knew it was too dark for him to see the face of his watch, let alone its hands.

They walked back in silence through the labyrinth of roads to the Elrod tent. She recalled every moment along the way, her own reference markers. Coleton grabbed Camilla's duffel bag from the steps and led her to the new coaches: one for him and one for George.

"Home sweet home." Coleton smiled shyly. These words were a blatant peace offering. Camilla accepted it.

"They're beautiful coaches."

"That's George's coach there." Coleton bounded up the two steps and pulled open the door. "And this one is all for—"

Camilla couldn't see past his broad shoulders, but knew something was wrong. He just stood in the doorway, framed by the light.

"What, Coleton? What is it?"

Camilla pushed past him. At the far end in the bedroom lay a beautiful, busty brunette in black lace lingerie, garters and stockings.

Coleton pulled the door shut. He didn't know what else to do, and he knew there was about to be an explosion. This could not end well. Camilla was frozen, her lips parted in shock. She looked from the girl back to Coleton, as if she couldn't piece it together.

"Wow. AWK-ward!" the girl said. Her voice was husky. She sprang from the bed and walked non-chalantly toward Coleton, as if to give him a kiss, but he held his palms out to keep her at bay. She didn't bother to cover up.

"You must be the new Miss Long Beach." She held her hand out. Camilla just stared at it. "No worries."

"You should leave," Coleton said to the girl cooly.

"You sure?" she asked, genuinely surprised. She looked down at her full chest and perfect body. "You sure about that?"

"Positive." Coleton swung the door open.

"You want me to leave in this?" Her laugh was loud and harsh. She turned and strutted back to the master bedroom to gather her things. The second she was out of sight, it was as if the spell was broken, and Camilla clicked back to life.

"What the *fuck* Coleton!" Camilla whispered harshly. Camilla said the F-word. She meant to.

"Camilla, please. I had no idea she—"

"This is absolute bullshit!" Camilla turned and tried to push past Coleton toward the door.

"Where the hell are you going?" Coleton said, stopping her in the doorway.

"I'm not staying here."

"Camilla, be serious. Where are you going? I had no idea this girl would be here. She just showed up. They do that. Did that."

"Well, she certainly seems to know you."

"I haven't seen that girl for a year. Okay? A year! I met her at Long Beach last year, and we planned to meet here again this year, and I completely forgot about it. Come on, Camilla. Why would I invite you here, if I wanted to be with her? I want to be with you, and I'm in just as much shock as you are."

"Doubtful."

"Is it okay if I leave now?" the girl asked. She was back, things packed, and waiting to leave the coach, but Coleton and Camilla were on the steps, blocking the doorway. She was fully clothed, technically, in a black mini-skirt and wife beater. "I mean, before this turns into a domestic violence crime scene. I've seen it before, believe me."

She looked at Camilla and smiled. "Unless *you* want me to stay."

Just then, the other coach door flew open, and George stepped out onto the top step in his boxers and an open bathrobe. "What's going on out here?" he demanded, his voice gruff. Then, he saw Camilla.

"Hey there, Camilla!" George exclaimed with a good-natured smile. Then he saw the look on Camilla's face, and he knew something was wrong even before he noticed the other girl.

"George. Can you please tell Camilla that—"

"Yes!" George interrupted, jumping to attention. "Yes, Camilla, she is with me. I'm so sorry—she must have got the coaches mixed up!" George started to hustle down the steps toward the girl.

"George! Shut the fuck up! I already told her the truth."

George stared at Coleton. Clearly, he was unsure what the actual truth was, or if "the truth" was even really the truth.

Coleton's face clouded over. He had lost control of the entire situation, an emotion he was not used to dealing with. So, he exploded.

"You!" Coleton yelled at the girl, standing with her hand on her hip. "Leave. I'm sorry, but it's over. Last year was … last year, and I have a wonderful woman in my life now." Seeing that he was serious, the girl spun on her heel and skulked into the dark paddock.

Turning, he pointed at George. "You! Get your ass back to bed, you lying bastard, before you make things worse."

George shrugged. "Ungrateful prick." He stomped up the steps into his coach and slammed the door.

"Camilla, inside!" Coleton said. "If you want to leave—fine! But, first you're going to know all the details, before we do something that can't be undone."

Giving Coleton a stony look, Camilla turned and stamped up the stairs into the coach. Coleton paused a moment, clenching and unclenching his hands, trying to breathe out the rage before going inside to reason with her. Camilla's weekend bag still sat in front of the door, a clear symbol of her indecision.

She sat at the dinette with her elbows on the tabletop. Her eyes were dry, her expression flinty.

"Camilla, look—"

There was a sudden resounding bang on the door. They both jumped. Coleton pulled back the curtain.

"It's Pamela!" He swung the door open, and she ploughed into the room without an invitation.

"Coleton! You have to help me. It's an emergency!" Her eyes were wide and her French braid was splayed out in every direction as if pulled by static electricity.

"What? What is it?"

Pamela nodded at Camilla in a solemn greeting. "Can I borrow your boyfriend for half an hour?"

"Be my guest," Camilla said, remembering Pamela from her hospitality tent. "I have no use for him at the moment."

Pamela gave Camilla a quick double take, as she pulled Coleton forcefully by the arm out of the coach and onto the pavement.

"Okay, okay. Give me my arm back. What's going on?"

"Follow me," Pamela ordered. "And be quiet about it."

They scurried through the maze of trucks and tents, keeping away from the main roads and skirting the pools of light from streetlamps. When Coleton saw Pamela vault over a low fence into the Indy paddock, he put his foot down.

"Pamela! What is going on?" Coleton whispered harshly, halting in the darkness.

She turned to face him and squared her shoulders confrontationally. "Are you going to help me or not? In or out?" Her eyes shone like a wild cat's.

There was such determination in her voice, and when Coleton saw her gray hair radiating in the moonlight away from her pale, shining face, right then, he made a decision. "Of course. In," he said, then gave Pamela a firm, resigned nod.

"Good." She accepted his nod of allegiance. He had just agreed to follow her into anything. "Then shut up and follow me!" With that, she spun away into the dark.

Near the main entrance to the track, Pamela slowed and crept in the shadows around the side of a parked Coca-Cola truck. She took a knee, and Coleton knelt beside her, careful to keep concealed in the shadows.

"You see that forklift?" Past a patch of scrawny grass, by the temporary guardhouse, was an industrial yellow forklift.

"Yeah, I see it."

"I'm going to steal it, and you're going to drive it."

"Are you fucking crazy?"

"Yes. And I will wash your mouth out for language like that."

Coleton sat back on his heels.

"We need the key," he said.

"It's probably under the seat or in the side door, or on top of a wheel," she said. "Construction workers always leave the keys lying around."

"How do you know?"

"I used to be married to one."

"I thought he was a dentist."

"Before him."

"Jerry, the pilot?"

"After Jerry."

"Weren't you a lesbian for three years then?"

"I'm old, I get it. Now come on." She sprinted off.

"Old and busy," Coleton mumbled, and sprinted after her, as fast as possible while hunched over at half-height.

He rounded the back of the forklift. Pamela already had the door open and was struggling to pull herself up. Coleton threw his shoulder under her bottom and hoisted her into the driver seat.

"The guardhouse is right there!" Coleton whispered. "This is insane! You think they won't hear you start this puppy?" Then, for emphasis, he added, "The guards here are dicks!"

Pamela looked down at Coleton. "Some kind soul *may* have drugged them with a gift of decaf coffee laced with a month's worth of Lunesta and my new specialty—fresh Melatonin muffins!" She giggled devilishly.

"God, remind me to stay on your good side!" Coleton swung himself in, pushing Pamela out of the way. "Let's find the keys."

"Right here, Cupcake." Pamela let them dangle from her fingertip. "They were under the floor mat."

"Classic. Here goes nothing." Coleton turned the key and revved the engine to life. "I hope your drugs are strong. Where are we taking this beast?"

"My tent. Make a right here."

"Down the main road?" Coleton exclaimed.

"That's the only way we'll fit."

The forklift chugged forward, its wheels churning up the dirt. They watched the guardhouse, holding their breath, seeing nothing, but expecting a flurry of black uniformed guards to swarm out like an angry army. All remained quiet on the western front.

Coleton pulled the forklift up to the front of Pamela's hospitality tent. Surprisingly, no one had come out to stop or even questioned them. Pamela threw open the back of a semi-tractor trailer parked, nose-in next to her tent. She waved Coleton in and yelled up through his open window, "That pallet—you've got to get that new refrigerator out of the truck."

"Right, that should be easy," Coleton scoffed.

"The old one is broken, and if I don't get the new one plugged in and the food switched over everything will be spoiled by morning."

It took him a few minutes, pulling different knobs and pushing levers up and down to figure out the general mechanics of the machine. Coleton prided himself on being a motorhead and never doubted that he could master a three-ton stolen forklift in the middle of the night. He lifted the refrigerator and backed out. In the meantime, Pamela had thrown open the wings of the tent and all of the tables had been pushed to the side. Coleton drove in and dropped the refrigerator neatly into position next to the old one.

"Perfect!" Pamela exclaimed, wild-eyed. "Now, I've got to get everything moved over. You take the forklift back."

"*There's* a sentence I wasn't expecting to hear tonight." Coleton laughed, and threw the forklift into reverse. Just as Coleton pulled out into the main street, Pamela ran out, waving her arms.

"Colt! Wait," she yelled, her face glowing.

"I know, I know … you're welcome," Coleton yelled down over the roar of the engine.

Pamela beamed up at him and waved goodbye. Coleton chugged back toward the guardhouse. As he rounded the corner, he saw a silhouette at the guardhouse window.

"Ohhhh, shit."

Coleton pulled the forklift back perfectly into the place where they had found it. He turned it off, replaced the key under the floor mat, threw his shoulder into the door and swung to the ground. The guard stood a few feet from him, hands on his hips and thumbs hooked in his belt.

"Thought it was a good night for a joy ride, did you?" the guard asked, and moved toward Coleton. He reached for his … Handcuffs? Gun? Coleton wasn't sure which, but neither was a good sign. For the second time that night, Coleton held out the palms of his hands to keep someone at bay. He took a step backwards.

"Joyride? No … I wouldn't say that." Coleton took another step back. "But I'm *fairly* certain I *didn't* see a guard too comatose at his post to see anyone take this forklift." Coleton prayed his emphasis would hit its mark. It did, and the guard's eyes widened slightly. "I mean," Coleton continued. "That's pretty much all a night guard has to do, right? *Not* fall asleep."

The security guard made a fist with his right hand and punched it into the palm of his left, but didn't say anything. He just continued to stare at Coleton.

"Well, no harm done," Coleton said firmly. "Just don't let it happen again." He took another step back, then spun and walked confidently, if not a little too fast, back across the open grass, hoping to God the guard didn't call after him to stop.

Coleton jogged back to the coach in the dark, grinning all the way. Breakfast had been saved. As he passed through the Elrod tent toward the coaches beyond, he noticed a fire burning in a trashcan in the center of the open space. Beyond it, his coach was completely dark, all of the lights had been turned out. He hoped Camilla had merely gone to sleep and not fled the neighborhood.

Coleton let himself in, stripped to his boxers, put on a clean undershirt and let himself into the master bedroom. He could just make out Camilla's sleeping form in the darkness, and he heaved a sigh of relief that she hadn't left. He lowered himself soundlessly into the bed, so as not to wake her.

After a moment, he cleared his throat and spoke up into the darkness. "Um, Camilla?" he asked, breaking the silence. "Are we sleeping on—*towels*?"

"Mmm-hmm," she murmured, half asleep.

"Camilla ... *why* are we sleeping on bath towels?" Camilla sighed and rolled over with her back to him.

"Because!"

"Cammmilla?" Coleton drew the answer out of her.

"Because ... I lit our sheets on fire."

"What!"

"I didn't realize they were our only set!"

"You didn't like the color?"

"I didn't want to sleep in them after that crazy bitch had been lounging in them all evening. They smelled like Captain Morgan and skank."

Coleton started to laugh. "Wait. You lit our sheets on fire, and she's the crazy bitch?" Now, he roared. It had been such a bizarre, crazy, beautiful night that all of a sudden he just couldn't stop laughing.

He heard Camilla, with her back to him, give a soft sort of snort. As soon as he heard that sound, he knew it was mendable. He knew she was smiling too, and they would be fine. Although it may have been the exhaustion, as she let him wrap his arms around her, with that snort, he was in love.

Coleton kissed her shoulder lightly, a butterfly kiss, then pulled back a few inches, leaving his breath to caress the same spot. After two long, slow breaths, she touched the place with her fingertips.

He gently drew her hair back and kissed her neck, searchingly. Her skin was warm and pliant beneath his lips. He heard a hitch in her breathing. She was wide-awake.

"Coleton, don't start something you can't finish," she murmured, and he heard the smile in her voice.

"Ohhh," he said softly into her ear. "I can ... finish."

She turned her head to peer at him over her shoulder. "What are you talking about? You have a race tomorrow."

His right arm wrapped tighter around her to caress her smooth stomach.

"Coleton," she said, slapping a hand over his to still its movement. "What about *the Rule*?"

Coleton slipped his hand out from under hers, cupped her hipbone, then rolled her backwards, flat on her back. He propped himself on an elbow, and his eyes burned with longing as he looked down at her. His right palm still rested on her abdomen, slowly rising and falling with each breath. Light from a nearby streetlamp slid through the cracks in the horizontal blinds and onto the bed, illuminating her face.

"Rules are made to be broken."

Camilla giggled. "No, you *can't*. I won't be the cause of you losing your race!"

"Okay," Coleton said. He swooped down to kiss her on the neck, then trailed his lips up under her jawbone. She rested her hands on his shoulders, and let her eyes fall closed as she squirmed under his delicious kiss. "I'll take the blame," he said.

She moved her hands into his hair, then pulled his face back.

"Right now?" she breathed.

"We've waited too long already. It needs to happen before we screw something up."

She wiggled her toes, a few inches beyond the bottom of the towel. Coleton smiled into the dark. He pulled himself into a crunch and tugged his t-shirt over his head. Even in the dim light, she could make out each chiseled muscle in his torso, and then, as her eyes adjusted, she saw ones she'd never noticed before. It was like an anatomy handbook.

"Now works for me," she said.

She yanked him toward her, and he rolled on top of her, an elbow on either side of her head.

"Camilla," he said, his eyes burning into hers. "You know … right?"

That you like me? That you care about me? She thought about making him spell it out. *That you love me?* But, as she paused, looking into his glorious face, his eyes brimming with emotion, she knew she didn't need to.

"Yes," she breathed. "I know."

Race day dawned bright and cold, perfect weather for a Grand Prix. Coleton felt the wind cut through the gabs in his helmet like a switchblade. The cold air burned his eyes, but sharpened his senses, like pure oxygen, as he adjusted his grip on the steering wheel. Coleton rounded Turn 11, the last corner of the pace lap, and sped onto the front straight. As soon as the green flag waved, it would be on.

"Green, green, green!" Nelson yelled over the radio.

Coleton flattened the accelerator and swept over the start/finish line. He grabbed the paddle and shifted into fifth. In an instant, Coleton was cleanly around the P2 qualifying car. He pushed into sixth gear and topped 180 mph. He had Klaus Ulrick in his sights in P1.

Coleton looked down the long front straight into Turn 1. There would likely be carnage there in seconds as the pack hurtled toward it, all jammed together from the start. The cars around him roared, loving the cold air that poured cleanly into their engines. He needed to drive defensively for the first few laps, especially since Long Beach is such a tight street circuit.

"Okay, boys … who's gonna fuck up my day today?" Coleton asked.

Coleton set his shoulders and clenched his biceps for absolute control over the wheel. Things could get hairy. His eyes flicked to his mirrors, though he knew he should focus on the road. In an instant he was into Turn 1 and saw the Sargento sign, his reference marker, but it was too late. The sign was in the wrong place.

"Holy shit!"

Coleton manhandled the car into the corner and felt it grasp the edge of adhesion with its fingertips. It danced out of the corner, slid sideways and narrowly missed the concrete barrier.

Coleton depressed the radio button on his steering wheel. "They moved the sign! They moved the goddamn Sargento sign! I almost ended up in Chicago. Nelson, get on this! This is going to be a shit show!"

Just as Coleton finished his transmission he heard tires squeal behind him.

Coleton's eyes flicked to his mirrors again just in time to see two GT cars collide and spin into the barrier. Apparently, they had chosen a similar reference marker.

"Talking to race control now," Nelson told him calmly. "Yes, the signs were re-arranged. Something about a new last-minute series sponsor." Coleton waited for Nelson to yell at him for cursing over the radio, but he didn't. *He must have given up on that wasted effort. Good man.*

"Unbelievable," Coleton said.

"Double yellow flag. No passing. Repeat: double yellow," Nelson told him.

"I saw the accident—I know!" Coleton spun through Turn 3 and saw the corner worker leaning through a gap in the high chain link fence, waving two yellow flags, one above the other.

"It's a pretty bad shunt. Expect a long yellow," Nelson said.

"Copy," Coleton growled. Now he would have to stare at Ulrick's tailpipes while he lapped the track, unable to pass, unable to fight for P1 where he belonged, until the track was cleared of debris.

"Ѕhe sure is a beauty," Elrod said. He adjusted his position on the bench, and turned to the man on his left. Kurt Carter was dressed in an ill-fitting mechanic's fire-suit the team had lying around, but he felt like a Champion driver as he sat in the Elrod pit cart in the middle of the action. "So, what do you think?"

"I'm hooked."

"You can see for yourself, we run a tight ship. We're going to get a podium today. And, if we make a deal right now, I will honor my original quote. If you buy the car later, with another podium under its belt, well then, I will of course have to charge you more."

The man idly zipped and unzipped the top of his racing suit, as he thought about the offer.

"It's a lot of money. Nine hundred grand isn't chump change."

"Believe me, it's a bargain. This car will be worth twice what you pay by the end of the season. Its provenance increases its value every race, every podium—like a racehorse. By Petit Le Mans, you'll have a real asset on your hands, something to pass on to your son one day."

Kurt looked down at the sandy blond head of his son, Oscar. He put his arm around his shoulders and pulled him a few inches closer. Oscar was transfixed, his head thrown back, staring hungrily at the television monitors overhead.

"So, we have a deal?" Elrod extended his hand.

"Hey, kid!" an authoritative voice yelled. They looked down from the pit cart. One of the firemen who pace the pits during the race and look for technical infractions and safety hazards had spotted Oscar. "Children are not allowed in the pits."

Elrod ignored the fireman and pushed his hand a few inches closer to Kurt. "Do we have a deal?"

"Ohhh—" Kurt paused, thinking. "All right." His hand accepted Elrod's. Elrod pumped it up and down and clapped him on the back.

"Smith," Elrod called, and his security guard stepped into view.

"Yes, sir?" Smith filled out every inch of his XXL racing suit. Despite his sporty attire, he exuded cold authority through the set of his eyes, the stance of his feet and his hands clasped behind his back. Smith stepped into place between Elrod and the fireman.

"Please take Kurt and Oscar here in a team golf cart to a few of the best viewing areas around the track."

Smith nodded, and then helped the father and son down from the pit cart.

As soon as they were out of sight, Elrod clapped his hands together and rubbed them back and forth. "Let's play ball!" He sat forward, ready to savor the rest of the race.

"Still a yellow?" Elrod grumbled to himself. His phone vibrated in his pocket. "Speak," he ordered.

"It's me, Blake."

"Out with it."

"Sorry, sir."

Elrod sat up. "What did you fuck up now?"

"Oil closed at 119 yesterday."

"I know," Elrod said, but the blood drained from his face even on the second telling.

"I've been checking all the numbers, trying to syphon some money into our margin account, but we don't have enough to cover. There's no more fancy footwork left."

"Blake, like I told you yesterday, this is the apogee. It's done: over. Oil prices are going to fall. Mark my words. I want you to sell more calls at 121."

"I can't do that, sir. I just told you we don't have enough to cover as it is."

"I have a few wires coming in first thing Monday, and I'll roll them straight into the margin account. Relax, and grow a pair. If it was easy, everyone would be as rich as me."

"I'm going to write a memo to the file voicing my concerns, sir."

"What do you think, I'm going to DK on you?" Elrod's laugh was hard and cold. "Hmmm," he said, stroking his chin. "I taught you well. Do whatever bureaucratic CYA bullshit you want, but follow my instructions. Got it?"

"Yes."

"Now, get back to work before you fuck up my mood."

Elrod hung up the thin phone and clapped it between his hands, as he brought them to his lips, prayer-like, and raised his eyes to the television monitors.

It had been 20 minutes since the accident. The track was clear of debris, but still under yellow, and Coleton felt like a bottle of champagne in a paint mixer.

"The safety car just pulled into the pits. Get ready to go green," Nelson told him, although he didn't have to. Coleton was chomping at the bit, swerving back and forth to keep his tires hot.

"Green, green, green!" Nelson yelled. Coleton matted the accelerator.

The long slow yellow gave Coleton a slightly longer stint; the car could now last longer on its fuel and tires. But he still only had about 15 minutes left in his seat, and he needed to make them count.

Coleton fought through the corners, braking later and later, and tracking out dangerously close to the concrete barriers.

"Colt, we need Championship points, Mate!" Max Cross's voice crackled over the radio. Normally, only Nelson talked to Coleton during a race. Coleton knew Max must really want to make a point. "Don't auger in over P1. We'll take the second place points, Bud."

Coleton growled. Long Beach was the track to take Ulrick on, and this was the moment. They needed a win, and Turn 5 was his best chance.

He rounded Turn 11, the slowest corner of the track, but all he could see in his head was Turn 5. He knew he could get around Ulrick there if he could roll enough speed through the corner. Coleton played it in his head as he braked into Turn 1, careful to turn in early, since the Sargento sign was now useless.

All of a sudden Coleton felt his car pull to the left.

"Something's wrong!"

"We have no telemetry data, so I can't see your tire pressures. Does it feel like a tire? Maybe you hit some debris from the crash."

"Fuck me!" Coleton yelled. The car pulled sharply and he had to fight to keep it out of the wall.

"You're going to have to bring her in. Now. Pit next lap."

"No shit, Nelson!" Coleton said, as he ground his teeth and leaned into the wheel to keep the car straight. "Get the boys ready. We've got to make this quick!"

"We're in the pit window now, so we'll do fuel, tire change and driver change while you're in. Repeat: fuel, tires and driver change."

"Copy," Coleton snarled.

Coleton hit the forehead of his helmet with his closed fist. It was the right call, but he was pissed. He guided his limping machine back to the pits. There would be no theatric pass on Ulrick for him, and the unexpected tire change might put them out of contention for a podium at all.

"Yellow flag! Yellow flag!" Nelson yelled.

"What? Where?" Coleton demanded, his eye widening with hope.

"Two GT cars into Turn 8!"

"Fuck yeah!" Coleton yelled, and slammed his fist into the wheel. He pressed down on the pit limiter as he turned in to pit lane, loosening his seatbelts. "Perfect timing!"

Coleton knew the whole field would have to slow down behind the pace car until the debris was cleared yet again. Since everyone else on track was going slower, their time in the pits would be less detrimental.

Max swung their #37 pit board back and forth in the middle of pit lane. He followed it in, turned off the engine, pulled the steering wheel off its column and set it on the dash.

Ten crewmembers leapt over the wall and swarmed around the car. Someone hooked an air jack into the back of the car and it elevated a few inches. Matt the fuel man shoved in the fuel probe, and Coleton heard the rhythmic chug of fuel entering the car.

Two crewmembers were stationed at each tire, new tires resting upright and ready to fly on the car as soon as the re-fueling process was over. They had to wait or risk a penalty. When fuel is going in, no other work can be performed: nothing, not even the cleaning of air vents. The team had learned that one the hard way earlier in the season.

Suddenly George was next to him, moving with lightning speed to help him out of his belts. Coleton leapt from his seat and hurtled over the wall out of the way. By the time he turned, George was already in the seat, being strapped in by the driver's assistant. Once in, he calmly clicked the steering wheel back into place, testing it back and forth. Fuel done, Matt jumped back and the tires flew on, one wheel nut per tire.

George looked at Coleton, helmet still on and catching his breath. Coleton gave him a thumbs-up. George returned it, as the air jack dropped.

George lit up the tires and squealed into pit lane. Just as George made it out, all the other cars started pouring into pit lane to taking advantage of the yellow for their pit stop. Nelson looked down to the Porscheworks box. "Ulrick is getting out! They're putting in Hans." He jumped down from the pit wall. "George can take him!"

"We're still in this, Mate." Max clapped Coleton on the back. Coleton took his helmet off, and drained an entire liter of water in one go.

"Where's Camilla?" Coleton asked, wiping his upper lip.

"She's watching from Pamela's. She said she'll see you at the podium." Coleton smiled. A little presumptuous, but it was nice that she had faith in their operation.

All he could do now was sit back and hope George had what it took. He climbed up into the pit cart next to Elrod. Elrod was so nervous that he didn't notice Coleton's arrival. He stared at a live track feed, his steepled fingers pressed into his lips, making an indentation.

On the last lap, George was still in P2.

"Come on, Georgey," Coleton mumbled.

George had to make a move now, but Vanderscot darted back and forth to protect his line, and George couldn't pass him.

"Come on ... lap traffic. Use lap traffic," Coleton chanted. "Tell him to use lap traffic!" Coleton called down to Nelson, who was sitting on a barstool in front of a bank of computer screens. The entire crew was standing, watching. This was it: now or never.

Up ahead of the two battling LMP1 machines, a lone Patron Ferrari limped along with some bodywork damage. When Vanderscot slowed to avoid the back of it, George pressed his accelerator slowly. He flicked his wrists to the right and drove off line. His car bucked as he nailed the outside curbing, but he held fast to the accelerator. He had two wheels off in the marbles, and was risking a spin, but he held it and passed Vanderscot.

George shot through the last turn and sprinted past the finish line to take the checkered flag. There was a roar as the pit crew exploded in euphoria. They had done it! They had won their first race of the season.

"You did it, Buddy!" Nelson yelled hoarsely over the radio. "You did it!"

George slowed the car and was finally able to see the cheering crowd on either side of the track. His eyes welled with emotion, as he waved from the cockpit. Tens of thousands of people with their noses pressed to the chain-link fence cheered for him, wild with excitement. Even the fronds of the giant palm trees that lined the track seemed to shake with applause. As George rounded Turn 2, he slowed even more to appreciate the picturesque Monte Carlo-like fountain on his right, with row upon row of bright flowers bejeweling its base.

In the pits, the crewmembers leapt up and down in unison, hugging and cheering, as the Elrod machine made its victory lap around the historic Long Beach circuit.

"Awesome drive, George!" Coleton had grabbed Nelson's headset, and his voice crackled over the radio to George.

"It was you that did it, man. I just took a leisurely drive after you set it up for me."

"See you at the podium, Bud," Coleton cried happily. George would drive the car straight to the podium area where it would be put on display and later moved to Parc Ferme for its final technical inspection.

Coleton high-fived everyone in the crew, jumped over the wall and hugged Matt, the hardworking fuel man who had the most dangerous job.

Elrod jumped down and shook his head. "Jesus, that was nerve-wracking," he said through a broad smile. He clapped Coleton on the back. "You drove like an animal!"

"It was a team effort." Coleton smiled.

"And without engine codes!" Elrod exclaimed. "See, we didn't even need them."

"We got lucky, this time," Coleton said, suddenly sober at Elrod's words. "Let's make sure we get the damn codes by our next test session. Agreed?"

"Anything you want!" Elrod clamored with genuine joy in his eyes. "Come on. It's trophy time!"

Coleton clapped him on the back and smiled. It was a remarkable feat to win without telemetry data, a remarkable feat he wasn't sure they could repeat.

Elrod and Coleton joined the river of people moving toward the end of the pits where the winning car from each class would be lined up and the podium would be erected. They were eager to get there, but not rushed. They had won and everyone would wait for them. The walkway was so congested that Coleton let Elrod walk ahead. Coleton smiled at Elrod's swagger as he pushed his way through the crowd. He was a happy team owner, and a happy team owner could go a long way toward a Championship.

Suddenly, a man's shoulder checked Coleton hard in the chest. Coleton's breath hissed from his lungs. He thought it had to be an accident, so he looked into the man's eyes. He glared at Coleton with hatred and then spit on the ground.

"You should be more careful," Coleton instructed him firmly. *Was this guy crazy?* He was about a foot shorter than Coleton. The man looked over Coleton's shoulder, as if asking someone behind Coleton what he should do next.

Coleton spun around and found himself face to face with Jose Gomez.

"Jose," Coleton spat. "What the fuck are *you* doing here?"

Gomez took a menacing step forward.

"Thought you were pretty cute with that engine code trick?" Coleton said, enraged and taunting. His body still buzzed with adrenaline from the dogfight of his stint, and now he could barely control himself. "You dumb asshole, we didn't even need the codes to win!"

"If your incompetent crew couldn't enter an engine code properly, that's not my fault."

Nikki Street had spotted them and was motioning frantically to her cameraman. He zoomed in just as their noses came within inches of one another.

"There appears to be a fight brewing between Coleton Loren and Jose Gomez," Nikki said, smoothing her hair and moving into the shot. She stared wide-eyed at the two men searching her brain for something to say. "I imagine this has something to do with the legal battle they are involved in over the ownership of some sponsors that Loren brought to Gomez's team last year." Nikki inched closer to the men.

Instead of airing the interviews, which were taking place as the top finishers exited their respective cockpits at the end of pit lane, the producer decided to hone in on this impromptu action. The network picked up the loop and now millions of people watched them on the brink of a fistfight, live on national television.

"Everyone knows you're *through* in this series," Coleton prodded. "Maybe the taxi cabs in NASCAR would suit you better."

"Whatever, Loren. Go back to kissing your new owner's ass." Gomez pointed towards Elrod who was disappearing into the crowd.

As the word "ass" left Jose's mouth, a screw came loose in Coleton's head. He didn't even hear the rest of the sentence. He never kissed anyone's ass, and in this particular situation, he was going to make sure that this guy, who stood inches from his nose, understood that.

"I'll drop you where you stand!"

"Oh yeah?" Gomez smiled with relish, looking over his shoulder at his friends.

Coleton was not intimidated by a couple of overweight thugs stupid enough to go gangster on a hyped-up racecar driver in peak physical condition.

"I'll drop all three of you fuckers!" said Coleton in a loud, but controlled voice. He was calculating his attack, which would come only after he got Gomez to throw the first punch. Coleton wouldn't risk an assault and battery charge for Gomez, but he sure as hell would relish crushing him in self-defense.

A sudden movement caught Coleton's eye, and he looked over his shoulder to see Nikki Street and her cameraman zooming in on them.

Gomez seized the moment and shoved him. The man behind Coleton pinned his arms behind his back.

"Good enough for me!" Coleton exclaimed. In one fluid movement he shook his arms free and swung a solid right hook into Gomez's nose. Gomez's jaw fell slack and his eyes bulged. He went down in slow motion. Someone screamed and the crowed pressed back, opening a circle around Gomez, who had sunk to one knee, covering his face.

For a brief moment, everyone watched Gomez. Then, the thug who had pinned Coleton's arms swung wildly at Coleton with his right, then left. Coleton ducked through both punches and using his attacker's forward momentum he pirouetted, hurling the man headfirst into the BAR1 pit cart. In that moment, the third crony jumped on Coleton's back. Coleton staggered, grabbed the man's right arm and threw him swiftly over his shoulder and onto the concrete.

All the while, Elrod was still steaming happily toward the podium. He caught a glimpse of a Jumbotron screen and gasped. There was his golden boy and star driver being assaulted live on the SPEED channel.

"Fuck!" Elrod yelled. He spun around and sprinted back up pit lane, pushing people out of the way, but it was too late.

Coleton stood by blankly in the aftermath. He looked around. Gomez was still on the ground, one of his friends lay next to him, rocking side-to-side and moaning, and his other friend was tangled in a mess of tables and chairs with blood dripping from a gash at his hairline.

The crowd was in awe. Nikki Street was in awe. The network was in awe. Nikki had her mouth open and eyes wide as her producer yelled into her ear bud, "Nikki! Let's go! Pick it up, this is great stuff!"

"Um, well, it appears Coleton Loren has concluded the fight with Gomez." Nikki had no idea what to say.

Just then, her colleague Brian Horn sprinted to her side. Nikki lowered her microphone. "Oh my God, Brian! Coleton just kicked the shit out of Gomez and his boys!"

Brian tried to knock the microphone out of her hand, but it was too late. The whole world had heard her expletive. Nikki smacked her hand over her mouth in horror. Brian switched on his microphone, stepped into the circle and nodded at his cameraman.

"Well, Chuck. Back to you in the studio," Brian said with a confident smile, trying to salvage the blunder.

"Well, aanyhooo," Charles "Chuck" Grant chimed in as he folded his hands on the glossy oak reporting desk and smiled deeply into the studio camera. "It appears Nikki is in a hot situation down in Long Beach, huh Brian?" The action was too good on pit lane to keep the camera in the studio. The producer cut back to the live feed.

"Uh, yes, Chuck. The race is over, but the pits are still hot!" Brian took this re-direction of attention as his cue to continue. He left Nikki and marched up to Coleton who was still standing alone, bodies at his feet.

"Let's see what the winner of today's Long Beach Grand Prix has to say, shall we?" Brian said, smiling over his shoulder at the camera as he approached Coleton. "Mr. Loren, what a fantastic race today. You absolutely dominated the field! How was the car during the race?"

"The car was great," said Coleton, still glaring down at Gomez. Then, Coleton shook his head as if to clear it, and smiled into the camera.

"I see you are quite a street fighter too," Brian chuckled nervously. Two paramedics rushed onto the scene and began to assess the carnage. Coleton looked at Brian. Brian looked at Coleton. Neither one of them knew what to say. After an awkward second, they both began to chuckle, then they broke into laughter. It was media mayhem.

"That fucker stole my interview!" screamed Nikki, as she glared at her cameraman. He leapt forward in horror and ripped the microphone out of her hand.

"That's great, Nikki. Now the world knows too," the cameraman said as he switched off her microphone. "Jesus, Nikki. A 'fuck' and a 'shit' in the same day? We're gonna get fired!"

"Well, it appears there is a lot of fun happening down there in the pits," said Charles Grant, as the camera cut back to the studio. "More on that, and the podium ceremony when we return." He shook his head and chuckled, as the network cut to the safety of a commercial. "Amateurs."

The producer smacked his palm against his forehead. "Unfuckinbelievable!" he said to himself. "We're in such trouble, but I love it!"

CHAPTER 14
LONG BEACH, CALIFORNIA

As the Long Beach Grand Prix first place LMP1 trophy was unveiled before the excited crowd, a barrage of glimmering pyrotechnics exploded in the sky above the podium. Ira Goldstein, however, didn't see a single sparkle. From the cramped bedroom of Coleton's coach, Ira heard the final resounding boom of the last firework as it dissipated into the night air, and he smiled.

Ira folded his arms behind his head and let out a long contented sigh. He could hear Veronica moving around the darkened coach collecting her things. She hadn't mentioned it, but he knew she was looking for her envelope: the small tightly packed envelope that he left for her each year. To Ira, it represented the only sour note in their whole time together. Ira had been unable to find a girl that could hold his interest for more than a night, so it never failed to surprise him when Veronica captivated his whole weekend. In fact, if she hadn't been a full-fledged prostitute, he thought they might even have a shot at a real relationship.

"What a weekend," Ira said, and smiled again into the dark coach. Veronica either didn't hear him or chose not to respond. She appeared at the foot of the bed.

"Sure you don't want me to go to the celebration dinner with you? Nelson said everyone is heading over to Strikes."

"Oh, no. That's okay," Ira said.

This year, he had brought her to the team tent and introduced her to a few of the crew, against his better judgment. He knew that by now everyone knew the truth about their "relationship," but she just looked so damn hot this year, he decided he didn't care who knew what. She was a hot piece of ass that deserved to be flaunted, whether it had been paid for or not. But tonight was Coleton's night. With their first victory of the season hot off the press, there would be business to conduct, new sponsors to scout and deals to cut, and Ira wanted no distractions.

Veronica placed a knee on the bed and leaned over to kiss him goodbye.

"Well, there's always next year, baby," she cooed. *She must have found the envelope*, Ira guessed. He wondered if she'd already counted it and found the extra two hundred he'd included as a little inflation index from the year before. He liked to keep his employees happy and his women wanting more, so the extra tip was a no-brainer. Veronica rose from the bed, straightened her mini-skirt and with one last smile, she left the coach.

Ira gazed up at the egg-colored ceiling and smiled into the darkness. *Could life get any better?*

Coleton stood on the top step of the podium searching the crowd. The fireworks had ended, the confetti bomb had been detonated and the sponsors had gotten their fill of photographs. Coleton was finally released to his own celebrations for a few minutes before he was due in the media tent for an on-camera interview. His Alpinestars racing suit was completely soaked and heavy with champagne, and he was plastered from head to toe with bits of silver and gold confetti. At last, he found what he was looking for and his eyes lit up.

Camilla waved both arms overhead and he waved happily back. He made his way down the stairs, brandishing a champagne bottle in one hand, and a mammoth silver trophy proudly in the other. He waded into the crowd as if from the bank of a river, and at the sudden proximity of his glorified presence, camera bulbs flashed amidst cries of delight, and fans grabbed pinches of his suit as he picked his way through them.

He grabbed Camilla in an awkward bear hug, his trophy and champagne bottle still in his hands. "That's my boy!" Camilla smiled proudly. All around them flashbulbs popped as people tried to squeeze themselves into a picture with Coleton Loren, bragging rights for their Facebook pages.

"I have a driver interview now, and then everyone is meeting up. I know all our stuff is packed, but can you grab me some dry clothes? Oh, and my keys. I forgot my keys in the coach. And, then we'll meet at the rental car."

"Okay," Camilla agreed.

Coleton took a long swig of champagne straight from the Magnum-sized bottle. "Wow! Shitty champagne never tasted so good!" he exclaimed. "Here. You try!" He shoved the bottle into Camilla's hand. As she took a timid sip, Coleton peeled off his brand new, sopping-wet Le Mans Champion hat and put it on her head.

"Yuck! Thanks a lot," she screeched, as a drip of champagne slid down her temple.

"That hat suits you! Get used to it." Coleton smiled back. His face was flushed with excitement.

I ra quickly pulled on his jeans in the semi-dark. The podium ceremony he could miss, but he knew Coleton would expect him in the media tent for a few quick pointers before the interviews began.

He rushed out of the coach and was halfway through the team tent, when something stopped him dead in his tracks. The door to the transporter was flung wide open. Everything should have been locked up tight; everyone from the team should be at the trophy ceremony, or already headed to dinner. Why was that door open? The team had valuable equipment in there.

Ira took the iron steps two at a time and looked down the long narrow hallway. Veronica was leaning over one of the desks, typing away on a laptop. His first thought was: God, her legs are long. His second thought was: What the hell is she doing?

"What the hell are you doing?" Ira demanded roughly. Veronica shot up abruptly and almost tumbled backwards on her high heels. "How did you get in here?"

"Oh, Ira. You scared me! Oh, nothing. I'm not doing anything," she assured him. But, Ira was on the scent. He hustled down the narrow hall and pushed roughly past her.

"Are you kidding me?" Ira screamed when he saw Nelson's laptop booted up, its screen an open book. Enraged, he turned, ready for a fight, ready to throw her to the ground, outraged at the raw treachery. But, she was already out of the transporter, clattering down its steps. She wouldn't get far in those heels.

He raced onto the garage mats, grabbing Coleton's keys out of the lock as he went. They were the same set of keys that had been sitting on the kitchen dinette in the coach. Veronica saw him coming, and she positioned herself on the opposite side of a rolling toolbox.

"Ira. Okay. We need to talk." She looped her purse over her head and under one arm like a pageant sash, secure and ready for a quick escape.

"Talk? You fucked me!" Ira screamed. His face was violent red. "Did you just steal from my team? Did you honestly just steal telemetry data?"

"Ira. Calm down," Veronica demanded. "Let me explain."

"Explain?" Ira shrieked. His voice strained. "There is nothing to explain, you treacherous bitch!" Ira shoved the toolbox that separated them and it rolled back a few feet toward Veronica. She jumped back, and the wall of the tent touched her shoulder blades.

"Who'd you do it for?" Ira demanded.

"Porscheworks."

"Those sons of bitches!"

"Ira, don't hate me!" She brandished a flash drive in the air. "You know what Porsche offered to pay me for this information? Fifteen thousand dollars!"

"Bullshit!"

"It's true, Ira. And, I need the money. I don't want to be doing *this* forever."

"This is unbelieveable!" Ira ran his hand through his thinning hair. He was beginning to sweat, as he thought through the implications. "You can't do this!" Ira took another step forward.

"Okay, so you buy it from me," she offered. "And, no one has to be the wiser." Ira unconsciously patted his pocket, weighing his options: He could resort to physical violence, or he could be shaken down by a rook. "You could just give me your watch, if you want."

It took exactly two seconds for Ira's brain to process these words, then he exploded. He stepped forward and slammed his palms into the toolbox. It skidded backwards and pinned the girl against the wall of the tent. She squealed in shock.

"Ira Goldstein! What the *hell* are you doing?" Camilla yelled. She had just pulled back one of the large tent flaps and was shocked by what she saw. She rushed forward. Both Ira and Veronica froze. This was uncharted territory.

Camilla grabbed the end of the toolbox and spun it widely away from the tent wall, freeing Veronica.

"Are you okay?" she demanded, rushing to her side and throwing a protective arm around her shoulder.

"Camilla, get back!" Ira warned. "She just stole information from the team and she's trying to blackmail me!"

"What?"

"She stole in-for-mation! Telemetry data. From our car. The information is on *that* flash disk." Both women looked down at the flash disk that was still in Veronica's hand.

"No," Camilla said, shaking her head.

"Yes, Camilla. It's true." Ira was getting annoyed now.

"No, I mean … that's not possible."

"What do you mean, she has it right there!" Ira screamed, gesturing wildly at Veronica. This was all too much for him. He hated when people slowed down the moment.

"Ira!" Camilla raised her voice to meet his. "Relax!" Camilla took a large step sideways, away from Veronica. "She doesn't have anything."

"What do you mean?" Ira demanded, both angry and irritated.

"She has nothing!" Camilla replied again, this time with a smile. "There was no telemetry data from the LMP1 car today. Something about engine codes. They couldn't get any information off the car. She couldn't have stolen anything."

Ira stared at Camilla blankly, processing the information. Then, in slow motion they both turned to stare at Veronica. Her reaction was as damning as a verdict from the bench: She dropped her eyes.

"You worthless slut!" Ira screamed with such force that both women jumped. "'You could just give me your watch?'" he mimicked her. "You were trying to shake me down? And, all along you had nothing!"

Camilla took a step toward Ira now, her arms low and outstretched.

"Just let her go, Ira. No harm. No foul. She didn't get any information. She didn't get anything."

"Fuck that! Let's burn the bitch! Where's a phone—call the police!"

Camilla turned back to Veronica, who was slowly but methodically inching away. She had taken off her heels and was ready to make a quick getaway.

"Get out of here," Camilla hissed, and the girl catapulted from the tent.

"Camilla! What are you thinking?" Ira demanded, outraged not only at the outcome, but that he had let a woman take control of the situation.

"Relax, Ira," Camilla smirked. "You're going to call the police and tell them your prostitute tried to blackmail you? Come on, think that one through!"

Ira's face was flaming and his adrenaline was still pumping. But, Camilla had a point. He took a deep breath and counted to 10, just like his anger management coach had instructed him.

"Are those Coleton's?" Camilla asked, pointing at the keys in his hand.

Ira looked down and nodded. Camilla motioned for him to toss them to her. She caught them and turned toward the coach.

"I've got to bring Coleton some dry clothes, and then we're heading to Strikes to meet the rest of the team. Want to ride with us?"

Ira was shocked that she was dropping it so quickly. But Camilla had come to realize, despite his faults, Ira was a true and loyal friend in a cutthroat world. Coleton needed him.

"We're leaving in 15 minutes," Camilla called over her shoulder. Then she spun toward Ira and pulled something from her back pocket. "Oh, and Ira—" He looked up at her, still dazed. She brandished a small white envelope and gave it a little toss up in the air, testing its weight. "Yours?" She acknowledged its weight with a raised eyebrow. At least he paid well. She tossed it to him with a shared smile of victory.

Enzo's iPhone began to ring. The girl he had brought back with him had withdrawn to the bathroom and closed the door. He heard the water running and wondered if she was drawing a bath in the oversized tub carved from a single slab of marble. Maybe he should join her.

To say that Enzo was disappointed in his finish at the Long Beach Grand Prix, would be an understatement. His teammate had cost them a shot at the podium when he rear-ended another GT car between Turns 2 and 3. Rookie mistake. It wasn't easy for Enzo to let anything go, but this—this was beyond his capacity for clemency. It was a Mickey Mouse curve around a fountain. All he had to do was carry speed and not hit the car in front of him.

To assuage his anger, Enzo had taken the Penthouse of the SLS hotel in Beverly Hills for the rest of the weekend. The room cost more than he made driving the entire race, but that never even crossed his mind. And, the girl—she had been an afterthought, but a good one. He wondered if he might be too exhausted from the race for his planned activities, but arousal was beginning to tilt the scale.

Enzo watched his phone vibrate as it rang and considered ignoring it. With great effort and no sense of urgency, he rolled onto his side and snatched the phone off the nightstand. The caller ID read: *Private*. Now, he was interested. He sighed and brought the phone to his ear.

"Yes?"

"Hey Enzo, it's Arthur Elrod."

Enzo pulled the phone away from his ear and looked at it in disbelief. He put the phone back to his ear and sat up in bed. He cleared his throat.

"Hey, man. How's it going? Congrats on the win. That was major." Enzo fixed his gaze on the white orchid in a red glazed pot on the other side of the suite.

"Thanks, yeah," Elrod said, distractedly. "We had some luck with the timing of the yellow flags ..." Elrod's voice carried away at the end of the sentence, as both men realized that it could have been

Enzo's crash that won them the race.

"Well, like I said, congratulations, man," Enzo added awkwardly, although he knew Elrod wasn't calling to be congratulated. Elrod didn't respond, but Enzo heard his slow breathing on the other end of the phone.

"I hope I didn't call too late?" Elrod asked finally. He was stalling.

The bathroom door opened. The bulbs in the bathroom were brighter than in the bedroom, and the door cut a straight catwalk of light onto the carpet that stretched all the way to the bed. The woman stood in the doorway, her thin silhouette highlighted in gold. She placed a hand on either side of the doorframe, waiting. She wanted his full attention before she entered the room. She had changed into a knee length black nightgown and high heels. The nightgown was completely transparent, and looking into the light, Enzo could tell she had nothing on underneath. He wondered where the nightgown had come from. It must have been folded up in her purse the whole time.

"No. No, it's fine. I'm awake." Enzo looked down at his watch. It was one a.m.

"Well, hey," Elrod continued. "I was just calling to see—" He paused, just before getting to the heart of it. "—to see if you were maybe still out with Scarlett? Justine hasn't come home yet, and I thought she might be out with Scarlett. And, I thought if you were with Scarlett then you might know where Justine is."

The woman pulled the bathroom door closed behind her, apparently giving up on the idea of a grand entrance. She walked slowly, purposefully toward the king-sized bed, accentuating each step. She stepped out of her heels and crawled onto the rumpled bedspread. She moved in to kiss Enzo on the neck, but he stopped her with his left hand on her breastbone and pushed her roughly back.

"No, I'm not. I'm already back to my room and heading to bed, actually. It's been a long day. Tough race … tough competition." Enzo forced a smile that he hoped would work its way into the inflection of his words.

The woman sat back on her heels, her knees in the air, and

looked at Enzo. She was confused.

"Who is—" she started, but Enzo cut her off and mouthed harshly, "Shut up!" There was a look in his eyes that scared her. She had never seen it before.

"Oh," Elrod said dejectedly. "Well, they must be out together somewhere. It was all such a blur when we won. I can't even be certain I saw Justine at the trophy ceremony. Then, we all went to Strikes to celebrate and I figured she'd catch a ride there with someone from the team. But, she never showed up. Maybe she and Scarlett went out together?"

"Yeah, I'm really not sure," Enzo said. "I left the track before the trophy ceremony. But, she probably caught a ride with Scarlett. Are you sure she wasn't at the restaurant? It would have been easy to miss her."

"Yeah, maybe I just missed her."

"Why don't you call her mobile?"

"You think I haven't?" Elrod snapped, then softened his tone. "She never answers her phone. It's probably dead. I love my wife, but sometimes I could kill her when she doesn't answer her goddamn phone."

"I'm sure she's fine. She'll turn up."

"I'm sure you're right," Elrod said quietly. "Well, do you think you can just call Scarlett for me? I don't have her number and I don't really even know her. Just call and see if Justine is with her. I want to know that she's safe before I go to bed."

"Sure. You know I would call for you, but Scarlett and I—well, things are pretty *off* between us." Enzo paused to let the information sink in. "I guarantee she wouldn't answer my call right now. Besides, Justine will show up. You don't want her to think you're too controlling, do you? You know, tracking her down. I'm sure she's safe."

Justine was frozen, still perched, leaning back on her heels. Enzo could tell by her posture, suddenly rigid, that she'd figured it out. She knew who was on the phone and what it meant. She didn't move, didn't dare breathe, she just watched Enzo's lips move in slow motion, each word carefully weighed.

"You're probably right. Well, thanks anyway."

"Sure," Enzo answered. "Anytime."

Neither man spoke for a moment; both were thinking.

"Oh, wait!" Elrod exclaimed. "Hold on a minute." There was a forced pause before he continued. "I think I hear her at the door! Yes, there she is. You were right. Justine is back. She's just walking in."

Enzo didn't respond. He looked at Justine and shook his head slowly, silently in disgust.

"Sorry to bother you so late," Elrod continued. "What a relief."

Enzo looked her right in the eye.

"Great. See, I told you it would be fine."

"Yeah, you were right. Goodnight."

Enzo hung up the phone without looking at it. He dropped it to the satin bedspread. Then, with a sigh, he dropped his head in his hands and ran his fingers through his thick black hair.

"What did he say?" Justine demanded. Her voice was high and taut like a violin string about to snap. He lifted his head to look at her, but this time he looked through her.

"Nothing. I think you should go."

"What? *Why?* He doesn't know anything," she whined.

"Look, it's over," he said quietly. But, she didn't move. "Jesus Christ!" he exploded. "Just get out!" Her whole body jolted as if he'd hit her.

He rolled off the bed, walked across the room and grabbed her purse off the glass table. He tossed it roughly at her.

"Just get your shit and get out. Go home."

"You're such an asshole," she spat.

"Pretty much."

She stared at him, clutching her purse to her chest. She was used to curious lust from men, then open infatuation. It was a familiar progression. This burst of hatred was something she'd never experienced. Her limbs refused to work.

Enzo stood in the middle of the room, all of a sudden awkward. He was unwilling to sit back on the edge of the bed, but he had nowhere else to go. Justine cart wheeled her legs off the bed and stood chest to chest with him. She threw her purse on the floor.

"Don't you judge me," she yelled wildly. "Don't you *dare* judge me." She pointed a finger at his chest.

He turned his cheek at an angle against her and found the stark white orchid again, tall and bright against the silver flecked paint. He thought about grabbing her by the throat with the V between his thumb and index finger and throwing her to the ground. He thought about slapping her across the cheek with the back of his hand. She deserved it. But, he'd never hit a woman before, and tonight, he decided, was not the moment to start.

There was nothing left to say, but he said it anyway. "Go home to your husband. Nothing happened, and nothing is going to happen."

He brushed past her into the bathroom and slammed the door behind him. He pressed his shoulder blades against the closed door and listened. He could just hear her through the door, gathering her things, picking up her purse, putting on her clothes. When he heard the loud, definite click of the door closing, he let out a long sigh, suddenly realizing that he'd been holding it in. Enzo braced his hands on the damp vanity and leaned over the sink. He looked up, and for the first time in a long time, he stared into his own black eyes.

"Nothing happened," he said again, out loud, but he still couldn't look away from his dark eyes in the mirror.

CHAPTER 15

TORONTO, CANADA

Coleton roared through Turn 4 at the Canadian Tire Motorsports Park without lifting and gave a cowboy yelp of exhilaration. He fought through the camber that tended to toss cars to the right, and exited the corner parallel to the left edge of the track. With his right foot pegged to the floor, he reached the bottom of the hill and turned into the hairpin at Moss Corner. His last lap time had been the fastest lap of the race. He could feel his tires grip the asphalt beneath him. They were fresh and hot and he was able to push farther and brake later into each corner. This lap might be even faster than the last.

Although he was making record time, Coleton was only able to cling to first position with his fingernails. He could feel the shadow of Klaus Ulrick less than a second behind in the Porscheworks #99 LMP1 car, nipping at his heels and just waiting for a mistake. Coleton piloted neatly through Moss Corner: Turn 5a, 5b and the almost non-turn of 5c. The tachometer danced as he rocketed through the gears and shot full-speed down the back straightaway. The car quickly and easily reached 186 mph, and Coleton capitalized on his only free seconds to stretch out his fingers and roll back his shoulders. He sprinted through the slight bends of Turn 6 and 7, which are really only turns in name, full throttle without difficulty.

The Porscheworks team had fielded two cars for the race, and as Coleton hurtled down the straightaway, he suddenly had Bruno König in the other Porscheworks #98 LMP1 car in his sights. In a blink, he came up on the car like it was standing still. Into Turn 8 at the end of the long straight, the #98 hung toward the middle of the track.

Seeing his opportunity, Coleton nudged to the right edge of the track, ready to stove-it into the corner. With his tires hot and sweet, Coleton knew he could out brake anyone, so he planned to slam down the inside and take the #98 car. Coleton crested the hill, let the car settle briefly and was about to brake, when without warning, König slammed his brakes so hard the rear of his car squirmed wildly left and right. Coleton jammed down the brake pedal. His tires squealed, as he veered left to avoid slamming into the back of the #98 car on the fastest turn of the track.

"What the hell?" Coleton yelled. Now well into the Esses, Coleton only had a few paces to gather up the car before heading into a quick Turn 9: brake, downshift, turn, back to gas.

"That asshole just shut the door on me!" Coleton yelled over the radio. "And, now my tires are flat spotted from slamming the brakes!"

"Stay calm, Mate," Nelson's voice crackled to life in Coleton's headset.

Out of Turn 9, Coleton lined the car up on the left, gently tapped the brake and manned the speed into the right-hander of Turn 10 to boost his exit speed. If he carried enough velocity through Turn 10 he could pass the #98 car on the short straight in front of pit row. Mid-corner, Coleton pegged the accelerator to the floor and let the car track out, grabbing some new pavement on the outside of the curbing—a little trick he found that gave him a jump start across the start/finish line. On the straight, Coleton jerked to the left, then sharply right, trying to get a line around the other car, but every time he moved, the German mirrored his movement to block him. Coleton had to brake to keep from hitting the slower #98 car, when he should have been full throttle.

"Fuck!" Coleton screamed, furious at being forced to waste his hard-earned momentum with a tap on the brakes. He remained inches behind the #98 car as they raced down the straight.

"The car in front of you is down a lap. Repeat. The car in front of you is *not* fighting for position."

"Copy," Coleton growled.

"Do not tangle with him, Mate. Give him some space until you can pass cleanly. They'd love to take you out of the race with their B team."

Coleton swerved back and forth inches behind the bumper of the Porscheworks LMP1 in front of him. He had the speed to pass into Turn 1 and Turn 2, which is a dangerous and completely blind downhill turn, but the #98 LMP1 swerved erratically to protect his line into both corners.

"There's still an hour left in the race. Don't do anything rash," Nelson warned again.

Into bumpy Turn 3, Coleton knew that the natural camber slopes away from the apex and if you get back to power too quickly you get tossed off at the exit. Coleton slowed slightly. In a flash, the other Porscheworks car, the #99 LMP1, blurred past him and shot past the #98 car, which suddenly jogged right allowing his teammate to pass and catch the best section of exit curbing.

"What the hell!" Coleton exploded. "I just got passed by Ulrick!" Coleton jammed down the accelerator trying to freight-train Ulrick and get past the #98 car while there was a small gap. Seeing this move coming, the #98 car swerved roughly sideways and Coleton had to brake to prevent contact. The #98 wanted a sacrificial shunt. Porscheworks was taunting him, hoping to end his day at the races with their slower car to ensure the victory of their faster one.

Coleton knew he could take Turn 4 flat, but stuck behind the #98 he had to brake into the corner. He was livid. Coleton painfully trailed the #98 LMP1 car through the hairpin of Moss Corner and had no room to pass on the back straight or the Esses.

"Lap time?" Coleton demanded into his headset, as they again flew bumper to bumper down the front straight past the start/finish.

"1:10:682."

"I'm down three seconds because of this asshole!"

"We've already contacted race control, but they haven't called it yet."

"What bullshit!" Coleton roared.

Sitting high up in the Elrod pit cart, George saw the #98 LMP1 bob and weave in front of their car. He threw his hands into the air in anger. "This is unbelievable! It's not even sporting. How is race control *not* penalizing them for this?" He looked to Elrod, who was sitting on the leather bench next to him, in disbelief.

Always quick to take control, Elrod turned and yelled down from the pit box. "Nelson, I demand that you do something!" Nelson sat on a barstool analyzing data in front of a bank of monitors. "They're fighting dirty! Coleton can't get around him. And Ulrick's getting away!"

With his back still turned to Elrod, Nelson rolled his eyes. He had already contacted race control to no avail. There was not much more he could do. Coleton was a superior driver and eventually the #98 car would make a mistake and Coleton would blow past him. But, when? Coleton was losing his patience. Nelson looked between two computer monitors to Max Cross on the other side of the table.

"Max, run down to the Porscheworks pit box and tell them to get control of their driver!"

Max nodded, recognizing this for what it was: a concession to a team owner not used to feeling powerless. This strategy of politics rarely worked, but at least he could try to disrupt the other team by making a scene and calling them out on their dirty plays face-to-face. He stood up and jogged down pit row toward the Porscheworks pit box.

Nelson looked up into the pit cart, past Elrod to meet George's eyes. They both knew it was going to get ugly. Coleton was enraged and was quickly approaching his tipping point. If they didn't get him out of the car, he would try something risky. Maybe it would work, but maybe it wouldn't and they'd be out of the race in a flash. George gave him a firm nod, then slid past Elrod and hopped down from the pit cart. He quickly drained a bottle of water and pulled on his fireproof balaclava.

Nelson pulled the small microphone attached to his headset close to his lips. "Pit this lap," he instructed Coleton calmly. "Pit this lap. We're losing too much time behind this Kraut. Come in for new tires, fuel and a driver change. George will go out with fresh rubber and clean air."

"Copy," Coleton growled.

Coleton knew that when a competitor isn't playing by the rules and race control won't call it, a team often brings their car in for an early pit stop. By the time the car reenters the race, it will be at a different part of the track than the offending car and it can get safely back to race pace. It was the appropriate call to make, but Coleton hated to concede to foul play. He wanted to fight fire with fire.

Camilla took a small sip of champagne. It was serious champagne and she let the bubbles dance on her tongue. She twisted the crystal stem between her fingers and looked down nonchalantly for the make. *Of course it's Baccarat.*

"Cheers, darling." Justine raised her glass to Camilla and smiled.

Camilla returned the smile and took a longer sip. She looked around the crowded suite, full to the brim with Miller Sunglasses' top retailers from around the world. Elrod had rented out the suite and organized a trackside party for the Millers as a little perk for their sponsorship dollars.

Trackside suites were usually just concrete boxes with air-conditioning and an elevated view of the track. But, Justine had put her mark on this one. She had framed vintage racing posters on the walls and expensive carpets covering the industrial gray carpeting. There was an immense flat screen TV mounted in the upper right hand corner of the wall of glass overlooking the track, so in a single glance you could see the television footage of the race and the live action on the front straight.

"Coleton seemed off the pace, no?" Justine asked. The corners of her lips curled into a smile; she was pleased with herself for picking up the lingo. "George better hold third position—at least! I want a podium. I'm having a great hair day and I deserve to be up there getting photographed."

"It looked like Coleton was being blocked," Camilla responded tartly, not answering the question. Camilla knew Justine couldn't care less about racing. Justine was a fickle fan and attended races only for the win. She justified her husband's entire investment in racing for the few seconds of fame, and pictures with handsome sweaty drivers glowing with victory to rub in the noses of her friends—the fabulously rich, but enduringly desperate housewives of New York City.

They watched the television as a camera zoomed in on the Elrod Racing LMP1. George was just catching up to a Porscheworks LMP1 car at the end of the long, tree-lined straight. Camilla suddenly thought about Grace. Quiet, sweet Grace was somewhere at the track. It was the first race Grace had attended all year. She had been quick to deflect Camilla's invitation to the crowded Miller suite, and Camilla hadn't seen her since.

"Isn't that the car that was blocking Coleton before?" Camilla asked intently, staring up at the television screen, as their LMP1 zigzagged behind the black and green #98 car.

"You're asking *me*?" Justine raised an eyebrow. She drained her flute and stood up from the small table. It was a clear message to Camilla that she was boring her. "If you will excuse me?"

Camilla nodded, and when Justine was out of earshot, she added, "With pleasure." Camilla looked down at her watch. She would give Coleton 15 minutes in the pit box to review data with the engineers and cool-down from his stint, and then she'd find him so they could watch the rest of the race together.

Now that he was out of the car safely, she gave a slow sigh of relief. She didn't realize how much tension she had been holding in her neck, and now she purposefully let her shoulders drop and rolled them backwards. She re-directed her attention to the television screen. It was difficult to keep up with the race from the suite. It wasn't like being in the pits. She knew Coleton wanted her to be social with his sponsors. It was good for business, but it made her nervous to be removed from the action.

The sun beat down on the black roof of the pit cart. Elrod wiped a bead of sweat off his forehead. His eyes were glued to the bank of television screens above his head. He was happy with the pit stop: fairly efficient, no penalties for stupid mistakes, and now George was out on the track on fresh rubber.

He drummed his fingers on his knees, waiting for George to make a move, to fight his way back into first place. That's what he paid him for: to pull a rabbit out of the hat.

"George has the knife between his teeth!" Nelson called up to the pit box to encourage Elrod. "His elbows are in the mud. Give him two laps, and we'll be in the lead."

Elrod nodded in agreement. All of a sudden, his phone began to vibrate in his pocket. He pulled it into the sunlight. *Blake Falcon.*

"Shit." Elrod never ignored Blake's calls, especially now after the recent catastrophe. He couldn't afford to. He hopped down from the pit cart and made his way out of the pit box.

"Go ahead," Elrod demanded, his index finger plugged his left ear, his phone pressed tightly to the right. He was standing with his back against the chain link fence that separated Pit Row from the paddock, as far from the roaring cars as he could get without actually removing himself from the combat.

"So, I got a call from Roger," Blake began.

"Speak up!" Elrod demanded, bowing his head to hear better. Elrod could only hear every few seconds, when there was a lull on the front straight. The conversation would be relegated to quick, punctuated bursts.

"We don't have enough to cover our margin."

"What?" Elrod yelled into his phone above the roaring engines.

"The price of oil is up to 121 a barrel, and unless we direct liquid funds to our margin account, then—"

"I know what a margin call is, you imbecile!" Elrod erupted. "I gave that little shit a start in this business. He used to be my intern! He couldn't even make a decent cup of coffee and now *he's* calling *us?*"

"We better come up with the cash fast, because Roger can liquidate our position and solidify our losses without consulting us, per the margin agreement."

"My money is tied up in other places right now!" Elrod yelled, but a Corvette GT car passed on the front straight and drowned out his words.

"We're way over levered and this could implode our entire—"

Elrod let the phone drop away from his ear, as the Elrod Racing engineers leapt to their feet all at once, shouting and pointing at their computer monitors. Then, a hush fell. Jaws dropped in silence as an image broadcast on their screens.

Camilla watched the movement on the television in the VIP suite, but the picture was incomprehensible to her: bright glints of twisted carbon fiber could just be seen through the thick black smoke. She watched the television, horrified and frozen, eyes glued to the screen, as the broadcast began the replay. It was their car.

George had quickly caught up to the #98 LMP1, and desperate to pass him, got reckless into Turn 2, a completely blind downhill turn. In a split second, as George crested the hill, he saw a broken Corvette GT car in the middle of the track. But, it was too late. He had carried too much speed into the corner and the car had almost no down force as it crested the top of the hill. There was not enough weight bearing down on the wheels and not enough grip to dodge left.

George crashed into the Corvette, and with little down force on his side, the car shot up. Time seemed to blur into slow motion as the LMP1 soared. Then with a cry of twisting metal his front bumper caught the ground and handsprung the car. It slid upside down for a few feet and rocked slowly to a stop.

Back to the live feed, seconds stretched to interminable minutes as Camilla waited in the crowded suite. There was no movement on the screen, and the silence of the room was punctuated by only a few hushed expletives. Through the smoke and mess of crumpled metal, finally George emerged from the car, somehow on his own power. He took a step from the wreck, but stumbled and fell. No one in the suite moved. They watched him spring to his feet. Someone whistled low in relief. Then, George swayed. Camilla gasped. He slowly laid back down on the ground, spread eagle on his back as if preparing for a snow angel, and he didn't move again. It was a bad sign, a very bad sign.

With a start, Camilla felt the blood rush through her veins. She realized her hand was still clapped over her mouth. She knew she needed to move. She had to find Grace, and quick. *Where could she be and did she know?* She turned without a word and fled the crowded suite.

Grace had settled in at a table in a quiet corner of Pamela's hospitality tent. Only one other person was under the large tent, a mechanic with a Flying Lizard racing t-shirt. He was slowly, methodically eating a plate of spaghetti. Everyone else was either working in the pits or stationed around the track to watch the race. Pamela was enthroned at her card table near the entrance to the tent, entering individual names and teams into a log book to remind her who had lunched at her buffet that afternoon, while her memory was still fresh.

Grace felt uncomfortable hanging around the pits with nothing to do while George was in the car. She hated feeling like she needed to make small talk with the sponsors, or with passing mechanics that were too busy to chat but trying not to be rude. Not to mention, Arthur Elrod quite frankly scared her. So, on the rare occasion she did attend one of George's races, Pamela's tent became her hideout. As soon as George got in the car, she would disappear to Pamela's, where she could sit quietly with a cup of coffee and watch the race on one of the television screens without the need for forced small talk about a sport she knew little and with people she didn't know at all. Pamela was the only one wise to her routine, and she knew enough to leave Grace alone.

It was the tone of the announcer's voice that brought Pamela's nose from her ledgers. She looked up at the television screen. She had been on the circuit long enough that her eye was trained. In a second, she knew there was an accident, she knew it was bad and she could just make out through the smoke that it was George's car, all before the announcer could begin on the details. She pushed her chair back so quickly that it tipped over, but she was already standing. She rushed to the far end of the tent toward Grace.

Grace was sitting straight-backed. Her lips were pursed and her eyes wide, but her face was otherwise devoid of emotion. Pamela rushed in front of her, blocking her view of the television. Grace did not move to see around Pamela, she just stared blankly in front of her.

"Your phone, sweetie. Give me your phone." Grace looked vacantly up at Pamela. Pamela saw Grace's iPhone on the chair next to her. Careful to remain between Grace and the television screen, she snatched it up. Luckily, it wasn't locked with a code, and she scrolled through Grace's contact list until she saw Camilla Harlow's name. She hit the call button.

"Grace!" It was Camilla's voice, high-pitched, but recognizable.

"No. It's Pamela. She's with me." Camilla's only response was to hang up the phone and sprint. It only took a few minutes for her to arrive at Pamela's. She rushed through the tent flaps, and immediately saw Grace in the corner, still seated. Pamela was sitting next to her, holding one of Grace's hands between the palms of her own, as if trying to warm it up.

"Grace!"

Grace looked slowly up, tilting her head back to see Camilla. Her eyes flickered with recognition, and then she began to sob. She slumped over the table, her shoulders shaking. Camilla wrapped her arm around Grace's shoulders and looked wildly at Pamela. But, Pamela looked back at her equally unsure of what to do.

"Take my Corolla. You've got to meet them at the hospital. Just worry about getting Grace there. Coleton will take care of George."

"Where will they take him?"

"I'm not sure. There is a local hospital near here. But, if it is bad—they'll take him straight to Toronto General." Pamela paused, thinking. Unconsciously, she glanced back at the television screen. "I would head toward Toronto. It's about an hour drive."

Camilla nodded gravely.

Coleton couldn't hear the phone ringing in his pocket. The noise in the helicopter was physically abrasive. Camilla had been trying him over and over: redial, hang-up, redial, since they left the racetrack. But, she couldn't get through. Coleton sat in the co-pilot seat, but was turned as far around as possible. There were three paramedics working on George who lay flat out in the aisle in a makeshift triage. All of a sudden, Coleton felt his phone vibrate against his leg. He pulled it out of his pocket and answered.

"Camilla?" he yelled above the noise. "We're in a helicopter headed for Toronto General Hospital. Can you hear me?"

"Yes!" Camilla yelled into her cell phone. She reached over and squeezed Grace's hand. "I can hear you."

"Thank God Nico had this bird at the track. It's one of his client's. I can't believe they didn't have a medical chopper at the most dangerous track in the series. It was a big point of contention at the driver's meeting this morning."

"What's that?" Camilla asked, pressing the phone even tighter to her ear, trying to hear him.

"You're with Grace?"

"Yes, I have Grace."

"Meet us at Toronto General."

"We're headed there now."

Grace hadn't said a word since they left the racetrack. She had just stared straight ahead, biting her lip. Camilla had somehow managed to sustain a steady buzz of comforting words, a metronomic drone of sympathy and hope. Now that Camilla had finally gotten through to someone who was with George, Grace came alive and began to plead with her.

"Please, please let me talk to George." Her voice was small and childlike, desperate.

"Grace wants to talk to George."

"Are you high?" Coleton responded harshly. "George has been fully unconscious since we left the track. It's bad, Camilla. It's really bad." Camilla sucked in her breath, not at his words, but at his tone. Until that moment, she didn't know how bad it was. But when she heard the unfamiliar note of terror in Coleton's voice, she knew it was serious. She knew it was life or death.

Camilla glanced back at Grace's face. "He's fine Grace. He's going to be just fine. But he has an oxygen mask on, so you can't talk to him right now." Camilla nodded encouragingly. "But he'll be fine."

A sleek black limousine paused at a guardhouse before pulling through a high chain-link fence onto the smooth tarmac of the Toronto Buttonville private airport. Through the tinted window Elrod saw his silver G-4 waiting for him, engines warming up. The sun was just beginning to set and he saw its final rays glinting orange and red as it rolled off the side of the plane. A carpet had been unrolled before the set of compact steps that lead to the fuselage. A beautiful blonde flight attendant stood at the top of the steps and waved at the limo as it came to a stop.

The chauffer hustled to open Elrod's door, but as he cracked it open, Elrod motioned for him to shut it again.

Elrod sunk into the comfortable leather seat and let his head fall backward. He sat like this, motionless for a few moments, thinking. The terrorist attacks on the oil refinery, the crash at the track—God only knew if he still had two living drivers and how much it would cost to get the car back together, the phone call from Blake about the margin call, everything seemed to be crashing down around his shoulders. He needed liquidity to stay afloat and he didn't have it.

"Fuck it," he said out loud. He raised his cell phone and pressed the call button. The number was already on the screen and at his touch the call initiated.

"I will take the meeting," Elrod began with no pleasantries, without even a simple greeting. "I am interested in his offer, and will meet his man in New York—tomorrow. Tell me where and what time."

Elrod hung up without waiting for a response. They would get back to him with the details. He continued to sit alone in the limo, his head thrown back. He could hear the jet engines running warm outside, but continued to stare at the silent black ceiling, thinking.

The last push of moonlight filtered through the horizontal blinds into the small, cold hospital room as night slowly eased toward day. Coleton sat at one end of a black vinyl couch, and Camilla lay asleep with her head in his lap. She had to pull her knees to her chest in order to fit beside him.

On the opposite side of the hospital bed that dominated the room, Grace sat in a straight-back chair that she'd pulled as close to George as she could get. He had yet to stir since they had brought him in from surgery a few hours earlier. Grace rested her forehead on the bed's metal guardrail.

After a few quiet minutes, Coleton guessed Grace was finally asleep. Coleton stroked Camilla's hair back off her forehead. He was the only conscious one in the room, the only one aware that the long night had finally given way to dawn. He pulled the thin hospital blanket up around Camilla's shoulder.

The door swung open, and a woman rushed in. She was dressed in a fitted sweater dress, had a scarf tied Hepburn-style around her hair and black sunglasses that covered most of her face. As she passed the threshold of the door, she swept back the scarf and shook out her softly curled auburn hair. In a fluid motion she shook off her sunglasses, dropped them into her green Hermès Kelly purse and stopped at the foot of George's bed.

"Oh, George!" she moaned. One of his legs was suspended in the air in a sling, and she dropped her head to kiss it gently.

Grace lifted her head, blinking her swollen eyelids at their beautiful, but unannounced guest.

"Can I help you?" Grace asked, as she painfully rolled first one, then the other shoulder back into an upright position.

"Who are you?" the woman demanded of Grace. She adjusted the scarf, which now hung in a loose knot around her neck, framing her face. "Never mind that. How is he? They said he is in a medically induced coma?" she asked in a strong confident tone that demanded more than it inquired.

"Who am I?" Grace asked, ignoring the woman's other questions. Now she sat straighter, waking up. "Who am *I*?" she repeated. "Who are *you*?"

"Cheryl Grayson."

Grace stared at her blankly; it just wasn't making sense. "I'm sorry. Who?" Grace asked again, with a little less force.

"Oh, you must be the *wife*," Cheryl spat back. Grace's face clouded in confusion, then her eyes narrowed.

At the woman's enunciation of these small quick words, Coleton clicked into motion. Until then, he had remained silent on the couch, not believing what he knew was happening. He should have predicted it and taken measures to prevent it. But, now it was too late. He slipped out from under Camilla, who woke with the movement and rubbed her eyes.

"Hello there," Coleton said, as he moved toward the woman. His arms were extended in right angles as if to corral her away from Grace.

"No!" Cheryl said harshly, as Coleton's hand brushed against her shoulder. "I want to know how George is. Oh, George!" She leaned forward again over the bed. Her eyes welled with tears.

"Who the hell *are* you?" Grace asked with a raised voice. She was standing now.

"Oh, please, doll. You know who I am. Do you really want to get into that right now? I want to know how he is. Has he asked for me?"

Coleton allowed this seemingly civil exchange of words, with his arms still extended between the two women. Coleton stared at Grace, waiting to see how she would react. It was up to her how this would all go down. Grace exhaled her breath in a hiss and took a step backwards as if the words had hit her full in the chest.

Grace looked down at her socked feet. Then, she looked up daringly at the woman. "I don't know who you are. But, get the hell out of here. *Now!*" Her voice didn't waiver.

"I exist," Cheryl said menacingly. "You may as well accept it. George wanted me in his life, and I have every right to be here." She reached out and laid her hand softly almost protectively on the lump of George's motionless foot.

"Don't you dare touch my husband," Grace said loudly, and took a step forward. "Get the *fuck* out!" Even Coleton jolted at the expletive. Her eyes had slipped from resolute to wild, her face contorted with rage.

"Okay, you heard her." Coleton moved in now, pushing the woman slowly back. She teetered on her high sling-back heels. Coleton steadied her with one hand, but continued his movement, ushering her toward the door. "Outside. We'll talk outside."

With this, the woman spun on her heel and strode from the room. Coleton followed closely behind and shut the door carefully.

"You're telling me she didn't know that George has been having an affair for the past two years?" Cheryl demanded as soon as they were in the hall.

"Of course. I mean—" Coleton paused, then shrugged. "She probably did. I don't know. But, now is not the time to go parading into her life. You're a goddamn news anchor for Chrissake. Show some decorum. You can't expect her to deal with this right now."

Cheryl broke down and tears streamed down her cheeks. Coleton held out an arm and she fell into his shoulder.

"I love him. I really love him." She sobbed into his chest. Her words were barely audible.

"How the hell did you even get in here?" Coleton asked idly over her shoulder as he looked down the hall toward the nurses' station. He needed to make sure they ramped up the security, first thing.

"Please ..." the woman sniffed, raising her tear streaked, but still proud face. "You think they don't watch the nightly news? Like they—" She nodded toward the nurse station. "—are going to turn me around?"

Coleton took a crunching bite out of his triangle of toast. Then, with his mouth still full of crumbs he called out, "Sure you don't want any of this? I mean, it is room service—" Coleton scrunched up his nose. "—but the omelet is pretty decent."

Camilla was stretched out on the striped couch across the room with her crossed ankles propped up on one of the armrests. All Coleton could see from where he sat at the breakfast table was the back of the couch and her small, socked feet protruding from the end of the couch.

"I'm fine," Camilla said. Coleton heard the crinkling of newspaper as she noisily turned the page and continued to read. "I can't believe this made the paper. I hope to God Grace doesn't see the story. It'll kill her."

Coleton buttered his last remaining piece of toast. "It must be a damn Canadian fascination," he said. "If every American news anchor's affair made headlines there would be no room to print anything else!"

"There's even a picture." Camilla held the paper up over the top of the couch and shook it, pointing to a square of color for Coleton to see. "It's Cheryl with a scarf over her head, running through the hospital doors," Camilla interpreted out loud. "What a shmuck."

"Don't talk about George like that."

"He's a cheating shmuck."

"Camilla!"

"Fine. He's a nice guy, but he should never have done something like that to Grace. She is so sweet and loyal. And, she's such a great mom."

"Well, George *is* on the road more than half the year."

"What!" Camilla exclaimed. She flung herself upright and glared over the back of the couch at Coleton. Her hair was still messy from sleep. "That's an excuse? It's okay that he cheated because he's away from home half the year?"

"No, it's not an excuse. He shouldn't have cheated on Grace. I'm not justifying it."

"You're gone more than half the year," she said, unwilling to let it drop. She glared at him. "It's okay for you to cheat on me?"

"Don't be ridiculous."

Camilla pulled the lapels of her robe closer together and maneuvered onto her knees, so that she was facing him squarely over the back of the couch.

"There is a big difference between me and George," he continued.

Camilla folded her arms. "By all means, do explain."

"George and Grace got married when they were still in college, and George never really had a lot of girls before her." Coleton shook his head. "Those are the kind of guys that you have to worry about. At some point in life, they are going to snap and want to know what they've missed. I'm already done with that phase of my life."

Camilla settled back on her haunches and rested her chin on the back of the couch. They had had this conversation before, and 51% of her believed him, just enough to tilt the scale.

"Let's drop it," he said. "We're both exhausted." They had only gotten a few hours of troubled sleep since the accident, and their tempers were scratchy and red. "If you thought I was capable of cheating, you wouldn't be here. Am I wrong?" Camilla wiggled her nose and shook her head no. She flopped backwards onto the couch, hidden from view.

"Well, I think Grace needs to get out of that hospital room today," Camilla said. "She needs some decent food. I'm going to take her to that little café in Yorkville that Justine told me about."

"Good idea," Coleton said, glad she was letting it drop.

He picked up the last grape on his plate and tossed it into his mouth.

Under the great spreading arms of the elm trees that flank Central Park West, Arthur Elrod stopped to buy a cup of coffee at a food-stand near 72nd Street. He wore a button-up shirt and neatly tailored slacks, even though it was the weekend. It was not an orthodox day for a business meeting, but then again, this was far from orthodox business.

"Sure is a hot one today, huh?" the man behind the cart said good-naturedly. Elrod nodded stiffly. Coins of sunlight slipped down through the treetops high above and dappled the sidewalk. "Sure you don't want to make this iced?" the guy asked as he handed Elrod a Styrofoam cup. Elrod's response was a five-dollar bill dropped on the counter before he walked away.

Elrod made his way east along Terrace Drive into Central Park and then turned onto a footpath. He looked for a good bench: out of the way, out of earshot, and where the meeting wouldn't attract any attention. He had been surprised, annoyed even, when they told him the location, but he wasn't in a position to argue. He had received a text and all it said was: *Strawberry Fields Forever. Tomorrow at 11. Come alone and pick a bench.*

Elrod picked a bench and sat down, suddenly wishing he had brought a newspaper or something to do while he waited. Elrod hadn't actually stepped foot in Central Park in years. He didn't have time for things like walks in the park. He took the lid off his coffee to let it cool and set it on the bench.

Elrod looked out over the broad green spaces where carefree students spread out their blankets in the grass to read books and children played Frisbee with their dogs. It was a normal Sunday in the Park, and Elrod scowled at its cheerful inhabitants. *Do these people really have nothing better to do?*

Elrod was so intent on the scene before him, that he didn't notice the man until he sat down. Elrod turned slightly to look at him out of the corner of his eye. He was over-weight and middle-aged, with a thick beard, '70s aviator glasses and an old-school Members Only jacket that billowed around his thick frame. He had a fat little Dachshund on a worn-out leash. Elrod opened his mouth to tell the man to get lost—he was waiting for a business associate, but with a start Elrod realized the man could be hiding anything from a penknife to an Uzi under his jacket, and his blood suddenly ran cold.

"You're Dieter Fleischer's man?"

"Vell, hello der, Artur," the man said with a yellowed smile. He had a heavy Austrian German accent. Elrod nodded slowly, then looked down the path suddenly hopping for a steady stream of joggers.

"Interesting spot for a meeting."

"Yes, vell—" The man smiled darkly. "Dars no cameras here."

Elrod gulped, and then to hide this nervous tell, he picked up his cup and took a sip.

"If you vanted a loan in broad daylight, ven you could valk wwrrright into a bank. Couldn't you?" the man asked gleefully. "But, you don't vant anyone to know how bad you need it, yah?"

Elrod remained silent and drew his lips back into a grimace.

"Vell, then—" The man smiled again. "Vee vill help you out of your little situation, and keep it to our ownselves. No-ones vill hear. For a price, ov course. Silence can be quite—expensive."

Elrod nodded again, grimacing as if in pain.

"How much do you need?"

"Thirty million."

The man giggled. "Okay, ven you vill have your thirty million for six months. And, *he* vill take an extra six for the effort. You have the account ready?"

Elrod pulled a thin, folded envelope from the pocket of his pants. "It's a Swiss account, untraceable." The man nodded and unzipped his jacket to slip the envelope inside. Elrod thought he could just make out the butt of a revolver and shivered despite the New York summer heat.

"Interest is payable once a month. In cash."

"Now, hold on a minute," Elrod said, straightening up. "I thought interest and principal would be due at the end of the term."

"*Nein! Nein! Nein!*" the fat man barked with harsh finality. Then, he softened his tone, "Do I vook like a balloon to you?" He chuckled and pointed his finger into Elrod's chest. Elrod felt something unspoken, yet very hostile in the gesture. "I vill see you in four veeks."

Elrod cleared his throat to speak again, but the man stood up, shook out the creases in his khaki pants and walked away with his tiny dog in tow.

In an unprecedented show of emotion, Elrod let his head sink into his hands, and 20 minutes passed before he too stood from the bench and made his way out of the park.

Although Grace wouldn't leave the hospital, she finally agreed to meet Camilla downstairs in the cafeteria for a quick lunch. It was the first time she'd left George's side, and the nurses told Camilla they hadn't seen her eat anything since George was admitted. Camilla was almost as worried about Grace as she was about George.

Camilla picked a table by a bay window, and left a chair with its back bathed in the sunlight open and ready for Grace. She hoped it would remind her that life outside was still moving forward, the earth was still spinning on its axis.

As she waited, Camilla looked around the quiet cafeteria and was surprised to feel at home. She took it for granted how familiar she had become with this space over the years of her medical training. Not this particular space but hospital cafeterias in general, regardless of their location, had always been a place of refuge for her, a place for collecting her clearest thoughts. The air perpetually seemed a few degrees warmer than the rest of the freezing hospital, and perhaps a bit less—antiseptic. A fresh pot of coffee was constantly brewing, its scent filling the air. And, a seat in the sun could always be found near a window where she could pretend for a few minutes to be a fat, lazy housecat basking in the Vitamin D.

When Camilla saw Grace enter the cafeteria, small and alone, she almost didn't recognize her. Dark circles shadowed Grace's eyes and she looked gaunt, as if she hadn't eaten in weeks, not hours. Camilla stood up, hoping to give her a hug as she approached, but Grace just nodded at her and pulled out the empty chair to sit.

Camilla smiled at Grace as consolingly as she could and opened her mouth to speak, but suddenly had nothing to say. Grace stared back vacantly.

Camilla lifted a shopping bag onto the tabletop to break the ice.

"Here. I picked up some things for you. Clean clothes, underwear, toothbrush, other toiletries."

Grace gave her a weak smile for her kindness and pulled the bag to her side of the table.

"Thank you, Camilla," Grace began. Camilla smiled. Then, in the same breath, Grace added abruptly, "I'm leaving him." Camilla's smile froze.

For the first time, Grace met Camilla's eyes. Her gaze was strong and decided. Camilla straightened-up in her chair and cleared her throat, but was at a loss for words.

"I'd pretty much decided—to leave him," Grace continued, picking her way carefully around those last words as if their edges were sharp. "Before we even came to Canada." Camilla nodded like she understood and agreed, but she was flying blind and remained silent.

"I found a few messages on his phone from *her*, from a Canadian cell phone. That's why I came to Canada. I figured he would try to see her while he was here. I had no idea it would be under these circumstances." Grace looked down at her hands and folded them neatly in her lap.

"And the crash, doesn't that change things?" Camilla wondered out loud.

"Should it?" Grace shrugged her shoulders. Then, she shook her head no. "I thought he was going to retire at the end of last year. I thought once he did, he would re-dedicate himself to the family, and to me. Be there for us. But, racing is in his blood like a flaw in his DNA, and he's not going to give it up."

"Well, he might *have* to, now that—" Camilla tried.

"No." Grace shook her head gravely. "Now I'm afraid his drive to win will be even greater. Now he'll say he *has* to have a comeback, to show everyone that he's a fighter. And, I can't take it anymore."

"You need to eat something, Grace. And sleep. You need to rest. Don't make any drastic decisions under these conditions."

Grace sighed. "It's been a long time coming, I'm afraid."

"Let me get you something to eat—a sandwich? A cup of soup? Doesn't that sound nice?"

"I just got part of a protein bar down. I'm fine, really I am. I couldn't eat real food right now if you put a gun to my head. Let's just go back upstairs. I want you to decipher some of his charts for me. The nurses aren't telling me anything."

Camilla nodded, hoping Coleton wouldn't blame her for her inability to talk Grace out of her plan. It would be a tough blow to George given his condition, but not necessarily one he didn't deserve.

As Camilla and Grace walked to the bank of elevators and rose toward George's room, Camilla was surprised. Not just by Grace's revelation, but also by the complete change in her demeanor. By telling someone and airing her plans, Grace seemed to have absorbed a whole new persona. The set of her shoulders and the swing of her arms as she walked through the sterile hallway belied a stronger and more decided woman. They were going to survive this: George, the injuries and her, the heartbreak.

Grace pushed open the door to George's room and halted abruptly halfway through the doorway. Camilla bumped into her not expecting the sudden stop, then peeked over her shoulder.

"I thought," Grace spat out. "I thought I made it *very* clear that you are not welcome here."

Cheryl Grayson stood next to the hospital bed. Afternoon light poured in through the half-drawn blinds and lit up the high cheekbones and full lips of her camera-ready face. In bed, George lay in the same position, his leg still elevated at the same degree. He had finally regained consciousness, but was now in a deep medicated sleep, his body slowly healing in silence.

"Oh, relax," Cheryl said with a dismissive flick of her wrist. "We're all adults here."

"Relax?" Grace asked, shocked. "*Relax*?"

"Yeah, you know—relax. Chill the hell out. George is practically comatose. He doesn't even know I'm here."

"Well, I'm not comatose and unless you want to be—you better get *out*. How dare you—"

"Look, not that I owe you anything, because I don't. But, I'll give you something. A little piece of information: I'm just here to say my goodbyes."

Grace went silent at this and seemed to retract within herself unsure of how to respond.

"You can have him. He's all yours. The scandal of this affair is too much. I'm married too you know. And, my marriage, and more importantly my career, can't handle a prolonged scandal right now."

Grace just stared at her, so Cheryl enunciated the words again, moving her lips slowly, forming the words as if speaking to a child, "He's—all—yours."

As she spoke these final words, Cheryl threw her jet-black coat loosely around her shoulders and breezed past Grace, shaking her head as she went. Camilla watched Cheryl stride confidently down the hallway, looking straight ahead. And then, she was gone.

Grace continued to stand in the doorway, looking at George's motionless form. All of a sudden she dropped her face into the palms of her hands, and broke down. She let her emotions go, not halfway, but like releasing a helium balloon into a blue sky. All or nothing, and no going back. "Oh, Grace. I'm so sorry." Camilla draped her arms around Grace's shoulders, but Grace only cried harder. Camilla tightened her embrace into a bear hug, as if trying to keep Grace from breaking into pieces.

"Are you still going to leave him?" Camilla asked softly, thinking the words out loud. But, there was no response.

CHAPTER 16

MIAMI, FLORIDA

At 8:30 a.m. Coleton jogged up the granite steps of the Citi Bank building on Biscayne Boulevard in downtown Miami, ready for war. Ira was already waiting for him at the entrance, busy on his BlackBerry and leaning against the wall in a dark blue suit.

"Will you look at this guy?" Coleton asked, pinching an inch of the fabric. "What is this Armani?"

"Yeah, isn't it great? Picked it up at the Neiman's Outlet at Sawgrass Mills mall. Fifty off." Ira bobbed his head with a smug, satisfied smile, as if expecting Coleton's praise.

"Nice cufflinks too," Coleton added. "Checkered flags?"

"Oh yeahhh," Ira giggled. He raised both fists in the air: double pump to the left, double pump to the right.

Ira pushed open one of the large glass doors, held it for Coleton and followed him into the entrance hall, "You ready for this?"

"I'm ready to tear out his heart with my bare hands, show it to him in his last dying breath, and then shove it down his fat throat to make asphyxiation his official cause of death."

"Jesus Christ! That's lovely."

Coleton chuckled and shook his head. It always made him laugh when Ira slipped into this particular expletive, considering what Ira's religion believed about the guy.

They stopped at the front desk and were greeted by a stately receptionist replete with a collar of fat pearls.

"Loren and Goldstein here for the nine o'clock arbitration at Shutts & Bowen."

"Mr. Gomez and his lawyers are waiting for you in the conference room on the 18th floor."

"They're already here?" Coleton asked, incredulous. "But, we're half an hour early!"

The woman nodded. "Will you be expecting additional counsel?" She looked skeptically at Ira. "I will be sure to send them right up."

"Oh, he's not my lawyer. And, no. No additional counsel. I'm representing myself." The receptionist raised an eyebrow, as if even she knew better than to attempt this misguided strategy.

"Floor 18," she said again, and pointed to a bank of elevators with a wry smile on her lips.

"Great." Coleton scowled.

Part pride and part stratagem, Coleton had decided not to hire an attorney since counsel was not technically required in arbitration. He was aware of the risk, but believed that he could use his perceived naivety of the legal system and lack of knowledge regarding the regulations of the arbitration procedures to his advantage. He planned to pull some unorthodox moves and hoped to get away with them by pleading ignorance.

"Maybe it isn't such a great idea for you to represent yourself," Ira said, and pressed the button for the 18th floor.

"Now you tell me," Coleton muttered, as the doors slid closed.

They made their way to the end of a corridor. A row of bay windows on their left looked into a large conference room. A skinny, balding man sat at the head of a long table and four suited men sat all on one side, their backs to the hallway. The other side of the table was empty. Beyond the table, a wall of windows looked east over the glimmering Biscayne Bay dotted with emerald green islands, the Port of Miami and the blue Atlantic beyond.

"There's no mistaking that fat fuck." Ira pointed at the back of Gomez's head, where a few rolls of flesh bulged over his collar. "Guess we're at the right place."

Inside the conference room, Gomez made a broad gesture with both hands, and the other men began to laugh, even the Arbitrator in his beige sweater vest cracked up at the joke.

"We better get in there," Coleton said. But before he pushed open the oak double doors, he paused and said to Ira, "Let me do all the talking. Got it? I don't want to hear a word out of you. Keep it in check." Ira nodded. Coleton looked him in the eye to make sure Ira knew he meant business.

"Good morning, Gentlemen," Coleton said brightly. The men stopped laughing and straightened. Gomez and his three lawyers turned in unison to glare at the new arrivals.

"Mr. Loren. Mr. Goldstein. Please take your seats." The Arbitrator nodded to them as they took over the empty side of the table. "You're late and tardiness will not be accepted in this arbitration."

"What?" Ira gasped. Coleton immediately quieted him.

"I was specifically told this arbitration would begin at nine o'clock," Coleton said in a dignified voice.

"Eight thirty," the Arbitrator corrected sharply, shaking his head. "And, I suggest you be on time from now on, or as an agent of the court, I will be forced to hold you in contempt of court." The Arbitrator turned back to the other side of the table. "Shall we begin?"

"*What the*—?" Ira mouthed to Coleton. Coleton shrugged.

Coleton settled into his chair, then glared with hatred across the table at Gomez, hoping to intimidate his opponent. Gomez had dark yellowish semi-circles under both eyes, lingering testament to the broken nose Coleton had given him at the Long Beach Grand Prix. This arbitration wasn't just about the money.

Coleton pointed to his own eyes, then pointed to Gomez and gave him a thumbs-up. "Looking good," Coleton mouthed with a smile, then piled a wink on top. Gomez glared at him in return with a look of seething hatred.

"My name is Mr. Rosen," the Arbitrator began. "And in this arbitration, I will hear the evidence presented by both sides and will come to a final decision that is legally binding on both parties, unless we reach a mutually agreeable settlement before hand." He paused to adjust his glasses. They were the exact size and shape of silver dollars. "The agenda of this proceeding is as follows: first, we will hear opening remarks from both sides, then, Mr. Gomez you will have the opportunity as the Plaintiff to present your case, and Mr. Loren you will be given the opportunity to respond to each issue as we go. Mr. Gomez will then depose any witnesses, before we will turn back to you, Mr. Loren, so that you can present your case and depose any witnesses that you might have. We will then hear closing remarks from both sides. Are we all clear on the order of the proceeding?"

The Arbitrator nodded to Gomez, who in turn nudged the lawyer on his right. The lawyer scribbled a few things on his yellow legal pad, while everyone waited, cleared his throat in a protracted *ah-ah-ah-ahem*, then began.

"Good morning. My name is Thomas Rank. I represent the Plaintiff, Jose Gomez, the sole owner of Gomez Racing, LLC, a Delaware Limited Liability Company, in this arbitration. On January 3rd of last year, Mr. Gomez entered into a written contract with the defendant, Loren Racing, which is owned 90% by Mr. Loren and 10% by Mr. Goldstein, both present here today. In this contract, copies of which have been furnished to all relevant parties, Mr. Loren agreed to pay Gomez Racing the sum of $2 million, broken down into a $1 million payment each year for two years."

"Wait, wait," Coleton spoke up. "I mean, I object! I only had to make the second payment if I continued to race for him for *two* years."

"Mr. Loren," said the Arbitrator. "You may *not* interrupt Mr. Rank. You will have the chance to make your own opening remarks in a few minutes."

"Thank you, Mr. Rosen." The lawyer glanced at Coleton sharply before continuing. "Mr. Gomez has been forced to invoke the arbitration provisions of that contract, as Mr. Loren has adamantly refused to make the second $1 million payment due and owing for this year. My client has done nothing wrong. It is not his fault that Mr. Loren has decided, treacherously I might add, to race for a new team this season."

"Treacherously?" Coleton ducked his head and muttered under his breath to Ira. "That's a bit much, don't you think?" Ira's nervous giggle was only perceptible by the slight shake of his belly.

"My client," the lawyer continued, glaring at Coleton, "is fully justified in seeking full performance of the contract, which Mr. Loren signed, and under which Mr. Gomez is still owed the sum of $1 million." The attorney then nodded at the Arbitrator, who motioned dismissively to Coleton.

"Okay, Mr. Loren, now you may proceed."

"This arbitration is *completely* ludicrous, because the sponsor we're talking about—" Coleton paused for effect. "—Phantom Jets is *bankrupt!*" He had been holding this information in for the past five minutes, dying to blurt it out.

"I had a contract with Phantom Jets to pay me $2 million a year for two years. Based on that contract, I agreed to pay Gomez Racing $1 million a year for two years. For the first year, last year, I made the $1 million payment to these fat cats, as required. However, Phantom Jets has yet to make my second payment of $2 million, so I can't possibly be expected to make another payment to Gomez." Coleton sat back smugly in his chair as if this revelation would immediately end the proceeding. Silence hung in the air.

The Arbitrator cleared his throat. "Would you care to make any other opening remarks, Mr. Loren?"

"What else do I need to say? The sponsor is now bankrupt and therefore it was a one-year deal. How am I supposed to give him another million, when Phantom isn't around to give it to me? I mean, I already gave this asshole one mill—"

"Refrain from offensive language in this proceeding!" the Arbitrator demanded, cutting Coleton off. He banged his fist on the table. "I will not tolerate it." Everyone at the table straightened.

"Sorry," Coleton said, accepting the reprimand. He felt a sinking, liquid feeling in the pit of his stomach.

"Anything else, Mr. Loren?" The Arbitrator glared at him.

Coleton was flustered, but continued, "And, most importantly, I'm not even racing for Gomez anymore, so why should I have to pay him anything?"

"Okay, we have now concluded opening remarks." The Arbitrator turned to Gomez's side of the table. "Mr. Rank, you may now present your case."

"Thank you, Mr. Rosen. Okay, Mr. Loren, since you brought it up. Let's begin with Phantom Jets: the sponsor. Your contract with Mr. Gomez does not reference any agreement you might have had with Phantom Jets. The contract merely states that you agree to pay Gomez Racing $1 million each year for two years. You made the payment in year one, and now you must make the second payment for year two. Quite frankly, it doesn't matter where you get the money as long as you fulfill the contract, and any further discussion of Phantom Jets is not relevant to this proceeding."

Coleton started to speak, but stopped himself and looked to the Arbitrator. "Can I respond now?" he asked. The Arbitrator checked with Mr. Rank, then nodded. Coleton took a deep breath. "Excuse me, but how the hell is Phantom Jets *not* relevant to this proceeding?" Coleton turned to the Arbitrator. "Let me explain a few things." Coleton straightened the papers in front of him before continuing.

"In racing, contracts are always quickly drafted and informal, if you even have one. Usually, we operate on handshakes. That's just the way it is. Everyone in the industry knows: when the money runs out, the money runs out. What does it matter what a piece of paper says if there's no money on the table? It's a big boy's club in the paddock."

The Arbitrator looked down at his paperwork, and didn't make eye contact with Coleton. Coleton changed strategies and looked right at Gomez. "Not to mention, why should I pay you anything when I'm not even driving for you this year?"

"That brings us to the next issue, if I may?" Mr. Rank asked the Arbitrator.

"Please, continue."

"For our second issue, if you look to the body of the contract, the four corners if you will, then you will see that the payments owed to Gomez Racing are in no way predicated on Coleton's continued performance as a driver for Gomez Racing. Coleton is free to race for whatever team he chooses, however, the second payment on this contract is still due."

"Did you *not* just hear me?" Coleton blurted out. "Racing contracts are never that specific!"

"Mr. Loren!" the Arbitrator interjected. "Please—"

Coleton ignored him and continued quickly, "Of course I don't owe him more if I'm not driving for him! That's a given!" Ira reached across and put his palm to Coleton's chest to quiet him.

The Arbitrator's face was beginning to redden. "Mr. Loren, this is the last time—"

"No, it's okay," Mr. Rank piped up, with a smug smile. "I was pretty much done with that issue anyway. Take it away, Mr. Loren."

"First, I think the record should reflect that it was *not* my personal choice to leave Gomez Racing. The team ran out of money. I couldn't tell you what he did with the first million I gave him, but all I know is that we barely made it to the last two races and left a series of debts in the paddock at Petit Le Mans last year. I can't waste my talent with a team that can't afford to run a serious program. Getting to the podium doesn't just take talent."

"Mr. Loren, you will have a chance to present you case later in the proceeding. Please limit your comments at this point to rebutting the issues raised by Mr. Rank."

Frustrated, Coleton fiddled with the papers in front of him. "Okay, fine. So what's the issue?" The row of lawyers on the other side snickered. Coleton almost lost it, but with great effort managed to remain silent … until he couldn't. "And, I guess it *isn't* relevant to this proceeding that Jose Gomez and two of his cronies physically attacked me on Pit Row at the Long Beach Grand Prix? Literally tried to do me physical harm? That doesn't matter at all, right?"

"Mr. Loren!" The Arbitrator banged his fist on the table for a second time.

"And, who cares that he withheld engine codes from the car he sold my new team? Who cares that he broke the law and tried to screw me over, just to be a vindictive asshole? And, while we're at it, who cares that this scumbag makes his money by exploiting women in strip clubs and bookstores."

"Mr. Loren those comments are *not* relevant!" the Arbitrator said, now livid.

"Isn't this guy supposed to be a neutral third party?" Ira whispered to Coleton.

"Yeah, aren't you supposed to be neutral?" Coleton asked loudly. "What happened to that little technicality? You decided to throw it by the wayside?"

"Okay, then, Mr. Rank." The Arbitrator turned to the other side, ignoring Coleton in an attempt to control himself. "It appears you may now continue to the next issue."

"Well, I think we've pretty much summed up our case," Rank said cheerily. "We just want to enforce the terms of the contract. It is quite clear that Mr. Loren owes my client $1 million."

"Did you *not* hear anything I just said?" Coleton demanded. "This is ridiculous. Are these hearings recorded?" He looked up into the corners of the room for a camera or audio recording device.

"No, they aren't. Only if it's specifically requested by you or your attorney," the Arbitrator responded smugly.

"Great," Coleton muttered, glaring at him. "So, when I want to appeal this, let me guess, nothing I've brought up will make it into your notes?"

Coleton felt sick. He sighed and leaned back in his chair. The wound to his pride would certainly be as painful as the hit to his bank account. The Arbitrator was just following the formalities now. Coleton could tell his mind was already made up.

Just then, Coleton's phone vibrated on the tabletop. Coleton silenced it and looked down at the caller ID. He snatched up the phone, his finger poised over the accept button. He looked at the Arbitrator, then back down at the phone. It continued to blink in his hand.

"I've got to take this."

"Absolutely not," the Arbitrator said, sitting up straight.

"I'm sorry, but I have to." Coleton pushed back his chair.

"Colt, no." Ira tried to stop him, afraid to infuriate the Arbitrator even further.

"It's okay, I've got it," Coleton said, then hustled out of the room into the hallway and answered the call.

"Coleton? William Crowne here," a deep voice came through his BlackBerry.

"Hello, sir," Coleton said, still surprised by the identity of the caller. He continued down the hall past the bay of windows to avoid the prying eyes of the men still in the conference room.

"So, I heard through the grapevine you have an arbitration with Jose Gomez today?"

"You really do know everything," Coleton laughed nervously, but with true admiration in his voice. "I'm in the middle of it—right now! I shouldn't have taken your call."

"Don't let that criminal jerk you around."

"I don't plan on it, but things aren't going well to be honest. I think he's bribed the Arbitrator somehow. It's an absolute dog show."

"The Arbitrator is superfluous. These kinds of things can be easily resolved."

"Okay—" Coleton said hesitantly, unwilling to contradict Crowne, but knowing there was no way Gomez would let this drop. Coleton couldn't see any way out.

"All you need to do," Crowne said, his voice deep and calm like a nighttime radio announcer, "is go back into the room and say a simple, yet key phrase."

Despite the stress, Coleton felt a smile tug at the corner of his mouth—the first fragile stirring of hope.

"Yes?" Coleton asked. He leaned forward and pressed the phone tightly to his ear.

"Ask Gomez if he really thinks the Mob won't find out about Agent McKenzie."

"What?" Coleton asked, confused. Surely he hadn't heard correctly. *McKenzie?* The name sounded slightly familiar. "What about the mob?"

"Ask him," Crowne said slowly, repeating himself, "if he really thinks the mob won't find out about Agent McKenzie. That's all you have to say."

"But what does—"

"I'm just walking into a meeting at BMW headquarters in Munich. I'm working out the details of an interesting new idea for next season. We'll catch up soon. Give my regards to Victoria."

"Um ... okay. Of course I will," Coleton said, still in shock. "Thank you," he added, but he heard the line go dead with a solid click and wasn't sure if his final words had carried across the Atlantic.

Coleton looked down quizzically at the BlackBerry in the palm of his hand. *What the hell was that all about?* He walked back down the hallway, and paused for a second to think before he rolled his shoulders back and pulled open the solid oak door. *What do I have to lose?* All arms in the room were crossed, Gomez and his three smug attorneys on one side of the table, and Ira, alone but ready for a scrap, on the other.

"Please forgive the interruption—" Coleton began.

"Mr. Loren, this kind of behavior will not be tolerated in my arbitration. As an agent of the court, you disrespect not only me, but also—"

Coleton cleared his throat loudly. The Arbitrator startled at the sound. His glasses slid down the bridge of his nose, and he lifted his chin to glare at Coleton through them.

"I see your point," Coleton said. "However, this whole meeting is a farce." The Arbitrator gulped in surprise and his glassy eyes bulged. Coleton turned to Gomez. "You want to settle this thing? You, me, outside, in private. Like real men."

Mr. Rank began whispering harshly into Gomez's ear. The other lawyers made violent but silent gestures as if calling plays from a football playbook. Gomez cocked his head to the side and looked only at Coleton, clearly unconcerned with his lawyers' advice.

"Okay, Loren … I'm interested." Gomez lifted his hand to silence his lawyers who were reaching a state of frenzy, unused to the sudden redirection of authority. Then, he followed Coleton into the hallway.

As soon as the door swung shut behind them, Coleton dove in. What did he have to lose? "Did you really think the mob wouldn't find out about Agent McKenzie?"

At first Gomez shook his head, confused. Then, after a few seconds, he froze. He narrowed his eyes to study Coleton's face.

"You little shit!" Gomez exploded. "*You* don't know anything about it."

"No?" Coleton taunted with a confidence he didn't quite own, but it was getting closer every second. Coleton's mind raced, trying to put all the puzzle pieces together in time to use them. *Strip clubs. Adult bookstores. A federal agent. The mob. Agent McKenzie?* Coleton's brain jumped from fact to fact, trying to connect all the information he knew about Gomez into something useful. *Jim McKenzie!* And just like that, it all clicked into place. Coleton's eyes lit up.

"Your new business manager, Jim McKenzie, is an undercover federal agent?" It came out as a question, but Coleton saw Gomez flinch. *Bingo.* "I mean, seriously?" Coleton recovered, pretending he had known the full and shocking truth the entire time.

"What do the Feds have on you? Prostitution? Did a girl lie about her age on her application? Must be bad, if you're letting an undercover agent tag around with you. Looking to bust someone bigger, no doubt."

Gomez stared at Coleton in outrage, his eyes bulging.

"*The Mafia?*" Coleton blurted out, making another connection in his head. "Shit, man! What, did they bank roll your operation? And let me guess—" Coleton said, fishing a little. "The feds also seized some of your assets? That's why you're tits up! No pun intended."

"What the fuck do you know about it?" Gomez growled.

"Plenty." Coleton smiled sweetly. "And so will the rest of the world when I get through."

Gomez exploded with an animalistic howl and shoved Coleton up against the wall. Inside the conference room, Ira leapt from the table, as did Gomez's lawyers, and they all crashed into each other as they bolted toward the door. Coleton wiggled his right arm free and motioned through the window for the men to stop. Although he was the one pinned up against the wall, Coleton had Gomez right where he wanted him.

"How did you find out about this?" Gomez demanded, but he had already begun to loosen his grip on Coleton. He dropped his arms to his sides and took a step backward.

"That's irrelevant, I'm afraid." Coleton clapped him on the shoulder. Gomez flinched away from the touch. He had suddenly taken on the lax expression and loose body language of a defeated man. "But don't worry. It's not common knowledge and your secret *can* be safe. I don't like you, but I'd really rather not be responsible for you getting wacked."

Gomez flinched again, as if he'd been slapped. His olive skin had gone gray, and he looked up at Coleton with a pleading expression. His darkest fears had just surfaced to haunt him.

"Look it is very simple," Coleton explained, taking control of the logistics. "The next few minutes will go by quickly and easily. We will go back inside. You will sign some papers dropping this silly lawsuit. In return, I will file safely away all the information I know about you and your, shall we say, interesting choice of friends."

Coleton turned Gomez around by the shoulders and gave him a small push toward the conference room door. Five noses were pressed to the glass, watching every move, trying to figure out what had just happened.

A s Coleton pushed open the broad glass doors and stepped into the Florida sunshine, he tasted the incredible sweet relief of victory. He felt special and chosen, like the sunlight on the crown of his head and tops of his shoulders was a divine benediction. He held in a deep breath, then let it slowly pass his lips. It was finally over, and it couldn't have turned out better.

"Now, it's time to go to France!" Coleton smiled at Ira, ready to make plans again. "Le Mans here we come!"

"Let's ride together to lunch. It's on me—to celebrate," Ira chortled.

Genuinely surprised by the gesture, Coleton smiled at Ira's flush, happy face and clapped him on the back. "Victory suits you!"

As they waited for the valet to bring Coleton's car around, they saw Gomez and his team of lawyers hustle out of the building and down the steps toward a waiting Escalade. Gomez ducked his head as if he expected a flock of reporters and a barrage of flash bulbs to expose his guilt as he fled the building.

"Hey, Gomez," Ira called out.

On reflex, Gomez turned to look at Ira, immediately wishing he hadn't directed his attention to him.

Ira held out a carefully folded $20 bill. "Good show! Here's a little something extra for ya, sugar. Tuck it in your garter."

Before he ducked through the open door of the Escalade, Gomez turned and flicked Ira off with such animosity, such sheer brutal hostility, that Ira couldn't help but giggle with delight.

CHAPTER 17
LE MANS, FRANCE

The TGV train from Charles De Gaulle Airport arrived promptly at 11:28 a.m. Camilla waited under one of the many arches of Gare du Mans for 30 minutes, but Coleton was late. She checked her watch for the 20th time and heaved a sigh.

Three schoolgirls walked by holding half-sized baguettes, the ends pinched off. The smell made her even more hungry, and the hungrier she got the more irritable she was. It's *not* like she had traveled halfway around the world to meet him *and* had arrived precisely at the appointed time. Coleton knew time; he was intimate with it. In the racecar he measured it in hundredths and thousandths of a second. The least he could do was be there on time to retrieve her.

"This is ridiculous," Camilla said, as she wrangled her two heavy suitcases across Boulevard Robert Jarry. After a measuring look into the gray sky, Camilla picked a bistro table outside Le Corail, but under the edge of its royal blue awning. A young waiter with a white apron tied around his waist presented a menu. She skimmed the laminated page, then handed it back, deciding to try out her rusty French with her breakfast order.

"*Une omelette aux légumes et un café Viennois, s'il vous plaît.*"

"*Bien sûr,*" he replied.

"*Et un carabe d'eau,*" Camilla added, pleased by his subtle smile. After he left, she had a sinking feeling and checked the dictionary in her phone. *Carafe* d'eau! She had just ordered a water beetle.

The trip had been comfortable enough. Camilla had found a leather seat by the window, and let her thoughts slip lazily through her head like the patchwork fields that slid by as the train sped southwest from Paris. The ride was so smooth that there had barely been a ripple in her bottle of water, yet she had gone nearly as fast as Coleton's LMP1 on a straightaway.

At each stop, she had watched passengers board and off-load: farmers, businessmen, mothers with children in tow and the tops of baguettes bobbing along in their *fourre-touts*. Each one with a different destination, a distinctive view of life, each with their own scars and neuroses, heartaches and hopes, each with a different dream fluttering behind their eyelids.

Camilla opened the glossy *Vogue Paris* she had purchased in the airport and flipped through the pages. The magazine took up most of the bistro table. She pulled a page close to her nose to smell a peel-away sample of *Noir*. Camilla startled. The fragrance was all Coleton: warm and cozy vanilla with hints of bergamot. *So, he's a Tom Ford man.* Smiling, Camilla lowered the page and startled again. A tall man stood in front of her table, staring at her.

"*Bonjour!*" he said. He had short brown hair parted on the side, a thin face and warm brown eyes. His hair was gelled and carefully combed down, but the cut was too short and here and there it spiked upward.

"*Je m'appelle Bertrand.*"

Camilla clutched her copy of *Vogue* to her chest, as if he might snatch it away.

"*Vous êtes seule, Mademoiselle?*"

"*Je ne comprends pas,*" Camilla said, wrinkling her brow. "*Je suis Américaine.*"

"Can I join you?" he asked in English. He nodded at the chair next to her. Camilla glanced at the empty chair, then down the row of empty tables.

"*Je suis désolée, mais*—I'm waiting for someone."

"Sure?" he asked, a smile tugging at the corner of his mouth. "How about a quick coffee?"

She shook her head no, not enjoying the way he paused between "quick" and "coffee." Bertrand shrugged and turned. Camilla checked the time.

"Wait," she called. She motioned to a chair at the next bistro table, so they could talk, but have a chair between them.

Bertrand tossed out the back of his navy blazer as he sat so as not to wrinkle the fabric. He turned in the chair and, as if on cue, the waiter popped his head out the door.

"*Bonjour Allain. Un café noir,*" he said, and then turned to Camilla. "Are you here for the race?"

Camilla nodded. His aftershave was strong and cheap.

"You like racing?"

"I'm learning to," she said. "My boyfriend is a driver."

"*Ooh-la-lahhh,*" Bertrand said, letting his breath out in a rush. "How can I compete with that?" His eyes twinkled. "What team?"

"Elrod Racing. You know it?"

"American team?" he asked.

The waiter arrived and set down their coffees. Hers had a swirl of whip cream on top. Bertrand let his arm rest on the back of the chair between them. All of a sudden, an engine revved angrily.

Camilla looked up and saw a black Alfa Romeo idling in the middle of the Boulevard. The engine roared again, impatiently.

"Here comes the cavalry," Camilla mumbled, squinting her eyes to see into the car. Then she slowly scooped a spoonful of whip cream into her mouth. She turned back to Bertrand and smiled as she swallowed.

The driver-side door flew open. Coleton left the car running in the middle of the street and sauntered toward Camilla. He wore dark fitted jeans and a stone colored cashmere sweater. In the shifting light, his eyes were forest green. Camilla hadn't seen him for more than a week and she felt her stomach go molten.

Coleton didn't say a word when he reached her. He just leaned down and planted a hard, lingering kiss on her lips, his hand on the back of her neck. Camilla flushed.

"I have food coming, and I still need to get *l'addition.*"

Coleton pulled out his "wallet," which consisted of a number of bills folded over a quarter inch of plastic credit cards secured with a rubber band. He peeled away two 20 euro notes and dropped them on the table.

"When you see the lunch they're preparing at the château, you'd kill me if I let you eat here."

Camilla wrinkled up her nose, but didn't stop him from grabbing her large suitcases.

"What the hell do you have in here? Your sister?" He chuckled at his joke. He was tanned and relaxed and she would have grabbed him for another kiss if Bertrand wasn't there.

She stood, took a long sip from her *café Viennois*, wiped her upper lip. She turned to say goodbye, but Bertrand had ducked his head below the spread wings of a newspaper.

"Was that guy hitting on you?" Coleton demanded the second she shut her door.

"You were late," she said.

Still in neutral, Coleton floored the engine and held the pedal. The RPMs danced into the red.

"Coleton—" Camilla warned. She jerked her seatbelt forward and clicked it into place. Coleton smiled at her, an angelic pink-cheeked grin.

Then his eyes blazed as he jammed the stick into first, and the car lurched forward. Coleton cranked the wheel and pressed the accelerator even farther. The car spun in a sharp right-hander onto Avenue de General Leclerc.

"You should have brushed him off."

"You were late," Camilla called over the roar of the engine. "And, next time—you don't have to pee all over me just because someone's talking to me."

Coleton's lips curled at the corners, but he focused on the road. He pulled the handbrake and skidded left onto Rue Gastelier, tires squealing. Camilla's body slammed forward, caught by the seatbelt, then inertia pushed her toward the doorframe.

At a red light, the engine creaked and the fan belts whirred loudly. Camilla was able to take her first full breath of the ride.

"So, how's the racecar?"

"Great," Coleton said. "We had night practice last night. Every driver had to put in a minimum number of laps and achieve minimum lap times. One team actually failed the 107% rule, which was a bit of a shock."

"The 107% rule?"

"It means that the lap time differential between the fastest and slowest car on the track must be less than 107%. If you're slower than that, you get sent home."

The light changed green and their car shot forward. Camilla braced herself into the back of her seat. She would have to wait until they arrived for any meaningful conversation.

As the car roared from the small town and through a nest of winding country roads, Camilla lost count of the turns. A plume of fine dust billowed behind them. At last, a thick evergreen hedge rose up on their right and the sweeping French countryside sloped down into a broad valley on their left.

Without warning Coleton jammed his left foot down on the brake and cranked the wheel. The rear tires squealed and spun out, sending gravel flying out in a wave of dust. The car shifted sideways threatening to spin out of control. Camilla braced herself against the door jam and squeezed her eyes shut. But, Coleton modulated the steering wheel, with quick tight movements.

"Coleton!" Camilla screeched. "Was that necessary?"

"Sorry, that turn really snuck up on me," Coleton chuckled.

"Selective blindness is not an excuse to get the car sideways. We could have crashed into that hedge!"

"Yeah, we could have been picking leaves out of our teeth," Coleton said. His eyes were gleaming. He drove carefully through the open iron gates and crawled up the cobbled drive, staring at Camilla to make a point. He was driving slowly, painfully slow, just for her. After their wild ride it felt ridiculous even to Camilla.

"Holy Mother of—" Camilla said, as they rounded the final bend in the driveway.

Before them at the top of a rise, set back in a grove of trees was not a house, but a mansion, a true French château worthy of its grandiose name.

"We're staying here?" Camilla chirped.

"Stick around, kid."

As this was the first year that Arthur Elrod brought his Le Mans team to the world famous 24 Heures du Mans, he had decided to go all out. He had taken the entire Château de Charmont for the week of the race to house the team's entourage, including the team sponsors, whom Elrod planned to lavishly entertain as a thank-you gift of sorts, strategically timed to help solidify sponsor commitments for the following year. Once the ancestral home of a noble family,

Château de Charmont had been converted to a five-star resort with 86 staff members for its 19 bedrooms, 26 bathrooms, six tennis courts, a parsonage with a 400 year old chapel, and a stable with riding trails throughout its 40 forested acres.

"I've never seen anything like this. This is how fairytales start."

As they pulled up to the entrance, their car was met by two gloved valets.

"What's that smell?" Camilla asked. "Something's burning."

"Just the brakes, baby." Coleton smiled.

Outside the car, the smell was even stronger and the valets looked at each other with appreciative glances. They had already witnessed a week of Coleton's coming and goings as he prepared for the race, but it never ceased to surprise them how he could work his rented racehorse to a lather.

A valet opened Camilla's door and extended a gloved hand for hers.

"Keep the car out and running. I'll be back down in 10 minutes," Coleton called to the valet, as he followed Camilla up the front marble steps.

"*D'accord, Monsieur.*"

"Ten minutes? Where are we going?" Camilla asked. "I had some other plans for you." She pulled him close. Coleton's eyes widened and he leaned in to kiss her.

"I've got to head back to town for an impact test at 1:30 and I can't miss it."

"An impact test?"

"They give you a series of memory and cognitive tests, to set the 'before' bar. Then, when you auger in during the race, they re-test you to see if you can get back in the car, or if you have problems."

"*When* you auger in?" Camilla pulled back from him.

"Sorry, *if.* Just a precaution."

"A precaution to measure future brain damage? Lovely. Should I come with you?"

"Settle in here, enjoy lunch in the courtyard and get ready for tonight while I'm gone."

"For tonight?" she asked.

"The welcome dinner. You know, the Grand Gala."

"Grand Gala?" Camilla gasped. "No, I ... You never ... Don't you know that galas require time for accessory selection and successive rounds of garment alterations—both of which require notice!"

"I'm sure you've got something in there you can wear," Coleton said, motioning at the valets as they wrangled her behemoth suitcases up the marble stairs. "You've really got to learn to MFM."

"MFM?"

"Maintain Field Mobility. You sure as hell aren't field mobile, sweetheart."

Coleton always traveled light and prided himself on his ability to move in any direction, call an audible, maneuver, relocate, switch activities, plot a new, sometimes covert operation—and all at a moments notice.

"Field mobility is for the battlefield, darling. We're in France," Camilla said. "Here it's social mobility that counts. A fine, but rather important distinction. Try to keep up."

Coleton rolled his eyes.

"Let's agree to disagree, shall we?" Camilla asked. Coleton clamped his mouth shut. He never agreed for the sake of agreeing.

"Look at this guy. He can move!" Camilla said changing the subject. A valet had already packed her bags onto a gold-toned trolley and was charging through the expansive foyer.

"His name is Marcus and we have him slated as our back-up driver," Coleton joked.

As Camilla stepped over the threshold, she froze. "It's a Jane Austin novel," she said in a hushed voice that echoed upward into the expansive foyer.

Checkerboard marble spilled from the oak double doors down the entrance hall to another set of tall double doors leading to a larger room. Twin staircases, paved with ruby red carpets, rose on either side of the room and connected in a second floor balcony along the back of the room that lead to the guest quarters. A Lalique chandelier the size of a Mini Cooper hovered above an antique table crowned with a vase of brilliant red Stargazer lilies.

A woman stepped onto the marble floor blocking their progress. She was dressed in neat white pants and a rose-colored silk blouse that tied in a bow at her neck.

"This must be Mrs. Loren?" she asked.

"Oh, no we're not—" Camilla began.

"Yes, this is Camilla," Coleton interrupted.

"*Je m'appelle Madame Beatrice.*" She limply placed her hand in Camilla's, but did not move it. "*Enchantée,*" she added.

Madame Beatrice had shortly cropped silver hair that fell in gentle waves behind her ears. She spun and motioned for them to follow her. "I am the *tenancier,* or manager as you say, of the property. *Permettez-moi* to show you to your suite."

Just as they began to follow her, Coleton noticed motion through the double doors at the far end of the checkerboard hall. He squinted, then smiled.

"Hey, Hilton!" Coleton called. His voice echoed down the hall. "Come meet one of my co-drivers," he said, turning to Camilla.

All of a sudden, Hilton slid into the room on the slippery soles of a new pair of alligator loafers. Camilla recognized Hilton Crowne immediately. He looked just like his twin sister, Juliette, whom she'd seen in tabloids for years. He had a handsome narrow face, softly curled blond hair that brushed the tops of his shoulders and bright blue eyes. He looked soft and fun loving, but his eyes had a glint, a sharpness Camilla recognized as intelligence.

Hilton threw his arm around Coleton's shoulders.

"This is Camilla," Coleton said.

"Hi Camilla! Finally we meet." Hilton's cheeks were flushed pink and Camilla noticed the sweet smell of alcohol on his breath. "Come join us! We've just begun to celebrate."

"Celebrate?"

"Didn't he tell you? Coleton qualified our car in third place this morning. The session ran really late, but on his last lap he pulled it off."

"That's why you were late?" Camilla asked, turning to Coleton. He smiled, then shrugged.

"Shouldn't you save the celebration for Saturday night?" Coleton asked darkly. "That's when it counts."

"It's my first Le Mans and I'm starting from third!" Hilton's eyes widened. "I'll drink to that."

The previous year Hilton had finished second in the Indy Lights Championship. When a young driver finishes well in Indy Lights, he has to choose the direction of his career: Indy car, Le Mans or the feeder series to Formula 1. If Hilton had been more focused than spoiled, William Crowne would have pushed him toward GP3, GP2 and then on to Formula 1, which is considered the pinnacle of racing. Hilton had the looks, the charisma, the money and probably the talent to make it to Formula 1, but even all those things combined won't guarantee you a seat. You also have to be singularly insatiable for victory. Indy car was also an option, but Hilton disliked driving on oval tracks, and since they are exceedingly more dangerous, as are the Indy cars themselves, William Crowne pushed his son to the Le Mans series.

"This guy is like a big brother," Hilton continued to Camilla. "He used to bail me out of trouble when we were growing up."

"Used to?" Coleton mocked.

A tall girl with chocolate brown hair stepped into the doorway to the Great Room. She was dressed in a black and white French maid's outfit, complete with a starched lace headband, and the tops of her black stocking were only just visible with the sway of her short skirt. She held up a bottle of Moët by its neck and let it swing slowly from side to side.

"*Chéri*," she called to Hilton.

Madame Beatrice glared at the girl, before turning her burning gaze on Hilton. He grinned in response, unabashed.

"Come join us after you get settled," Hilton said. Coleton nodded, not bothering to explain their plans wouldn't coincide.

"Was that a real French maid?" Camilla asked as they walked away. "Or maybe she was an FME?"

"A what?"

"The French maid version of a GFE," Camilla said with a mischievous grin. Coleton laughed out loud.

"I'm not actually sure," he said, still smiling. "Maybe *Madame* B does manage more than just this old place." He gave her a conspiratorial wink.

Their suite was on the second floor and by the time they had climbed one of the grand staircases and walked down the long east corridor, the valet had arranged her suitcases and thrown open the windows. The living room had three broad windows draped in white curtains that puddled on the floor and framed the view of a large traditional French garden. Camilla leaned out the middle window in awe.

The sky was still gray even though it was midday and the garden had a misty morning quality. Topiaries cut the garden into a radiating geometric pattern, with sharply defined diamond-shaped boxes. Each leafy square was packed with jewel-toned roses: amethyst, ruby, tourmaline, pink sapphire, rose quartz. In the center of the garden, three stone women stood elevated back to back, pouring out their vases into the pool of clear water at their feet.

"It's been a real tough week," Coleton said.

"Clearly."

Coleton came up behind her, wrapped his arms around her in a barrel hug and lowered his chin onto her shoulder. Camilla turned in his arms and gave him a long lingering kiss. He looked deep into her eyes, then bit his bottom lip and glanced at their cornflower blue canopy bed. He knew exactly what biting his lip did to her. True to form, she went weak at the knees.

"I guess I could be 20 minutes late ..."

The clock on the dashboard read: 6:50.
Shit.

Coleton was going to be late for the gala. The impact test had taken longer than he expected, and it was more difficult than the one in the States. He couldn't remember the order of all those shapes when he was in perfect health, let alone after a crash. He made a left onto Avenue Bollée and skidded to a stop at a red light. He glared at the light. Red lights always infuriated him. Like a bull, he only wanted to charge when he saw red. He drummed his fingers on the steering wheel, then peered at the driver in the car next to him.

"What are the odds," Coleton laughed, his expression instantly shifting.

Coleton released the clutch an inch and let the Alfa Romeo roll forward to be certain. Sure enough: Anderson Green. Instinctually, the other driver released his clutch and evened up his front axle to his neighbor.

Andy was the star driver for the factory Aston Martin GT team, one of the fastest, most professional teams in the GT paddock. He was a funny Brit with a propensity for practical jokes, a trait he acquired during his childhood. He had been raised by his father in a small blue-collar town north of London with five brothers and no mother, so his upbringing was quite loose. He happened to be in the right place at the right time and had lucked into his first drive, which earned him his second drive and so on. Drivers like Andy are a bit of an anomaly in today's motorsports world.

In the '60s and '70s drivers could go from mechanic to driver just by catching the right man's eye and performing on command. Team owners were willing to harvest raw talent in that era. In the modern racing world, however, drivers need more than just raw talent or a lucky break. They need sponsorship dollars, business acumen, an endorsement-friendly face and if they can drive—that doesn't hurt either.

Andy was one of the hungriest and hardest working guys in the paddock, but he was also the most laid back. He never got frazzled and emotional. Some drivers are crybabies or drama queens and report anything with an inkling of merit to race control, most of which gets noted and promptly thrown out. Andy never ran to the officials. Even if another driver pulled a blatantly bad move, Andy would just make a mental note and return the favor when he got the chance. Coleton liked Andy Green.

Coleton motioned for Andy to roll down his window. "What's happening, you limey bastard?"

"Not much, you Yankee wanna-be Euro trash!" Andy retorted with a huge smile revealing a mouthful of spectacularly awful teeth.

"Wanna trade paint?" Coleton smirked.

"Does a one-legged duck swim in circles?"

Coleton pegged his accelerator to the floor with the clutch depressed. His tachometer bounced repeatedly into the red. Andy reciprocated with his rental car, a lime green Citroën. This would be the perfect street race, two rentals with full collision insurance. The light turned green. Both drivers dumped the clutch and their front wheels spun out plumes of smoke. They jolted forward, shifting to second gear at the same time, then third, then fourth.

Andy put a wheel on the inside of Coleton and boxed him behind another car to take the lead. With a growl, Coleton pulled from behind the slower car and caught up. He couldn't make a pass because there was traffic on both sides, so he started to ram Andy's bumper. Andy smiled into his rearview mirror and responded with a brake check. Surprised by the move, Coleton slammed his brakes, but still ploughed into Andy's bumper so hard that its attachments broke and it fell off, along with Coleton's front license plate.

"You crazy wanker!" Coleton laughed as his front wheels bucked over Andy's bumper. Stuck under Coleton's chassis, it made an awful screeching noise on the asphalt. This minor setback did not waiver Coleton's determination.

Coleton grinned from ear to ear as he pulled alongside the Citroën. Andy flashed him a matching maniacal grin. They made eye contact for a split second, and with that quick look, the agreement was finalized. The fun would not stop until one of the vehicles was inoperable.

Coleton decided to make a right onto Rue 33EME Mobiles, which required a quick lane change. He was half a car length in front of Andy and began to merge right. Andy didn't respond quickly enough, and Coleton helped him to the same decision, nudging him over bit by bit and destroying his own rear quarter panel in the process.

By the time they reached the far right lane, Coleton gave a quick jerk to the steering wheel, and both cars shot airborne as they launched over the median, rolled down the grassy slope and rocked onto the off ramp. Their respective landings resulted in more carnage: Andy lost his muffler and Coleton sacrificed two hubcaps that rolled past both cars before peeling off the road of their own accord. Coleton tested the accelerator and realized the maneuver had succeeding in dislodging Andy's bumper from under him. His rear tires rolled over it like a speed bump.

Coleton gave a wild whoop. "No more drag, better aero!"

They raced down Rue de 33EME Mobiles, passing the imposing Théâtre Municipal on their right. Ahead the Cathédrale de St-Julien du Mans rose up, dead-ending the road with its flying buttresses, gothic spires and stained glass windows. All of a sudden, they screeched to a halt in gridlock traffic. Two long segmented orange buses blocked the right hand lane onto Avenue de Paderborn. Andy was behind Coleton and both cars idled at a dead stop. Andy spotted a flight of stairs on his right that led to Jacobin Park.

"Right," said Andy. "I guess it's down the old apples and pears, Mate."

He pulled onto the shoulder of the road on Coleton's right, revved his engine and made for the historic stairs.

Not to be outdone, Coleton spun onto the shoulder and followed Andy on his suicide mission without even calculating the risk. Sparks flew as the cars slid down the stairs, both drivers modulating the throttle to keep from stalling. More car parts scattered behind them, like the entrails of a wild beast being tracked through the African bush. Andy's car hit the ground at the bottom of the stairs and stuck fast, its rear wheels a few inches off the steps. Coleton carried more speed down the stairs and slammed into him. The collision pushed the Citroën forward, setting it free. Coleton's car rolled down the last step and rocked to a standstill.

"How about that for an impact test?" Coleton yelled through the windshield. "How many fingers am I holding up?" Coleton flourished his middle finger at the eyes he saw in Andy's rearview mirror.

Coleton took a deep breath, released and re-gripped the steering wheel, then broke into loud laughter. A few feet from the smoking car, an old woman with a cable knit sweater was walking on the park path. She moved forward, leaned over to make eye contact with Coleton through the windshield, and with a resounding *THWACK*, she smacked her long umbrella into his hood, leaving an indentation. Suddenly sheepish, Coleton raised a hand in apology, and offered her a smile of the type he knew to be very effect with women. In response, she brandished her umbrella overhead, shaking it like a weapon of war, and yelled, "*Espece de connard!*"

Coleton ducked his head, but inched forward. After a few feet, he pressed the accelerator and shot after Andy, who had started off through the park, kicking up a plume of dust from the pathway. Coleton gained on him quickly, but the path took a sudden 90-degree turn. They both had to handbrake, and sliding sideways, almost ended up in the bushes.

"Whose the rally king?" Coleton yelled, modulating the steering wheel with quick precise movements to reign in the oversteer. Rolling speed through the corner, Coleton quickly caught up to Andy and nudged his exposed bodywork with his bumper. The Citroën looked naked without its rear bumper.

Andy looked up and gasped. Ahead, the pathway dead-ended in a row of trees and a low stone wall. Andy jogged left, through a narrow opening in the trees. His car stepped over the curb and back into the street. With fighter pilot instincts Coleton followed, as if his front bumper was glued to Andy's car.

Coleton was possessed. He had to figure a way to force Andy into an unrecoverable shunt. He saw a fire hydrant up the way and began to concoct a plan.

Andy slammed on his brakes and skidded to a stop at an intersection. Behind him, Coleton hit his brake pedal hard with his left foot and screeched to a stop with inches to spare. The idling machines creaked and fan belts whirred, as smoke lifted from their hoods. There were no other cars in the four-way stop, so Coleton laid on the horn. Andy's right hand shot up between the seats of his car: all five fingers perfectly straight in a halting motion. Coleton released his palm from the horn, but his hand hovered over the spot.

Slowly, almost gingerly, Andy crawled forward in first gear through the intersection. As he moved out of the way, Coleton saw down the avenue ahead. Parked along the side of the street was a *Police Nationale* car topped with a bar of blue and white lights.

"Fuck me running!" Coleton yelped.

He inched forward cautiously and put on his left blinker for the first time that day. The indicator light on his dash clicked in double time. The bulb was definitely broken. Coleton brought the car to a complete stop well before the stop sign, paused for a moment, then eased forward and turned left, careful not to make eye contact with the policeman sitting at the wheel of his parked car.

"Cheeky bugga," Coleton chuckled, as he lost sight of the Brit. "I'll see your limey ass on the track!"

By the time the tall hedge appeared on Coleton's right, the clock on the dash read 7:40.

Coleton had lost his top end gears and had to drive all the way home in second. He pressed the accelerator to the floor, and the car erupted with a cacophony of new squeaks and groans. He had 20 minutes to shower, slip into a tuxedo and be in the ballroom before dinner was served. Cocktails would already be in full swing. Camilla was going to kill him.

Coleton hit a late apex and cut sharply into the long drive of Château de Charmont. The car clamored up the drive, but as he neared the entrance he dropped to first gear. A line of Rolls Royces, Bentleys, and Maybachs crowded the drive, waiting to deliver their glittering passengers to the marble steps. This wasn't just a dinner for the Elrod team principals and sponsors. It looked like the elite of the entire racing community was waiting to make a grand entrance.

Normally, Coleton didn't care what anyone thought. But, for just a moment, a flash of decency reminded him that the cars were filled with sponsors, actual and potential, and the highest echelons of racing royalty. Coleton realized that racing up in a smoking Alfa with burnt brakes, dented bodywork, broken headlights and dragging bumper, not to mention an umbrella shaped dent in the hood, wouldn't fast track his career. He parked in the bushes a few hundred feet away and went through the gardens to the east side of the château. When he saw the fountain of the three women, he cut left to look for a side entrance.

There were a few doors in the side of the château, but they were painted shut and didn't budge to his shoulder. He walked along the building, until he could just make out their open window with white curtains fluttering in the breeze above his head.

"Camilla!" Coleton called, his head thrown back, but there was no response. The first stars were winking from the darkening sky.

An old lichen-covered trellis laced the wall of the château up to the second story windows. Coleton gave it a little pull, testing it. The quicker he moved, the more likely it would hold his weight. Coleton looked down at his watch in the dim light. He didn't have a choice.

"How the hell do I get myself into these things?" he asked out loud. Coleton backed three paces away, inhaled then exhaled loudly.

He swung his arms, first one then the other, before sprinting toward the wall and pulling himself up. The trellis began to give under his weight. He climbed faster, knowing he only had a few seconds to get to the top.

He got his fingers over the edge of the windowsill. He did a pull up, then threw his leg over the sill and rolled onto the floor of the plush living area.

"Camilla, I'm back!" he called. "You're not going to believe–"

As Coleton stood up and picked a leaf out of his hair, he gasped. It was not their room. Their room was done in a smattering of different blue patterns, not fern green fleur-de-lis. Coleton's eyes widened. He tiptoed toward the door, holding his breath. He almost made it, if he had fallen forward he would have touched it, when from down the short hall he heard a voice purr his name, "Coleton Lorrrren?"

Coleton cringed and pivoted slowly toward the sound. The master bedroom door was flung open and the king sized bed rested only a cartwheel away. Justine Elrod lay on the bed like an odalisque, naked except for a diamond necklace. She sat up, her knees steepled in front of her, but made not the slightest effort to cover her breasts.

"Hello, dear," she cooed. Coleton looked down at his jeans and felt as naked as she was.

"Wrong room." Coleton blushed. "I just—" He didn't know where to begin. He heard water running and guessed that Elrod was in the shower.

"Are you sure? You're always welcome in my room." She raised an eyebrow and her artificially plump lips curled into a feline smile. She let one knee drop outward.

"Oh, God," Coleton said, the words slipping from his mouth. He had no idea how to respond.

Justine had always been flirty, but he thought it was just a diversion, a game for her to play at like the other cougars he knew. Nothing about this situation felt like a game, especially that simple, outward motion.

Coleton checked his watch with an exaggerated pantomime. "Shit," he muttered. "I'm going to be so late to dinner. So are you, by the way."

"Yes, but I'm the money, and the money is always forgiven. Drivers on the other hand must *perform* if they want to join our little party."

"I always perform," Coleton said with a wink.

"Come back anytime," Justine laughed. "But next time—" She paused. Coleton paused too, his hand already on the doorknob. "Next time," she continued. "Leave the mud outside, won't you?"

Coleton looked down at his shoes, caked with muck, and the trail he'd left across the plush carpet.

"Shit, sorry! What will you tell—" He nodded toward the bathroom.

Justine shrugged a bare shoulder, unconcerned.

Coleton slipped into the hallway. Over the balustrade he saw the string of formally clad guests walking through the marbled entrance hall below. He stuck close to the wall and hurried toward his suite.

The first rays of sunlight woke Coleton as they spilled across the embroidered coverlet. He sat up in bed and rubbed his eyes, disgusted with himself. He was hung-over. He only had the faintest trace of a headache, but on the day before the biggest race of the year, it was far from acceptable.

As a rule, Coleton never drank during the race season. In fact, he had once gone two years without even a champagne toast. But, this year had been different from the very start. Taking to drink after he broke his leg had seemed the superior alternative to pain pills, but it had been too easy to keep up the habit socially after his leg had healed.

Race or no race, Coleton had always appreciated fine wine. When Elrod produced a bottle of 1973 Château Mouton Rothschild, the year the wine achieved Premier Cru status after 120 years of domination by the four other Premier crus, Coleton salivated. After that, Elrod fired up a tasting of the remaining four first growths of Bordeaux: a 1982 Château Margaux, 2000 Château Haut-Brion, 1982 Château Latour, a 1982 Château Lafite Rothschild. All the best Bordeaux, all the best years. It never occurred to Coleton to abstain, although it should have.

Racecar drivers lose up to five pounds of water weight during a race of two or three hours. In a 24 hour endurance race like Le Mans, where a single driver will be behind the wheel for at least eight hours, his liquid intake must be massive before, during and after the event. Beginning a week before a race, Coleton drank at least two gallons of water a day. A hangover the day before an endurance race was rookie behavior.

Coleton shielded his eyes from the sunlight. An anal-retentive freak about closing the shades, he preferred to wake up in complete darkness. *Two strikes already and I'm still between the sheets.* He snatched a glass bottle of water off his nightstand and drained the entire liter into his stomach in one go, poised like a Greek statute in the morning light. He looked around for more. He rolled out of bed, careful not to wake Camilla, and grabbed a second liter off her nightstand, which he downed in two long gulps. *That's a start.*

Coleton showered quickly, but quietly. Camilla would want to join him, but he preferred to eat breakfast alone during a race week. He didn't want to make small talk. He needed a few precious moments of silence, the only time he would have for the rest of the day to prepare his mind. He scribbled a quick note for her and left it on his pillow.

Coleton could hear his footfall in the plush carpet as he descended the grand staircase of the sleeping château. The soles of his driving loafers thundered on the marble in the foyer. To get to the breakfast room, he passed through the cavernous Great Room. Its whitewashed walls were a patchwork of old master paintings scattered up to the rafters, and imposing stone fire places rose on either end of the hall. Embers still smoldered from the evening before. Coleton guessed the party had adjourned there for scotch after he had turned in, as the smell of Cohiba Esplendido cigars still lingered in the air.

A curious muffled sound gave Coleton pause. It was almost a hiss. He froze, one foot poised above the floor, listening. Again, he heard it—this time it was more of a sigh. He followed the sound to a seating group, and peered over the back of a couch upholstered in a tapestry hunt scene.

Hilton's head was flung back on the arm of the couch, and he was wearing a white lace headband. His mouth gapped to reveal the tips of a row of perfect teeth, his left arm and leg, dangled over the edge of the couch. His pants were unzipped and his right hand rested protectively over the Crowne family jewels. His custom shirt was crumpled, and three buttons were undone to reveal lipstick on his neck, a big garish red kiss. Coleton laughed out loud. Hilton didn't stir, as another soft snore sighed from his lips.

Coleton shook his head. *Breakfast.* He made his way to the Crystal Room, named for the collection of antique chandeliers that hung like stalactites from the painted ceiling. Tables clothed in white and set with silver waited for the breakfast bustle. A pair of broad French doors had been thrown open to a courtyard lined with pots of miniature orange trees and fragrant lavender. Coleton nodded to the liveried attendant and took a seat at an iron bistro in the courtyard. The air was cool and damp, the morning dew still falling. Coleton felt it settle on his skin as it sifted down, slowly down, through the air around him.

Coleton pulled a crumpled track map from his pocket, and flattened it on the table. His handwritten scribbles brought back thoughts, visions, memories of the track. Reference points, shift markers, lines in the pavement, trees in the peripheral vision, undulations in the road, were all personal markers committed to memory that made him faster around the track.

After giving his breakfast order to the waiter, Coleton closed his eyes. With a deep inhalation and a metered exhalation, he consciously moved into what Jackie Stewart referred to as the "deflate the ball stage." The stage before a race, when a driver must let all emotion—excitement, anxiety, fear, hope—drain from the body, leaving behind a calm and focused core, as cool and smooth as a stone. The easiest way to drive is with anger and passion, spit and fire, throwing up your hand at the cars that dodge and weave around you, but these emotions burn out during an endurance race.

Drivers who mainline the quick drug of adrenaline and rely on its rush, never reach the podium, or at least not at an endurance race. Coleton let his breathing settle into the slow rhythm of ocean waves, as his every sense awoke and the small courtyard came to life in its own microcosm of morning sounds.

Then, Coleton began to race laps in his head. He visualized each corner, felt each turn. Like other top professionals in his field, Coleton could trace a lap in his head while timing it on a stopwatch. His head moved perceptibly to the right into Turn 1, his foot tapped the gravel where the brake would be. He could feel the shudder of each change of pavement. He remembered precisely the length of each straightaway, the exact moment to shift and the succession of gears. When he opened his eyes and hit the stop button, his lap time would be within a second from what it would be on race day. Driving is more than an instinctual feat of adrenaline and abandon, it's careful mental and physical practice, a form of art.

With a loud crunch, the waiter stepped over the doorsill into the gray gravel and Coleton's eyes shot open. He brandished a silver tray loaded with plates: an egg white omelet for protein, a plate of ripe berries packed with antioxidants, a carafe of orange juice to regulate his blood sugar and boost his vitamin C. Coleton smiled at the perfectly groomed waiter. The French view food as art and Coleton admired anyone obsessed with perfection.

Woof. Woof-woof, woof. Coleton looked around the still courtyard. *What is that?* He frowned and pulled out his cell phone. Ira's picture filled the screen. Camilla must have changed Ira's ring tone.

"Is that hot little French tart of Elrod's there?"

"What?" Coleton asked, pushing the phone tighter to his ear. He heard loud thumping music in the background. "Who?"

"His secretary."

"Who knows? All the girls here are French."

"I think the French part might be an act, but she is *smoking*. If I was there, I'd totally take that down."

"Great. Is that why you called? And, remind me why you're *not* here?"

"I told you. I have to entertain some Canadian businessmen this weekend."

"I'm sure they can hire a hooker without your fat finger dialing the number."

"You're missing the point. They're on the board of an energy drink. Great potential sponsor."

"Nice try. Be honest—you're not here because you ran out of credit card mile upgrades."

Ira giggled. "No regrets for me. I'm at Mynt," he said. "And I've got this sophomore all over me. Krystal from Kansas. Ohhh yeah."

"You're at Mynt?"

"In the bathroom."

"And where's Krista?"

"Krystal, with a 'y.' She's outside."

"Better hurry, you might lose her."

"No way. I reeled her in with the 'Who lies more, men or women?' opener, dropped a couple subtle *negs*, and got her all the way through the Cube Routine, all the great PUA stuff … major kino!"

"What language is that? PUA?"

"Pick Up Artist," Ira said. "Google it. Works like magic! Not all of us are handsome racecar drivers, you know. Some of us need game."

"You need—a therapist. What time is it?"

"Two."

"Two a.m. on a Thursday. Don't you work, you lazy bastard?"

"I *am* working! I'm doing research for this weekend. Now listen, is Miller there?"

"At my breakfast table?"

"You need to have a sit down and ask why he didn't make his payment to Elrod yesterday."

"Ira. I'm leaving for the *Grande Parade des Pilotes* now, and I have a race tomorrow. Don't fuck with my head."

"I can't get ahold of him."

"Well, keep trying. That's what I pay you for." Coleton hung up the phone and shook his head to refocus on his job—winning Le Mans.

As he took his last sip of green tea and rose, Coleton peered down into the bottom of the fine porcelain cup at the dark flakes— just to check. But, he couldn't make out anything of his future in the pattern of the leaves. The cup rattled as he dropped it back to its saucer.

"*Bonjour, Ami!*"

Coleton turned. "Hey Seb," Coleton replied to his co-driver. They shook hands.

Sébastien Babineaux grew up in Tours, a city along the Loire, an hour south of Le Mans, and he had been to Le Mans as a spectator or driver every year of his life. He was tall for a professional driver at six-foot-two, almost too tall to fit in a closed cockpit car, but he made it work. Babineaux had raced for Audi as a factory driver for three years, and had won two first place trophies, but wasn't asked back for a fourth year after a horrible shunt that totaled the car and landed him in the hospital. After that, he became a journeyman driver, traveling from team to team to the highest bidder, with his helmet in hand. He didn't bring sponsors with him, just talent, and Elrod paid handsomely not only for his skill and knowledge of the track, but also for his celebrity. Sébastien Babineaux was a crowd favorite, a local gone pro, and the crowd wanted to see him back on top.

Coleton looked down at his watch. "We better make tracks."

"*Oui.* They'll start closing roads to prepare for the parade."

"There should be a limo out front." Coleton looked out the stone archway that led from the courtyard to the front drive. "Have you eaten?"

"In my room. Quite a party last night, no?" Sébastien asked, scratching his head.

"Elrod can certainly throw a *fête.*"

"*Oú est* Hilton *ce matin?*" Sébastien asked. "The last time I saw him he was drinking champagne from the bottle and pissing in a fireplace."

Coleton laughed. "Don't worry. I know where to collect him. But he's going to need an espresso."

"Tonight we lock him in his room."

"Camilla, you sit here. Right by me," Elrod said, pulling out a white painted bistro chair.

Elrod's secretary, Marie-Claire, had found a café along the parade route, and Elrod had rented the entire establishment for his entourage of 40 guests and sponsors. La Petite Vache was only a block from the Place de la République, where the parade would begin, and from its white-linened tables arranged along the street, they could see the spire of the square's Gothic cathedral.

Camilla accepted the seat. Olivia Miller took the chair on her left, and Justine the one on Elrod's right. Their party bus and its escort of police motorcycles pulled away from the curb, and a band struck up the *La Marseillaise* in the Place de la République. The streets had been cordoned off and the sidewalks were packed with thousands of fans, eager to see their favorite drivers. The band would march out any minute, followed by 55 antique convertibles, each one carrying the three drivers of a racing team.

"How exciting!" Justine cried, leaning over Elrod's lap to talk with her new friend, Olivia. She clapped her hands like a little girl. "I can't wait to see all the handsome drivers."

"This is the *only* way to watch it!" cried Olivia. "Just look at the people!" She pointed across the street, where a chain-link fence held back a mob of excited fans.

"Oh, here comes the marching band! Looks at the uniforms. Only the French!"

Camilla sat up in her chair to see. Everyone was cheering, laughing and waving flags of their country or favorite team. Excited energy shook the leaves in the spreading arms of the plane and boxwood trees above their heads.

"Arthur Elrod?" a gruff voice asked, loud enough to be heard over the music.

Elrod and Camilla turned. A tall, barrel chested man stood behind them, his chest so broad it cast a shadow over the pair. He had slim black sunglasses on his square face and his hands were clasped behind his back.

"Yes?"

"Come with me."

Elrod's eyes darted around the tables looking for Smith, but couldn't find him. "No, I don't think I will. Who are you?"

"Dieter Fleischer requests your presence."

"Where?" Elrod asked, the color draining from his face.

"Upstairs."

Elrod looked up at the balcony, then swallowed back some words. He took another closer look at the boulder-like man and saw an inch of curled plastic behind his right ear.

Elrod pushed back his chair and stood.

"Everything okay?" Camilla asked.

"Fine," Elrod said. He straightened his sport coat, pulled the lapels closed, then let them spread open, flexing his shoulders. "Dieter's an old friend."

Camilla glanced at Justine for confirmation, but Justine was chatting to Olivia, oblivious.

The crowd began to cheer as the first car came into site. Three drivers in royal blue racing suits sat side-by-side on an antique Bugatti, their feet resting on the backseats, waving their hands in small slow movements like beauty queens.

Elrod followed the man into the café, keeping an eye on the fabric of his lapel in the breeze, but he couldn't see a weapon. Smith emerged from the restroom. He wiped his hands on his pants and adjusted his skinny black tie. Elrod made wild-eyed, silent gestures at him behind the large man's back.

"Useless son of a bitch!" Elrod mouthed. Smith wrinkled his brow and cocked his head. Elrod held up his hand to stop him. He pointed up the stairs, then drew a line over his throat. Smith startled.

"If I'm not back in five minutes," Elrod mouthed, holding up five fingers. "Raise hell!" Elrod flailed his hands on "raise hell" and started up the narrow wooden staircase. Smith nodded and turned his back to the stairwell, arms folded over his chest.

The wooden beams of the second floor landing bowed and creaked under their weight. A sea of empty tables stretched onto the balcony. A man sat near the railing, his back turned to them. He had on a maroon sport coat and had a full head of yellowish white hair.

Dieter's guard pulled out a chair for Elrod, facing the parade. Elrod watched the cars crawl like a row of ants down the tree-lined street, as the crowd went wild with excitement.

"Arthur," Dieter inclined his head in greeting.

Elrod's face was drawn into a tight pale mask. He tried to see through Dieter's mirrored sunglasses and read his eyes.

Dieter pushed the sleeves of his sport coat up a few inches, then rested his elbows on the table. Elrod's mouth gaped. Circling Dieter's right wrist was a heavy gold bracelet, with a collection of skull beads that clinked dully.

Dieter looked at Elrod's pale face and chuckled. "No one ever believes, until they see it." As he spoke, Dieter slid each bead to the right, as if counting on an abacus. The beads wrapped all the way around his thick wrist.

Each skull represented a person whose life Dieter had taken with his own hands, by strangling, shooting, cutting, crushing. Dieter had a wide array of tools at his disposal. Elrod's thoughts suddenly flicked to the hundreds of victims that hadn't merited such personal attention. The rumors, Elrod could now believe, might be true.

Sometimes Dieter let his victims trade an especially beautiful woman for their lives; a few he had turned into assassins like him, his loyal agents, bodyguards and lovers. True or not, Dieter let the stories spread across Europe. His victims were half dead with terror when he met them, ready for him to put them out of their misery.

Elrod gulped, and his dry throat made a guttural strangling sound.

"I have room for a few more beads," Dieter said. His lips curled ever so slightly at the corners. "We both know what you've done, or should I say—have failed to do."

"I … I'll get you your money," Elrod stuttered. "It's a non-issue. I just need a few days because my associate's payment is late, and—"

"I never read the middle of a novel, Mr. Elrod. The ups and downs of the plot, the nuances of character, the waste of pages on romance and cheap inspiration, I skip it and go straight to the end. Do you know what the playwright Chekhov said?"

"No, I don't."

"He said in Act One there must be an unused weapon. An old rifle, perhaps, mounted on the wall above the warm, inviting fireplace. And in Act Three—you see, it doesn't matter what children have snuggled by that fire, what some geriatric recalls about the hunting trips of his youth, what two little idiots in love see reflected in each other's eyes, none of it matters. Because, in Act Three, that old rifle must fire a bullet into someone's head. That's what interests me, Mr. Elrod. How will this story end?"

He jangled his bracelet of skulls and laughed. Elrod wanted to throw up.

"I gave you 30 million," Dieter continued. "And you can't even come up with the first interest payment?"

Elrod blanched. "No, I can. I will."

"Beautiful ring." Dieter stared intently at Elrod's ring finger. "You always wear it, don't you?"

Dieter extended his hand, palm up. Elrod looked down at his ring finger with horror. The large ruby glinted in the sunlight, ripe and red like a bloody berry.

Dieter wiggled his fingers, looked Elrod in the eye and nodded at his open palm.

"Don't be silly." Elrod forced a chuckle. "I'll have a million for your man tomorrow."

Boom!

Dieter slammed his palm on the table. Elrod's eyes bulged at the sound.

"Right, then," Elrod said. He gritted his teeth and worked the gold ring right and left, forcing it over his knuckle and slowly off his finger. He dropped it into Dieter's outstretched hand and watched his fist close around it.

"Tomorrow," Dieter said, with the first smile of the sitting. "And make it two million." Elrod's mouth dropped open. "Late fee," Dieter explained with a shrug. Elrod shivered, and Dieter pulled his lips back to reveal a row of large yellow teeth.

"Did you see me?" Coleton called, as he loped up to La Petite Vache with Sébastien and Hilton in tow. Now that the parade was over the streets were flooded with pedestrians, better dressed than the fans at Sebring, more wine, fewer coolers, but otherwise the same—drunk and excited. The drivers still wore their fire red race suits, and the crowd parted to make way. Glory suited Coleton.

"Of course," Camilla smiled. "Didn't you see me waving?"

Coleton nodded through a little boy smile. "Where's Elrod?"

"He went upstairs." Camilla looked over her shoulder, but the balcony looked empty now.

"What, these seats weren't good enough?"

"I think he had to meet someone."

Coleton frowned. "Well, want to walk around town before we head back?"

"I think we'd be mobbed!"

Flashbulbs popped as fans pressed against the knee-high picket fence that separated La Petite Vache's area from the public domain. Someone called Coleton's name, but they didn't look up.

"My wrist *is* a little tired from signing autographs," Coleton said. He put his arm around Camilla's shoulders and turned to pose for a picture. The crowd cheered. "I asked Madame Beatrice to have dinner sent up to our suite. So, we can have a nice, early night. I have to be up at the crack."

"A nice early night? Plenty of time to lounge in bed?" Camilla raised an eyebrow.

Coleton smiled. "No *lounging* until after the race."

"But, wait. What about Long Beach?" she asked. "You shot your own theory when you won. Maybe it's good luck!"

"Long Beach was an anomaly. We didn't have engine codes either, remember? Doesn't mean I'm going to walk into Le Mans tomorrow with no data."

Camilla stuck out her lower lip. Coleton ducked his head in a flash and kissed it, sucking it into his mouth. Camilla pushed back, laughing.

"But nice try," he said. "I like where your head's at."

Sirens cut through the noise of the crowd. Blue strobe lights flashed on faces and storefronts, as three police motorcycles rolled forward in the shape of a V, parting the crowd for a vehicle behind them.

"There's Elrod's party bus." Camilla pointed.

"Now we're talking!"

Elrod's guests migrated toward the curb, taking their plastic cups of beer with them. Camilla and Coleton let the crowd move them forward as well.

"Coleton Loren!" a voice called from the crowded street, deep and melodious, sexy.

A brightly manicured hand waved at Coleton, and a pair of dark almond eyes sparkled a few inches above the crowd. Coleton smiled and waved the woman over the low fence into the La Petite Vache area. The crowd parted. She wore a skin-tight Peugeot polo that revealed a tanned throat, a backpack and white A-line skirt. She walked up to them, then spun so they could see—not a backpack, but a baby sling.

Coleton's mouth dropped open. The baby boy had soft brown hair and snappy hazel eyes. Coleton stepped forward and shook his little outstretched hand, up and down. The baby pulled Coleton's hand to his mouth to chew on his index finger. Coleton leaned in to kiss the woman warmly on the cheek.

"He's incredible!" Coleton smiled.

"Isn't he?" she agreed, then laughed. "You look like a ghost, Coleton." Her laugh was rich. "Don't worry, he's not yours."

Camilla's eyes widened. "I'll see you on the bus," she said quietly to Coleton, and turned without waiting for an introduction. Coleton watched Camilla for a moment, before turning back to the woman.

Camilla picked a seat by the window and watched the pair talk. Each time the woman grabbed Coleton's arm and threw back her head to laugh, Camilla felt the heat in her cheeks strengthen. *Who is that woman?* Everyone was now seated and the driver was waiting to close the door. Camilla heard Hilton tell the driver to wait.

Finally, Coleton gave the woman a kiss on the cheek and sprinted up the steps into the bus. He shuffled down the aisle. Camilla continued to stare out the window, as the woman with her bouncing baby melted back into the crowd.

"Excuse me, Dr. Harlow. Is this seat taken?"

Camilla said nothing.

"Jealous?" he asked. She shook her head no, but looked out the window.

"Coulda fooled me." Coleton smiled. Camilla waited for him to explain the woman, but he just settled into his seat, looking around to see who was sitting near them.

"So he's not yours?" Camilla finally asked.

"No."

"How do you know?"

"Simple. I never *lounged* with her." Coleton couldn't suppress his smile. "Or to put it another way—"

"I get it! I'm glad you think this is funny. So why would she say, 'Don't worry he's not yours'?"

"It's a long story."

Camilla settled back into her seat. "I'm listening."

"You want to hear it?"

"I *would* like to know if there are any little Coleton's running around."

Coleton laughed. "And winning every tricycle race! Look, as far as I know you have nothing to worry about."

"Wonderful."

"You really want the story?" Camilla nodded, studying the seat fabric, which had bright droplets of color woven into it.

"Her name is Claudia Hershenheim. Her grandfather was a famous Le Mans driver, who drove in the first Le Mans in 1923 and her father started a pharmaceutical company in Austria that's now worth a billion, maybe two. She's the only heir. She used to come to Miami for the season every year to party, and I met her through Ira. One night she pulled me aside at Living Room, and, well … she asked me to be her donor."

"Donor?"

"She wanted a baby, but not a husband."

"Why?" Camilla asked.

"She has plenty of cash, but never met the right guy—for her. Most men are intimidated by the 'B' word."

"Bitch?"

"Billion. And, I guess she thought my gene pool might be a nice place to swim."

"What'd you say?"

"I said no, of course." Coleton leaned closer. "But Ira somehow found out about it and went bat shit. He was offended she didn't ask him."

"Like she'd want her kid to grow up fat, short and pushy?" Camilla blurted out, then covered her mouth.

Coleton laughed. "Exactly. So he gallantly offered to be the donor, but really I think deep down he thought it could be a meal ticket."

"But Ira makes plenty of money."

"There's no such thing as too much money. I believe his exact words to me were, 'I've been making free donations for years. Might as well cash in after all that practice.'"

"Eww," Camilla said. "Well, if she said no to Ira, then who's the donor?"

"Don't know. Don't know for sure she even said no to Ira."

They both grew quiet at the thought. Camilla looked out the bus window and watched the sunlight dapple the swale as it broke through the tree cover. She breathed a silent sigh of relief, but Claudia had walked out of the crowd holding in her baby sling a dangerous thought: a surprise down the road Camilla could never truly rule out.

CHAPTER 18

24 HEURES DU MANS

"Where the hell is Hilton?" Coleton yelled above the roar of the Augusta 109. Its rotor spun like a ceiling fan on the lowest setting, warming up. Sébastien Babineaux sat in one of the three bench seats, facing forward. He shrugged, then peered into a duffle bag, double-checking he had everything he might need for the race. A cool breeze ruffled the grass and swept in the side opening of the chopper.

"Perfect weather for a race," Sébastien said. Coleton looked out the open door into the cloudless sky. The sun had only been up for a little over an hour, but the first rays slanting in were already warm and golden.

Coleton yanked the metal buckle of his seatbelt and threw it off his lap. "I'll pull that little asshole out of bed by his hair!"

Just as Coleton grabbed the vertical bar along the door, Hilton rushed out of the château. He paused, dropped his bags to the ground, shuffled down a few feet, turned and urinated in the grass.

"Is that really necessary? The château has 26 bathrooms!" Coleton said, settling back into his seat. "He better not be hung over." As the words left Coleton's mouth he remembered his own mild headache the morning before and clamped his mouth shut.

Hilton rushed across the lawn and tossed his bags one at a time to Coleton. Then, Coleton grabbed Hilton by the wrist and hoisted him into the helicopter.

"Ready to go." Coleton patted the pilot on the shoulder.

A liveried staff member slid the door into place from the outside, then gave the pilot's window two resounding thumps with the palm of his hand.

"Roger," the pilot said. His voice rang clear in their headsets, as he placed his feet on the pedals to control the rear rotor.

Coleton turned in his seat to watch the pilot. With his right hand on the stick, the pilot twisted the collective bar with his left, as if revving the throttle of a motorcycle, then gently lifted it. In response, the helicopter rose from the ground, its nose remaining a few feet lower than its tail.

"You don't have an auto throttle?" Coleton asked, nodding as the pilot twisted the collective bar again.

"This bird's older than she looks," the pilot said over his shoulder.

Coleton raised an eyebrow.

"Fresh coat of paint and some new seat cushions, and she's as good as new."

"That's a comfort."

"Don't worry, she's also got a new Jesus nut."

"The nut that holds the hub to the mast?" Coleton asked.

The pilot nodded, impressed. "If it fails, the next person you see'll be Jesus."

After gaining altitude, the pilot moved the stick forward and the chopper responded. Coleton looked down at the château, shrinking below him, and saw it from a whole new perspective. It had another wing to the north that he'd never seen. More than 40 chimneystacks rose from its gray slate roof giving it the imposing feel of a gothic cathedral. In the courtyard, the first lone guest of the morning enjoyed a quiet breakfast. He saw the French garden to the east, and its geometric pattern was even more beautiful and complicated from the air. He guessed which window Camilla was behind, still sleeping soundly.

As they rose higher, Coleton saw the long front drive lined with oak trees. A Rolls Royce phantom with blacked out windows pulled to a stop in front of the marble steps. Four burly men in dark suits and sunglasses bailed out of the car at the same time. Coleton sat forward.

A man in a burgundy smoking jacket emerged from the château. He jogged down the steps and approached the closest of the suited men. There was no sign of greeting, no handshake, no exchange of pleasantries. He pulled a white envelope from an inside jacket pocket, then heard the helicopter and craned his neck. Coleton recognized Arthur Elrod's upturned face instantly. For a moment, the envelope appeared to float in the air. All the men watched the helicopter. Elrod shook the envelope to regain the man's attention. The man folded it in half and put it in the breast pocket of his coat. He twirled an index finger in the air, and the men piled back into the Phantom.

"What's that all about?" Coleton wondered. Elrod's contribution as team owner could be summed up in one word—*money*, and if he was in bed with the wrong people, Coleton wanted to know. He looked over to see if Sébastien or Hilton had seen the exchange, but Hilton was adjusting his headphones, and Sébastien was studying a track map.

The pilot's voice crackled over his headset. "Sit back and relax, we'll be landing in approximately eight minutes."

Dark green forests passed below, and the serpentine country roads were already clogged with cars, all headed in the same direction—toward the historic Circuit de la Sarthe.

As they approached the epicenter of the track, the massive grandstands that line either side of the front straight came into focus. The VIP grandstand, the larger of the two, rests above the team garages that border Pit Row. Above them, rise 40 feet of sheet glass to keep the VIP suites in climate-controlled comfort. Above the VIP suites, stretch row upon row of covered outdoor seating. And at the very tiptop garish flags flutter in the wind, representing with colors and shapes all the participating countries.

The helicopter landed in a field only a few hundred feet from the public grandstand. Early fans were packed on the far side of a chain link fence, and they snapped pictures as the three drivers strutted from the helicopter, the rotor spinning in slow motion over their heads. Two girls waved a banner that read, "We love you Sébastien!" When they recognized him, they started to scream his name and jump up and down.

"Poor girls. They have no idea," Coleton said.

"What, that I'm more likely to steal their boyfriends than their hearts?"

Coleton chuckled. "Such a waste of sexual energy."

"Ah, let them keep their fantasy." Sébastien shrugged, as a smile spread across his handsome face.

They crossed the field and flashed their credentials for entry into the tunnel. They proceeded under the public grandstand, under the front straight, and under the VIP grandstand to emerge into the morning light in the paddock. All the team transporters were lined up behind their garages, and behind the trailers was Paddock Road with a smattering of hospitality tents beyond.

Coleton, Hilton and Sébastien reported to the Elrod team trailer for their first debrief of the day. Max Cross held open the transporter door as they scaled the aluminum steps. Around the conference table, the team of engineers had already assembled, each with a thick white mug of steaming coffee. The track map was splashed across a flat screen television fixed on one wall. The drivers exchanged solemn nods with the rest of the team. All of the faces were familiar from the week of practice and training, except one.

"This is Jacques Girard," Nelson spoke up. "He is a veteran here at Le Mans, and he will be our technical director, helping with track specific issues, fuel strategy and last-minute calls."

Each driver shook hands with the new addition. Coleton narrowed his eyes at Girard. He didn't like introducing anyone unproven onto the team at the last minute.

"We've reviewed all of your lap times from the practice sessions and have evaluated your strengths and weaknesses," Nelson began, taking charge of the meeting. "And, we've determined that you, Coleton, will begin *and* end the race, and will drive three quadruple stints. You're most familiar with the car, and your lap times in practice were the quickest. We expect carnage right out of the gate, so we need you to be quick, but cautious to start."

Coleton nodded grimly, but a flicker of pride lit his eyes. Quadruple stints were mentally and physically exhausting, downright numbing, but he knew he could do it, and he was glad they trusted him. It would give them an advantage over teams that only triple stinted their drivers. Triple stints were also grueling, but putting a driver in for anything less than three hours at a go would result in too many lengthy driver changes and make them uncompetitive.

"Sébastien, you will be in for sunset and sunrise, as you're the most experienced around the track," Nelson said. "With the sun in your eyes you won't be able to see brake boards and turn-ins well and may have to drive from memory. You and Hilton will both drive two triple stints."

"There's incredibly tough competition in the LMP1 class this year," Max spoke up. "Of course Audi and Peugeot are fielding two cars each, and are in a race all their own, then there are two Porscheworks cars, and the new Toyota entry that can't be dismissed. The three other privateer entries have substantially slower times, so lets keep our eyes on the front runners."

"We won't always have the fastest lap times," Nelson said. "But if our pit stops are perfect, and we quadruple as often as possible, we've got a chance to make a podium. Questions?"

Everyone looked around the table, but no one said a word.

"It's 8:45," Nelson said. The men all looked down at their watches. "Coleton, you're in first for the warm-up, so go ahead and suit up."

Coleton walked through the cool air to the changing room in the other transporter. First, he put on a fresh set of black Carbonex, screened with his sponsors logos, then his three layer made-to-measure race suit, Nomex socks and custom Stand 21 shoes.

Emerging from the transporter, Coleton walked straight through the garage and got in the car. He wanted to feel the seat insert Max had been working on the night before. Fitment is very important to a driver, especially in long races, so a little tweaking is always worthwhile. Since Sébastien was the biggest, the seat was made to his dimensions. Coleton and Hilton each had an insert molded to their body that would be thrown in during their driver change.

As the insert molded around his lower extremities, Coleton nodded. "That'll work," he said. "No one knows my ass better than you, Maxy."

"Well, for the next 24 hours I own it," Max said with a smile, as Coleton crawled out the small cockpit door. "Now get to work."

Unlike their car in the States, the LMP1 Elrod leased in France had a roof, which made getting in and out more difficult in pit stops, but gave the drivers protection from inclement weather. Rain at some point during the 24 Heures du Mans is a foregone conclusion and teams plan for it in their race strategies.

Coleton reached for his earplugs, form fitted for each of his ears. The red one was for his right ear and the left one was blue. He inserted them slowly, knowing that this was the last step before he would switch to race mode. They were designed for radio communication, not sound muffling. He could still hear talking once he inserted them, but they were a clear signal to the world that nothing they said mattered anymore.

After draining one last bottle of water, Coleton pulled on his balaclava, ducked under the HANS device, worked his helmet on and finally slipped on his Alpinestars gloves. He dragged the toes of each foot slowly on the ground, like a bull preparing to charge, to make sure they were dry and climbed into the cockpit ready to be strapped in for the warm-up.

Coleton wiped his brow on his shoulder and heaved a sigh of relief. He carefully arranged his racing things on a row of built-in shelves along the back wall of the garage, where he could find them in a hurry.

There's nothing more nerve-wracking to a driver than watching teammates lap the track during the warm-up session, praying they don't get into trouble. At almost every race, someone does something stupid and ends their day at the races before it officially begins. To crash in a race is disappointing, but to crash in the warm-up is disgraceful.

Coleton patted Hilton on the back. "Good work, Brother. You turned some really respectable times."

"That was just the warm-up." Hilton smiled.

Coleton and Hilton had raced go-karts a few times together as teenagers at Palm Beach International Raceway, but Coleton had never driven with him on a professional level. While Hilton's off-track behavior the past week had been a bit worrisome, on-track he'd given Coleton no reason to complain. Hilton had demonstrated real aptitude behind the wheel. Although he was inexperienced with the lap traffic of different types of cars all racing at the same time, Coleton knew if he put his head down, Hilton would go far in the Le Mans Series.

The final team debrief went quickly and smoothly with little for the drivers to report, except that the car felt good. Coleton walked across Paddock Road to Pamela's hospitality tent. He had three hours to kill before the parade lap.

He pulled open the heavy glass door. Pamela's European setup never ceased to impress him. At Le Mans, her tent sported hardwood floors, crystal chandeliers, linen napkins, and food and service to match. Coleton went straight toward the table in the back where Pamela sat bent over a ledger.

"Hello, love," he cooed.

Her head shot up and she smiled brightly. "Hello, Colt. Looked like you boys had a good warm-up?" she said, and pointed to the closest of the many suspended television screens that broadcast a live feed from the track.

Coleton nodded. "Car feels good."

"Must have felt better than Klaus Ulrick's. Did you see that ass eat it in Indianapolis corner this morning?"

"No, I didn't," Coleton said. His eyes sparkled.

"Serves the bastard right."

"For what he did to George in Toronto?"

"No, that was just racing. For not eating in my tent! Apparently, my cooking's not good enough."

"Believe me, you're better off without him."

"Sure am. But, I'd like to be the one to tell him!" she huffed. "That reminds me ..." Her voice trailed off as she changed the subject.

Pamela's fingers skipped along a row of different colored files held upright by two fleur-de-lis bookends. She pulled out a hunter green folder and spread it open. She touched each name down the column with the point of her neatly sharpened pencil and stopped at Coleton's name.

"Here we are," she said. "I have you booked with Jesus for a stretch, massage and B-vitamin shot in your cabin." She looked down at her watch. "In 10 minutes. Good thing you stopped in, or he'd a had to go looking for you."

Celimo Jesus Peña, known by the racing world as Jesus, was a Colombian-born therapist renowned on the racing circuit for his unique and fluid combination of electro-acupuncture, chiropractic adjustments, vitamin shots, stretching and deep tissue work, all in a single session. You never knew if Jesus was going to suddenly crack your neck or stick a needle in your buttocks, which was unnerving until you learned to trust him. But, at six-foot-two and 220 pounds, he was strong enough to apply the deep pressure that drivers needed between races to pulverize knots, and smart enough to switch to Swedish techniques to get blood flowing and protect muscle just before a race. Over the years, he and Coleton had become close friends. Jesus traveled to all of the racing venues with Pamela and helped her set up and close down. In return, she helped book and organize his appointments.

"Call it an early birthday present ... or a late one," Pamela said. "When's your birthday again?"

Coleton walked around the desk and planted a kiss on her cheek.

"You're the best."

"Don't think you're not going to pay for it!" she said, wagging her finger at him. "I just saved the best time slot for you."

"No, that's fine. Thank you!"

"And, I'll have Sarah take a plate of food and a protein shake to your cabin for an early lunch."

Coleton sighed. He felt a tension he didn't know he was holding release in his shoulders. "You really are a Fairy Godmother. That's just what I need."

"Of course it is," she said. "You're not the first racecar driver I've favored, you know."

"Right, wasn't that André LaGache in 1923?"

"Watch it."

"You spoil me, you old broad."

"More than you deserve, you arrogant upstart."

She nodded sternly at the exit, a door cut from a glass wall that made up the front of the tent, but a smile flickered in her eyes.

When Coleton stepped back onto Paddock Road, the sun was high and morning's chill had burned off. He unzipped his racing suit, then slipped out of the sleeves and tied them around his waist to reveal a long-sleeved Carbonex top underneath. He set off for his cabin with a spring in his step.

Behind the hospitality tents, rows of tiny cabins stood in the field, separated by grass roads too narrow for cars. Each cabin was big enough for a twin bed, a small table with two folding chairs, an antiquated television and a small bathroom with a shower. There weren't enough cabins for every driver, or even every team, but with Pamela's help Elrod managed to get three. The cabins were a refuge for the drivers: a quiet place for a quick nap or shower, room for a massage and a way to avoid sponsors or team owners.

Coleton started down a path between two rows of cabins. He heard a familiar voice behind him and turned.

Klaus Ulrick, still suited from the warm-up and carrying his helmet, walked up the path followed by Heidi. She was wearing red patent leather wedges and from the way she picked her way through the grass and lagged behind her husband, Coleton could tell they hurt, or maybe they were an excuse not to keep up.

Coleton turned around, but continued to walk backwards.

"Hey Ulrick," Coleton called. "Still behind me? Looks like it's becoming a pattern."

At the sound of Coleton's voice Heidi looked up from behind Ulrick. Her lips softened when she saw him. Not a full-fledged smile, but Coleton noted the movement.

Coleton stopped walking and Ulrick continued until they were standing face to face.

"Karma's a bitch," Coleton said.

Ulrick grunted like an animal and pushed Coleton out of his way.

"After what you did in Toronto, you deserved that shunt," Coleton taunted.

Ulrick spun, straightened to his full height and puffed out his chest.

"How could I have done anything to your aging friend?" Ulrick spat. "I wasn't even near him."

"We both know *exactly* what you did."

Heidi stood beside Ulrick, with her thumbs hooked through the belt loops of her white shorts. She tossed her golden hair over one shoulder and furrowed her brow. Coleton realized she probably knew nothing about Ulrick's foul play.

"Look, I don't have time for empty accusations." Ulrick said, looking down at his wrist. "Where's my watch?" He turned toward Heidi.

Heidi blanched, her tan skin lightening ever so slightly.

"Where is it?" he demanded, steel behind the words.

"It must be in the garage," she said softly.

"What do you mean?"

Heidi looked at the ground and dug the toe of her cherry red shoe into the grass.

Ulrick spat on the ground, and then leaned toward her menacingly. Coleton took a tiny step backward.

"I told you to hold it for me. Not leave it *in the garage*," he said, screwing up his face and mocking her voice. She stared at him blankly.

"I set it on the shelf next to your other things."

"How stupid *are* you?" Ulrick exploded, making Heidi flinch. "You don't leave a $40,000 watch lying around a garage!"

Heidi stared hard at the ground, her cheeks now flaming. Her silence seemed to infuriate him further.

"*Dumme Schlampe!*"

He lashed out, punching his helmet forward. It narrowly missed her. She jumped backwards, her eyes wide.

Coleton stepped forward. "Hey, hey. Easy there," he said to Ulrick, stepping between them.

"It's just a watch. Believe me *she* looks better on you arm than some stupid watch."

"*Fick dich,*" Ulrick spat. He reached over Coleton's shoulder to point at Heidi. "You better find it!"

He gave Coleton a shove, whirled around and stormed off toward his cabin. Coleton turned back to speak to Heidi, to brush it off, make a joke or apologize for all mankind, but she was already walking back toward the garages with her head down.

A s Coleton drove the car around the track on the parade lap, the sheer mass of spectators that occupied every inch of the 8.469-mile circuit shocked him. The race director had told them earlier in the week to expect a crowd of 750,000. From the cockpit, it seemed there were more than a million spectators on hand.

Coleton waved to a few fans that caught his attention. Some held banners with his name, others had pennants with his race number waving above their campsites. The number of different cultures that motorsports attracted had always amazed Coleton. He saw French, British, Italian, German, Dutch and American flags swaying above the crowd. And, the race footage would be broadcast in over 107 countries.

As 55 multi-million dollar racing machines slid into place on the grid, the crowd poured onto the tarmac around them: co-drivers, crew, team owners and sponsors gathered around their respective entries and the fans lucky or rich enough to garner the proper credentials, gawked and photographed the spectacle.

Not all of Elrod's guests were on the grid. Passes were too difficult and expensive to obtain for all. Only the top sponsors were allowed. The others had their noses pressed to the glass wall of the VIP suite Elrod rented right above the Elrod Racing garage. They had a clear view of the front straight and waved down at their team gathered around the crouching machine.

Elrod and Jack Miller smiled and chatted in front of the racecar. Coleton noticed their friendliness with one another, which he found comforting and alarming at the same time. Suddenly Elrod peeled away and walked over to throw his arm around his shoulder.

"Drive it like you stole it today," Elrod said and slapped Coleton on the back. The gesture felt like an insult and Coleton's entire torso froze under his hand.

Coleton had heard that saying so many times that its banality annoyed him. Coleton did not drive cars like he stole them—with wild, reckless abandon. That's what amateurs did: joyride. He drove like a decorated fighter pilot: precise. A jockey on a Triple Crown thoroughbred. Attentive, reverent, but always ready to throw down and show the animal who's boss.

Coleton bit back his retort. *Deflate the ball. Deflaaate the ball. He's just the money.*

"Good," Elrod continued. Then, a serious look came over his face. "Oh, and another thing, I don't think Miller's wire has hit yet."

"Well, I'm sure it will, Arthur. It's not like he's unhappy with the program."

Coleton pointed at Jack Miller's happy face. He had each arm around a "Miller Model" and a huge smile plastered on his face for a picture in front of the racecar. Olivia was talking animatedly to the driver of the car that would be starting behind them. Coleton also knew that the Millers had cut a deal with Target at the 12 Hours of Sebring to deploy Miller sunglasses in all of Target's domestic locations. That deal alone had to be worth north of two million in EBITDA. If that wasn't enough, Ira was negotiating a private label deal for Miller to produce sunglasses for a Brazilian conglomerate. Coleton wasn't worried about the Miller's commitment to the program.

If there was one thing Coleton couldn't stand, it was talking business on race day. That's what all the other weeks and months of the year were for, all the conference calls and expensive dinners. Game day was for blistering focus beforehand and raucous celebration after. Over the years, however, every single team owner had done it to Coleton, and it made his blood boil. It was always the same thing, "When's the payment coming?" or "Payment's late."

Camilla waded through the crowd and found Coleton leaning against the straightaway wall by himself behind the racecar, brooding. His arms were folded across his chest; his earplugs jammed into his ears.

"What's wrong, baby?" she asked. She knew he could hear her even through the plastic.

"Nothing."

Camilla squared her shoulders to him and asked again with her eyes.

"Elrod is a social cripple. He just doesn't get it," Coleton replied with a grimace. He took out his blue earplug.

"What do you mean?"

"Well, let's see, I have to find the money, manage the money, deploy the money, keep the sponsors happy, stay fit and healthy and when I get around to it I have to drive the racecar too. And I have to drive perfect and on the limit. And … I can't crash! So reminding me of everything else *right* before I jump in the driver's seat *really* helps me keep my head in the game."

"Don't worry about it," said Camilla, as she placed a cautious hand on his shoulder. "I've got the Millers wrapped around my little finger." She held up her pinky and wiggled it. "Just go out there and kill it." She ran her fingers lightly over his lucky race-day stubble, then kissed her favorite spot, the softest part, where his perfectly trimmed sideburn just met his ear.

The announcer came over the PA with a quick French directive. Then, in English, Camilla heard, "Drivers in your cars."

"I'm not worried about it. I just wish for once I could just drive and not think about all this other shit. This is what Ira gets paid for—to be a filter. But he can't filter anything! Sometimes he's completely TOAB."

"TOAB?" she asked.

"Tits On A Bull. He's useless." Camilla giggled, but Coleton remained stony. "Yes, I'm hilarious. I know. But don't get me started on Ira."

Camilla grabbed Coleton by the shoulders and gave him a little shake. "Okay, forget about Ira, forget about Elrod. It's time to focus. I mean it, don't even think about the sexy lingerie I've been saving for after the race."

"*What?*" Coleton said, his jaw dropping a fraction.

"Don't think about the kinky things I'm planning to do to you. Some of which are illegal in the U.S.—"

Coleton stared at her in shock.

"See how easy it was to change your train of thought? Now *focus.*"

Despite himself, Coleton's lips curled into the hint of a smile.

"What do you say? Ready to drive around this town a few times real fast?"

"Yeah," he said.

"Good." She nodded once, forcefully, and put the blue earplug back in his ear. "Doctor's orders: All you have to do is go out there and drive your ass off."

Coleton didn't say thank you, but she saw it in his eyes.

"Get ready to go green," Nelson's voice crackled over the radio, hollow and distant as if it was a transmission from Mars.

"Roger," Coleton said, double-checking that the radio communication worked both ways.

Into the Ford Chicane, the front running cars slowed, bunching up the pack behind them to prepare for a sprint over the start/finish line. Coleton eyed up the tricky corner. The Ford Chicane would witness plenty of passing over the next 24 hours. Brake late enough and you can gain a position, brake too late and the next thing you know you'll be selling cars instead of driving them.

Down to third gear, Coleton hit the curb on the left, ran the curb on the right, then kept to the right for a clean exit, using the slower than normal pace to swerve back and forth and warm up his tires. Out of the Ford Chicane and onto the front straight, Coleton rocked through the gears: third, fourth, then fifth.

"Green, Green, Green," Nelson yelled the instant the green flag waved.

Coleton put the hammer down and roared wide open over the start/finish line. He jogged right to pass the Peugeot in front of him, but the front straight was too short to make a pass, and he had to brake hard and drop to second for the Dunlop S. After the tricky uphill curve, he crept up to third and roared under the Dunlop bridge, then into the Esses: up to fourth, then fifth. Coleton hit the brakes again hard, dropped to fourth and muscled the car left, while the car pushed to stay right: classic understeer. Out of the Esses, Coleton slingshot into Tertre Rouge, checking his exit speed was at least 145 mph to ensure a good run down the long straight.

Coleton's body buzzed with life, as every synapse stood to attention, electric and snapping, ready to send messages to neurons throughout his body like a fireworks display. He had been waiting for this moment for weeks: day after day of physical training, watching videos, practicing on racing simulators, grueling work outs, careful nutrition, memorizing track maps, and it all came down to the next 24 hours. *Game on, Assholes.*

A s the afternoon waned, the sky marbled with heavy clouds. The light gradually faded, as if someone had a steady finger on the dimmer switch. Sunset was near, but the sun's exact movements were masked by the clouds, indefinite.

After watching the start in the Elrod Racing garage, Camilla had quickly become disenchanted with their European set-up. In the US, she watched races from the Elrod pit cart and preferred to be in the middle of the action. In Europe, however, in lieu of pit carts, covered garages open to the pit boxes, where cars park for fuel and tire changes. Pit lane runs beyond the pit boxes, and on the far side of pit lane, overlooking the front straight are long, narrow countertops fronted by barstools and covered by plastic canopies.

Along the pit wall, there was only room for the engineers and race strategists, with one empty barstool for Max, the Crew Chief, who ran back and forth rallying the troops and relaying messages from the engineers to the mechanics. Camilla was relegated to one of the folding chairs in the garage with the mechanics. She couldn't help feeling in the way and quickly decided to make a move to Pamela's tent.

Camilla picked a table by the front glass wall of Pamela's. For a few hours, she had been content to watch a live feed of the race on a suspended television, but as the fourth hour of the race drew near, she turned to watching people hustle back and forth down Paddock Road and flipping idly through her *Vogue Paris*. As the sun clawed its way toward the horizon, exhaustion maneuvered its first finger hold on the faces she saw in the darkening street.

Camilla peered over the rim of her *chocolat chaud* to find the marshmallows had already melted. In the same moment, she felt hot breath on her ear. She jolted upward, rattling her cup on the table. Then she smelled him, warm and spicy, dry vanilla and bergamot. *Noir.* She smiled.

"Hello, beautiful," Coleton whispered, then pulled out a chair at the round table.

"Hello there," she said, unable to hold back the happiness in her voice. His first quadruple stint was over.

"Sébastien's holding steady to fourth. It's still early, but we're in it."

"Of course we are." Camilla tried to stifle her giddy smile. He'd done well, but more importantly, he was safe.

Coleton reached over to stroke her hair, resting the palm of his hand on the crown of her head for a second before separating a section and pulling his hand gently down from root to tip.

"Want me to get you a plate of food?" Camilla asked. Coleton looked over his shoulder at the long buffet tables.

"I'll go. You want anything?" Camilla shook her head no. She'd been snacking all afternoon. Pamela's spread at Le Mans was a profusion of everything you could possibly want to consume, with new dishes added hourly.

Coleton sauntered to the buffet line. He nodded to a table of British mechanics from the Creation team.

Camilla turned back to her cup, blew on the milky liquid and looked over its rim onto Paddock Road. A tall blonde approached in knee-high Christian Louboutin boots, followed by three men—standard issue hangers-on. Camilla sucked in her breath. *Keep walking.*

Juliette Crowne turned on her heel and came right for the door to Pamela's. One of her entourage jogged up the three steps and held the door. The other two followed behind, eyes glued to her backside.

In addition to her soft leather boots, Juliette wore dark fitted jeans and a quilted Burberry vest over a cashmere turtleneck. Camilla turned the page of her *Vogue Paris* and felt annoyed to find a model looking almost exactly like Juliette.

"Coleton Loren!" Juliette called. "There you are, you handsome devil."

Coleton greeted Juliette with surprise. They embraced, then she gestured widely to her friends.

"That's Jean Paul." She pointed at one of the men. "Or are you Pierre?" She swayed slightly. "And that one's Renault."

"Actually, it's Luc," the man said, extending a hand. "I drive a Renault."

Coleton shook it briefly. "Don't worry, she used to call me Citroën."

"Enjoying ourselves are we?" Coleton asked Juliette. He put his arm over her shoulder and turned her toward the start of the buffet line.

"Have you seen my brother?" she asked, pointing a wandering finger into his chest. "I've been looking everywhere for him."

"He's probably resting. Getting ready to get in the car."

"I'm here to support Hilton. I've been in Paris for three weeks staying in a darling suite at Le Maurice. Shame its next to Angelina's. I can't pass that window without buying something pastel and *deux mille* calories."

"A few extra pounds wouldn't hurt you," Coleton said, steadying her thin frame with a hand on the small of her back.

Not again. Camilla stood from the table, adjusting her loose sweater so that it fell off one shoulder.

"I thought your motto was a girl can never be too blonde, too skinny or have boobs that are too big," Juliette asked, as she looked down at her breasts that filled out her cashmere sweater. She swayed again, then giggled and threw her arm around Coleton's neck, letting him support most of her weight.

"Must have been some other guy," Coleton said with a sly smile.

"Hello, Juliette."

"Oh, hello!" Juliette said, leaving her lips in an open O and cocking her head. "Have we met?"

"I'm Camilla."

"My girlfriend," Coleton added.

Instead of extending her hand to shake Camilla's, Juliette shoved it into one of her deep vest pockets, then brandished a glittering flask with an intricately engraved crown on it encrusted with diamonds.

"Lovely to meet you," Juliette said. She let her head roll down, then back up, almost as if in a bow. Her smile was lopsided. She carefully unscrewed the cap and threw back her head to take a long swig.

"Having a good time, are we?" Coleton asked again. This time the edges of his words were sharp. He swept the upturned flask from her hand, but it was empty.

"Hey—" she slurred.

"Why don't you get some hot food and come join us. We're over—" Coleton waved his hand toward their table.

"I'm not hungry. What kind of champagne do they have here?"

Coleton took a step forward. "Juliette, you need to eat. Get a plate and come join us."

"Darling, don't be a bore." Juliette put a limp hand on his shoulder. Her nails were done in an outré French manicure—dark gray nail beds and metallic silver tips. "I couldn't eat if I tried."

"If she doesn't want to eat, she doesn't want to eat," Camilla said.

"Quite true. I'm not the one getting behind the wheel." Juliette grabbed the edge of the buffet table to steady herself and then looked over her shoulder. The three men who accompanied her were a few paces away huddled under a suspended television catching up on the race.

"Jean Luc," she called, as if addressing a member of her court. One of the Frenchmen turned. "A glass of rosé champagne, *si'l vous plaît.*"

"*Il n'y en a pas ici.*"

"Then go *find* some." Juliette waved her hand. The man's eyes darkened, but he left the tent.

"I need to go find Hilton," Juliette said, and hiccupped. "I want to wish him a good race, or happy trails, or whatever it is you're supposed to say."

"Not in your state," Coleton said. "He doesn't need any distractions right now. This is an important race for him. Lots of people will be watching."

As if she didn't hear him, Juliette turned toward the front door. "Okay, then. Lovely to have seen you, Coleton."

Coleton followed her and nodded for Camilla to do the same. Camilla hurried to the table and grabbed her purse. *This ought to be interesting.*

Camilla pulled open the door to the first gusts of night air and zipped up her jacket. The temperature had dropped while she was inside. The first few electric lights buzzed to life along Paddock Road. The rhythmic roar of lapping cars droned on incessantly.

"You need to lie down for a while," Coleton said.

"I'm fine," Juliette said, but her eyelids drooped.

"I'll throw you over my shoulder if I have to."

"Sweetie, not in front of your *girlfriend!*" Juliette's eyes sparkled for an instant, then she tripped on the last step. Coleton caught her by the shoulder and pulled her arm around his neck.

"Don't take this personally," she said.

"What?"

In an exaggerated stage whisper, Juliette said, "I don't like her."

Coleton looked back at Camilla, who rolled her eyes.

"Where's your bodyguard?" Coleton asked, but Juliette let her head roll down again. "Let's get her to our cabin before she gets sick."

"So she can get sick there?" Camilla asked. "Brilliant."

Juliette snored softly, fully clothed, and with a starchy white sheet pulled to her chin. Coleton had stripped the linens from the bed in Hilton's cabin and let her pass out in them.

Coleton and Camilla sat at the small square table and drank green tea out of mismatched cups. She had to heat the water through a single cup coffee maker, and the tea tasted like hard water and tin.

They had thrown open the front door and slid up the small window to let in as much evening air as possible, but a sickly sweet smell still filled the small cabin.

"Surely she's finished," Camilla giggled. She took a sip of hot tea, rotating the cup to avoid a large chip in its rim. "Her royal highness couldn't possibly have anything left in her stomach."

"Doctors aren't supposed to giggle when people are sick."

"Oh, please," Camilla said. "Now don't take this *persssssonally.*"

"Stop."

"But, I don't like her," Camilla whispered loudly.

"Cut her some slack," Coleton said. "She's young. She only just turned 22."

"I never acted like that when I was 22."

"You never got drunk?"

"I never got wasted in a foreign country with three men I didn't know and imposed myself on a nice couple minding their own business."

Coleton chuckled. "I've got to get back to the pits. And I still need to eat something."

"Let's go," Camilla said. "Sleeping Beauty will be out for a while."

"You should stay here and keep an eye on her."

"Oh, please no."

"What about your Hippopotamus Oath—"

"She's not going anywhere. I want to watch you from the pits."

"What if she has alcohol poisoning?"

"She's fine. Sweetheart just drank all the vodka out of her diamond flask." They both looked at the flask glittering on the table like a Fabergé egg.

"Are we sure it was just vodka?"

"You think she Roofied herself?"

"Or Valium. And yes," Coleton said.

"Ugh, debutantes."

"You're a doctor. Show some character." Coleton grabbed the remote control and turned on the small TV. "You can watch the race from here."

"Did you seriously just tell *me* to show some character? Priceless! You ask your girlfriend to miss her first Le Mans and watch over your little *fling*—"

"She was never a fling," Coleton said sharply. "She's a family friend. Nothing more."

"Okay," Camilla said, changing tactics. "Doesn't your *family friend* have a bodyguard? Someone who's actually paid to babysit her?"

"She usually does." Coleton furrowed his brow. "That's what worries me."

Coleton shook off the thought, like shrugging out of a coat. "Get it in check, Camilla. I don't have time for—"

"Distractions. I know, I know." She picked up her cup with both hands and brought it close to her mouth, brooding. The rising warmth felt good on her face.

"Close the door, will you? It's getting cold."

Coleton kissed the top of her head, before zipping up the chest of his racing suit and walking out the door.

"The cockpit smells like smoke," Coleton said over the radio. His voice was calm, despite the importance of the transmission.

Coleton was halfway through his third stint, and each stint he'd pushed harder than the last. He was in the rhythm, making great times, and he didn't want any problems to ruin his position. They were back in third, where they'd started.

"Standby," Nelson instructed. "We are checking our readings."

Coleton narrowed his eyes, trying to see the smoke in the cockpit, as he floored out of Tertre Rouge onto the Mulsanne straight. It lingered like a haze in the car—but where was it coming from? As the straight opened up and the car accelerated toward 200 mph, Coleton knew this was the only moment to find the source before he launched back into negotiating the track's corners.

He searched the dash, but the wind sucked some of the smoke out the gaps around the window. As he braked for the first chicane, the smoke began to billow upward again.

"Definitely smoke in the cockpit," Coleton said, then coughed. "It appears to be coming from the dash."

Camilla sat on the end of the bed to get closer to the boxy television perched on a plywood credenza. She flipped through the channels, each one a different corner of the track, but she couldn't pick out Elrod's car. There was too little light on the track and the cars would pass through the turns too quickly. Finally she settled on the network feed, but it focused on the race leaders. Audi and Peugeot were fighting over the order of the top two spots.

All of a sudden, she heard a string of French that was too rapid for her to understand. A camera reeled wildly, zooming in on an LMP1 that was off the pace, crawling down the back straight. Camilla leapt from her seat. It was Coleton.

She rushed across the room and pulled the large blue team headphones from her purse. She clapped them over her ears and ratcheted up the volume.

"Hold steady," Nelson instructed. "It's probably just a hot fuse."

As the car came out of the second chicane, Coleton frantically searched for the source of the fire. The smoke was building and his time was running out. He coughed again and realized he would have to stop.

"Try to make it back to the pits and we'll take a look."

318

"Are you crazy?" Coleton said over the radio. "I can't make it another six miles!" Smoke billowed from the dash and he began to choke. "Something's on fire. I can't even see."

"Roger. Do what you need to."

As the smoke began to burn his eyes and nose, Coleton said, "I'm pulling over."

Approaching Mulsanne Corner, one of the slowest on the track, Coleton knew this was as safe a place as any to pull off. Into the tight right-hander, Coleton held to the right, refusing to let the car track out left like it wanted. He dropped to second gear, then first as he pulled onto the grass on his right. As the car slowed the smoke intensified.

On the television screen, Camilla saw Coleton pull to the side of the track.

"Do not walk away from the car," Nelson warned over the radio. "Repeat, you must stay with the car or we'll be disqualified."

Over the team headphones, Camilla heard Coleton cough, as he clicked on the radio to speak.

"Roger."

She covered her throat with her hand. Her own throat felt raw with smoke.

Fire and racing fuel are not a good combination, and Camilla could suddenly picture the car exploding into flames, incinerating itself out of existence.

"Get out, Coleton. Please get out," she chanted.

Finally Coleton leapt from the car, and smoke billowed from the tiny open door. It was difficult to see him on the darkened television screen, but Camilla could just make out his broad shoulders and large helmet strobe lit by the headlights of each passing car, as he inched away from the machine.

Camilla gave one quick look at Juliette, a softly snoring lump in the bed. She grabbed her jacket and pulled it on as she raced out the door and toward the pits.

Coleton stood at the side of the road. His earplugs were eerily silent. When he had jumped out of the car, the cord connecting them to the radio had been jerked from the plug. Coleton put his hands on his hips and stared at the car.

If he walked away from the car they would be DQed. If he didn't make it back to the pits they would be DQed. Coleton counted to 10. It seemed like an eternity. Every second, cars zoomed by him. Coleton stepped closer to the car and peered inside. He couldn't see any flames. The clock was ticking.

Coleton let out a long measured exhale, then sucked in a full free-diving breath: his diaphragm, then lungs, then the last small space under his traps filled with air as he lifted his chin. He dove into the cockpit headfirst, letting his feet dangle out suspended in a cloud of smoke.

Coleton found the source under the dash. A melted fuse had caused a small glue fire. He pounded at the dash with his fireproof gloves until he was satisfied the fire was extinguished. He wormed his way back out onto the pavement and waved the door open and shut to clear the smoke. Then, he jumped back in the seat and buckled his belts.

He made sure all ignition switches were on before he placed his thumb over the starter. Shutting his eyes, he pushed firmly down on the button. The engine roared to life. Coleton opened one eye at a time, and looked at the dashboard. All of the dashboard electronics were out: shift lights, gauges, temperature readings, but he hadn't blown up.

Coleton reconnected his radio cord. The entire crew was on their feet, faces upturned to the suspended television monitors.

"Coming into the pits."

At the sound of Coleton's voice a cheer went up.

"Holy hell, Mate. You had us worried," said Nelson.

Coleton burned out his tires with the clutch release and smiled with stolen relish. Wheel spin in the pits at Le Mans is forbidden.

"Pit this lap. Pit this lap," Nelson said, recovering his composure.

Through the next series of corners, Coleton babied the car, testing it. Into Indianapolis, a heavily banked left hander, the car felt planted. Shifting was flawless; the brakes felt good. He approached the Porsche Curves: left, right, left again, then right.

"The car seems fine," Coleton said over the radio. "The only problem is my dash lights are out. Keep an eye on my temps for me and I'll stay out until we're in the pit window."

"Roger. I'll keep you posted." Nelson smiled with relief.

Coleton shot past the pit entrance. The grandstands on both sides of the front straight were packed with cheering fans, as he roared between them.

Camilla was only inches away, but Coleton couldn't see her clearly in the dark. At Circuit de la Sarthe when you move beyond the edge of the bright floodlights, it's like falling off a cliff into the dark. Coleton reached out for Camilla, caught her upper arm and followed it down to hold her hand, as they headed toward their cabin.

"I need about a gallon of water and a nap," he said. His arms felt heavy, leaden.

"Mmmhmm," she said. "I can't believe how tired I am. I can barely keep my eyes open."

A cold wind picked up. Coleton was grateful for his Carbonex and three-layer suit, but it felt nice as it cooled the skin on his hands and face. From focusing into the dark for the past four hours, Coleton had a slight tension headache. He pinched the bridge of his nose and squeezed his eyes shut, but they were still scratchy and tired when he opened them.

"I thought doctors were supposed to be on a first name basis with sleep deprivation?"

"I'm more tired now than after an entire night shift, and it's only three a.m. Must be all the stress."

"Stress? What do you have to be worried about?" Coleton asked. "It's not like you're lapping the track in the dark at 180 with a dashboard fire."

"Maybe I'd prefer to keep you around for a while," she said.

As they approached the cabin, the moon sashayed through the clouds and lit up the packed grass between two rows of cabins with the gentle sweep of a highlighter. Camilla pulled the door open, but paused at the threshold.

"Juliette's gone," she told Coleton over her shoulder.

"Did she leave a note?"

Camilla moved inside, and Coleton began to follow, but heard a sound.

"Hey, Coleton," a voice called softly from the shadows.

Coleton peered into the dark. In the shadow of the eves of the neighboring cabin a man leaned forward, then took a step into the moonlight. It lit up his high cheekbones and straight Roman nose.

"Hey, Enzo," Coleton called. He pushed the door shut and they met in the shallow dip between the cabins. "How you doing?"

"Been better. You hear about our shunt?"

"That was you?" Coleton asked. "They told me over the radio, but I didn't know it was you."

"I was coming out of Tertre Rouge completely flat and this Ferrari GT was just sitting there, in the middle of the road, smiling right at me. I had nowhere to go. My car caught about four feet of air and landed on the wheels, but broke everything in the suspension."

"What can you do?" Coleton shrugged. "That's racing, buddy."

"I have an idea," Enzo said. "A sweet Swedish consolation prize."

Coleton smiled blankly, but didn't understand him.

"Heidi Ulrick."

"Oh, dream on," Coleton scoffed.

"She's right in there," Enzo said, pointing across the path and down two cabins. "I figured I'd knock on the door and see if she wants to go a few rounds."

A mix of exhaustion and mirth, Coleton's laugh turned giddy. "You actually think you're going to shag Klaus's wife right under his nose?"

"Of course not. He left 20 minutes ago to get back in the car. I'm just waiting for—" Enzo's words dropped off. "That." He nodded at the window of the cabin that had just gone dark.

"Holy shit! You're serious?"

"Of course." Enzo smiled, and his dark eyes glinted with determination.

"No ... You can't, Enzo. I've seen you get away with a lot of crazy shit, but this is too much."

"Mr. Loren, you should never underestimate the power of the Italian man and his way with a beautiful woman. We are, how do you say?" He waved his hand in the air. "Another breed altogether."

Enzo patted Coleton on the shoulder twice. To Coleton it felt like a solemn farewell. Enzo walked across the path, shoulders thrown back and head held high. He knocked shave-a-haircut on the door. Coleton counted to 15. The lights turned on, and the door cracked open. Enzo leaned forward as he spoke. Then he rested against the doorframe. Suddenly his body folded inward as if pulled inside, and the door shut with a bang.

Coleton's jaw dropped. He stood outside in the cold for five minutes, but the door didn't reopen. Heidi certainly hadn't let Enzo in at three a.m. while her husband was racing to play cards.

"There's been a horrible accident." Enzo softened his snappy eyes to warm and apologetic.

Heidi gasped. *"Jag mår dåligt!"* Her big blue eyes widened and she raised her hand to her forehead as if she might faint.

Enzo folded forward to catch her, but she stepped back and stared at him in shock. Her black eyelash extensions fluttered.

"You should sit down for this."

"What happened?" She took another step backwards and he followed her in.

Enzo heard a frantic scratching sound and cocked his head to one side, listening. Napoleon raced to Enzo's feet, his little toenails scraping the linoleum and jumped his front paws onto Enzo's leg, again and again, as if on a tiny trampoline.

"Ciao Cucciolo," Enzo said, and scooped up the dog before he shut the door. Heidi sunk to a chair at the table, her head in her hands.

"I knew this would happen—someday," she said. Her voice wavered.

Enzo opened the cabinet and looked for glasses. Only one chipped mug and a tall Sunday style ice-cream glass sat on the particleboard shelf. He placed them on the table, but she didn't look up.

He pulled a new quart sized bottle from the inside pocket of his cream suede jacket. He took a seat in the chair facing her and carefully poured three fingers of Cuban rum into both of the glasses. He slid the mug across the table toward her.

"Here," he said. "Drink."

She reached out both hands, wrapped them around the mug and shot the whole glass in two gulps. She coughed and sputtered and squeezed her eyes shut. She put the mug on the table and pushed it toward Enzo to refill.

"Please …" Heidi said. "Tell me what happened. I can take it. Whatever it is."

"Okay," Enzo said. "If you're sure …" He cleared his throat. "I was coming out of Tertre Rouge and there was a Ferrari GT just sitting in the middle of the road." He paused to let the information sink in. "I had nowhere to go and smashed right into him at a 140 miles an hour."

"*You?*" Heidi asked, wrinkling her brow.

"And now I'm out of the race." Enzo hung his head. "They thought I had a concussion." Enzo scratched the back of his neck. "But I checked out okay."

Heidi squinted her eyes and shook her head. "So what?"

"So, that leaves us the rest of the evening."

A ripple of anger flashed through her eyes. Enzo patted his knee, and Napoleon jumped his front legs up, stretching his back, and begging with his beady black eyes for Enzo to pick him up. Enzo swept the little palomino dog up and kissed the top of his head.

"You better leave, *now*. My husband will kill you if he finds you here."

Enzo bowed his head, hugged Napoleon close with one arm and stared into the remaining sip of rum in the bottom of the thick-lipped Sunday glass. "'My life were better ended by his hate.'"

"What did you just say?" She sat straight up, rubbing her upper arm with one fingertip. "Get out. I don't even know your name."

"'By a name, I know not how to tell thee who I am. My name, dear saint, is *hateful* to myself,'" Enzo spit out the word, then softened his face. "'Because it is an enemy to thee. Had I it written, I would tear the word.'"

Heidi looked around the room and bit her bottom lip. She looked at Enzo out of the corner of her eye, then said, "'My ears have not yet drunk a hundred words of your tongue's uttering, yet I know the sound.' Art thou not Enzo, and a BMW driver?"

Enzo sat forward. "'Neither, fair maid, if either thee dislike.'"

"'How camest thou hither,'" Heidi said, her voice strengthening. "'Tell me, and wherefore? The orchard walls are high and hard to climb. And the place *death*, considering who thou art,' if my husband finds you here."

"'With love's light wings did I o'erperch these walls, for stony limits cannot hold love out, and what love can do, that *dares love attempt.*' Therefore thy husband is no stop to me!" Enzo shook his fist in the air.

Heidi's shoulders shook as she giggled. Then, she looked into her mug, took another sip and said softly, "'If he sees you—he *will* murder thee.'"

"'Alack!'" Enzo cried, his black eyes flashing. "'There lies more peril in thine eye, than twenty of his swords. Look thou but sweet, and I am proof against his enmity.'"

"'I would not for the world he saw thee here.'"

"'I have night's cloak to hide me from his eyes, and but thou love me, let him find me here. My life were better ended by his hate than death proroguèd, wanting of thy love.'"

Enzo reached his hand across the table, open palmed, asking for hers. She stared at him for a second, then stretched out her long thin arm. In one fluid motion, he drew her hand to his lips as he stood and pulled her into his arms.

"Oh, Enzo," she murmured, as he kissed her neck, leaving a trail of warm saliva. With his hand on the small of her back, he pulled her tight to his body.

"Heidi, I've been waiting for this moment for months," he said into her warm, smooth neck.

She grabbed him by the back of the neck. Her gaze lingered on his full lips, then she bit his bottom lip and pulled back releasing it. She stared into his obsidian eyes.

"Kiss me," she said. "*Now!*" Enzo's mouth ravaged hers. He

knotted his hands in her hair and yanked her head back, separating their lips. She gasped, then a smiled curled up her lips and she narrowed her eyes.

"Are you sure?" he asked.

She attacked him, pushing him backwards. He fell onto the twin bed, his legs flailed outward as he bounced. He grabbed the mattress to keep from being tossed off. Heidi took two sauntering steps to the door and spun on her heel. He pushed himself up on his elbow. *Did she change her mind?*

Her blue eyes sparkled. In one swift move, she peeled her turtleneck over her head. She wasn't wearing a bra, and as she lowered her arms, her full breasts settled above her perfectly flat stomach.

Enzo's mouth fell open. "*Mamma Mia!*" He'd never seen anything so beautiful.

Her mouth curled into a hungry smile. She lifted her hand like it was a dance move and flicked off the lights. In the dark, he heard a solid click as she locked the door.

A low rumble of thunder woke Elrod from a light sleep. As he blinked his eyes, he heard rain pattering the windowpane and sat up in bed, arranging the silk-cased pillows to prop himself up. Justine slept next to him with a black eyeshade covering her eyes. He picked up the remote control off the nightstand and with his thumb hovering over the mute button, he turned on the TV and silenced it in the same motion. Justine moaned something and rolled over, but didn't wake.

"Sixth?" Elrod said out loud, as he looked at the timing and scoring channel. "Fuck!" he whispered with little sound and great vehemence. "What the hell are they doing out there?"

Elrod thought about all of his sponsors snuggled into their soft down mattresses as the rain pelted the gray slate roof, in happy exhaustion from their long day at the track. But, this wasn't enough. Elrod was a businessman, and he knew the only thing sponsors truly care about is quantifiable exposure value. The only way to solidify sponsor commitments for the next year was a high Joyce Julius & Associates rating, calculated by comparing the on-screen television time that sponsor logos appear clear and in-focus, as well as their number of mentions, to the estimated cost of a commercial spot during the race. To get a high rating, Elrod Racing needed to follow the cardinal rule: *spin, crash or win.*

If you aren't going to win, you better go out with a bang and get some quality television coverage. The sponsor's exposure value is minimal on a car that finishes strong but out of the top three with no media coverage, no interviews after the race and only a quiet, unnoted slide into ignominy.

The only thing that could save Elrod's financial position was some serious sponsor commitments. He had managed a spectacular show on the hospitality side, but now the team better perform or it could jeopardize the whole program.

Elrod grabbed his BlackBerry off the nightstand.

"Smith," he whispered, when he heard the line connect.

"Yes, sir?" the voice sounded wide-awake despite the hour.

"Call Jacques Girard."

"Yes, sir."

"I need him to *understand* the *importance of media coverage,*" Elrod said, carefully emphasizing each word. "If we aren't going to win, if we won't have our drivers on the podium, we need to make headlines *another* way. Do you understand me?"

"Yes, sir."

"Good. Make sure *he* understands."

Coleton awoke and peered at the glowing digits on the alarm clock. Camilla stirred next to him, then began to roll over.

Coleton's arm shot out and he caught her by the hip, just before she rolled off the narrow twin bed.

"What time is it?" she asked, rubbing her eyes.

"Five twenty-two," Coleton said, then sighed. "I better get up."

"I'll come with you," Camilla said, sitting up. Her hair was disheveled from sleep. Coleton smiled, and ruffled it up even more.

"You should look like this all the time. So cute," Coleton said, as he picked up his phone.

"Don't you dare take a photo. I know that look."

"Sébastien should be back in the car. I want to catch Hilton while he's still in the garage. See how his first stint went."

"Okay," Camilla said, she flopped back into her pillow and covered her eyes with the inside of her elbow. "Maybe I'll just sleep for five more minutes."

"If we leave now, we can watch sunrise together before breakfast," Coleton taunted.

Camilla lifted her arm an inch and opened one eye to peer at Coleton.

"I know just the place," he added, tilting the scale.

"Okay, I'm up. I'm up," she grumbled, but a smile played at her lips.

Coleton threw back the covers and kicked both feet high in the air, letting the downward momentum propel him out of the bed.

"Where do you get your energy?" Camilla moaned.

"Money never sleeps, baby!"

"Oh, God. You're channeling Gordon Gekko? At 5:22—" Camilla rolled over and looked at the alarm clock. "At 5:24 in the morning?"

Camilla peeled back the drapes of the cabin window. "Oh no, it's raining!"

"Shit," Coleton said. He sat on the edge of the bed and leaned over to wiggle his toes through the leg of some fresh Carbonex.

"Sorry, babe. Rain makes the track really dangerous?"

"No, its not that—I'm worried it won't hold until I get back in the car."

"*What?*"

"I love driving in the rain. It separates the men from the boys. Other drivers become more cautious and their lap times slip. Not me, I put my foot down even harder. Sliding around doesn't bother me."

"You really have a screw loose. You know that?"

"As long as it's in my head and not my car," Coleton chuckled. He pulled on the bottom half of his racing suit then stood to slip his arm into the sleeves. "You want to know my secret to driving in the rain? Lots of drivers don't get it."

Camilla nodded and sat up on her knees, then fell back on her haunches.

"In normal conditions, there is an ideal line that's the most efficient way around the track. Every car traces this line lap after lap to within centimeters. When it rains, the track is slippery and the line goes out the window. Your new line is wherever you can find the *best grip*. You've got to be creative to find this grip and test the limits of the tire and track surface."

"And you're creative?"

Coleton nodded and ruffled up her hair again.

"Get dressed before I give away all my secrets. Let's go find Hilton."

Hilton paced back and forth in the garage, behind the loose group of folding chairs. His hair was slicked to his neck with sweat, his helmet still clamped between his elbow and ribcage. Eyes wide and glinting with adrenaline, he looked like a lathered racehorse. With the action of the pit stop over, the mechanics began slumping back into their folding chairs to sleep for 15 or 20 minutes before they would have to be back on their feet.

"Hey, Brother. How'd you do?" Coleton asked, walking into the garage. He and Camilla threw back the hoods of their Elrod Racing rain jackets.

"Pretty happy with my times." Hilton grinned.

Coleton felt a little tension in his shoulders relax. Onscreen were the field's lap times. He followed Sébastien's name across to his latest time: 3:26:156.

"He's already settled into a good pace," Hilton added, standing behind Coleton.

"Not bad," Coleton agreed. "Especially in the rain."

"I got a little sideways coming into Indianapolis one lap. Almost looped it."

"Yeah, you've got to be careful there. Really stay to the outside until you dive in," Coleton said. "That corner has a ridiculous amount of banking, more than any other corner on our whole calendar. That's why it's named after Indianapolis Motor Speedway. Have you ever walked the corner?"

"No."

"Next year, we'll walk it together. It'll give you a whole new perspective on its dynamics."

Hilton nodded.

"For now, just use the camber, and once you dive into the corner, don't fight the exit. The banking will catch you."

"Have you seen your sister?" Camilla asked Hilton.

"My dad said she flew back to Paris on his chopper. Can't believe she'd come here to see me and leave without saying goodbye."

"That *is* weird," Coleton said, giving Camilla a meaningful look. "Where's your dad watching the race from? I couldn't find him in the BMW pits."

"He's all over the place: pits, engineer booth on pit wall, hospitality tent, VIP suite."

"I need to catch up with him. There's something I need to thank him for …" Hilton raised an eyebrow. "He helped me with an arbitration."

Hilton shrugged. "He's around. I'm sure you'll run into him."

"We're going to watch sunrise from the grandstand upstairs," Camilla said. "Want to come?"

"No, thanks. I'm going to Pamela's for a quick bite, then maybe a 30 minute nap before my next stint."

Coleton shrugged. "Make *sure* Nelson and Max know where you're going, and make sure you set an alarm."

"Okay, okay." Hilton smiled. "I won't oversleep. I'm too excited!"

A girl in a white apron pushed open the hidden service door into the Crystal Room, which had been paneled and painted to match the wall. At the creaking of the door, every head turned. Each of the eight round tables, set with crystal and fine china, was full. All of Elrod's guests were accounted for, watching the flat screen televisions that had been wheeled into the breakfast room to broadcast the race.

At the sudden attention, the girl curtsied, then held the door for a parade of white-gloved waiters. Some balanced large silver trays on their shoulders, some carried bottles of Dom Pérignon by the neck, others carried carafes of citrus colored juices: orange, yellow, ruby red. A ripple of excitement passed through the tables and hunger quickly outweighed any interest in the race re-cap.

The rain had subsided around sunrise, and now the sun slanted in through the French doors that led to the courtyard. The light through the beveled glass scattered bright skyscrapers across the white tablecloths.

Waiters surrounded each table and at Elrod's nod, they leaned in unison over the guests' right shoulders to serve the breakfast feast. There was an excited tinkling of silver and china, as napkins were slipped from rings and forks were grabbed, poised, ready to dig in.

Elrod clinked his butter knife on his champagne glass three times. The sounds of excited preparation continued. Elrod clinked again and stood from his chair. He cleared his throat. Steam rose from the plates of farm fresh eggs, thick bacon, bread still warm from the ovens, homemade jam from wild strawberries.

"Good morning to all. Before we begin, I would like to inform you that Elrod Racing is in fifth position. We have persevered through the night, and the rain, and a failure in dash circuitry, and now we are gaining. Soon we will re-take fourth!"

There was a ripple of soft applause, more tapping of palms than real clapping. One portly man simply banged his fork and knife together. The guests stared at their plates in anticipation.

"There are five hours left in the race and we're on the offensive."

Smith walked into the room, dressed in a navy suit. He paused at Elrod's elbow, but didn't interrupt. Elrod leaned down so Smith could speak in his ear.

"Wonderful," Elrod said, then leveled his gaze to Smith's eyes. "Did you make the call we discussed?"

Smith nodded. Satisfied, Elrod turned back to his guests and raised his voice and his glass.

"A fleet of limos awaits to take us to the track." Elrod motioned with his glass out the French doors, through the courtyard, where a sliver of cobbled drive could be seen. Then, he raised his glass higher. "A toast to team Elrod Racing!"

In unison, the guests raised their cut crystal glasses. Some looked worried. Would breakfast go with them? The same eager man jabbed a sausage from the tray and finished it in two bites.

Coleton paused, head thrown back, waiting for the last drop from a water bottle to plop into his mouth. Then, he tossed it across the room at the trashcan. It missed and rolled across the floor.

"The water's freezing!" Camilla screeched. Her voice carried through the hollow bathroom door. Coleton peeked his head in.

"What's a matter princess? Never had a cold shower? How do you think I've stuck to the no lounging rule?"

Camilla pulled back the thin plastic curtain and stuck her tongue out.

"I'm headed back to the office," he said.

"Wait. Come here."

He approached the shower warily. She had water dripping down her face, but she pushed out her lips. He gave her a quick wet kiss, then stepped back before she could drip on him.

"I'll see you on the podium," he said with a smile. His eyes looked tired, but the set of his jaw was determined.

"Good luck, babe."

Coleton stepped out into the sunshine and closed the door behind him. He looked down the path and saw Heidi Ulrick striding toward him. Her eyes were red and raccooned with mascara, her arms were folded over her chest. She passed him without noticing, threw open the door to Enzo's cabin without knocking and slammed it behind her.

"This is going to get interesting."

With one hour left in the race, Coleton pulled into the Elrod Racing pit box. He stretched his neck as far as his HANS device would allow, flexed his wrists and extended his fingers. He pinched his shoulders up, then dropped them. The cockpit door flew open and a crewmember dove in, flipped up his visor and stuck a plastic straw in his mouth.

Sometimes the pit crew is too busy to remember things as trivial as driver hydration, but after three straight hours in the car, Coleton could have kissed the guy. He drank as quickly as he could and although the water tasted like plastic and chlorine, it was the best drink he'd ever had.

In a flash, the straw was gone, his visor down and the door closed. Someone dove over the windshield and pulled off a plastic tear sheet, removing with it a layer of dirt, oil and smeared bug remains. A web of tiny cracks remained in the screen from the car's continuous body flexing.

Coleton looked out the windshield and saw the sign: an index finger making fast circles. He fired up the car and pulled out of the pits, careful not to spin his wheels.

Back on track in fourth position, Coleton settled into the cockpit. He was back up to full power by the banking area for the Esses. He felt like a fighter pilot locked on target, with the taillights of Ulrick's LMP1 in sight.

Ulrick drove off line into every corner. Lap after lap, he blocked, making as many as three moves on the straightaway, but the officials didn't call him on it. At every deft movement, Coleton felt his blood pressure spike higher.

"He's pulling the same shit he did in Toronto!"

He knew the only way to make a pass stick was to do something ridiculous, dangerous and unexpected. He was literally inches from the rear diffuser of the Porscheworks machine. Should he stove it in to Dunlop curve, or try to sneak by in Tertre Rouge? He couldn't wait until the final corners of the track. There was definitely no getting by in the Porsche curves.

Coleton rarely thought about moves when overtaking, he just reacted on instinct. But, he knew he had to outsmart Ulrick with something calculated. The two cars came out of Tertre Rouge side by side, and the avenue of majestic trees rose up on their left. Coleton had a good run out of the corner and tried a head fake, dodging right, but Ulrick didn't budge. Both cars approached 220 mph as they reached the 200 meter brake board, the braking zone for the first chicane.

"Go fuck yourself," Coleton said in his helmet as Ulrick came over on him. Coleton held his line and the cars touched. Both cars squirmed under braking as they dropped to 100 mph in third gear and touched again.

They came through the corner two abreast and roared through

the gears: fourth, fifth, sixth. A long stretch of the three and a half mile straight undulated in front of them. Coleton saw a café full of spectators flash past, then he saw the clump of trees that conceal a small hump before the Mulsanne Kink. This second chicane was the same fire drill as the first. Except this time Coleton was done playing.

Coleton gritted his teeth, as he hit the brakes. "This is for George."

Both cars squirmed under braking, but Coleton slowed more than Ulrick, then suddenly cut left, bumping Ulrick's rear quarter panel. The impact sent Ulrick into a spin. Coleton dodged out of the way and had to jump the blue and yellow curbs at the apex on his right, which scraped the bottom of his car and sent sparks flying.

"Elegant," Coleton muttered.

He straightened his wheel and got back to full power.

He looked in the mirror attached to his left wheel flair and saw Ulrick, just getting back on the track. Coleton gave a whoop in his helmet.

"Shit!" Coleton yelled. "Toyota just got by!"

The Toyota LMP1 had carried more speed through the chicane and was able to pass Coleton as if he were standing still. Coleton hadn't seen him coming.

"Who's in the Toyota?" Coleton demanded.

"Jimenez."

"I can catch him," Coleton said. Pegging the accelerator to the floor, he raced toward Mulsanne Corner. He waited as late as he could, then hit the brakes at the 250 meter brake board, but they didn't jump up and respond. Coleton pumped them back to life and dropped to second gear, the car over revving loudly. He had to jump back up to third and muscle the speed through the tight, slow corner.

"My brakes are going way," Coleton said.

"Roger," Nelson said.

"Is it from the impact?" Coleton asked.

"Possibly" was Nelson's only response. They both knew there was nothing Nelson could do about the brakes. All Coleton could do was try to pump them up, but with only a handful of laps left, they certainly couldn't pit to investigate the problem.

"If his brakes are going, there's no way he'll retake third position," Jacques said to his computer screen. He shifted on his stool, and then looked at Nelson.

"It will be difficult," Nelson agreed.

Exhaustion etched their faces to haggard masks. While the mechanics and drivers had breaks from time to time and catnaps here or there, the engineers on the pit wall remained shoulder-to-shoulder, calculating, monitoring, communicating, from start to finish.

Jacques shook his head sadly, removed his thick glasses to clean them, and then replaced them on the bridge of his oily nose. He looked at the numbers on his computer screen and shook his head. *"Merde,"* he said to himself.

"We need a fuel reading," he told Nelson. Nelson looked at him sharply, but clicked on his microphone.

"Fuel reading, Coleton," Nelson said.

Coleton was startled by the transmission. Pit wall usually only called for physical fuel readings when the computer data indicated the car might run out. Coleton was completely focused on the final stages of the race, catching up to the Toyota, as he roared into the Porsche Curves at 200 mph, and the request rattled his nerves. It was the worst possible section of the track for him to take his eyes off the road and check a gauge. They would have to wait.

Into the Porsche Curves, Coleton dropped down a gear, then cut toward the apex on the right hand side. In an instant he was flat out in fourth gear, then fifth at 180 mph down the narrow road, the barrier only feet from his side panel. Safely out of the Porsche Curves and headed for the Ford Chicane, Coleton had an instant to glance down.

"36.5, 36.5," Coleton said.

"Roger."

At Coleton's words, Jacques began scribbling on a pad of paper, and then looked back to the fuel grid on his screen. He grabbed his calculator, typed in a few numbers, divided by the number of laps left and held it close to his face. He removed his glasses and squinted at the number, just to be sure.

Nelson grabbed Max by the shoulder and peeled back one of his earphones. "This idiot better not run us out of fuel."

Jacques looked at the large Rolex timer that sat on the other side of the front straight: 18 minutes, 37 seconds left. He began to sweat. He knew what Arthur Elrod wanted and now he knew how to make it happen.

"Fuel reading, please," Nelson asked Coleton, without waiting for Jacques to request it.

"31.4, 31.4" Coleton said. "Do we need a splash?"

All the engineers along the desk looked down the row at Jacques. He leaned over his notepad and calculator: more squinting, more calculations, more sweating.

"Do we need a splash and go?" Nelson asked Jacques sharply.

"No, no. We'll make it," Jacques said, looking up with watery eyes.

"Are you sure? We can dive in for a splash."

"I'm sure."

Nelson turned back to his screen and transmitted, "Conserve fuel. I repeat, conserve fuel."

Coleton felt sick. "How the fuck am I supposed to do that? I've got P3 in my sights. I'm not giving up the podium."

Nelson braced at the expletive over the radio frequency, but let it go.

"Do your best, Mate. If we pit we lose the position anyway, so do what you can to save fuel."

"If I push, I might run out of fuel. If I conserve, I'll never retake third," Coleton said. There was no response from pit wall.

Coleton ground his teeth. "Why does the driver always take the fall for other people's errors?" To the television audience and track spectators, it would look as if he had lost his edge to exhaustion.

His next lap, Coleton short shifted and lifted off a bit on the straights. His lap time dropped by three seconds. Roaring down the Mulsanne Straight he could see the Toyota now about 11 seconds ahead.

"Fuck it." Coleton shook his head angrily and pushed down the accelerator. He had to go for it. He didn't know how to drive halfway.

Fireworks exploded in the sky, as the last cars sprinted past the finish line and started their cool down lap. Thousands of excited fans migrated toward pit lane for the podium ceremony.

The Elrod mechanics wandered around the garage without purpose like a bunch of houseflies. There was no point in attending the podium ceremony, but they couldn't leave the track either. Not until the hook truck picked Coleton up from the side of the track where he'd run out of fuel and brought him back to the pits. Only then could they finish their job of cleaning and dismantling the car, packing up the trucks and finally head home for the last night at their cheap motels near the track.

"I feel bad for the bugger," one of the mechanics said and shook his head. In their team headphones, they could all hear Coleton's rant. He had been screaming and cursing at the top of his lungs for eight minutes straight.

While the checkered flag still waved in the air over the front straight, Elrod grabbed Jacques from the pit wall and pulled him through the garage and into one of the team transporters.

"I said a *crash!*" Elrod exploded. "Something dramatic to attract some goddamn attention." He flailed his arms in the air. "Not run out of fuel. How anticlimactic, you imbecile!"

Jacques Girard paled. "No one told me that. I'd never agree to risk lives for the sake of media coverage."

"Then what the *hell* did I pay you for?"

Jacques opened his mouth to speak, but Elrod held up a finger to silence him. An on-track interview filled the television screen on the wall of the transporter. Elrod turned up the volume. Coleton's face filled the screen. His eyes were bloodshot; his hair slicked back with sweat.

"Tell us. How did it feel after almost 24 hours of driving, of fighting with everything you had, to run out of fuel on the last lap?" the broadcaster asked.

Elrod's eyes were glued to the screen.

"We had an incredible team, a wonderful car, great support from our sponsors: Miller Sunglasses, Elrod Financial Enterprises, Organic Valley Market, and it's a real kick in the nu—" He caught himself. "—stomach to DNF on the last lap. It was a single miscalculation, after thousands of correct ones, and we paid the price with a podium."

Elrod's eyes snapped back to Jacques's. "At least we got an interview out of it. That should raise the Joyce Julius value." He slapped Jacques on the back, as he passed him and stepped out of the trailer. "It'd better be enough!" Elrod called over his shoulder.

CHAPTER 19
ST. TROPEZ, FRANCE

The sun was high overhead by the time Coleton finally accepted the fact he was fully awake. He had been tossing and turning, pulling the sheet overhead, ignoring the slices of sunlight slipping past cracks in the heavy silk drapes. He sat up, rubbed his eyes and only then realized that for possibly the first time, Camilla was up before him.

He pulled on a pair of board shorts and wrapped a terry cloth robe around his shoulders before climbing their curved, private staircase into the sun-filled salon of the yacht to look for her. Coleton was taken aback at the sight of the spotless dining table, which only hours ago had been extravagantly set for 12 with full place settings of fine china.

The immaculate décor had quickly been dismantled in drunken disorder as the dinner party spiraled from an elegant affair into nine foreign models dancing to Ibiza's finest on the table top in spike heels and doing lines of coke off each other's tan flesh. Coleton shook his head. He and Camilla had arrived on the yacht, expecting a luxurious weekend in St. Tropez aboard one of the most opulent yachts in the world, a place where he could rest and recuperate, relax from the stressful end to his 24 Heures du Mans. Instead, they found an Eastern Bloc party in full swing.

Looking toward the stern through the lavishly appointed, perfectly manicured salon that looked more like a royal sitting room in Versailles than a room on a boat, Coleton saw a group of people on the back deck. The far wall of the salon was solid glass, a pneumatic door that slid open silently as he approached.

As he stepped from taupe carpet onto oiled teak, an enthusiastic girl in a polo shirt brandished a silver tray, blocking his way.

"Orange juice?" she asked brightly. Coleton nodded and accepted a tall, crystal glass.

"Just orange juice?"

"Yes." The girl smiled. "Not a mimosa, but I can make it one."

Coleton shook his head no-thanks. He caught sight of Camilla in a lounge chair on the far side of the deck, angled out to sea. She was engrossed in a novel, a good one by the looks of it. The book was only a few inches from her nose. A barrage of catcalls sounded from a group of girls in the crowded hot tub as Coleton walked past.

"You! Hot car driver. Come dance with us!"

Coleton waved his hand in greeting and smiled in their collective direction, but knew better than to slow his pace. Seven of the models were accounted for, all standing thigh-deep in the water, moving back and forth mechanically to the techno music that blared from hidden speakers. Coleton lowered himself to the edge of Camilla's lounge chair and pushed her knees to the side with his back, making room to sit.

"Nice company, hey?" he asked with a wink.

He took a slow sip of orange juice. Camilla smiled absently, still intent in her book until she had finished her sentence. Then she looked up, beamed at Coleton, slapped the covers of her book together and sighed.

"They're drinking straight Patrón Platinum from champagne glasses, and I don't think they've slept yet."

"Not since last night or not since Al-Aziz imported them from Moscow?" Coleton quipped.

Camilla sat up from the lounge chair, rested her breastbone against Coleton's arm, her head on his shoulder. She extended her arm and pointed at a long-legged girl with short red hair and a gold lamé bikini. "That one doesn't speak a word of English."

"I imagine she gets by quite well regardless." Coleton smiled. "And, Al-Aziz? Is he accounted for this morning?"

Camilla shook her head no. "I doubt he'll make an appearance before dinner."

"Oh, wait 'till you see this," Camilla added, leaning over the edge of her chair. She grabbed a newspaper, folded open to the society page, off the deck. There was a large picture of Juliette Crowne, an action shot, showing her running out of a cabin, her hand raised to shield her face from the camera. The caption read, "Juliette Crowne Caught with New Boyfriend."

"What's this?" Coleton asked.

"They got a picture of Juliette leaving your cabin, and now the world thinks you're officially a couple."

"No way!" Coleton laughed, grabbing the paper.

"It's not that funny, dear," Camilla said. "Especially since you already have a girlfriend."

"If you hadn't left her there by herself, it wouldn't have happened."

"Well, *excuse me*, but I thought you and your fancy car were going to *explode* at the time."

Coleton's BlackBerry began to ring. He fumbled through the pocket of his robe and pulled it into the bright sunlight. He paused, staring at the number on the screen, then accepted the call on the last ring.

"Coleton!" the caller exclaimed before Coleton could speak. "I'm in trouble, Brother!"

Coleton stood up from the chair abruptly, his cheek pressed tightly to the phone.

"Where are you?" Coleton demanded. "What happened?"

Camilla pulled gently on the hem of Coleton's robe. "Who is it?" she mouthed. Coleton just stared ahead distractedly. When she tugged again, he mouthed back, "Enzo!"

"Okay, you need to stop. Right now. Pull the car over," Coleton instructed, trying to force a tone of calmness into his voice, but he had begun to pace back and forth.

The silver rented Peugeot shot like a bullet through the *carréfour* and careened the wrong way down a one-way street. The sound of the blaring police sirens that chased it lagged a few seconds behind the speeding car. Above, a helicopter hovered, following the car's erratic turns through the narrow Parisian side streets.

"No, it's a media helicopter. Not a police one," the handsome Italian yelled into his cell phone.

"Are you sure?"

Enzo rolled down the window and stuck his head out to get a better view. "Yes! I'm sure."

"Enzo, I'm scared. Stop the car," Heidi said quietly from the passenger seat. "Please." Enzo transferred the cell phone from his right to left hand, then held his right arm out straight, pinning Heidi to the back of her seat as he slammed on the brakes. Then, he spun the car into a sharp left turn. The road ended and he jumped the curb onto the grass. The car sped into the Champ de Mars park.

"I can outrun these bastards, Colt. Definitely."

"Enzo, you're joking. You can't out-run the French police!" Coleton exclaimed. "They'll make it a matter of national honor. You've got to stop. Just pull over and let Heidi out. You're scaring her."

"I can definitely out-run them."

Enzo floored the rented Peugeot through the thick grass of the park. Red and pink tulips spun out from beneath his tires. A flock of ducks waddled out of his way, quacking indignantly and wagging their tails.

"Pull over, get out and put your hands up." Coleton's tone of voice changed; it was an order.

"Colt, they'll shoot me. They're all hopped up with the chase, and who knows what Ulrick told them—*the brutto figlio di puttana bastardo!*"

Enzo looked over at Heidi. She had her eyes closed. Her right hand pressed the seatbelt tight, and her left clutched Napoleon in her oversized purse against her chest. Her lips moved slowly, silently in prayer. She looked beautiful, but Coleton was right, she was petrified. Enzo pulled the e-brake, and the car skid to an abrupt halt.

"Okay, *Amore*. Maybe you should get out here. Just keep moving and call me when you are safe in a hotel for the night. And, I will come to you."

Heidi looked at him and her eyes burned, but Enzo wasn't sure if it was hatred or fierce love he saw there. She made no sign, no sound, no acceptance or rejection, she just bailed out.

She scuttled from the car, her purse clutched tightly under her arm like a football. Her overnight bag slung over her shoulder rested against the small of her back. She ducked her head, shielded her face and bolted toward the trees. Like a vulture drawn to a kill the helicopter swooped down as low as it dared, as the news crew filmed with relish the super model's sprint into the bushes.

"Someone just exited the vehicle. It appears to be … yes, it is Heidi Ulrick! She's safe!" The newscaster motioned over his shoulder for the cameraman to zoom in on her figure as she scurried across the open lawn of the Parisian park toward the tree cover. When she had disappeared completely from view, the camera panned back to the newscaster. He had his microphone gripped firmly in his hands and perfectly positioned two inches below his bright white teeth. He was ready for the moment, ready to assume the posture his job required, ready to wrangle that heat-of-the-moment, calm-amidst-crisis Tom Brokaw persona that he'd practiced in front of his bedroom mirror since childhood.

"WXKM brings it to you first. We are here *live*, hovering over the Champ de Mars park, as the action unfolds. Just seconds ago, it appears the kidnapper released his hostage, Heidi Ulrick. Again, the details of this incident have not been confirmed, nor has the identity of the driver been released. It has been a long, scary day for us all since Klaus Ulrick reported his wife missing this morning. But, Heidi appears to have been released to safety, and the police continue their chase of the suspect who has once again entered the streets of Paris."

"Okay, it's just me, now," Enzo said calmly into his cell phone, but his knuckles whitened on the steering wheel. He made a sharp right, and the car stepped back down from the sidewalk into the street on the east side of the park. He sped down the street, and as he crossed the next intersection he saw the rotating blue and white lights of police cars speeding toward him at the perpendicular.

"*Merda!* I thought that would lose them!"

"Enzo, okay. Listen …" Coleton started, but he heard the engine rev angrily and Enzo mutter something under his breath. "Enzo! Listen to me!"

"Okay, what Brother?"

"Go to the Louvre. Where are you? Do you know where that is?"

"Yes. Of course," he replied, a true European.

"In front of the Louvre, the driveway by the glass pyramid. The cops would never shoot someone in front of all the tourists, Enzo. Go straight there, and turn yourself in."

"Call Crowne."

"Yes, I'll call Crowne. He can fix anything. But first, I want to know."

"Know what?"

"How did you do it?"

"Do what?"

"How did you bag Heidi Ulrick?"

Enzo chuckled. "Shakespeare. Helping men get laid since 1591."

"No way!" Coleton laughed out loud and shook his head. "Okay, I'll be in Paris in about four hours to bail you out."

"Bail me out? But I have done nothing wrong!"

"I know. But, I'm sure Ulrick cooked something up, and besides they'll book you just for running, not to mention the hundred or so traffic laws you've broken."

"*Cazzo!*"

Coleton heard a slight scrapping of metal, but Enzo's engine roared louder and continued on.

"I'll see you soon. Just stay calm and give them no excuse to make the charges worse. You hear me? Don't give them any reason to shoot you."

Coleton hung up the phone and slowly let his arm drop to his side. He stared at Camilla blankly. She was standing now too, her muscles taut, staring at Coleton.

"We're going to Paris?" she asked, but she already knew the answer.

"Pack our bags," Coleton instructed. "I'll find Al-Aziz and tell him."

"If he gets arrested at the Louvre, they'll take him to La Santé prison," Camilla said. She had picked up more from one side of the conversation than he had expected. "In the 14th arrondissement. That's where we should head."

"How the hell do you know where the jail is in Paris?"

"I spent a semester abroad in Paris during undergrad," she said, then smiled mischievously. "Don't ask."

"We'll talk about this later. Go pack!"

Coleton rushed through the thick techno music, past the hot tub that appeared to be getting even hotter. The girls, rather than sluggish with exhaustion, seemed to be just waking up, their narrow hips thrusting to the music in the midday sun.

Coleton rushed through the salon, then down the portside hallway toward the master staircase. He paused for a second, looking at the solid door that led to the descending staircase. He threw his shoulder into it for emphasis, but it easily gave way. He rushed down into the full-beam master stateroom. The Stark carpet beneath his feet disappeared in darkness as he neared the bottom, which opened up into an expansive, completely dark room that had the size and general feeling of a lion's den.

After the last step, Coleton slid his foot slowly forward making sure he was in fact to the bottom of the stairs, then he turned left and took shuffling steps toward the side of the yacht, his arms extended in the blackness like a swimmer coasting toward the edge of the pool. At last he reached the wall, then he turned toward the bow and inched forward until his fingers felt drapes. He pulled them from the wall and a spotlight of sun shot across the broad room.

There was an enormous custom bed, bigger than a King size, pushed against one wall. He adjusted the curtain to train the light on the bed. At the sudden attack of light, a large lump rolled sideways. He heard a distinct moan farther off, and he adjusted the curtain to train the light toward the far side of the wall. Another form lay on the ground: clearly naked, clearly female.

"*Fermez la fenêtre maintenant!*" a hoarse feminine voice on the ground near his feet demanded. Coleton startled. "It's too bright." If he had taken one more step he would have stepped on her. Models #8 and #9 were accounted for.

Coleton cleared his throat with more noise than necessary. "Al-Aziz?" he asked into the darkness.

The large lump on the massive bed moaned. Then, Al-Aziz sat up. "By Allah!" he said, grasping the sheet to his chest, then began to chant, "There is no God but Allah, and Mohammed is his prophet! There is no—"

"Relax, it's just me—Coleton." Coleton smiled in the dark.

"Who?" He squinted. "Coleton?"

"Yes. I'm sorry to wake you."

"Hello, friend!" Al-Aziz said cheerfully, followed by a grimace. "Ow! My friend, the light—"

"Hey, listen, my friend needs help. You know Enzo Ferrini the BMW factory driver? He is in trouble, in Paris. I must go to him." His words took on the gravitas of a divine mission as he spoke them into the dark room.

"By all means!" Al-Aziz agreed. "Yes, by all means, take my helicopter. I insist." Al-Aziz extended his heavy arm in blessing. Coleton smiled broadly at Al-Aziz's gesture; it felt like the toss of a set of car keys. "I insist, my friend," Al-Aziz continued. "Think nothing of it. Tell a staff member to awaken the pilot. He had quite a late night last night with us. He will still be sleeping. But he is on the clock. My clock. And, he can be ready in 10 minutes for your trip. Godspeed." With that, Al-Aziz fell back into the cloud of bedding.

"Thank you. I won't forget this, and neither will Enzo. I'm sure."

Al-Aziz giggled and called out from flat on his back. "I've always been a closet BMW fan! Sorry my friend, but it's true."

Coleton shook his head, before sprinting by feel back up the stairs.

Fourteen minutes later, Al-Aziz's Sikorsky Executive S-76 lifted gently off the yacht's helipad, flew low over the city of St. Tropez and headed north, as the crow flies, toward the French capital.

Dim light sifted down from a row of antique globe streetlamps. Coleton lifted a large aluminum can in the air and watched the light roll slowly off its curves. Camilla's chin rested in the palm of her hand, her arm propped up by her knees. She was tired, but there was a spark of good humor in her eyes. She lifted her own can off the cold marble step that she sat on and clinked it dully against his.

Coleton threw back his head and took a long, slow swallow of Stella Artois. He had bought their drinks in the nick of time from the corner *boulangerie*. The stout clerk had repeatedly checked the face of her watch, as if willing to turn off her credit card machine mid-transaction if the minute hand slipped past the mark of closing time. She knew she was the last shop open and believed this gave her a blank check when it came to her attitude toward customers, especially when they were foreign, attractive and happy-looking. They had scored their purchases with seconds to spare: a baguette of stale French bread, two cans of beer and a block of cheese—for dinner.

"Not exactly what I had planned," Coleton said, through a mouth of crumbs. He tore off another bite, then passed the baguette to Camilla. "I was hoping to show you a good time in the lap of luxury this weekend."

"A good time? Al-Aziz's yacht? That 'lap' was more like a Petri dish!"

"Point made." Coleton chuckled, his thoughts resting on the nine models that were undoubtedly still partying like rock stars the night before a trip to rehab. "Well, it certainly wasn't what I expected, if that's any consolation. I can honestly say I'm over that phase in my life."

"Someone bring this man a medal," Camilla said with warmth in her voice.

"And, neither is this—what I expected." Coleton motioned with his beer can to the deserted Parisian streets that radiated in all different directions from their compass point.

"At least it's not raining," Camilla said, as she tore a bite from the crusty baguette with her molars, unleashing a flurry of dusty crumbs.

"It could be worse," he agreed. "Although, I never thought we'd be drinking beer out of cans, sitting on a dirty step in front of a police station in the middle of the night in Paris. Not exactly a night to remember."

Camilla bumped his shoulder softly with hers. "It's a beautiful evening, and I wouldn't want to be anywhere else."

"Camilla—" Coleton cleared his throat. He was suddenly aware of what he was about to say, like the words had a mind of their own and he was just the spokesperson. They were fully formed in his head although he had never thought them through before. He wasn't sure that he wanted to stop them; he was only aware that it was too late to try.

"I've been a lot of places in my life. I've done a lot of things and met a lot of people," he said. Camilla sat up straighter. Here is where she would normally make some joke about how she was well aware of his reputation. But, there was something in the tone of his voice, something she hadn't heard before. He was about to say something important.

"I've done just about everything. But, I think there is one thing I haven't. I've never been—in love."

Camilla's eyes lit up as she turned toward him. They were shoulder-to-shoulder, eyes locked in the dim light.

"Well, I'm glad I can be your first—something." Camilla smiled. A warm silence settled around their shoulders. "Your last first."

Coleton gazed into Camilla's eyes. Her pupils were large, her irises a dark navy, almost purple. "Your eyes are so beautiful in this light," he said.

"You know how they say eyes are the windows of the soul?"

"Mmm-hmm," he said, gazing at her.

"Well, it's true. Not just poetically, but scientifically."

"Oh yeah?"

"Your pupils don't just react to light. And, you can't control them—they're regulated by the autonomic nervous system, which also controls other unconscious reactions like goose bumps and your heart rate."

"Do you have any idea how sexy you are when you talk like that?"

Camilla smiled softly. "The brain secretes norepinephrine, which flexes the dilator muscles—in response to *attraction*. Pupils dilate when you see someone you want, and they don't lie."

"Say that again."

"What?" she asked.

"Norepinephrine."

She smiled. "Let me see your eyes," she said, and leaned closer.

Coleton shook his head. "That doesn't seem very fair ... using your medical knowledge to read me."

"You're an open book, Loren."

"So how do they look?" he asked, pulling her head closer. His fingers weaved through her hair. Their eyes floated inches from one another.

"Massive," she whispered.

CHAPTER 20
MEDITERRANEAN SEA

Elrod walked to the railing and looked overboard. The wind ruffled his hair and tugged at his khaki pants and white linen shirt. The water below the *Closing Bell* was Confederate gray in the morning light. Deceiving. It looked shallow, but he knew it free-fell hundreds of feet. Elrod shivered, and turned back. Even though the boat was drifting in the middle of the Mediterranean far from land, he still felt watched, exposed.

Elrod's toes sank into the plush carpet of the main salon, and left footprints as he walked to the bar. Out of the wind, he smoothed his hair back with both hands. He felt jostled, as if someone had elbowed him in a crowd without an apology. He lifted a martini glass off a shelf with a miniature silver railing. A slight tremor passed through his hand as he held it. His gaze shifted out the window, clouds rippled the sky like the scales of a fish. Startled by a thought, he looked at the glass in his hand, surprised that he held it. He set it on the mahogany bar top. He scanned the rows of bottles to jog his memory, but he couldn't remember what part to what goes in a martini.

"Smith!" Elrod called. He waited, but no one appeared.

He walked the slim hallway along the starboard side, past the staircase that led down to the master stateroom, and continued into the French kitchen. A stick-thin girl in her 20s, with fine, almost translucent blonde hair, stood at the window, mesmerized by something. She wore a white polo shirt, and white golf shorts crosscut with sky blue plaid. She turned at the sound of his footfall, then jumped to attention.

"Mr. Elrod, sir. What can I get you?"

"What were you looking at?"

"The gathering cirrocumulus clouds, sir." She pointed out the window at the growing veil of clouds. "You know what they say, 'Mackerel sky, storm is nigh.'"

"Right. Well, is it too much to ask for a martini?" His inflection made it clear it wasn't.

"No sir," she said, then added, "I just put on a fresh pot of coffee, if you'd like a cup."

He gave her a withering look. "Just the martini. I'll be in the salon."

Elrod started back down the hallway, but peered over the staircase at a sound. He saw the top of Justine's dark head, tramping up the stairs.

She wore a flowered dress, tightly belted around her slim waist, perfectly applied make-up, large diamond stud earrings, two necklaces and juicy-colored gemstone rings. A petal pink Birkin hung in the crook of one arm and a pair of strappy high heels dangled from the index finger of the other.

"Hello, darling," she said, halting at the sight of him. Her foot hovered over the top step.

"Where are you going?" he asked.

He looked past her and saw two staff members angling her Louis Vuitton luggage up the narrow staircase.

Elrod spun on his heel, and she followed him into the salon. He took a seat on one of the opposing couches. He threw one arm over the top of the cushions and slouched back into the fine linen fabric. Justine sat next to him, on the edge of the couch, back straight.

"So?" Elrod asked. "Speak."

Justine took a breath. "I had those papers prepared."

"What papers?"

Justine pushed back the lip of her Birkin with one finger and produced a manila envelope. She unsheathed a stack of papers and set them on the coffee table.

"Divorce papers."

"What the hell are you talking about?" he snapped.

"Oh, dear," she said with a note bordering sympathy. "If you sign these papers I'll get to keep some of our US assets. If you don't, we'll both go down in flames. You think I don't know about our financial situation?"

Elrod's mouth dropped open.

"Just sign them. Let's not get all dramatic and sloppy."

Elrod stared at the papers, but didn't touch them. "I don't understand. Where are you going?"

The girl walked in with a martini on a silver tray. She set down a cocktail napkin on the table, carefully passing Elrod the martini glass. She opened her mouth, but when she saw the look on Justine's face she closed it and left the room.

"Back to New York."

"But, how?"

Elrod heard a gentle thrumming. He set down the glass without taking a sip, and a wave of cold clear liquid splashed onto the lacquered tabletop. The sound grew steadily louder. Elrod walked to the window and saw an approaching helicopter.

"Right," he said in a dejected voice. "The passports."

Outside, crewmembers scurried along the railing toward the helipad located on the far back deck. Justine leaned forward and plucked the clear plastic sword from his glass. Elrod watched it drip on the carpet: once, twice, as she slowly pulled off an olive from the skewer with her front teeth.

"Listen," he said. "You can't list all my assets in the open like this." He looked at the stack of papers.

"Relax. You can keep your super-secret Swiss account. I didn't mention it."

Elrod released a sigh of relief. He had plenty squirreled away in his apocalypse fund, and the federal bankruptcy court could take the rest. As for Dieter, Elrod would be long gone before he realized his next payment would never arrive.

Smith and a tall man with black aviator sunglasses and a brief case approached the pneumatic door that separated the salon from the sweeping back deck. The wind ruffled their hair and clothing. When the door slid open, Smith nodded for the man to enter, but remained outside as it closed.

"Elrod?" the man asked.

Elrod and Justine stared at him blankly.

"I have the documents you requested," he said walking toward Elrod and extending his hand.

At the sight of the man's outstretched hand, Elrod cleared his throat and stood up. They shook hands, but the man didn't introduce himself.

"Thank you for coming," Elrod said. The man nodded.

Elrod motioned him to the bar, but didn't offer a drink. The man placed his briefcase on the bar, clicked the double locks and lifted its top slowly like a treasure chest. He removed two dark green passports.

"You are now a citizen of the Kingdom of Morocco."

Elrod picked up one of the booklets. The words *Royaume du Maroc* floated above a crest encircling a star. On either side of the crest a lion reached up toward a crown. He opened it to the picture page. To the right of his picture was the name: Winston Murdock.

"And Morocco doesn't have an extradition treaty with the US?" Elrod asked.

The man smiled behind his dark glasses.

Elrod flipped open the other booklet and saw Justine's dark glittering eyes. "I only need the one for me. She's going home."

"You will be required to pay for both," the man said. "But, yes, I was told she would accompany me back to Spain."

"What else do you have?" Elrod asked.

The man removed a piece of thick white paper from the briefcase. "This is confirmation that the AIS tracking for *Closing Bell* has been removed. Additionally, the boat has been reflagged by the Kingdom of Morocco under the name *Contessa*, and will be untraceable to your former name."

"Good," Elrod said.

The man closed and locked his briefcase. Elrod pulled his cellphone from the pocket of his khaki pants and pushed the call button.

"Send the wire," he said.

Coleton downshifted to fourth and the sunflowers shook violently in their glass vase, beating their bright yellow heads against the dash.

"Careful of the flowers!" Camilla warned.

She held the vase with both hands tight to the seat between her legs. The arrangement was so full she couldn't see Coleton to the left or the road ahead. She gave up and sat back in her seat.

They roared up to a guardhouse, and the gate promptly lifted without anyone asking for identification.

"Do you have any idea where you're going?" Camilla asked, as Coleton pounded through the gears. Her head bumped the headrest as each gear caught.

"Of course."

Camilla raised an eyebrow, unconvinced by his tone. Then she took a bow face first into the flowers, as Coleton slammed on the brakes. The engine popped and sputtered in overrun, as the unused fuel in the 12 cylinders of the F12 burned off.

The car idled for a second, then jerked backwards. The engine whined as it accelerated in reverse. Coleton's eye met hers through the spray of flowers, and he smiled sheepishly.

Coleton spun the car 90-degrees, then sped down another curving road bordered by tall royal palms. Out the window, one beautiful home after another flicked by in succession like frames from an old nitrate film. Although each one had slightly different rooflines and cast-stone columns, they looked eerily similar.

"Here it is!" Coleton said brightly. He dropped the car to a crawl, and angled the car to climb the inclined driveway without scraping its lowered chassis.

"You sound awfully surprised for a man who knew where he was going."

Coleton pulled the e-brake, then twisted to grab a present strapped in the leather luggage rack, where the backseat would have been in a normal car. He had to use both hands to lift the heavy box.

They walked up a paver-set walkway through tropical landscape to a set of immense cut-glass double doors. Coleton rang the doorbell. They waited, but no one came. Coleton stepped forward and knocked firmly. Nothing.

"Maybe we should just go in?" Coleton asked, but he already had his hand on the door handle and pushed open the door.

"Coleton, wait!" Camilla said. "Don't be rude."

Coleton shrugged and pushed forward.

"I didn't peg George as a Boca-fabulous kinda guy," Coleton said, wrinkling up his nose.

A marble staircase with an intricate wrought-iron railing rose to their right. Above the entrance a gold leaf chandelier hung from the ceiling with a ring of electric candles complete with fake wax drippings. The walls were sponge-painted a warm terracotta and a series of painted cracks gave it the feeling of an old world villa. They walked around a cherry wood table topped with a vase of tall, silk lilies.

"Well, we are in Boca, dear."

They continued under an archway. A country kitchen opened up on their left, and on the right, a large living room. The back wall of the house was a series of towering glass doors that led to the lush backyard and, beyond it, the dark water of the intercostal waterway. Grace sat at the edge of the pool, with her pant legs pulled to her knees, as Christopher and Megan splashed in the aqua water.

"I'm going to say hi to Grace and the kids," Camilla said, setting the vase of flowers on the kitchen counter. "Why don't you go find George?" Coleton watched her open one of the tall glass doors and walk into the sunshine, before he turned.

"George?" he called. He waited for a second, listening, then called louder, "*Numbnuts!* Where are you?"

He heard George's voice and followed it down a hallway that led off the living room. He still had the present tucked under one arm, as he pushed open the hollow door.

"Hey, buddy. Great place!"

Large silk pillows with twisted fringe propped George up in a queen-sized bed. The blankets were neatly arranged around him. The bed faced sliding glass doors that led to a narrow concrete porch.

"Thanks." George said with a smile. "I really haven't been here all that much over the years."

"Great decoration," Coleton said, walking to the sliding glass door. He pushed back the silk brocade curtain to let in more light.

Beyond a stretch of grass, he saw the pool glint in the sunlight. Camilla sat next to Grace, her feet in the water now too.

"It's all Grace's doing," George said. Coleton looked around the room. "This is just a guest bedroom. I'm still not walking too well and can't make it up and down the stairs."

"I know the feeling," Coleton said. He turned and held out the present.

"You didn't have to do that." George smiled warmly. He rested the heavy present in his lap. "What's in here?" he asked.

Coleton shrugged and smiled with mischief, as George pulled the bow and loosened the satin ribbon.

"How you feeling?" Coleton asked. He sat on the edge of George's bed.

"Better everyday. It was touch and go to start, which put a different perspective on things, but I'm coming back. I have rehab in the pool four times a week and a great new trainer."

George lifted the lid of the box.

"You're shitting me!" he chuckled. He pulled out a baseball cap, and underneath was a six-pack of beer.

"How did you know?" George said, pulling a can loose from its plastic ring. "You're a true friend."

"You can't drink it warm!" Coleton warned, as George popped the top.

"Just try to stop me."

"Gross," Coleton laughed.

"I haven't had a beer in weeks. When we got back from Canada, Grace went on a rampage and threw out all the alcohol in the house. Most of it was hers I have to say. Said we were starting over." George took a sip of his warm beer and smacked his lips.

"And, what's this?" George asked. He set his beer on the nightstand and picked up the hat with both hands. He tilted it into the light to see its brim. "It's a Le Mans hat," he said. Coleton nodded. "An old one," he added. "And, hey, that's my signature!"

"Autograph," Coleton corrected.

"Where'd you get this?"

"At Sebring." Coleton said. He waited for George to look up at him. "When I was 11."

George's mouth dropped open. "I don't understand."

"I begged and begged my parents to take me to the 12 Hours of Sebring for my birthday. Of course, my dad said no. Finally, I convinced my mom, and we had to sneak out of the house and lie to him," Coleton said, his eyes crinkled at the memory. "You were my favorite driver. I wanted to be just like you."

George's eyes misted over. "I don't even remember this."

"Why would you? I was just a kid with stars in his eyes and a dream to be a driver."

"Why didn't you tell me? You never told me!"

Coleton smiled. "When you saw me karting with Hilton Crowne at PBIR that Saturday, and pulled me aside to tell me you thought I had talent, I thought my heart was going to explode out of my chest."

"I remember that day."

"If you hadn't called your contact at Skip Barber and gotten my tuition waived, I wouldn't be a driver today. Did you know I told my dad I made the Lacrosse team, when I was really sneaking off to race after school?"

George shook his head no.

"By the time my parents found out, I'd already risen to the top of the class, and had too much attention on me for them to kill it. I won a scholarship from Skip Barber and was able to work my way up from prize money."

"I always knew you had talent, and a killer instinct. I'm proud of how far you've come," George said, wiping a moist eye.

"Last year was supposed to be my final year in the Series." George looked down at where the blankets mountained over the bulky cast on his leg. "But, when the opportunity to be your teammate came up, I knew I couldn't retire. I'd seen you grow from the very beginning, and I wanted to help you win your first Championship." George looked down at the baseball hat and turned it over in his hands.

"Now I've fucked it all up."

"Nah, we've still got a shot," Coleton said.

George looked out the glass door at the pool, and Coleton realized he wasn't just talking about the Championship. Camilla tossed a beach ball high into the air, and Megan leapt from the side of the pool to catch it mid-air.

"I thought I had some things left to teach you, but it seems you have a thing or two to teach me." He nodded at Camilla. "I took my family and my wife for granted for too long. Camilla seems like a really special girl. I see the way you look at her. Don't take that for granted."

The wind picked up and rocked the yacht from side to side in the moonlight. It had top-of-the-line stabilizers to minimize the roll, but even they weren't able to smooth the troubled waves under her hull.

Elrod lay in his bed with the down comforter drawn over his head. He pulled his knees to his chest and moaned. He prided himself on never getting seasick, but tonight he felt miserable and found it convenient to shift the blame to the waves.

There was a knock on the door. Elrod shuffled his feet under the bedding, as if pedaling a bicycle, and pushed himself to a sitting position. He'd left the lights on, and his eyes darted around the room looking for something he could use as a weapon. The only items within reach were a lamp glued to the nightstand and a Deepak Chopra book Justine had left behind.

"Yes?" Elrod called. He pulled the comforter up and peered over the edge.

Smith opened the door. "It's me, sir."

"Oh, come in, come in," Elrod said, dropping the fabric and motioning him in.

"The additional men you requested are inbound, half a mile away."

Elrod breathed a deep sigh of relief. Smith had sourced and hired a team of six top grade Israeli mercenaries that boasted round-the-clock protection.

"And you're sure their boat hasn't been followed?" Elrod asked, grasping a corner of his comforter and slowly wringing it.

"Positive."

Elrod watched Smith out of the corner of his eye. "And the woman I requested?"

Smith nodded. "Yes, sir. She's on the boat."

"Good," Elrod said. His eyes glittered. "Pass me my robe. I'll come on deck with you to greet them."

"Only if you're feeling well enough, sir."

"I'm fine," Elrod spat back, as Smith handed him his burgundy smoking jacket with the velvet shawl collar.

Elrod followed Smith through the twists and turns, staircases and pneumatic doors, onto the bottom deck. Smith handed him a set of binoculars and pointed out into the waves. Elrod followed the angle of his arm and searched the moonlit whitecaps.

"I see them," Elrod finally called.

A sleek center console cut through the waves. He twisted the binoculars to focus them, but couldn't pick out which figure among them was the woman. He couldn't wait to see what she looked like.

During the past 11 years of faithful marriage, all he could think about was ruffling his nose into the thick hair at the nape of a beautiful blonde's neck. And, that's only where the fantasy started.

As the boat neared the yacht, the captain spun the wheel and pulled back the throttle to drop the four Mercury motors to an idle. He let the momentum inch the boat into place along the starboard side of the yacht's wide transom.

Six men in black foul weather gear stepped off the boat, each carrying a sturdy dark grip. Then, a woman appeared from behind the console. The captain helped her onto the transom and into the broad lights that crisscrossed the back deck. She had a dark scarf over her head, and it was tucked into a fitted black trench coat. Elrod noted with glee that long tendrils of blonde hair had escaped around her face.

Elrod trotted down the four teak steps onto the transom and extended his hand to her. "Allow me," he said. Elrod brought her up to the salon. Smith and the six new recruits waited outside.

"Anything else for the evening, sir? I want to take them to the crew quarters and brief them."

"That will be all." Elrod smiled, already feeling at ease. "I'm sure we can entertain ourselves." He looked back to the woman, who walked into the warm glow of the salon.

She pulled off the scarf and shook out her long blonde hair. She checked to make sure Elrod was watching before she undid the top button of her coat to reveal the sweetheart top of a black negligee.

"Carry on," Elrod told Smith, and hustled into the salon.

"Would you like a drink?" Elrod asked her, nodding at the bar.

She shook her head slowly left, then right. Long eyelashes curled above her midnight blue eyes. She had a dark mole above her lip, and Elrod shivered with ecstasy when he saw it.

"Come with me, my dear," Elrod said with sudden urgency. She followed him along the hallway, down the stairs and to the master stateroom.

"I hope you brought a suitcase. I have a feeling we'll be seeing quite a lot of each other."

Elrod turned on the lights, then carefully dimmed them. On an impulse, he rushed across the room and slid the self-help book off the nightstand and onto the floor. He turned, and motioned her to him.

He ran his thumb over her lips, so full and ripe. He kissed her gently, exploring, and she tasted just as he'd hoped. A smile tugged up the corners of his mouth at the taste of strawberry lip balm. He pulled back for an instant to appreciate the beautiful creature that he was free to ravish in any manner he chose.

"La Perla?" he asked, stroking her lacy black negligee with the back of his knuckles.

Elrod's blood raced, he looked down at the rise in his boxers. He was aroused, very aroused. He tore the shoulders of her coat back, but it was still tied at her waist. She pulled first one arm, then the other out of the sleeves, and placed them on his shoulders. He pressed his body against hers so she could feel him.

He tangled his fingers in her hair and yanked her head back to kiss her hard on the lips. He pulled harder, exposing her soft white throat. His lips moved down to kiss under her jawbone. Her skin was soft, and so sweet. He rested his forehead on her breastbone. Something red glinted between her breasts. He pulled back. He placed the V of his hand around her neck, then slid his fingers down the long gold chain around her neck and picked up the charm in his hand. It was a ring.

He rolled it in his palm: a large ruby ring. It glinted softly, greedily in the low light. He saw his reflection in the table of the blood red stone, and gasped. He dropped the ring as if he'd been bit and stumbled backwards.

"*Shhhh—*" the woman said. Her eyes were smoky, as she stepped toward him. Her lips curled into her first smile.

"Where … where did you get that ring?" he demanded. Fear sprang loose, wild in his eyes.

In a swift, fluid movement, she swept a Desert Eagle .50 from a holster strapped to her thigh and aimed it into Elrod's chest. His eyes locked on the gun, and his mouth worked open and shut like a dying fish. He looked into her eyes, pleading. She shrugged, then gave him a wink. A blinding flash filled his vision.

CHAPTER 21

BRASELTON, GEORGIA

Milky gray light sifted through the glass atrium and down three stories onto a flock of empty tables in the breakfast area of Château Élan. A chef dressed all in white adjusted his towering *toque blanche* with one hand and gave his frying pan a last little shake before he slid a perfectly white omelet onto a warm breakfast plate. He continued to hold the plate for a moment, considering whether or not to hand over his flawless creation. Finally, the chef passed the steaming plate to Coleton but not without a look of regret.

Coleton chose a two-top near the wall. On race weekends, he always woke early and preferred to eat alone. Today, the first day of official practice sessions for Petit Le Mans at Road Atlanta, was no exception. Coleton used these early morning moments to reflect, relax and prepare for the day ahead, to clear his thoughts and drive through each corner of the track, noting in his mind each reference marker and gear change.

A waitress arrived and set down a porcelain cup of green tea. She gave him such a high-beam smile, it made Coleton chuckle. She didn't care who he was exactly, it was enough that he was attractive and had team credentials around his neck. He thanked her for the tea, but she didn't move or dim her smile.

"Okay, thank you," Coleton said again, trying to dismiss her. In the face of her perma-grin he couldn't help but chuckle again, and she took this as a sign of encouragement. She made a movement as if to sit down, "You look like you could use some comp–"

"Heya Colt!" They both jumped. Ira Goldstein stood at the top of the grand staircase that led down to the breakfast area.

"Oh, great," Coleton muttered. His quiet breakfast was shot. The girl looked up at Ira hustling down the stairs, then back at Coleton's handsome face.

"Well, you let me know if you need anything, love. Anything ..." she cooed. Coleton smiled up at her, relieved that one obstacle was removing herself. Now, if only he could get rid of Ira, he could return to his thoughts.

Coleton just managed to fork a small piece of omelet into his mouth before Ira descended on him in a huff.

"Just landed. I've always loved this place," Ira said, looking up at the vast glass atrium laced with ironwork like the Musée d'Orsay. "I mean, it *is* kind of a farce to build a French château is the middle of Georgia, but—" Ira giggled.

"I don't see you staying anywhere else."

"*God*, no. I booked a year in advance for this weekend. How's the car?"

"The car is okay," Coleton replied, chewing his food slowly and waiting for Ira to ask why the car was only okay, and not good. But, Ira had something to share first, something big enough to eclipse any other thought.

"So, I got the contract signed with Pinkberry frozen yogurt yesterday," Ira boasted. "They're giving us two hundred grand for just this one race. Not a bad day at the office. I already booked three 'convention' models to squeeze into Pinkberry tank tops and hand out samples." Ira made air-quotes around the word convention.

"Convention models?" Coleton asked.

"Yeah, they're not real fashion models. Fashion models are always hungry and pissed off. Convention models are the girls that work trade shows at convention centers. You know the ones—they've got massive boobs and the right attitude."

"The right attitude?" Coleton laughed out loud. "You mean they'll sleep with you if you book them?"

"Look, we need some—" Ira paused to choose his adjective carefully. "—spicy girls that will bring a lot of attention to the sponsor."

"Right," Coleton scoffed. "Good thinking."

"Oh, and I already talked to Nelson and emailed him the Pinkberry logos late last night, and he's going to get them on the car by the first practice session this morning."

"The first practice session? You know it starts at 10, right? That doesn't give them much time, and they've got some gear box issues to focus on that I think are a little more important at the moment."

"Relax. What's more important than money?" Ira giggled.

Ira made 10% on all sponsorship dollars that came in, so he just raked-in twenty grand for himself, and no bad humor on Coleton's part could ruin his mood.

"Easy for you to say," Coleton replied. "You're not driving that puppy around the track at 180."

"So, how'd Hilton drive in the practice session yesterday?" Ira asked.

"Surprisingly fast. He's young, but he's really talented. He's only about a half second off my lap times."

"Really?" Ira inclined his head in disbelief. "Well, that's a relief."

"It's Trotter we need to worry about. I think he's actually gotten worse since Sebring."

"Wow, Elrod's letting that fucker race again even after he crashed the car?"

"Politics—" Coleton grimaced and took a small sip of green tea. "He's Elrod's nephew, remember?"

"How could I forget?" Ira said. "He'd never get a ride with a serious team otherwise."

"Well, Hilton turned some great lap times yesterday. We've got a shot at the podium, if we're lucky and manage to keep Trotter out of the cockpit as long as possible."

"What about Audi and Peugeot?"

"Thanks for bringing them up." Coleton cringed. "I said a podium, not a win. There is no way we're going to beat Audi or Peugeot, with their full factory support and multi-million dollar budgets. The European factory teams really screw up our averages when they join the Series for the endurance races."

"And, they're running two LMP1 entries each again this year?"

Coleton nodded grimly.

"Remember last year?" Ira asked, unnecessarily. Coleton remembered the race vividly: the European factory teams had dominated the field. Both had entered two cars and took positions one through four like it was a walk in the park. "Trotter's only got to drive one stint, right?"

"Yeah, we'll probably give him an hour of seat time for the books, to shut him up and keep Elrod happy. And, as long as he keeps it out of the wall, we'll be fine. He's about three seconds off the pace, but if Hilton and I drive our balls off, we can make up for that. Hilton drove really well in France this year, and now he's got some endurance practice under his belt. The gloves are off. We're just going to man-through the 10 hours between the two of us."

"Speaking of Elrod, is he around?" Ira asked.

"I haven't seen or heard from him. But, I'm sure he'll turn up this weekend to soak up a little glory."

"I need to talk to him about a few ideas I have for next year."

"He'll turn up. Oh, and by the way, I need you to do me a favor."

"What is it?" Ira sat back in his chair looking skeptical. He was happy to do anything for Coleton, as long as it made him money. And, although it was true that Ira would lie down in the street and die for Coleton, he'd charge him 10% for the effort.

"I need you to pick Camilla up at the airport tonight. She's flying in to ATL just in time for night practice."

Ira looked down at Coleton's untouched ice water, pulled it to his side of the table and took a long sip. "Sure, no problem."

"What do you mean, 'sure, no problem'?" Coleton stared at him with open shock.

"I'll pick her up." Ira took another sip and looked off over the empty tables.

"Ira, I've known you since we were too young to fuck. When have you ever willingly done a favor for me that didn't line your pocket? You *do* know the airport is 45 minutes away?"

"What, you want me to change my mind?"

"No, no." Coleton took another bite of his omelet. "I just want to know what's gotten into you."

"I like her. That's all."

"You like Camilla?" Coleton said the three words slowly, trying to read Ira's facial expressions, looking for one of his tells.

"Yes, I think she's a great girl." Ira smiled slightly, remembering Camilla's heroics in the face of espionage at the Long Beach Grand Prix.

"What's she got on you?" Coleton demanded.

"No, nothing. I just think she's a quality person—that's all."

"Okay," Coleton agreed with a smile, willing to let it drop. "So do I."

The waitress came back to their table. Her gaze lingered on Coleton, but his teacup was still full and he didn't ask for anything. Finally, she turned toward Ira.

"Want to order something off the menu or you want the buffet?"

"Has your menu changed since last year?" Ira asked. The girl paused to think.

"No, I don't think so. Only the soup and the catch changes."

"Great, I've been fantasizing about your mascarpone French toast for the past year." Ira smiled with delight. "And, I'll also take a side of scrambled eggs, bacon, and a cappuccino."

"No wonder you're a fat kid," Coleton laughed and shook his head. He finished the last bite of his egg white omelet and dropped his napkin onto his plate. "I've got to get to the track."

Ira parked the golf cart at the start of the Audi bridge, which spanned the width of the track, and Camilla bailed out. They stood shoulder to shoulder with their fingers hooked into the chain link fence, watching in the dark for the racecars to approach, and then in a split second zoom underneath them and into the bend of Turn 11.

"How can they see the track?" Camilla asked. Surprisingly, there were few street lamps to illuminate the track, and the drivers had to depend on their headlights, which from where Camilla stood didn't seem very bright, and their muscle memory from previous laps.

"The drivers know this track like the top of their dicks," Ira said, then startled. "Oh, sorry. I mean—they know this track *very well*."

Camilla couldn't help but giggle. Although Ira was offensive by nature, she appreciated the effort at least.

"They could probably run it with their eyes closed," he added.

"Which one is Coleton?"

"It's hard to say. The LMP1 cars have white lights, and the GT cars have yellow ones. And, you can hear when the diesel LMP1 cars go by. They are much quieter and make more of a high pitched whine when they pass."

"Oh," Camilla replied, politely pretending he had answered her question, but she waited, hoping he would continue.

"So, Coleton is in one of the non-diesel LMP1 cars, but which one is hard to tell. They have small illuminated numbers on their sides for identification, but they move so fast it's hard to read them."

"Why do they have to practice at night?"

"Night practice is very important because Petit Le Mans is a 10 hour race, and the teams will run well into the night. There really aren't any other races where they get to practice their night driving skills, except Sebring and Le Mans in France, of course, but only a few of the American drivers make it across the pond. So, this is really their only chance."

"Wow, 10 hours," Camilla mused.

"Well, more precisely it's 1,000 miles or 10 hours, whichever comes first."

Camilla tried to picture Coleton in one of the cars that were zooming below them, rattling around the cockpit in the dark, but it was hard for her to imagine. She pulled the lapels of her jacket closer together against the cool evening breeze.

Ira looked down at his gold Submariner. "It's almost nine. There are only 10 minutes left in the session. Want to go to the pits and see Coleton when he gets out?" Ira could see her bright-white smiled answer even in the dark.

On Friday morning, the main entrance to Road Atlanta racetrack was clogged with cars, and it wasn't even race day. Camilla waited in the long line of cars in Coleton's rented C class Mercedes. He had left the hotel room before she was awake, but had thought ahead, opting to hitchhike to work with another driver, and had left her the car keys and scribbled pace notes on how to get to the track. *Don't bother with breakfast,* he wrote. *Pamela will be offended if you don't stop by for a visit.*

Camilla smiled at the thought of visiting Pamela in her hospitality tent kingdom. She was beginning to see that once you developed friendships within the Series, you were no longer an isolated itinerant in a different city every other week, but rather part of a family, a crazy traveling circus.

Finally through the entrance gates, Camilla crawled straight up the steep hill, and then following Coleton's hand drawn map, she turned left and crossed the Audi bridge where she had watched night practice with Ira. Then, she continued straight past the Corvette and Porsche corrals.

These "corrals" are parking lots designated for specific makes of cars, and are set up at every race venue. The Series knows that grouping fans based on their predilections breeds tailgate parties and new friendships, enhances the overall fan experience and ultimately promotes Series loyalty. The corrals are always packed with cars, each owner eager to show off a hard earned beauty to a ready-made fan base.

After the corrals, she made another left and crept back down the hill, careful not to bump any pedestrians. The closer she got to the paddock, however, the more crowded it became, until she could barely maneuver the car. She came to a complete stop.

Camilla nudged the car forward again, and all of a sudden, someone yelled, "Watch out!" She panicked. There was a loud knock on her window. Someone bent low to glare into her window. She couldn't help but laugh in relief when she saw Ira's shiny smiling face inches from hers.

"Move over, Shorty. You'll never get through here!"

Ira pulled open her door and without waiting for her to move, he began to sit and pushed her into the right seat. As soon as he took the wheel, he rolled down the windows, put on the emergency flashers and laid on the horn. Camilla covered her ears.

"Ira!"

"You want to get to the paddock or not? You're lucky I found you. You were shipwrecked!" Then, he stuck his head out the window and yelled, "Get out of the way! Coming through! Are you deaf?" and continued to honk the horn without shame.

Camilla watched in awe as the crowd parted in front of them like a herd of cattle. Ira pushed the car forward, a little too quickly for Camilla's taste, and possibly brushed a few shinbones in the process, but he got the job done. At the bottom of the hill they turned right, and now in the paddock there was a little more space to move. Ira weaved in and out of pedestrians, port-o-lets, pit carts and mechanics rolling tires by hand down the road. Finally, he made a sharp left and pulled the e-brake, sliding into a parking spot behind a large white tent.

"Here we are!"

Camilla followed Ira through the back of the tent, which opened up into the makeshift garage. There sat the Elrod LMP1 car in all its shiny glory, surrounded by mechanics tinkering and polishing its bright side panels. The front of the tent was open to the pedestrian-laden Paddock Road, but roped off, and a solid wall of fans stood shoulder-to-shoulder taking pictures of the machine.

"Wow, the car looks great this weekend! It has a new paint job?" Camilla asked, pointing at the large Pinkberry logo.

"Well, no. It's not painted. It's wrapped."

"Wrapped?"

"Paint is too heavy. A single gallon of paint weighs about 10 pounds, but every ounce matters, so they wrap the cars with plastic."

"You're always *full* of useful information, Ira."

At the front of the tent, they saw the Elrod Racing LMP1 autograph session in full swing. She immediately recognized the back of Coleton's head, sitting between his co-drivers at a folding table, facing Paddock Road. There was a long line of fans waiting for an autograph and the chance of a handshake.

Camilla went straight for him, planning to surprise him by placing her hands over his eyes, but something she saw made her take a step backwards. Two scantily clad women stood at the front of the autograph line, and Coleton stood up and leaned over the table. Camilla gasped, as the beaming women pulled down the scooped necks of their skin-tight tank tops to expose their bare breasts. Coleton leaned over the table, his head right above their cleavage.

"What is he doing?"

"That's my boy!" Ira laughed.

Coleton uncapped a gold Sharpie and proceed to autograph one ample breast on each of the women. The women glowed with pleasure, gave Coleton a kiss on the cheek and then continued down Paddock Road.

"Busted!" Ira called. When Coleton turned around and saw Camilla, his eyes lit up.

"Hello, love!" He grabbed her in a hug. "I have 15 minutes left here, and then we can go straight to Pamela's for a quick bite. I've got to be in the car to qualify at 3:30."

"Did you just autograph a boob?" Camilla asked, more incredulous than angry.

"No ... two!" Coleton laughed. "Don't get upset. Some other woman just had me autograph her baby's bald head. Our fans are crazy! I love it!"

Camilla rolled her eyes in exasperation, but deep down she was impressed. She hadn't realized how many fans the team had developed over the season.

"Okay, Colt. The tires are warming up nicely. Get ready to set a hot one down. This should be your golden lap."

"Roger," Coleton replied calmly, his tone belying how high the stakes had climbed for the qualifying session.

The term "golden lap" refers to the first lap in a session after the car and tires are fully up to temperature and ready to rip. A driver's golden lap is almost always the quickest lap of the session, as drivers maximize this opportunity and commonly push with all-or-nothing abandon before their tires "fall off" and begin to lose their grip.

Coleton hurtled under the Audi bridge, bent into Turn 11 and 12 and felt the G forces kick in, a steady hand pushing his helmet firmly toward his left shoulder. Coleton blazed past the entrance to the pits and onto the front straight: his golden lap had begun.

Coleton rode the revs until the limiter whined and then tapped the paddle shifter solidly with the fingers of his right hand. He pushed the car into sixth gear and flew down the front straight, gathering as much speed as possible. Coleton inhaled deeply, counting to five as he slowly exhaled, to slow his heart rate and pack his blood with oxygen. Then, in an instant, he saw his reference marker, the 200-meter brake board. He brushed the brake and shifted down to fifth.

He gathered up the car and muscled her into the right-hander of Turn 1. The car squirmed at the turn in, but he hit the apex perfectly, coming as close to the inside curbing as possible, but not actually touching it. Coleton felt the slight indentation in the pavement he was waiting for, a reference marker. The instant he felt it he went back to full power, accelerator pegged to the floor, sprinting uphill and bending right toward the next section of the track.

Coleton smiled to himself. There was no denying it—he had felt the speed he carried through Turn 1 pressing down like a smooth stone in the pit of his stomach. The corner had been a good one, a good start to a great golden lap.

Coleton kept the accelerator flat until he crested the top of the hill, then he hit the brake and slapped the paddle shifter down through the gears: fourth, third, in rapid succession, to set up the car for the next set of turns. From the sudden deceleration, he felt all of his weight pinned against the few points of contact his seat belts made with his body.

In third gear, he jumped the curb with the right side of his car. Some curbs could be hit, and others would bottom out the car. Coleton knew the difference. He piloted expertly through the right-left-right complex from Turn 3 down through the serpentine section of track called the Esses, all in a few quick flicks of his wrist. He felt the car solid and responsive beneath him, but with a sudden jolt, he lurched forward.

His initial reaction was that the gearbox had broken, and he glanced down at the shift lights, but then the car shifted sideways. It began to slide, slowly, as if hydroplaning. He looked into his rear-view mirrors, but couldn't see anyone.

All of a sudden his rear wheels caught grip, tossing the car into a spin. In a rush, Coleton saw the Peugeot that had hit him and it all made sense. One of the Peugeots had carried too much speed into the Esses and had been forced to detour through the run-off area. He had pushed into Coleton's rear quarter panel as he tried to re-enter the track, and Coleton had never seen him coming.

Coleton spun onto the grass on the infield side of the track and rocked to a stop, pointing in the wrong direction. As the adrenaline roared loud in his ears, Coleton watched the other LMP1 cars skate past him in total selfish annoyance that their golden laps were being slowed by a cautionary yellow flag.

The Peugeot to blame was on the far side of the track. Its accelerator must have jammed or its brakes failed, because after it had smashed into the back of his car, it had continued across the track, plowed through the gravel trap and exploded into the tire barrier on the far side of the course. It was now a tangled, smoking mess of metal, and the corner workers were just pulling the driver out.

"Confirm you are okay," Nelson said over the radio.

"That fucker hit me!" Coleton yelled.

"Confirm you are okay."

"That fucker hit me!"

"Would you please confirm that you are okay?"

"I'm fine!"

"Can you make it back to the pits?"

"I'm not sure."

The engine had cut out and the dash still read third gear, so Coleton clicked the paddle shifter two times with the fingers of his left hand, then jammed in the clutch and fired up the engine. Because there was no reverse gear in his LMP1, Coleton had to light up the tires and crank the wheel.

He spun the car until he was headed in the right direction, then carefully inched forward, first lightly tapping the brakes to test them, then tugging the wheel back and forth to make sure the tire rods and A-arms were intact.

"It feels like something is dragging, but I am able to move. I'll get her back to the pits, but it might take a while," Coleton said.

A familiar rush pumped through his veins, but he knew it was his job to keep it in check, to focus until he got the rig safely back to the pits. He checked for traffic and limped back onto the track.

Then, he spun his wheels to get off the clag—stray pieces of debris and rubber marbles from the tires of other cars he'd picked up from running offline. It would be a long lap to get back to the pits.

As he chugged through each corner, dragging his right rear panel and sending sparks flying, the quick chemical exchange from raw adrenaline to red testosterone began to take place. By the time he stopped the car at his #37 pit board, Coleton wasn't ready to rage—he was already there. The instant his driver assistant unhooked his belts, Coleton leapt out of the car and screamed through the flipped-up visor of his helmet.

"Fucked! I got fucked!"

The mechanics looked at Coleton wide-eyed, clearly afraid of his fury, afraid to make any gesture on the off chance it might be misinterpreted and invoke the brunt of his mad wrath. Coleton ripped off first one glove, which he spiked to the concrete, then the other. He unbuckled his helmet and tore it off with a flourish, just barely checking himself before he threw it to the ground in a move that would have ruined its four thousand dollar paint job.

"What the hell was he thinking? On my golden lap!" Coleton yelled, rage contorting his attractive face. "I thought these European bastards were supposed to be professionals. The Series treats them like they're gods, and they are just as fucking fucked as the rest of us!"

Ira hopped down from the pit cart and started for Coleton, ready for crisis control. Coleton was still ranting blindly, shaking his helmet in the air for emphasis.

"Colt, calm down," Ira said coolly. He took Coleton's helmet from him, trying to shut down the spectacle.

"I'm going to kill that bastard!" Coleton yelled. He spun and started down pit lane toward the Peugeot pit box. Ira trotted quickly after him.

"Coleton, no. Don't do anything stupid!" Ira said. "It's *Fernando Garza* for Chrissakes! What are you going to do? You can't yell at Fernando Garza."

"Why the hell not? He fucked me! We'll be lucky to get the car back together by tomorrow … if we can even source the parts!"

"We'll get the parts, Colt. Don't worry. I've got Michel Burnie from ORECA wrapped around my little finger."

"And, on my golden lap! I didn't even set down one single lousy decent lap before he hit me. We'll have to start from last—*from last!*" Coleton shook his fist in the air. His eyes were completely wild and he continued to bull-walk down pit lane, shaking out his arms as if preparing for battle. But as the Peugeot box came into sight, Coleton stopped abruptly.

Fernando Garza was sitting on a cheap folding chair, his handsome head in his hands. Two red-faced Peugeot principals hovered above him, screaming in French and waving their arms in indignation. The paramedics were standing by the wayside like shy prom dates, waiting for a lull in the ferocity to swoop in and take Fernando to the medical tent.

"It must have been that poor bastard's fault." Ira shrugged with a giggle he couldn't suppress. "And, I thought it was the steering column that broke." Coleton continued to stare coldly at the Peugeot team, his gaze shifted darkly and indiscriminately from mechanic to engineer to Garza to water boy then to the far side of the pit wall. The hook truck was just arriving, dragging the mangled car home, its tangled side panels glinting in the sun like a broken pinwheel as it dropped solidly to the asphalt. It was clearly a total loss.

"Coleton, look at the bright side—"

"Fuck you."

"No, listen. At least this Peugeot is out, or likely out, for tomorrow. And, with only one more Peugeot and two Audis in the field, if only one of them DNFs we've got a real shot at a podium!"

Coleton paused to consider Ira's words, then shook his head. "They'll be back together tomorrow and better than ever. They're machines!" Coleton said the words with conviction, but the same note of anger didn't ring through his words.

Throughout his whole in-lap, Coleton had Garza by the throat and he was shaking him in the air—in his head. Now that Coleton was here, at the Peugeot pit, it didn't seem quite so black and white.

"Well, that's racing." Ira sighed, placing a hand on Coleton's shoulder. The two words used by every driving coach from the beginning of time to explain something inexplicable, or patently unfair—that's racing.

"Shut up," Coleton directed. But, a tiny pinprick of light had punctured his anger. It stretched and grew until he was lucid enough to know that Ira was right. Coleton spun on his heel and headed back to the Elrod pit, but by the time he got back, the pit box was empty. The wreckage of the car was gone. The mechanics were already hard at work, fighting in their own real way for the Championship.

CHAPTER 22
PETIT LE MANS, OCTOBER 2ND

"Today … is … race day!" Nikki Street beamed into the camera. "Welcome to the action! We're here … live! … at Road Atlanta for the final race of the season. And, race fans are literally pouring through the gates." She looked over her shoulder at the lines of cars, campers and golf cars waiting to get through to the track infield. "Estimates put the crowd at well over 100,000, and it's still an hour from race time!" She smiled proudly, as if crowd attendance was somehow her own doing. "And the weather—" She looked up dramatically at the gray sky. "Is just holding on." Her voice dropped to a somber note. "But, will it hold on for the race?" She arched an eyebrow and smiled into the camera like she knew the answer. "How are things looking down on pit lane, Brian?"

The television cut to Brian Horn, standing in the middle of pit lane. The camera took in the long line of cars behind him, each in front of its pit box for some last minute attention.

"Thank you, Nikki. Yes, I'm down on pit lane. And, as for the weather—" Brian also looked up to check the dark storm clouds rolling in, as if he hadn't already been briefed with a full meteorological report. "The first few drops have already started to come down. Looks like the start of the race will be wet. You can see behind me here, the cars are just getting a final few touches before they head out for their reconnaissance lap, then they will line up in their starting order on the grid."

"Look! There's Team Elrod Racing. Let's see how this changing weather will affect their race strategy!" Brian walked around the edge of the mean-looking LMP1 car and leaned against the pit wall looking into the Elrod pit box. Mechanics rushed around, and engineers typed frantically on their computers. Two drivers in red, black and white racing suits loitered at the far side of the pit box looking at a monitor, one had his back turned toward the camera and his suit had "Loren" written across its shoulders.

A team member shouted to Coleton and he turned to look at the camera. He patted Trotter on the back, told him to finish suiting up and jogged over to shake hands with Brian. Coleton exuded a calm-amidst-the-storm confidence and looked unflinchingly into the camera, his fan base growing by the second.

"How about this weather?" Brian asked.

"It's definitely thrown a wrench in the works." Coleton nodded. "It's been hot and sunny all week, so this is a bit of a surprise. But, luckily, our car is great in the rain. We just needed to make a few quick adjustments this morning."

"So, you got everything back together after that nasty crash in qualifying yesterday?"

"The crew had a pretty late night, but yes, we're as good as new this morning."

"And, are you feeling all right?"

"It certainly rang my bell." Coleton chuckled, rubbing his neck. Then, more serious, he added, "But, I was cleared by medical this morning, and I'm good to go. I think I'm *more* sore about starting last in our class. We had some of the quickest laps in the practice sessions, so we were expecting a good starting position, but we didn't get to finish qualifying because of the accident."

"That *is* a shame. But, there's a lot of time to make up the ground in a 1000-mile race. And, now with one of Peugeot's cars out, the playing field is a bit more level, huh?" Brian smiled. "That's got to make you feel a little better?"

"The Peugeot that hit us is still out?" Coleton asked. "They're taking a DNS? I hadn't heard!"

"That's a Did Not Start, for all you new fans out there."

Brian looked over Coleton's shoulder and saw Trotter pull on his fireproof balaclava, then his helmet. "You're not starting the race, then?"

"Trotter is in for the first stint, then Hilton Crowne will get in the car. The start will undoubtedly be messy. The wet weather is a real question mark for the teams so there is more likely to be a yellow flag or two in the first hour, which will allow us to make up any early time gaps before I get in the car."

"Is that a polite way of saying you're the fastest?" Brian laughed.

"It's just race strategy." Coleton winked. He gave Brian a friendly pat on the shoulder, before stepping away to help Trotter strap into the driver's seat.

Brian took a few steps backwards into the middle of pit lane and smiled brightly into the camera. "Well, it's all come down to this! Who will walk away with the Championship?" As if on cue, the cars behind Brian began to fire up their engines to head to the starting grid, and Brian covered his left ear with his free hand. "Today's winners … will decide!" With that, Brian ended the segment and scuttled out of the way with seconds to spare before the racecars spun out their wheels and hurtled down pit lane.

After the cars had completed a lap and parked in their starting order, track officials opened the grid and fans poured onto the front straight, surrounding the cars and photographing their favorites. Flag girls held the national flag of each team at the front of the cars, and drivers assembled to sign autographs and pose for pictures. Fat raindrops began to plop down on the shinning hoods of the lined-up machines, but the fans were not deterred as they swarmed around the battle-ready cars.

After 45 minutes, the track speakers crackled to life. "It's now time to clear the grid. Clear the grid."

Since they were starting last in their class, Coleton knew that they needed an incredible start to spirit them a few positions ahead. He had already convinced Nelson to let him call the start, so at the loudspeaker's first announcement, Coleton grabbed Camilla's hand.

"I'm calling the start. Want to help?" The question was rhetorical.

"Of course!"

They jogged through the crowd still amassed on the front straight and hopped the thick waist-high concrete wall onto pit lane. They hurried across pit lane to the Elrod pit box.

It would take the track officials a few minutes to clear the grid and get the race underway, and Coleton knew they needed every second to get in place. Coleton grabbed a team radio from the pit box and Camilla followed him along the chain link fence that separated the pits from the paddock until he found an opening. They made a u-turn back toward the Elrod transporter and garage, which was positioned directly behind their pit box on the other side of the chain link fence.

"Gentlemen, start your engines!" the loudspeakers demanded. The field of cars roared to life, loud and raw.

"We've got to move!" Coleton grabbed Camilla's hand and they sprinted to the transporter. There was a hydraulic lift in the back of the transporter that was used to lift and store cars on the upper level of the transporter. Coleton and Camilla jumped onto it and raised the platform until they were able to pull themselves onto the roof of the semi. The sky was curtained with heavy gray clouds, but the rain had stopped.

"Ok, see that guy?" Coleton asked Camilla, pointing at the official poised on the Firestone bridge. "See the green flag at his side? Glue your eyes to him, and the second he *begins* to raise his arm to wave the flag, I mean the very second, I need you to yell: green, green, green. Okay?"

Camilla nodded. She narrowed her eyes and focused on the official. She felt as if she'd never focused so hard on anything in her life.

"I'm going to watch the front straight for the first cars to appear." Coleton held up the radio and shook it slightly. "See, in a rolling start, the race starts for all the cars the instant the green flag waves, *not* as each car crosses the starting line."

Coleton's eyes were trained on Turn 12, the last turn of the track that led onto the front straight. "We'll be able to see the start a lot quicker than Trotter down in the car, and if I radio to him the exact second of the start, he can get cleanly past a few cars before they see the green flag themselves."

"Got it," Camilla breathed. The excitement tightened her lungs. Her chest felt full to bursting.

In an instant, the cars swept down the steep hill through Turn 12 and roared onto the front straight. Camilla's breath hitched in her chest. She was overwhelmed by the raw power and aggression of over 50,000 horsepower of energy, channeled into a pack of wild animals that devoured the track and rumbled toward her. Camilla peeled her eyes from the cars, which she wasn't supposed to be watching, just in time to see the race official begin to lift his arm with the green flag.

"Green, green, green!" Camilla screamed, forgetting Coleton was a matter of inches away. Coleton took up the cry in a nanosecond and relayed it to Trotter through the hand-held. The gleaming cars were already jumping and diving, jockeying for position.

Coleton and Camilla stood stock-still, shoulder-to-should on top of the semi, as the pack thundered past them. The noise was punishing and Camilla's hair blew back from her shoulders. Her eyes were wide and luminous with awe.

"What? It's like you've never seen a start before?" Coleton joked, but his smile was exuberant, and Camilla knew he had been touched by the same elation.

"Come on! Let's go to the pits. We may have picked up a position or two. We didn't pass a Giant, but it's a start."

"A Giant?"

"An Audi or Peugeot. Let's go!"

"Ready for some lunch?" Coleton asked, and squeezed Camilla's knee. She sat next to him in the pit cart watching the cars zoom by on the front straight. Camilla nodded and reached for her purse.

They had only been in the pits for the first half hour of the race, but Coleton felt comfortable that everything was under control. Although Trotter was in sixth position, he was keeping up with the leaders and was still on the lead lap. Coleton wouldn't be in the car for a few hours, not until after Hilton drove his double stint, so it was a good time for him to get out of the pits and relax before he got his head fully in the game.

"Where's my golf cart?" Coleton called to Nelson. Nelson was perched on a barstool in front of a bank of computer monitors. He pulled one of his puffy headphones away from his ear.

"What's that?" Nelson asked, screwing up his eyes, and trying to hear above the roar of the cars streaming past on the straightaway.

"My—" Coleton grabbed an invisible steering wheel and moved his hands back and forth. "Golf cart!"

"Oh, I gave it to Miller—Olivia Miller, and one of her friends. She said you offered it to her."

"Great," Coleton grumbled, hoping down from the pit cart, and offering Camilla his hand to help her down. Drivers are notoriously territorial about their golf carts during a race weekend, and Coleton was no exception.

"Sorry, Mate."

"No worries." Coleton managed a bleak smile.

"If you see Hilton, tell him to get his ass back here. We might need to put him in any minute."

Coleton nodded. He kept Camilla's hand in his and swung it broadly back and forth between them. "Guess we're walking to lunch."

"Is it far?"

"Try to keep up." Coleton winked.

They made their way up a steep hill toward Pamela's hospitality tent. Every square inch of infield was covered with parked cars, and the narrow roads were clogged with pedestrian fans drunk on the excitement of the first minutes of the race. From the top of the hill they could see Turn 1 where it rose into the quick jog of Turn 2, 3 and 4. Overhead a helicopter swooped down to improve the television footage of the leading cars as they dug into a fresh lap.

Coleton and Camilla flashed the team credentials hanging around their necks and entered the tent. Pamela was nowhere to be seen.

"Coleton!" They turned in unison as his name danced over the heads at the crowded tables. Hilton Crowne beckoned from a table near the edge of the tent. Coleton returned the wave, pulled Camilla's arm taut and made his way toward Hilton's table.

"Well, look who it is!" Coleton's eyes glimmered, as he glanced from face to face at the full table, where William Crowne sat next to his wife, her plate of food untouched. Across the table sat Crowne's daughter, Juliette, and next to her, Enzo and Hilton. "It's the entire Crowne colony. To what do we owe this pleasure?"

"Hello, Coleton." William Crowne wiped his mouth on a paper napkin with infinite poise, and smiled as he stood from the table. He clapped Coleton warmly on the back. "Good to see you."

"Why are you—" Coleton started, again taking in the other people at the table. "You have your own team hospitality tent. Why are you all here?"

"Yes and no. Our chef—who we've had for years—got poached by some primetime television show last week! His replacement is less than average, so I thought we'd give Pamela's a try. You know I used to eat in this very tent years ago when I was a driver."

"Surely this tent isn't that old, Daddy," Juliette piped up. "Wasn't that when the racecars had cranks in the hood?"

Juliette Crown stood from her chair to full height—more than full height. She was perched on platform heels, far from practical shoes for the racetrack. But, then again, practical wasn't a prized word in her vocabulary. She lifted the baseball cap off her head that she'd been using to shield her identity and with a flourish shook out her long blonde hair, allowing the room to recognize and appreciate her.

"Hello, Coleton," she said warmly. She batted her eyelashes and moved in for a hug. It certainly had the desired effect and the room of men made a collective gasp, every eye trained on her lithe limbs.

Camilla cleared her throat. Coleton turned quickly to her. "This is my girlfriend, Camilla Harlow. Remember meeting her in Le Mans?" he asked Juliette with a smile.

Juliette blushed. "Yes, of course." She stepped forward and shook Camilla's hand. "Well sort of ..." she added sheepishly. "Good to see you again, Camilla."

"Feeling better?" Camilla asked, trying to hide a smile, but not very hard.

William Crowne stepped forward. "I don't think we've met, but I've heard so much about you, Camilla." He shook her hand warmly.

"Really?" Camilla asked with a smile, turning a surprised look toward Coleton. "I've heard a lot about you too, sir."

"Please, call me William. And this is my wife, Muffy." Crowne turned stiffly and gestured at the elegant woman sitting by his elbow.

Making no effort to rise, Muffy gave Camilla a wan smile and then narrowed her eyes at Coleton. She returned her attention to William, pausing to study his face as well.

Muffy had Siberian blue eyes, and her light blonde hair was pulled back in a severe chignon. A coral Hermès scarf looped her neck and perfected her natural coloring. Coleton was surprised by how young she looked—mid-40s at the latest.

"And of course you know Hilton and Enzo," Crowne continued.

Hilton gave Camilla a bright smile, and she returned it with a friendly wave. Enzo was sitting next to Juliette, which made Coleton uneasy. He would need to talk to Enzo and soon. This was not a girl to mess about.

Coleton re-directed his attention to Muffy, hoping to make a good impression. He couldn't figure out why she was so rude. Housewives were usually the most loyal demographic of his admirers.

"Muffy?" Coleton asked, letting his smile dimple his cheeks and leaning toward her as he spoke. "That's short for?"

"Margaret Saxon-Duff. Duffy, Muffy. It's from my Cambridge days."

"I see," Coleton said.

"Cambridge days?" Juliette snapped. "*Really*, Mother? You were there for a two week secretarial course!"

"Juliette!"

Juliette gave an exaggerated eye roll. She pulled her baseball cap back down over her eyes, but not before giving Coleton a conspiratorial wink.

"Is this your first race?" Coleton asked Muffy, ignoring Juliette's outburst. "I don't think I've seen you in the paddock this year."

"Yes, well, I couldn't let the season end without seeing Hilton race." She gazed at her son fondly.

"Speaking of Hilton—racing." Coleton turned to look at Hilton, then demanded, "What are you still doing here?" Hilton smiled sheepishly. "Nelson wants you back in the pits. He's been looking all over for you. You know the strategy is to pull Trotter out at the first yellow. That could be any minute. You better get back."

"The first yellow?" Muffy asked. Her eyebrow tugged upward fighting the Botox to look inquisitive.

"The first yellow flag," Hilton said, as he stood. "A yellow, caution flag slows down the cars when there has been a crash on the track. With the rest of the cars on the track going slower, it's the best time to come into the pits for tires, fuel and driver change."

"You're just *waiting* for the first crash—that's part of your strategy?" Muffy demanded. She turned on her husband like a snake. "That's just wonderful!"

Hilton used the diversion of attention to make his escape. Enzo jumped up to follow him. With a sudden thought, Coleton swiped a bottle of chilled water off the table, shook off the condensation and tossed it to Hilton.

"Don't forget to hydrate," Coleton said. "It's really hot out there."

"You're telling *me* to hydrate?" Hilton laughed. "You're getting in the car after me, so that advice is not exactly in your best interest." Coleton rolled his eyes, remembering how Hilton had managed to pee in practically every public crevice of the château in France.

"I should be getting back, too," Enzo announced to the rest of the table, but no one was listening. Crowne and Muffy were now mid-squabble. "See you soon, *Amore*," Enzo said under his breath to Juliette as he swept up one of her hands to kiss it. Coleton narrowed his eyes at him, then pulled him aside with a nod.

Camilla claimed a table in the corner of the room and set to work gathering their drinks, silverware and napkins from the buffet line.

Enzo followed Coleton to the front of the tent.

"So," Coleton said. "Tell me."

"Tell you what?" Enzo said, stroking the top of his chest as if arranging his feathers.

"Last time we talked was on the steps of La Santé prison in Paris. What happened with Heidi?"

Enzo let out a long sigh, as if his shoulders had suddenly deflated. He shook his head, smiled and began. "After you made my bail, I found a message from Heidi on my phone. All it said was: *Le Meurice*. I walked all the way from the 14th arrondissement to the Jardin de Tuileries. I walked its broad gray paths, sat by that large round fountain and looked into the spray of the water, trying to

384

discern what it is I want. Finally, I decided I wanted Heidi. I jogged across the street into the hotel, couldn't wait for the elevator, sprinted up the stairs and when she threw open the door—*Dio Mio.* She was in a lacy black bra and black stockings with those little satin straps clipped to her panties. I knew I made the right choice."

"So she didn't go back to Ulrick?"

"Maybe she tried and he wouldn't take her. I don't know. But let me finish the story."

Coleton nodded.

"The next morning I woke up, with this incredible panic gripping at my throat." Enzo's hand wrapped around his neck. "I pushed it down, I didn't have a choice. We rented a car and drove from Paris to my family estate outside of Florence. Over the next few weeks, we baked in the sun around my pool, took long walks through the sunflower fields, went sightseeing in Sienna, somehow the panic slipped away."

"That's great, man."

"She's still there, waiting for me. My little brother is keeping her company every day on bike rides and swims. He thinks he's died and gone straight to heaven. No purgatory."

Coleton smiled. "So, you're really happy, then?" Enzo nodded, as a smile curled his lips. "Then what the hell are you trying to pull with Juliette?"

"Juliette?" Enzo blinked at Coleton, and then scratched the back of his neck. "What do you mean?"

"Kissing her hand, leaning in to whisper in her ear, she was lapping it up."

"Must have been instinct. Don't worry," he said, and frowned. "I have no plans for her."

"Good. Juliette's off limits."

Enzo raised an eyebrow suspiciously. "Why?"

Coleton looked flustered, a little lost for words. "She's like a sister, and no offense, but your track record with women is a little shoddy."

"Don't give it a second thought." Enzo patted him on the back. "I'm a changed man."

A corner worker leaned through a hole in the chain link fence at Turn 5 and frantically waved two yellow flags. Hilton caught the movement of the flags out of the corner of his eye as he negotiated the tricky corner.

"Hilton, double yellow. Double yellow!" Nelson barked into his ear. "It's a full course caution. No passing."

"Roger."

Hilton breathed a sigh of relief. He had only been slated to drive two stints, but there hadn't been a yellow flag, so he'd continued into a third. Driver changes take more time than routine stops, so teams wait for yellow flags when possible before calling their drivers back to the pits. After almost three hours behind the wheel, Hilton wanted out, and with a full course caution, they'd be calling him in sometime soon.

"Where's the accident?" Hilton asked, depressing the radio button on the steering wheel again. "Who augured in?"

"It's Audi *and* Peugeot!" Nelson cried, the surprise still in his voice. "Monteparnassus tried to stove-it into Turn 12 on the inside, but he clipped Bleeker and they both spun out into the middle of the track. Two GT cars came barreling down the hill, under the bridge, you know the turn in is almost blind, and they never saw the parked cars. It's horrific."

"Should I pit now?" Hilton asked.

He had caught up to the line of cars trailing behind the Porsche pace car like a conga line minus the mirth. If felt great to relax his hands on the wheel, stretch out his fingers, roll his shoulders back, wiggle his feet on the pedals. The freedom to blink his eyes and stretch his neck, although the HANS device that connected his helmet to his shoulders only gave him a little wiggle room, was a relief. At the sudden relaxing of his muscles, however, he was overwhelmed by the urge to urinate.

"Yes, we'll bring you in toward the end of the yellow. It's going to be a long one."

"Thank God. How long, you think?" Hilton asked, feeling the urge strengthen to a heavy pain in his bladder.

"Oh, maybe 15 to 20 minutes. There appears to be injuries. They'll take their time getting the guys out of the cars and onto boards."

"Shit! It does look bad," Hilton said, as he followed the pace car slowly through Turn 12 and saw the carnage for himself. "I don't know if I'll make it 20 minutes. I need to pit sooner rather than later."

"Well, the pits are still closed. But, once they re-open, we still want you out until the last possible minute: the less in the tank when we re-fuel the better. We need to minimize our number of fuel stops."

"Shit," Hilton mumbled and shifted uncomfortably in his seat. His bladder was definitely full, uncomfortably full, full to bursting. The safety harnesses held him back tightly, magnifying his discomfort. "Um," Hilton spoke up again. "I've got to get out of the car—soon!"

"What's wrong? Heat exhaustion? Just take a couple of deep breaths and relax."

"Umm, no ... I wouldn't say that."

Coleton was sitting in the pit cart listening to Hilton over the radio, ready to suit up for his stint at Nelson's call. Suddenly he straightened up and cursed to himself.

"Nelson! You tell that fucker, if he pees in the seat ... I'll kill him!"

Nelson looked up at Coleton and laughed silently, but didn't relay the message. Coleton seriously considered breaking the unwritten rule that only the lead engineer can talk to the cockpit and hijacking a headset that could transmit his words.

"This kid thinks the world is his goddamn urinal," fumed Coleton.

"We're keeping you out until right before the end of the yellow," Nelson repeated to Hilton. "Repeat, do *not* pit."

"Shit," Hilton mumbled to himself. "I'm not going to make it!"

But, then suddenly he had an idea. Embracing the long yellow, he quickly began loosening his belts, making sure to keep close to the car in front of him, trying to keep one hand on the wheel at all times. After much shimmying and wiggling, he was able to loosen the belts enough to unzip the front of his suit, raise his hips a few inches and angle his attachment toward the hollow door of the car.

Back in the pits, a race official, who had been pacing up and down pit lane looking for team infractions, stopped in front of the Elrod Racing pit box and pointed a finger at Nelson.

"Channel 8," he demanded, then pointed to his headset.

Nelson quickly adjusted his dial to the new channel.

"Nelson, Lead Engineer, Elrod Racing."

"Yes, Race Control here. We just had a report from the Audi pits ... about your car."

"Yes?" Nelson asked, leaning forward.

"Fluid is leaking out of your car. Their driver is right behind you and fluid is splashing onto his windshield."

"Oh, no! Thanks for letting us know."

"Check your data immediately, and if your car needs to come into the pits, do so at once. We need to keep the track safe."

"Of course. Thank you," Nelson said. He was already scanning data tables, checking gauges and fluid levels. No alarms had sounded and there was nothing out of the ordinary. He radioed Hilton.

"Hilton, there is fluid leaking out of the car. The pressures and fluid levels look normal, but we're calling you into the pits to double check. Stand by. As soon as they are open, dive in."

There was silence over the radio.

"Hilton, do you copy?" Nelson asked.

After a few more moments of silence, Hilton spoke up. "Guys," he said, then cleared his throat. "The car is fine. I can stay out."

"Hilton, there's fluid leaking—"

"I repeat," Hilton interrupted. "The car is fine. Take my word for it."

The mechanics and engineers exchanged confused glances that gave way to disbelieving smiles, then outright laughter. *No way!* The team broke into uproarious laughter.

"Everyone calm down," Nelson instructed over the radio for all to hear.

"Ask him how it felt to piss on Audi!" a mechanic called to Nelson. Nelson moved the microphone away from his mouth, and stifling a smile, yelled back, "Everyone keep your head down. We've still got a race to win!"

Then, Nelson turned to Coleton and gave him the nod he'd been waiting for. "Suit up."

With a smile on his lips, Coleton hopped down from the pit cart and pulled on his fireproof balaclava. At least the "fluid" was all over the track and not in his seat.

After a brief meeting with Nelson and a well-earned pat on the back for his flawless double stint, Coleton grabbed two bottles of water and climbed up into the pit cart next to Camilla. She had been watching the television monitors for the past two hours, barely breathing, face pale and jaw clenched, as his car lapped the track.

"Not bad, Loren. Not bad." Camilla beamed, relieved to have him next to her again, proud of his performance on the track. She grabbed his head with both hands and gave him a smacking kiss on the temple, oblivious to the sweat. He broke into a broad smile and took a long swig from his water. Now that Coleton was back safely in the pits, they slipped easily into the usual charade, where she pretended she hadn't been worried and he pretended to believe her.

Camilla passed Coleton his BlackBerry, which had rung a few times while he was in the car. Coleton swept up the phone and checked his messages, while draining another bottle of water.

"Okay, meet us by the Audi Bridge," Coleton said into his phone, still red-faced and sweating. He nodded to Camilla and she followed him out of the pit cart and down the narrow path behind the pit boxes toward an exit to the paddock. "We're headed there now," he added before hanging up.

"Who was that?" Camilla asked.

"Barney."

"Barney?" Camilla asked, trying to place him.

"You met him at Sebring, remember? He works for my family. The caretaker of our Palm Beach property."

"Oh, yes." Camilla smiled. "I like him! He came to watch your race? That's so nice!"

"No. He came to bring my mother."

Camilla blanched. She stopped walking so abruptly that someone on the crowded pathway bumped into her. She stared at Coleton. "You're kidding."

"Not really. She just flew in."

Coleton took Camilla's hand and pulled her around so he could look her full in face. "You're so pale!" Coleton laughed. "Are you afraid of Victoria?"

The sun was sinking low in the west and the shadows across the track were lengthening. It was close to that magic hour that photographers love so dearly, when the play of light and shadow lends everything an added note of meaning. Coleton lifted Camilla's chin and the soft light highlighted her cheekbones. They stared at each other for a second in silence.

"You didn't—" Camilla huffed, pulling back and breaking the spell. "I didn't know your mother was going to be here!"

"She'll love you! What's not to love?" Coleton smiled. "Except maybe this sweaty ponytail?" Coleton yanked her long, blonde ponytail playfully and then let it drop.

"Coleton Loren! We've been running around all day in the sun, and I—" Camilla was at a loss for words. "I'm a wreck."

"Relax, I'm kidding. She'll love you." He pulled Camilla into his arms for a quick embrace. "Come on, they're probably waiting. And, if we make her wait ... well, then she'll *definitely* hate you."

Camilla punched Coleton in the shoulder, and reluctantly allowed herself to be led up the hill. Nearing the Audi bridge, Camilla looked down at the track twisting below.

"That's the left right complex of Turn 10a and b," Coleton said, pointing. "The best place to pass." On the far side of Turn 10, a crude amphitheater cut the hillside into row upon row of narrow terraces where lawn chairs and blankets patch-worked the clay-red Georgian dirt.

To prevent people from clogging the Audi bridge, which is the main artery of spectator traffic, huge plywood walls reach into the air and block its spectacular birds-eye view of the track. On either end of the short bridge however, golf carts pull onto the narrow shoulder, and pedestrians press against the chain link fence to steal a few glances, before moving on.

As they approached, Camilla recognized Barney's stocky figure and salt and pepper hair. He stood against the fence looking down at Turn 10 and next to him was a slim woman in white linen pants and a lavender colored blouse. *That must be her, the Queen Bee.*

Victoria Loren turned toward them, and her face lit up at the sight of Coleton. Camilla's first thought was that she now knew where Coleton got his beauty. Victoria was tall and thin, with sparkling green eyes and rich brown hair that curled gracefully at her shoulders. Camilla's second thought was—*is she serious with that diamond?* Victoria had a diamond the size of a chestnut sparking from a sleek-linked chain around her neck. Her blouse was silk, and the diamond hung low and heavy between the curves of her breasts.

"I'm so glad you made it!" Coleton beamed and gave his mother a heart-felt kiss on the cheek. Turning toward Camilla, Victoria motioned her forward.

"You must be Camilla."

Camilla nodded. "What a pleasure."

"The pleasure is mine. I assure you," Victoria said, leaning forward to give her an air kiss on both cheeks. Victoria pulled back to study Camilla appraisingly. "I've never actually met one of my son's girlfriends before! He has always kept them well hidden."

"From what I've heard about them," Camilla said. "They were better off well hidden!"

Victoria smiled in agreement. "You better hang on to this one, Coleton. I like her already."

"Thanks for coming, Mom. I'm glad you're here."

"Well, don't get used to it," she said, but there was warmth in her voice. "You know these—" She motioned over the expanse of lawn chairs, as she searched for the word. "Events ... aren't really my thing. I can only stay for a few hours, before I need to jump back on the plane and head north."

"You're not staying for the finish?" Camilla asked, surprised. *If Victoria had finally made the effort to come to one of Coleton's race, wouldn't she want to stay for a while?*

"Oh, no. I'm meeting my girlfriends in New York, and we already have some big plans for this evening." She winked by way of explanation, and then reached up to touch Coleton's wet hair. "You already drove? I missed it?"

"Only two stints. I'll be back in the car in two hours to take it to the finish. We're running third right now, but we've got second in our sights," Coleton said with pride. "Sure you don't want to stay and see your son on the podium?"

"I can already picture it, my dear. And I couldn't be more proud." She broke into a broad white smile, a smile, like Coleton's, that got exactly what it wanted.

"Hmm," Coleton said, thinking out loud. "So we can't bum a ride home with you? We have back-up tickets on a commercial flight, but I'm desperate to JW home on something private."

Victoria ran her fingers through her son's hair again. "You really are spoiled rotten." Pride sparkled in her green eyes. "But I guess I'm to blame for that."

"I'm definitely your son. No doubt about that," Coleton laughed. "Well, while you're here, you want to go to the pits?"

"Not if I have to put on one of those suits!"

Camilla's cheeks flushed, as she looked down at the fire-red suit she was wearing. Like Coleton, she had the top pulled down to her waist, with the arms tied like a judo belt around her waist.

"Oh, I mean," Victoria said. "The suit looks very—*sporty* on you, my dear. But, for us old ladies, well—it's not really my look."

Camilla responded with a weak smile, and looked intently at Victoria. *Old lady?* Victoria was past 50, but she had the bright, clear skin of a woman in her early 40s. Camilla suddenly wished she knew more about the specialty of dermatology. She'd have to do some research. Clearly there had been a dermatological breakthrough not yet broadcast to the normal people of the world. Or maybe her genes were just *that* good.

"Why don't we go up to Pamela's tent, then?" Coleton asked, looking from one beautiful woman to the other. "If you don't want to come to the pits, I can set you up with your own table and a bottle of good wine. Err … well, probably average wine for your standards, but at least you can watch the race from there."

"Wherever you want me, darling. Just stick me someplace out of the way. And, as for the wine—" Victoria's eyes glittered. "Not to worry. I came prepared."

She nodded to Barney, back at the wheel of the golf cart. He nudged a Louis Vuitton duffle bag with the toe of his hiking boot, and mouthed the word, "Dom!"

Pamela's tent sparkled with light like Christmas. The inside walls of the tent were strung with twinkle lights and candles dotted the tables. From the thickening dark of sunset, they walked in and the smell of a holiday dinner party rose up to greet them from steaming silver trays: pork chops, truffle mash potatoes, crisp lemony asparagus, lobster rolls, chicken cutlets with white wine and capers. There was something for everyone, and the tables were filling with team principals, sponsors and guests.

"Oh, look! There's Mrs. Crowne," Camilla said, pointing to the corner of the tent at the woman she'd met earlier in the day. "Should we join her?"

Muffy Crowne was sitting alone at a table, with her back to them, a half-empty bottle of white wine on the table in an ice bucket. She held her wine glass by the bulb and let the stem swing back and forth like a clock pendulum. She was watching the closed circuit television screen intently, as it followed the leading cars around the track.

Camilla began to make her way through the crowded room toward Muffy's table, but Coleton pulled her back with a hand on her arm. She looked back at him questioningly, but her glance fell on his mother.

Victoria's face was twisted in an expression of distaste. "I wouldn't sit with that troll if you paid me."

"What?" Camilla did a double take. "Don't you know each other from Palm Beach."

"Camilla," Coleton said. "Leave it."

Just then, Muffy turned to glare at them. Camilla inwardly flinched at the expression of malice.

"Oh, we know each other all right," Victoria hissed.

"Don't be so dramatic, Mother," Coleton said, a note of irritation in his voice. "What, did she buy the same cashmere sweater set? Or no, I have it, she beat you once, unforgivably, at Hearts?"

"Quite the contrary."

"Why do you look so ruffled?" Coleton continued.

"Ruffled? Please—" Victoria replied, and as if to prove her point, she went straight for Muffy's table.

Coleton took Camilla by the hand, and they fell in behind Victoria. "I don't understand," Camilla said in a low voice. "Did I say something wrong?"

"It's not you," Coleton said, also in a low voice. "It's my mother."

As they approached the table, the stem of Muffy's wine glass twitched like a cat's tail. Muffy leveled her gaze at Victoria.

"Victoria." Muffy nodded, and then looked away as she took a long sip from her wine.

"Muffy." Victoria nodded back, as she inched forward. "It appears our sons are the talk of the track."

"Yes, Hilton is doing quite well." She raised her glass toward the television.

Victoria settled into a seat at the table and crossed her arms across her chest. Muffy glared at Victoria; their eyes locked in death rays. The room was alive with chatter, which made the heavy silence at the table all the more palpable.

Camilla arched an eyebrow and gave Coleton a what-is-this-all-about look. Coleton just shrugged and took a seat opposite.

"Well, I need to eat before I get back in the car," Coleton said. "Something light. Victoria, can I get you something?"

"No, thank you, dear. I ate on the G-4," Victoria replied, her eyes never leaving Muffy's.

As Coleton stood, Muffy's gaze flicked to his face. She narrowed her eyes as if searching his features for something.

"I'll join you," Camilla added nervously and pushed back her chair to follow Coleton.

"What was that about?" Camilla asked under her breath as they got in line at the buffet.

"They've hated each other for years, but I've never figured out why."

Ira Goldstein strutted into the tent with a flag girl tucked under his arm and the telltale flush of a well-formed alcohol buzz. His watery eyes lit up when he saw Coleton, and he quickly cut the line to join his friend.

"A Larry David chat and cut?" Coleton asked, peeking over Ira's shoulder to see if anyone was about to protest.

"What's up?" Ira demanded. His question wasn't a friendly greeting. He was already on a scent, he just didn't know what yet. Ira could recognize the sweet-sick smell of drama in the air. Following Coleton's glance, he looked across the room to the table where the two women were embroiled in heated conversation.

"Shit," Ira said. "Who put those Siamese fighting fish together?"

"Why do they hate each other so much?" Coleton asked, ignoring Ira's question.

Ira giggled. "You *don't* want me to answer that."

"What are you talking about?"

"Oh, come on, Colt. You know the rumors about Crowne and your mom."

"That's ridiculous. Just because you read something on a gossip blog doesn't make it true, Ira." Coleton rolled his eyes, but then narrowed them as he looked back to the equal foes squaring off.

"Yeah, well, it doesn't make it *not* true, and this rumor has stood the test of time."

Coleton shook his head as if to clear it. "Have you seen Elrod? I can't believe he didn't make the starting grid."

"No, and I've been looking for him."

"So strange," Coleton added. "What team owner fails to show for the last race of the season?"

"He'll turn up by the podium ceremony. I'm sure he wouldn't miss the chance to claim a trophy on stage."

Coleton looked down at his wrist, but his watch wasn't there. "I've got to get back to the pits."

Coleton reached over to Camilla's arm, where he had strapped his watch at the beginning of the day. He couldn't wear it in the car and didn't want it to get lost in the shuffle. It is common to see drivers' wives with two watches on race day. He rotated the heavy watch face from under her wrist back on top, where he could read the dial.

"We're in the pit window now. If a yellow flag comes out, then they'll throw me in. I better take this to go." Coleton looked down at his plate pilled high with vegetables and broiled chicken breast. He turned to Camilla. "Want to stay here or come back to the pits with me?"

Camilla glanced back to the table where Victoria and Muffy were growing more animated, red slowly clawing its way into their faces. For a moment, curiosity made her consider staying. But this wasn't going to end well.

"Back to the pits."

Coleton turned to Ira and pulled him a step out of line, so they could speak in private. "Ira, make yourself useful. Lose the flag girl and go sit with them." He nodded toward Muffy and Victoria. "Make sure they don't kill each other. Try to lighten the mood, will ya? Make use of that world-famous charm."

Ira grumbled something under his breath. "The shit I do for you, Coleton, you should double my percentage. Lucky for you, my real date's arriving in two hours. That's what I give you: two hours."

"Ira," Coleton said with a hint of sharpness. "Don't forget who keeps your lights on."

"I can't see a goddamn thing!" Coleton called over the radio to his crew in the pits. "Aren't you guys watching the Doppler? You're supposed to warn me about this shit!"

A misty rain had begun to fall on the far side of the track and Coleton bulldog-ed right into it, slipping and sliding through Turn 6 and 7.

"Sorry, Colt. It's still clear over here," Nelson said. He maximized a window on his computer and watched a wispy green patch float over the track map. "Yes, expect patches of rain." Then he looked down at his watch. "Should clear in 20 minutes."

"The rain is washing away the grip. Repeat: no grip!" Coleton barked as he fishtailed through the chicane of Turn 8. The rain pelted Coleton's helmet and began to slowly seep through the thick fabric of his racing suit.

"Can you hold out a while longer? Or do you need rain tires?"

Coleton fought through Turn 11 before answering, his rear tires locking in the wet. "There's only 10 laps left," Coleton said. "If I come in now, and the others don't, we won't even make the podium."

"Correct," Nelson agreed. "Audi is almost one full lap ahead. One Porscheworks is four seconds ahead, the other is six seconds behind."

"Then, there's no choice," Coleton muttered, as he sprinted past the pit entrance.

The rain gathered steadily on Coleton's helmet visor. Taking advantage of the front straight, Coleton reached up to clear it, but his glove only smeared the water and dirt across the plastic.

"It's really coming down," Coleton said over the radio. Coleton knew that if the water made its way down to his feet and affected the grip of his soles on the pedals, he wouldn't be able to modulate the throttle properly. He could feel the rain soaking through the arms and chest of his suit, making the fabric heavy. "This sucks!"

"Come in if you need to."

Coleton put his head down. The car was on the edge of adhesion and each slippery corner threatened to fling it off the track. He sprinted toward Turn 1, opening up the car for the first time since the rain began. He came up quickly on a Corvette GT car, but squeezed by on the right as he late braked into Turn 1.

In the rain, the GT car didn't see him. He turned into the corner too sharply and clipped Coleton's left rear. Coleton accelerated out of the corner, and the extra speed added just enough down force in his rear wheels to glue him to the track. The GT car wasn't as lucky and went into a tailspin, beaching itself in the middle of the track.

"Double yellow! Double yellow! Accident in Turn 1."

The radios in cockpits around the track went wild, as the warning flickered through the dark. But, it was too late for Audi. Only seconds behind Coleton, seconds from turning their lead into a full lap, the LMP1 barreled through Turn 1 and t-boned the Corvette. Carbon fiber splintered outward like fireworks.

"Coleton! Damage report?"

"He definitely hit me," Coleton confirmed.

Driving at half throttle, Coleton swerved back and forth to check the steering, suspension, tires. "Everything feels okay," he said as he accelerated to race pace and closed the gap to the next car.

"Pace car is out. Repeat: pace car is out."

"There's only nine laps left!" Coleton barked. "If we finish this race under yellow, I'm going to lose." Coleton saw the brake lights of the car in front of him.

"It's Porscheworks. They're right in front of me!" Coleton told Nelson. "Is it Ulrick?"

"No, it's the #98 car."

"Who's driving?"

"König."

"I can take that little bastard! We've *got* to go green."

"You're in P2 now. One lapped GT behind you, then Ulrick in P3."

"Roger."

The Elrod Racing crew huddled together on white folding chairs, like a flock of birds, sheltering under the tent. They watched the television screens in silence, listening for a word, waiting for the hint of a breath from Coleton in their headsets. In a microsecond they could be ready for anything—a change to rain tires, dismantling a twisted quarter panel, a new driver, more fuel, anything.

But, Coleton knew better than to come into the pits. He couldn't—wouldn't—give up the position. With Bruno König in his sights, all he could do was hope they cleared the track with enough time left in the race for him to make a move.

"Laps left?"

"Three."

"Fuck!"

"Looks like the accident is cleared, though. Pace car may come in this lap. Standby."

Coleton shook his head in the dark cockpit. He had to focus. As soon as the race went green he'd have to pull out a real trick.

"Pace car—*in!*"

"Copy."

Coleton swerved back and forth to work heat into his cold rain-soaked tires. As they warmed, he felt the rush of adrenaline through his veins warm his limbs as well.

"Green! Green! Green!"

Coleton floored it. He was inches from König's bumper. König swerved off line to protect his position into each turn.

"Two laps left."

"Got it. No more talking," Coleton instructed over the radio. Nelson nodded.

Two words floated through Coleton's brain: Stewart chassis. He suddenly remembered William Crowne's words from months before. *Porscheworks's new Stewart chassis has serious downforce issues, and they can throw in the towel if it rains.* Encouraged by this thought, Coleton flew down the front straight trailing a rooster tail of rainwater from his tires. The white flag waved ominously from the Firestone bridge: last lap. The rain had stopped, but there was a sheen of water over the asphalt. The grip of rubber that had developed during the race was gone and the track was slick.

In the Elrod pit, the crew was on their feet, staring at the live television feed in silence. Hilton stood behind Nelson's shoulder, watching the telemetry data. Perched in the pit cart, Camilla had her hands pressed prayer-like to her lips.

Coleton knew that even in perfect conditions, in cool dry air and the broad light of day, Turn 5 was a stupid place to pass. But, so did König. Coleton hoped König would focus on piloting his weak chassis through the tricky corner, and forget about protecting his line.

Coleton rolled as much speed through Turn 4 as possible to get a good run through the Esses. He roared toward Turn 5, inches from König's bumper, then faked left. König took the bait and dodged left to close the door on an inside pass. But, Coleton was already on the outside. He let centrifugal force pull his car to the edge of the track, as if a magnet was coaxing it to the tire barrier. Then the car began to drift sideways at the bare limit of control.

Rather than lifting, Coleton touched the accelerator, hoping for more grip to the rear wheels. His tires clung to the wet asphalt. Coleton cut back down from the outside, half a car length in front. Coleton pegged the throttle to the floor with impunity, but König stuck with him and began to inch forward.

"Wanna play?" Coleton yelled, and pushed the car into fifth. They barreled toward Turn 6, shoulder-to-shoulder, neither lifting, neither braking. Finally, Coleton saw König's car pull back as he braked for the turn in. Coleton counted to two, and then hit the brakes as hard as he could without locking them up. It was the latest brake into Turn 6 that Coleton had ever attempted, and he didn't know if he could hold it.

The car squirmed underneath him as he released the brake pedal. The rear of his car fishtailed on the wet asphalt. "Don't spin. Don't spin," Coleton chanted.

He didn't spin, and as he hit the apex of Turn 6, muscling the speed through the tight corner, he saw König's lights, bright eyes in the dark behind him. Coleton gave a whoop into his helmet. "Hell yeah!" He straightened his hands on the wheel for a breath, then made another tight turn to hit the apex of Turn 7.

Now Coleton was the one driving off line, protecting P1 through the quick left right complex of Turn 8, then he floored it down the back straight. The Elrod pit exploded in cheers. Hilton put his hands on Nelson's shoulders and did a leaping cheerleader split.

A radio transmission from their cockpit brought the crew back to silence. "Why's he dropping back?" Coleton asked, allowing himself a rare glimpse in his rearview mirror. Through the rain-streaked visor and into the darkness, Coleton could just make out König's LED headlights receding on the straight. "What's he doing?"

"Keep your head down, Mate. Worry about the last three turns. You've got this!"

Braking into Turn 10a, Coleton gave another glance into his mirror. "He's really off the pace!"

"Maybe he's conserving fuel to make the checker."

"Maybe." Coleton nodded in the dark.

As he shot through Turn 12, the final corner of the final race of the season, Coleton let his face relax and gave free reign to the victory smile that waited just below the surface.

"Come on!" Nelson shouted to Camilla, motioning her to follow him as he vaulted over the pit wall. The glow of electric lights danced in his eyes. They jogged the wrong way down pit lane, now safe and quiet, but streaked with rubber and oil from 10 hours of aggressive burnouts. Camilla could just make out the line of racecars parked in the order in which they finished at the far end of pit lane, adjacent to the stage area that had been set up for the trophy ceremony.

As they neared, drivers began to emerge from their machines, from hot cockpits to cool night air. Some drivers were still high and sharp with adrenaline as they fumbled with their nylon straps and pulled off their heavy helmets with a flourish.

Trying to make up time in the final hour, some of the best drivers in the Series had accepted the challenge of three and four hour stints, and they blinked dazedly into the flood lights, slowly extending numb limbs, stamping feet, stretching cramped necks from side to side. One by one the drivers tossed off the cloaks of exhaustion that pressed down on their shoulders, while throngs of fans and photographers swarmed around them. Excitement snapped and crackled in the air as the track loudspeakers blared a recap of the last few laps and the final race standings.

Camilla moved as quickly as she could through the thickening crowd, her chest tight with excitement and pride and the overwhelming relief that Coleton was safe. Her eyes welled with happy tears as she scanned the line of cars, trying to recognize theirs. Once bright with color and all sexy of line, the cars now sat like a row of ruined beauties, similarly painted with red Georgian dirt and smeared with oil, their carbon fiber body panels dented and fenders twisted.

No longer beautiful, but now proven, the cars remained proud of spirit, war heroes creaking and popping as their engines slowly cooled in the night air. Suddenly, Camilla realized she had gone too far down the line of cars as she recognized Enzo's BMW GT car. Since Coleton finished first, he should be at the head of the line. She turned to re-trace her steps, and then she saw him.

Coleton was standing on the tub of his LMP1 machine, his helmet under his arm, his uplifted face glowing with exaltation as he thrust his closed fist into the air in victory. The crowd below him went wild with cheering. Coleton Loren was clearly a favorite contender. Camilla ran to the car. Coleton jumped to the ground and crushed her into a big sweaty bear hug. Then, he pulled back for an instant, locked eyes with her and leaned down to plant a long, lingering kiss on her lips. The crowd went mad with whistling and cheering. Camilla couldn't help thinking he tasted like gasoline, but she'd never tasted anything sweeter.

A man pushed through the crowd and thrust out his hand. Coleton dropped his left arm around Camilla's shoulder and accepted the handshake.

"Kurt Carter," the man introduced himself, then stepped back to pull a young boy out from behind his legs. "And this is my son, Oscar."

"Well hello, Oscar!" Coleton ruffled the boy's soft sandy blond hair. "Did you enjoy the race?" The boy nodded enthusiastically.

"Oscar, tell Mr. Loren," the father instructed the boy. "Tell him thank you for bringing your car back in one piece." The boy smiled up at Coleton.

"Thank you," he said shyly, then hid his face in the pant leg of his father's jeans.

"Oh, you bought the car from Elrod?" Coleton asked.

"Yes. After Long Beach. And thanks to your work, it'll be worth a lot more after today's performance!" The man's eyes gleamed.

"My pleasure." Coleton smiled. "Well, if you will excuse us?" Coleton spoke to the man, but looked smokily at Camilla. "We have a trophy to collect!"

The man nodded and pushed his son toward the car. The engine was off, but fan belts still whirred and the car creaked as it cooled and settled, quiet after its long race, but refusing to be forgotten in the excitement.

"Want to sit in your car?" Kurt called warmly to his son, loud enough for the crowd to hear. "Excuse me. Watch out there," he said as he pushed his way forward.

As the crowd parted, he saw three flag girls in sports bras and spandex shorts draping themselves suggestively over the car as flashbulbs popped.

"Okay, did you get your picture?" Kurt asked a man who was posing with the models, his hand jauntily on his hip and sitting straight backed on the side of the tub. "I'd like to get a picture with my son now."

"Maybe in a minute." The man waved dismissively at Kurt, then motioned the photographer to continue snapping pictures.

"Let me put it to you another way—" Kurt moved forward. "This is *my* car. And, I want those girls off it—now!"

The man chuckled. "Nice try. But, you don't own this car. I do."

"I bought this car from Arthur Elrod after Long Beach." Kurt took another bullish step forward.

"That's not possible," the man replied, his tone matching the confidence of Kurt's. He lifted his chin an inch or two, but the color had begun to drain from his face. "I bought the car from Arthur Elrod after the 12 Hours of Sebring."

"Elrod couldn't possibly have sold the car—" Kurt paused for emphasis "Twice." It was meant to be a declaration or even an exclamation, but it sounded more like a question. They stared each other in the eye, murderously. Two opponents sizing each other up, knowing this to be the start of a long litigation.

"Where is that motherfucker?" the man screamed suddenly. In unison, as if a single being similarly vested in interest, the crowd looked around its shoulders, but Arthur Elrod was nowhere to be seen.

Camilla looked up into the black Georgian night. Even through the bank of temporary floodlights, she could see a mass of tangled stars winking down at the track as the race officials tried to corral the excited drivers and organize them back stage. The fever of the day had broken and the temperature was quickly dropping.

In the half an hour it took to get the podium ceremony rolling, Camilla had begun to shake. She put Coleton's dirty racing gloves on her hands to warm them and hugged her arms closer to her chest. She stood alone amidst the throng, surrounded by tightly packed groups of crew members waiting for their drivers to ascend the steps to glory and a barrage of flash bulbs. She craned her neck but couldn't locate the group of red and black shirts of the Elrod Racing crew.

"Hello, luv!" Camilla turned to see Pamela scuttle toward her. Pamela lugged a basket filled to the brim with mini champagne bottles. "Have you seen Arthur Elrod?"

Camilla shook her head. "No. I haven't seen him all weekend."

"That bastard," Pamela swore. "I tried to run his tab, but they kicked back my charge for insufficient funds."

"Really? That's horrible!"

"No, that's racing." Pamela rolled her eyes. "Don't worry, I'll track him down. It won't be the first time someone tried to pull a runner on ole Pamela." And with that, she gave Camilla a quick smile and dashed off with her basket of goodies, ready to bestow them on her favored supplicants.

Shivering again, Camilla looked behind her. A platform had been erected for the press, and photographers were now tightly packed on it, waiting for the winners. A throng of fans steadily amassed behind a guardrail, drawn from all corners of the track.

Camilla was shocked that so many thousands of spectators remained at the end of 10 long hours, hoping for one final glimpse of their favorite drivers. As she scanned the excited crowd, waving their team's posters, pennants, banners and flags: Ferrari, Porsche, BMW, she startled with recognition. In the front row, a beautiful woman with flame-colored hair pressed against the guardrail. Camilla couldn't quite place her face, but she remembered her hair from somewhere. The woman had a tiny baby wrapped in a blanket and clutched to her chest.

Music sounded, drawing Camilla's attention back to the podium as the announcer called forth the LMP1 first, second and third place winners. Coleton sauntered onto the stage, waving confidently to the crowd. Camilla had never seen a bigger smile on his face, as he took his place on the top step. The press went crazy, calling his name and snapping pictures. Bottles of champagne were placed on the front edge of the stage, one a few paces in front of each of the drivers. After receiving their large silvered trophies from scantily clad models and taking successive rounds of pictures in all the different sponsor hats, the announcer finally made the instruction they were all waiting for.

"*Rrrrr*-elease the confetti!"

With the sound of a canon, confetti burst overhead and rained down on the drivers. That was their cue. At the first syllable of the announcer's words, Coleton leapt forward giving reign to his quick reflexes and swept up his bottle of champagne, shaking it roughly as he straightened. In an instant, he popped the cork and went straight for Ulrick.

Caught off guard, Ulrick was just bending to reach his bottle and Coleton hit him full in the face with champagne. Coleton continued to shake the bottle as he held his thumb over the lip to strengthen the stream. Ulrick stumbled backwards holding his eyes and Coleton followed him relentlessly.

Finally, the power of Coleton's bottle weakened as his supply dwindled and he stepped backwards, laughing uproariously and waving to the crowd. Everyone cheered wildly. Ulrick lunged toward his bottle, which still sat proudly on the front of the stage, but at the movement Coleton made one final broad wave to the crowd, gave a quick bow and sprinted off the stage before Ulrick could enact his revenge. The crowd roared with laughter.

"Okay, let's clear the stage for the GT winners!" the announcer instructed. Ulrick remained behind to wipe his burning eyes on the sleeve of his racing suit. The second and third place GT drivers mounted the stage and headed toward their places, passing Ulrick as he slowly made his way toward the stage steps.

"Enzo Ferrini, please make your way to the stage," the announcer called. "Enzo Ferrini." Enzo peeked around the backdrop of the stage, but at the sight of Ulrick, he pulled himself back behind the white tarp like a turtle into its shell.

At the mention of Enzo's name, Ulrick turned sharply, scanning the back of the stage. Enzo peeked around the backdrop again. With one swift movement he dashed passed Ulrick and leapt up to the top step of the podium, beaming at the crowd and waving. Ulrick turned toward Enzo and smashed his fist into the palm of his hand. Enzo looked at the crowd and shrugged. Then, he turned slowly back to Ulrick and blew him a kiss. Ulrick made the ragged sound of a bull before it charges and lunged forward. But two race officials grabbed Ulrick by both arms, guiding him off the stage and down the stairs. The crowd went mad, drunk on the rivalry that is racing.

Clutching his trophy proudly, Coleton waded through the crowd of celebrating crewmembers. He must have seen Camilla from the podium because he made his way straight to her for a big stage kiss. The press went crazy again snapping away at the happy couple and calling after Coleton. For the first time, Camilla heard her name called from the lips of paparazzi. Without thinking, she snapped her head up at the sound and flash bulbs went off like boiling water. Another photographer took up her name and called out to her, then another. Coleton wrapped his arm around her shoulder and together they waved happily to the cameras.

"So Elrod didn't show after all?" Camilla asked under her breath.

"No. It's strange," Coleton said. "Very strange. Something must be wrong."

A firm hand clapped Coleton on the shoulder and he spun.

"Hey, Brother!" Coleton grabbed Ira into an embrace.

"Well done, Colt," Ira said, slapping him on the back. "That was the best pass I've ever seen you pull off."

"Really?" Coleton asked, scratching the back of his head with a satisfied smile.

"Seriously," Ira said. "I'm not just blowing smoke up your ass. You really wiped König's face on the floor!"

"That's the idea." Coleton laughed.

Nelson parted through the crowd. "There he is," Coleton said, sweeping the tall thin man into a hug. "Hug it out." They embraced for a moment and patted each other on the back.

"What a season," Nelson said, out of breath. His thin lips arched into a smile. "It's been a real pleasure working with you."

"Likewise," Coleton said.

"But, here. Before I forget," Nelson said sheepishly, and held out a sheet of paper folded in thirds.

"What's this?" Coleton asked, as he unfolded it.

"Your tab."

"Tab?"

"Eighteen thousand dollars in fines ... for cursing over the radio, accumulated over the season like you asked."

"You've got to be shitting me!" Coleton's mouth dropped open, then he broke into a loud full laugh. "It was worth every *fucking* cent."

Onstage, Enzo played up to the crowd, dancing the waltz with his large first place GT trophy. He pretended to dip the trophy, then turned to the crowd with a blinding white smile, assuring he had their full attention before he lowered his head and kissed it seductively. The crowd went wild, the women cheered and called his name.

Camilla looked over her shoulder to see the women in the crowd frenzied with lust. But she stopped short and the smile dropped from her lips. The woman with flaming red hair was frantic. She screamed

Enzo's name so loudly that those around her turned to stare. Camilla looked from the girl back to Enzo. He wasn't hamming it up anymore. He stood stock-still.

The girl held the baby up high and yelled, "Enzo. Your bambino!"

Enzo screwed up his face in confusion, but then a wave of recognition crossed his handsome features. The color drained from his face, but he continued to wave mechanically to the crowd.

"*Rrrrr*-elease the confetti!"

Enzo didn't even notice the glitter falling around his shoulders, as confetti rained down on the GT winners. He picked up his bottle of champagne, gave it a little reflexive shake and opened it without heart. The other drivers ran around the stage spraying each other, then turned their spray toward the crowd to shrieks of dismay.

"Coleton … Loren! There you are!" Coleton turned as Nikki Street bounded up, a cameraman in tow. "Charlie, get this on tape," she demanded. "How does it feel to have the Championship stolen away from you?"

"Excuse me?"

"The Championship. You heard what happened, right?"

Coleton stared at her blankly.

"Oh!" she exclaimed. "I didn't think I'd be the one to tell you! *Live* on national television!"

Coleton looked from her directly into the camera, and then back, realizing by her smile of relish that this was exactly what she'd hoped for.

"So, tell me," he demanded.

"On the last lap of the race, a Porscheworks engineer made a call over the radio to the #98 car. While the exact words weren't decipherable, Bruno König quickly allowed Klaus Ulrick to pass for second place. Because Ulrick came in second rather than third, the extra points he garnered pushed him past your total season point count—for the Championship victory!"

"Team orders." Coleton nodded gruffly. His handsome features had hardened into a mask devoid of emotion.

"Team orders that influence the outcome of a race are in clear violation of Le Mans regulations." Nikki turned to look deeply into the camera and raised her eyebrow. "However, since race control hasn't been able to decipher the exact words of the transmission, there is no way to prove Porscheworks actually instructed König to slow down."

"I see," Coleton said quietly, but anger burned in his eyes. Coleton was not new to the game of publicity, so he pulled himself together with a quick shake of his head and dove into the speech that was required of any driver in his position. "Well, when you get on track you hope everyone is playing by the same set of rules, but what can you do? We've fought fairly and hard all season long. Of course, this is difficult to accept, but—that's racing!" Coleton mustered a smile.

"This has been a difficult year for you, what with your teammate's heart-wrenching crash at the Canadian Tire and Motorsports Track, and now with this—"

"Yes, it has been difficult, but it has also been an incredible, wild ride. George is out of the hospital and doing well. And, I'm already working on some new prospects for next season." Coleton's eyes snapped back to themselves, bright and eager at the thought. "Porscheworks better hold on to that title tight. I'll be back next year, and they'll be hard pressed to keep it—no matter what means they employ!"

"Well, there you have it: the Le Mans fighting spirit at its finest! What an exciting, overwhelming, always entertaining season this has been! After almost a year of fierce competition, countless hours of practice, millions of dollars in sponsorship, feats of mechanical engineering and the devotion of hundreds of crew members, the Championship came down to this: the final lap of the final race. The winners separated from the losers by mere seconds." Nikki beamed into the camera.

"As racecar driver, Coleton Loren, so aptly put it—it has been an 'incredible, wild ride.' Thank you for joining us. This is Nikki Street, signing off from the Le Mans season finale here at Road Atlanta. We'll see you next year!"

CHAPTER 23

BRASELTON, GEORGIA

As soon as the cameraman clicked off the interview light and lowered the camera, Coleton hoisted his trophy over his shoulder and reached for Camilla's hand. When they were out of the reach of the floodlights and well into the paddock, Coleton pulled her to a stop.

All around them rose the quiet clinking and un-ratcheting of bolts, as tents dropped and equipment was stored, and although they were surrounded by these small sounds, for a moment the heavy night air draped their shoulders in damp silence. Camilla thought of a line from one of her favorite books, about the guests in Gatsby's garden and the champagne and the whisperings and the stars.

"We can still make our flight out of ATL, don't you think?" Coleton asked. His eyes sparkled, emerald dark and flecked with moonlight. "Wake up in our own bed?"

Camilla looked down at her watch skeptically, but before she could speak, Coleton grabbed her by the elbow and half-carried her into the sliver of space between two team transporters. He let his trophy slide to the wet pavement, and pushed her up against the side of the truck, pinning her hands above her head.

He traced down her arms with his fingertips, sending goose bumps throughout her body. She kept her arms up where he had left them, staring into his eyes and breathing heavily. Barely brushing the outer curve of her breasts, his hands settled around her waist, slender even in the thick racing suit.

Drawing her to him, he kissed her, softly and so slowly she ached. His lips were warm against hers and tasted of champagne.

"Camilla, you know … right?" he asked, pulling back for an instant. His eyes blazed even in the dark, insistent, demanding an answer. His gaze lingered on her lips.

"Yes. I know."

"Do you know *how much*?" Coleton asked again, his eyes molten. He gently brushed her bangs back off her cheekbone.

"This much?" Now, *she* kissed him.

Breathless, they stumbled back out into the paddock walkway and still holding her hand tightly, Coleton pulled her into a jog toward the Elrod transporters and their packed rental car.

They made their hurried goodbyes to the team and within minutes their car skidded out the gates of Road Atlanta.

"Do you really think we'll make our flight?" Camilla asked, looking at the long line of gridlocked cars.

Coleton revved the engine. "Of course. I know a shortcut." He made a sharp right onto Winder Highway, a grandiose name for a winding country road. The traffic crawled in the opposite direction. "Only the locals and truckers know about this little back road route. Sheep wait in line."

Camilla giggled. "You *are* going to obey the speed limit, aren't you?"

"See there? It says 185 ahead. I won't be going over 150."

"That's I-85!"

"Remind me," he said. "To take you out on moonlit nights and tell you jokes more often. I've never seen anything so beautiful as you are right now." Camilla beamed.

The night was almost pitch black, just the faintest sliver of moon silvered the tops of the passing trees, as they made a sharp right on New Liberty Church road. Coleton reached across the car and took Camilla's hand. He brought it back to rest just above his knee.

Grace rested her head on George's chest, and his right arm circled her. He grabbed the remote control from the coverlet and turned off the television. They continued to stare at the screen even after it faded to complete black.

"Are you awake?" George asked, jostling her gently.

"Mmmhmm," Grace said softly, and shifted under the silk bedspread. Far from asleep, Grace felt more alive than she had in ages. After years of frost, something new had sprouted in her like a bright red tulip.

"I hope Coleton is contesting that call right now," George said. "Before he even leaves the track. It's not too late."

Grace traced a figure on his chest with one hand and kissed his shoulder, relishing the new sensation of being in his arms the night of a race. She let her eyes fall shut and drew a slow breath deep into her lungs. He smelled warm and earthy, like the darkest cacao, and ever so faintly of Colgate.

"They can't let Porscheworks get away with that," he continued. "If it wasn't for their team orders, we'd have the Championship."

"Is it strange to see your team race without you?" she asked, rubbing her feet together under the sheets to warm them.

Strange didn't begin to cover the chaos of his emotions: angry, but hopeful; powerless, but proud; relieved, but … forgotten? Grace sensed his feeling of loss, as his car circled the track without him, and the whole sport carried on in his stead.

"Strange … yes, strange," he said.

She pulled her knees up and slid her toes into the space behind his right knee. After the crash, she had marveled at the warmth of his body, at how alive he was, something she would never take for granted again.

"Do you wish you were in Atlanta, right now?" Grace asked lightly, still staring at the dark screen. She bit her lip, glad he couldn't see her face.

"No." He pulled her close and ruffled her soft fawn-colored hair with his nose. "I wouldn't want to be anywhere else."

George leaned over her and clicked off the lamp. She felt a jolt in the dark, as if static electricity had jumped from his body to shock her. He kissed the top of her head, then inched down in bed. Her heartbeat quickened. He planted a soft, searching kiss where her neck met her collarbone. She shied away, tickled with delight and lifted a protective shoulder. George pushed her shoulder down with his cheek, and this time his kiss was lingering and wet.

"Oh, George," she moaned.

He reached over her, cupped his left hand around her hipbone, and rolled her toward him, meeting her face to face. She drew the coverlet over their heads, and they stared at each other, the contours of their faces emerging as their eyes adjusted to the darkness.

One hand on the side of her head, he brushed her cheekbone with his thumb. Then, he yanked her in for a kiss, a great show-stopping kiss, and her body melted against his. Even as her well-mannered hormones kicked up their heels in delicious abandon, she pulled back. A smile broke across her face, as she ran her fingertips over the stubble on his upper lip.

"You still grew your lucky mustache?"

"Of course." George smiled in the dark. "It was the least I could do."

The waitress lifted a tray overhead to squeeze through the crowd of merry people. The Saturday of Petit Le Mans is always the busiest night of the year at Paddy's Irish Pub, but her face was relaxed, and her brown hair pulled back in a ponytail, ready for the long haul.

She passed the bar and continued to a table near the far wall. One after another, she plopped down three pints of Guinness. Foam lava-crept over the edge and trailed down the side of the last glass she set down.

Like previous years, half the paddock crammed into the small, warm pub that had been imported piece by piece from Ireland and reassembled only miles from the track: some to revel in victory, some to drown their sorrow, most to carouse, but all to celebrate the close of the season.

"Anything else?" the waitress asked as she watched the slow foam drip to the sticky tabletop, ringed by a lifetime of spent glasses.

"We'll take one of *everything* on the menu," Hilton said, although the after-hours menu featured only four items: chicken wings, mozzarella sticks, BBQ pork sliders, and hamburgers with French fries.

"Oooh, boy. I can't wait." Juliette clapped her hands together in mock delight, but the smile on her face was genuine.

William Crowne swept up his glass, heedless of the dripping foam, and held it aloft. With a ringing, "I propose a toast!" he reigned in their attention. They had proudly displayed their trophies in the center of their table: William's first place GT, thanks to Enzo, and Hilton's first place LMP1, thanks to Coleton. William had to cock his head to the side to see Hilton across the four-top.

"To my son, and his first Le Mans podium!"

Hilton and Juliette raised their glasses.

"To the first of many!" Hilton called. A few people in the standing-room-only crowd returned with, "Here, here."

A steady stream of well-wishers had migrated past the Crowne table since they'd first taken their seats, paying their respects, jockeying for position, courting favor with the racing legend. Stares were tossed in their direction, as one-by-one newcomers recognized Crowne's iconic white hair, carefully combed back in a conservative pompadour. Murmurs of respect rippled through the crowd.

"Hey, isn't that Coleton's agent?" Hilton asked.

"I think you're right," Crowne said, shifting in his seat to get a better look. "Maybe Coleton's here too. Let's invite him over for a drink."

Across the pub, Ira leaned in to speak to a woman. His left hand gestured like an over-caffeinated conductor, every thrust threatening to spill his drink, as he spun a story into her ear. His face was red, as if he hadn't taken a breath in minutes.

Hilton parted the crowd and led Ira and his date back to the table. He pulled up an extra chair for Ira next to his father, just as the waitress set down their food.

Ira reached over and grabbed a handful of fries, before anyone else had even noticed their arrival. "It's hotter in here than two rats fucking in a wool sock," Ira said, peeling off his sweater. Beads of sweat had gathered on his forehead.

Juliette snorted into her half-empty pint glass. She never drank beer, but somehow in the warmth of the close pub, surrounded by family, it seemed just right. She'd forgotten how good fresh draught beer could smell, like baking bread.

"This is my date, Rhonda," Ira said proudly.

"Oh, hello," Crowne said, extending a strong, tan hand. "What a pleasure."

Rhoda's face lit up, as she unleashed her widest, whitest Chiclet smile. Crowne froze, then continued to smile and nod on autopilot. Nothing could ruffle his manners and good grace.

"Is Coleton here?" he managed to ask, turning to Ira.

"I think he's headed back to Miami tonight."

"I was hoping to talk to him before he left. I have some ideas for next year."

It was as if Crowne shook the dog bowl. Ira stopped mid sip, every fiber of his body focused, intent, hungry. He coughed as the alcohol puddled in the back of his throat.

"What do you have in mind?" he said, wiping a dribble of tequila from the corner of his mouth.

"I may have a BMW works deal on the table for next year. Enzo's done well this year, but he will need a new teammate."

"We could definitely disc—"

"LMP1."

"*What?*"

"LMP1." Crowne chuckled.

"BMW has never run a true LMP1!"

Crowne's eyes twinkled over the lip of his pint glass, as he took a measured sip of his dark beer and nodded.

Ira cleared his throat. "I mean, we'll have to talk money, of course," he said, trying to put a frown on his face. He didn't want to give away too much. "But, I think that's an opportunity Coleton would be interested in."

"Good," Crowne said, and gave Ira a swift, solid pat on the back.

Anytime a conversational windfall dropped in his lap, Ira liked to harvest his gain and change the subject. Scoop the jewel off the table and put it in his pocket, before it disappeared. Without a second thought, he leaned toward Crowne and angled his mouth away from the table.

"How about the rack on this one? *Eh?*" He nodded at Rhonda and jabbed an elbow into Crowne's ribs.

Crowne's eyebrows shuttle-lifted off his forehead. Then regaining facial control, he inclined his head appreciatively. "Quite … impressive."

"Y̶ou reek of champagne, Coleton." Camilla smiled, scrunching up her nose. She laid her arm against his shoulder, so she could twist a piece of hair at the nape of his neck, but snapped her hand back. "Your hair is still wet!"

Coleton laughed. "Get used to it, baby. It's the smell of victory!"

Camilla rolled her eyes, but when she looked across the car at his handsome face radiating in the dark, her breath caught in her chest. Whether it was the sheen of sweat or champagne or the lingering glow of raw adrenaline, Coleton was incandescent in the dark next to her, and she couldn't help but feel amazed by him. She shook her head to clear her thoughts. But they didn't clear. They settled in her, young and warm and happy.

"Just think," Coleton said. "All this happened because I let you see me naked that day in the hospital."

"Yeah, right," Camilla scoffed. "That's what did it."

"Admit it, love at first sight. One look at my ass and—"

"Oh, please."

She looked up at the moon through her window, bright and steady, while the world sped by them in a shadowy blur.

"It was your smile," she said softly after a few moments.

"Hmm?" he asked, stealing a glance at her.

"Even through the pain, you wanted to see me laugh."

She could picture the years ahead of them, outpacing sadness, negotiating the curves of fate. "Promise me you'll stay that way."

"Pantsless with multiple fractures?"

"No," she laughed, patting his arm. "Always meeting challenges with humor and bravery."

Coleton squeezed her hand, and she glanced at the speedometer.

"You should slow down," she said. Coleton shrugged, but didn't lift his foot. "If we don't make our flight, we'll just stay at a romantic hotel in Atlanta."

"There aren't any romantic hotels in Atlanta."

"The last thing we need is to get pulled over," she said. "I can just imagine you trying to talk your way out of a ticket while soaked in champagne."

"It's an easy sell—with that beauty in the backseat!" They looked over their shoulders at the large silvered trophy Coleton had seatbelted like a child into the back seat. Their eyes met and they broke into laughter.

At the sudden roar of the air horn, they both flinched. They blinked out the windshield, scanning the narrow yellow world illuminated by the headlights, but the piercing sound came from their right. In an instant, the car filled with blinding white light.

On impact, all of the windows shattered, and the right side of their car imploded with the sound of a percussion grenade. The tractor-trailer's brakes squealed, but its inertia pushed it forward, and with the dinosaur-scream of grinding metal it snowplowed their car off the road into a wide ditch.

W hen Coleton came to, he was hanging upside down, strapped in by his seat belt. His foot was still jammed down on the accelerator. He looked to his right, but there was blood in his eyes and he couldn't see clearly.

"Camilla," he called hoarsely. "Are you okay?"

There was no response. He shook his head to clear his vision and saw Camilla hanging limply from her tightened belts, her arms dangling.

"Camilla!"

*To find out what happens next
please visit
www.nakedpaddock.com
for the first chapter of the
second book in the series*

In loving memory
of Celimo Jesus Peña—
Gone, but not forgotten.

ACKNOWLEDGMENTS

A big heart-shaped Thank You to:

Chapman Ducote, my handsome, pushy, neurotic husband, the love of my life and one incredible driver, who never once lost faith in my ability to capture his crazy world and finish this book. Without him, and his relentless encouragement, *Naked Paddock* would never have happened.

Kay, my strong, beautiful mother and friend, for the years of her life she spent homeschooling me, taking my education by the bit and making me write everyday. For the hundreds of cathartic walks down Orange Drive, sometimes real walks, and sometimes, when I rang home from some far-flung country, only mental ones.

Wayne, my Papa-law, aka Clark (W. Griswold) and the Seagull (for his tendency to swoop in, leave a sloppy mess, and fly away), who demanded chapters of this book years before its completion, and bravely charged through its tattered plot line. For showing up and holding the pieces together when no one else could.

Vikram Rangala, editor, mentor, friend, and the only writing coach I've ever had. Hater of the unspecific, defender of the downtrodden, eternally succinct (Don't tell them, show them!). For the strongest axe arm for deadwood I've ever met. I've come a long way from the first day of your class, Writing & Love, when I took a seat in the back row my first semester of college, and I still have so much to learn.

Chauncey Mabe, for sweeping in and rolling up his sleeves. For giving a damn when it would have been easier to skate through.

Ian and Casanova (aka Supernova), my ninjas for hire, my guerilla everything team—marketing, graphic design, research, subversive ideas. Here's to the 12-hour day, you both deserve a drink on the house.

And last, but not least, Vinny for relaying the anatomy of a crash from his oh-so-personal experience.

ABOUT THE AUTHOR

M.K. Ducote grew up in the small town of Davie, Florida. Eager to see more of the world, M.K. studied abroad in Melbourne, Tokyo and Paris as an undergraduate, studying business finance, art history and classics. The eternal scholar, M.K. went on to law school and studied international law and human rights in Cape Town and Lima, graduating with a J.D. from the University of Florida and an LL.M. from the University of Miami.

Having seen the world, M.K. settled down to practice law and met her husband, Chapman Ducote, a professional racecar driver and entrepreneur with over 14 career podiums under his belt.

Tossed into the exciting and scandalous world of motorsports, M.K. was enthralled by the behind-the-scenes drama. M.K. quickly turned to her life-long passion and set pen to paper, plucking from real life the colorful settings and scenes of her fiction series, Naked Paddock.

Each year, M.K. Ducote embraces her passion for travel and writing, accompanying her husband to racing circuits all over the world and gathering inspiration for her high-octane novels. When not on the road, the couple calls home to Miami Beach, Florida. This is the first book in the Naked Paddock series.

www.mkducote.com
www.nakedpaddock.com